# CRITICAL ACCLAIM FOR ROBERT HARRIS' *FATHERLAND*

"A strong premise for a police thriller with rich foreign atmosphere and political texture galore? Absolutely!"

—*Entertainment Weekly*

"Fast-paced and ambitious in concept, *Fatherland* . . . takes a lot of chances—and succeeds. Historical fact is blended skillfully with fiction . . . a dazzler that should emerge as the summer's surprise blockbuster."

—*Detroit Free Press*

"A sly and scary page-turner."

—*Los Angeles Times*

"A well-plotted, well-written detective tale and a fascinating trek through parallel history."

—*Chicago Tribune*

"A solid thriller, vividly imagined and genuinely frightening, a novel written with intelligence and frequent humor."

—*The Atlanta Journal/Constitution*

"A novel that dances on Hitler's grave."

—*Kirkus Reviews*

*Continued . . .*

"*Fatherland* works on all levels. It's a triumph."
—*The Washington Times*

"Distinguished by vivid details based on impeccable research, the thriller is a crackling-good read in the le Carré tradition."
—*Time* (International Ed.)

"Wonderful."
—*New York Newsday*

"A gripping detective story as well as a chilling visit to the Germany that might have been. It is so plausibly written it seems quite real. Robert Harris is a name to watch for."
—*Book Page*

"I have to say that *Fatherland* is better [than *Gorky Park*]. *Fatherland* takes a history that never happened and makes us believe it. . . . A simply terrific job—and a rare case of what will undoubtedly be a significant bestseller that actually deserves the acclaim and success it gets."
—*Boston Sunday Herald*

"He [Harris] creates a fascinating tableau, if the nightmare of a victorious Germany can be considered."
—*Indianapolis News*

"*Fatherland* is a truly superior work, combining historical fact, detective mystery, alternate time lines and exploratory fiction. It is a master work by a dedicated craftsman who knows his material in great depth."
—*South Bend Tribune*

"The question remains as fascinating as always: What if . . . ?"
—*Roanoke Times*

"Well-crafted. The procedural aspects have a compelling authenticity, and the book moves at a finely calibrated pace."

—*American Way*

"This book has the dark, cynical foreboding atmosphere of *Gorky Park*. But even more so."

—Liz Smith, syndicated columnist

"Absorbing . . . expertly written."

—*The New York Times Book Review*

"*Fatherland* is, thankfully, fiction . . . an intriguing way to look at Germany's never-buried past."

—*Newsweek*

"Harris' narrative . . . erodes our solid past and shows our present to be less than inevitable. . . . His brooding, brown-and-black setting of a victorious Nazi regime is believable and troubling, the stuff of long nights of little sleep."

—*Time*

"Terrifying." —*FanFare*

"A singular achievement, displaying original and carefully wrought suspense all its own."

—*The Washington Post*

"Suicide? Accident? You've already guessed something more nefarious and you're only a couple of pages into the book."

—*Philadelphia Inquirer*

"[Harris] is a cunning maker of plots. . . . His imaginative portrayal has struck a still-sensitive nerve."

—*Maclean's*

"What makes it more than just a good detective page-turner is Harris' attention to small details."

—*The State* (Columbia, S.C.)

# FATHERLAND

## ROBERT HARRIS

HarperPaperbacks
*A Division of* HarperCollins*Publishers*

Permissions appear on page 381.

HarperPaperbacks *A Division of* HarperCollins*Publishers*
10 East 53rd Street, New York, N.Y. 10022



A hardcover edition of this book was published in 1992 by Random House, Inc. This work was originally published in Great Britain by Century Hutchinson, London.

Cover illustration by Kirk Reinert
Cartography by ML Design, London
Map on pages xii-xiii designed by John Grimwade

First HarperPaperbacks printing: May 1993

Printed in the United States of America

HarperPaperbacks and colophon are trademarks of HarperCollins*Publishers*

10 9 8

# ACKNOWLEDGMENTS

I thank the librarian and staff of the Wiener Library in London for their help over several years.

I also thank, for their wise advice and kind support, David Rosenthal and—especially—Robyn Sisman, without whose enthusiasm this book would not have been started, let alone finished.

TO GILL

The Greater German Reich, 1964
Atlantic Ocean
REICHSKOMMISSARIAT MUSCOVY
Ufa
St. Petersburg
Riga
Moscow
REICHSKOMMISSARIAT OSTLAND
Königsberg
Danzig
Hamburg
Berlin
GENERAL GOVERNMENT
REICHSKOMMISSARIAT UKRAINE
Rovno
MOSELLAND
PROTEKTORAT OF BOHEMIA AND MORAVIA
Krakau
WEST MARK
OSTMARK
GENERALKOMMISSARIAT TAURIDA
Melitopol
REICHSKOMMISSARIAT CAUCASUS
Caspian Sea
Gotenburg
Theoderichshafen
Tiflis
Kilometers
0
400
800
1200

The hundred million self-confident German masters were to be brutally installed in Europe, and secured in power by a monopoly of technical civilisation and the slave-labour of a dwindling native population of neglected, diseased, illiterate *cretins,* in order that they might have leisure to buzz along infinite *Autobahnen,* admire the Strength-Through-Joy Hostel, the Party headquarters, the Military Museum and the Planetarium which their Fuehrer would have built in Linz (his new Hitleropolis), trot round local picture-galleries, and listen over their cream buns to endless recordings of *The Merry Widow.* This was to be the German Millennium, from which even the imagination was to have no means of escape.

HUGH TREVOR-ROPER
*The Mind of Adolf Hitler*

People sometimes say to me: "Be careful! You will have twenty years of guerrilla warfare on your hands!" I am delighted at the prospect . . . Germany will remain in a state of perpetual alertness.

ADOLF HITLER
*August 29, 1942*

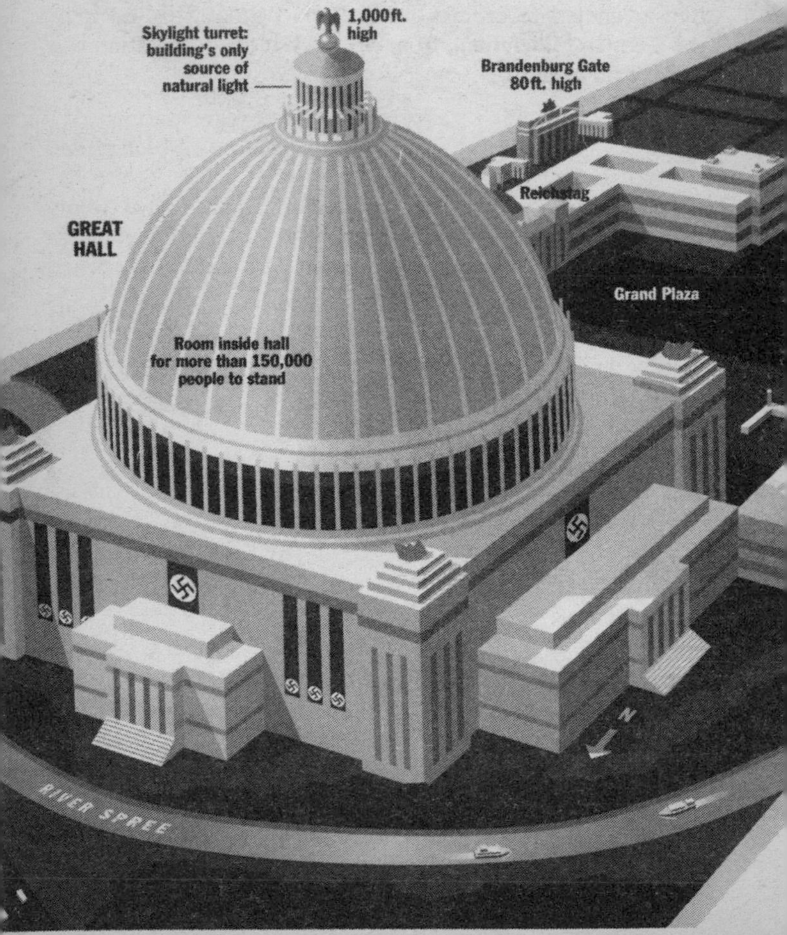

1,000 ft. high

Skylight turret: building's only source of natural light

Brandenburg Gate 80 ft. high

Reichstag

GREAT HALL

Grand Plaza

Room inside hall for more than 150,000 people to stand

N

RIVER SPREE

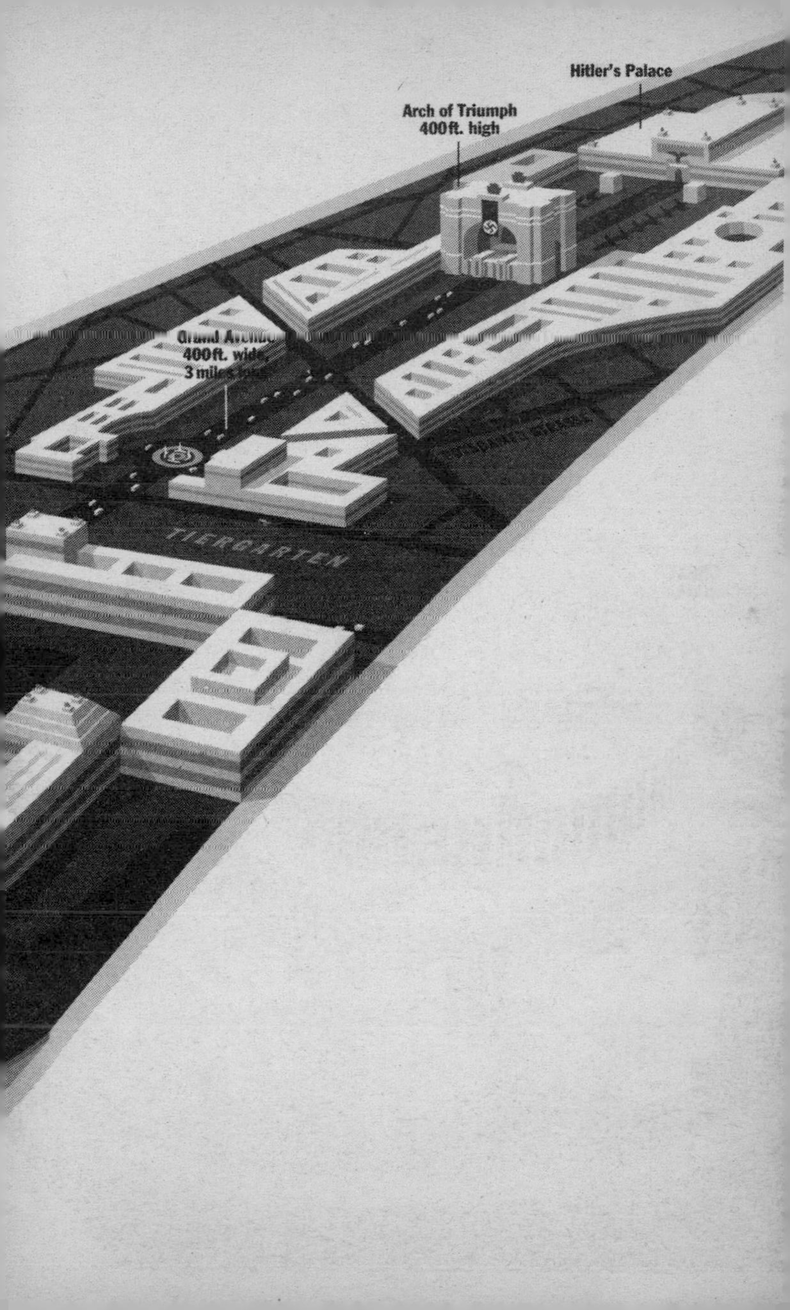
Hitler's Palace
Arch of Triumph
400ft. high
TIERGARTEN

# TUESDAY, APRIL 14, 1964

I swear to Thee, Adolf Hitler,
As Führer and Chancellor of the German Reich,
Loyalty and Bravery.
I vow to Thee and to the superiors
Whom Thou shalt appoint
Obedience unto Death,
So help me God.

SS OATH

Thick cloud had pressed down on Berlin all night, and now it was lingering into what passed for the morning. On the city's western outskirts, plumes of rain drifted across the surface of Lake Havel like smoke.

Sky and water merged into a sheet of gray, broken only by the dark line of the opposite bank. Nothing stirred there. No lights showed.

Xavier March, homicide investigator with the Berlin *Kriminalpolizei*—the Kripo—climbed out of his Volkswagen and tilted his face to the rain. He was a connoisseur of this particular rain. He knew the taste of it, the smell of it. It was Baltic rain from the north, cold and sea-scented, tangy with salt. For an instant he was back twenty years, in the conning tower of a U-boat, slipping out of Wilhelmshaven, lights doused, into the darkness.

He looked at his watch. It was just after seven in the morning.

Drawn up on the roadside before him were three other cars. The occupants of two were asleep in the drivers' seats. The third was a patrol car of the *Ordnungspolizei*—the Orpo, as every German called them. It was empty.

Through its open window came the crackle of static, sharp in the damp air, punctuated by jabbering bursts of speech. The revolving light on its roof lit up the forest beside the road: blue-black, blue-black, blue-black.

March looked around for the Orpo patrolmen and saw them sheltering by the lake under a dripping birch tree. Something gleamed pale in the mud at their feet. On a nearby log sat a young man in a black tracksuit, SS insignia on his breast pocket. He was hunched forward, elbows resting on his knees, hands pressed against the sides of his head—the image of misery.

March took a last draw on his cigarette and flicked it away. It fizzed and died on the wet road.

As he approached, one of the policemen raised his arm. "Heil, Hitler!"

March ignored him and slithered down the muddy bank to inspect the corpse.

It was an old man's body—cold, fat, hairless and shockingly white. From a distance, it could have been an alabaster statue dumped in the mud. Smeared with dirt, the corpse sprawled on its back half out of the water, arms flung wide, head tilted back. One eye was screwed shut, the other squinted balefully at the filthy sky.

"Your name, *Unterwachtmeister*?" March had a soft voice. Without taking his eyes off the body, he addressed the Orpo man who had saluted.

"Ratka, Herr *Sturmbannführer.*"

Sturmbannführer was an SS title, equivalent in Wehrmacht rank to major, and Ratka—dog tired and skin soaked though he was—seemed eager to show respect. March knew his type without even looking around: three applications to transfer to the Kripo, all turned down; a dutiful wife who had produced a football team of children for the Führer; an income of 200 Reichsmarks a month. A life lived in hope.

"Well, Ratka," said March in that soft voice again. "What time was he discovered?"

"Just over an hour ago, sir. We were at the end of our

shift, patrolling in Nikolassee. We took the call. Priority One. We were here in five minutes."

"Who found him?"

Ratka jerked his thumb over his shoulder.

The young man in the tracksuit rose to his feet. He could not have been more than eighteen. His hair was cropped so close the pink scalp showed through the dusting of light brown hair. March noticed how he avoided looking at the body.

"Your name?"

*"SS-Schütze* Hermann Jost, sir." He spoke with a Saxon accent—nervous, uncertain, anxious to please. "From the Sepp Dietrich training academy at Schlachtensee." March knew it: a monstrosity of concrete and asphalt built in the 1950s, just south of the Havel. "I run here most mornings. It was still dark. At first I thought it was a swan," he added helplessly.

Ratka snorted, contempt on his face. An SS cadet scared of one dead old man! No wonder the war in the Urals was dragging on forever.

"Did you see anyone else, Jost?" March spoke in a kindly tone, like an uncle.

"Nobody, sir. There's a telephone booth in the picnic area, half a kilometer back. I called, then came here and waited until the police arrived. There wasn't a soul on the road."

March looked again at the body. It was very fat. Maybe 110 kilos.

"Let's get him out of the water." He turned toward the road. "Time to raise our sleeping beauties." Ratka, shifting from foot to foot in the downpour, grinned.

It was raining harder now, and the Kladow side of the lake had virtually disappeared. Water pattered on the leaves of the trees and drummed on the car roofs. There was a heavy rain-smell of corruption: rich earth and rotting vegetation. March's hair was plastered to his scalp, water trickled down the back of his neck. He did not notice. For March, every case, however routine, held—at the start, at least—the promise of adventure.

He was forty-two years old—slim, with gray hair and cool gray eyes that matched the sky. During the war, the Propaganda Ministry had invented a nickname for the men of the U-boats—the "gray wolves"—and it would have been a good name for March in one sense, for he was a determined detective. But he was not by nature a wolf, did not run with the pack, was more reliant on brain than on muscle, so his colleagues called him "the Fox" instead.

*U-boat weather!*

He flung open the door of the white Skoda and was hit by a gust of hot, stale air from the car heater.

"Morning, Spiedel!" He shook the police photographer's bony shoulder. "Time to get wet." Spiedel jerked awake. He gave March a glare.

The driver's window of the other Skoda was already being wound down as March approached it. "All right, March. All right." It was SS Surgeon August Eisler, a Kripo pathologist, his voice a squeak of affronted dignity. "Save your barrack-room humor for those who appreciate it."

They gathered at the water's edge, all except Dr. Eisler, who stood apart, sheltering under an ancient black umbrella he did not offer to share. Spiedel screwed a flashbulb onto his camera and carefully planted his right foot on a lump of clay. He swore as the lake lapped over his shoe.

"Shit!"

The flash popped, freezing the scene for an instant: the white faces, the silver threads of rain, the darkness of the woods. A swan came scudding out of some nearby reeds to see what was happening and began circling a few meters away.

"Protecting her nest," said the young SS man.

"I want another here." March pointed. "And one here."

Spiedel cursed again and pulled his dripping foot out of the mud. The camera flashed twice more.

March bent down and grasped the body under the armpits. The flesh was hard, like cold rubber, and slippery.

"Help me."

The Orpo men each took an arm and together, grunting with the effort, they heaved, sliding the corpse out of the water, over the muddy bank and onto the sodden grass. As March straightened, he caught the look on Jost's face.

The old man had been wearing a pair of blue swimming trunks, which had worked their way down to his knees. In the freezing water, the genitals had shriveled to a tiny clutch of white eggs in a nest of black pubic hair.

The left foot was missing.

It had to be, thought March. This was a day when nothing would be simple. An adventure, indeed.

"Herr Doctor. Your opinion, please."

With a sigh of irritation, Eisler daintily stepped forward, removing a glove from one hand. The corpse's leg ended at the bottom of the calf. Still holding the umbrella, Eisler bent stiffly and ran his fingers around the stump.

"A propeller?" asked March. He had seen bodies dragged out of busy waterways—from the Tegelersee and the Spree in Berlin, from the Alster in Hamburg—that looked as if butchers had been at them.

"No." Eisler withdrew his hand. "An old amputation. Rather well done, in fact." He pressed hard on the chest with his fist. Muddy water gushed from the mouth and bubbled out of the nostrils. "Rigor mortis fairly advanced. Dead twelve hours. Maybe less." He pulled his glove back on.

A diesel engine rattled somewhere through the trees behind them.

"The ambulance," said Ratka. "They take their time."

March gestured to Spiedel. "Take another picture."

Looking down at the corpse, March lit a cigarette. Then

he squatted on his haunches and stared into the single, open eye. He stayed that way a long while. The camera flashed again. The swan reared up, flapped her wings and turned toward the center of the lake in search of food.

Kripo headquarters lie on the other side of Berlin, a twenty-five-minute drive from the Havel. March needed a statement from Jost and offered to drop him back at his barracks to change, but Jost said no: he would sooner make his statement quickly. So once the body had been stowed aboard the ambulance and dispatched to the morgue, they set off in March's little four-door Volkswagen through the rush hour traffic.

It was one of those dismal Berlin mornings when the famous *Berlinerluft* seems not so much bracing as merely raw, the moisture stinging the face and hands like a thousand frozen needles. On the Potsdamer-Chaussee, the spray from the wheels of the passing cars forced the few pedestrians close to the sides of the buildings. Watching them through the rain-flecked window, March imagined a city of blind men, feeling their way to work.

It was all so *normal.* Later, that was what would strike him most. It was like having an accident: before it, nothing out of the ordinary; then, the moment; and after it, a world that was changed forever. For there was nothing more routine than a body fished out of the Havel. It happened twice a month—derelicts and failed businessmen, reckless kids and lovelorn teenagers; accidents and suicides and murders; the desperate, the foolish, the sad.

The telephone had rung in his apartment in Ansbacher-Strasse shortly after 6:15. The call had not awakened him. He had been lying in the semidarkness with his eyes open, listening to the rain. For the past few months he had slept badly.

"March? We've got a report of a body in the Havel." It was Krause, the Kripo's night duty officer. "Go and take a look, there's a good fellow."

March had said he was not interested.

"Your interest or lack of it is beside the point."

"I am not interested," March had said, "because I am not on duty. I was on duty last week, and the week before." *And the week before that,* he might have added. "This is my day off. Look at your list again."

There had been a pause at the other end, then Krause had come back on the line, grudgingly apologetic. "You're in luck, March. I was looking at last week's rota. You can go back to sleep. Or—" he had sniggered "—whatever else it was you were doing."

A gust of wind had slashed rain against the window, rattling the pane.

There was a standard procedure when a body was discovered: a pathologist, a police photographer and an investigator had to attend the scene at once. The investigators worked off a rota kept at Kripo headquarters in Werderscher-Markt.

"Who's on today, as a matter of interest?"

"Max Jaeger."

Jaeger. March shared an office with Jaeger. He had looked at his alarm clock and thought of the little house in Pankow where Max lived with his wife and four daughters: during the week, breakfast was just about the only time he saw them. March, on the other hand, was divorced and lived alone. He had set aside the afternoon to spend with his son. But the long hours of the morning stretched ahead, a blank. The way he felt, it would be good to have something routine to distract him.

"Oh, leave him in peace," he had said. "I'm awake. I'll take it."

That had been nearly two hours ago. March glanced at his passenger in the rearview mirror. Jost had been silent ever since they had left the Havel. He sat stiffly in the backseat, staring at the gray buildings slipping by.

At the Brandenburg Gate, a policeman on a motorcycle flagged them to a halt.

In the middle of Pariser-Platz, an SA band in sodden brown uniforms wheeled and stamped in the puddles. Through the closed windows of the Volkswagen came the muffled thump of drums and trumpets pounding out an old Party marching song. Several dozen people had gathered outside the Academy of Arts to watch them, shoulders hunched against the rain.

It was impossible to drive across Berlin at this time of year without encountering a similar rehearsal. In six days' time it would be Adolf Hitler's birthday—the *Führertag,* a public holiday—and every band in the Reich would be on parade. The windshield wipers beat time like a metronome.

"Here we see the final proof," murmured March, watching the crowd, "that in the face of martial music, the German people are *mad.*"

He turned to Jost, who gave a thin smile.

A clash of cymbals ended the tune. There was a patter of damp applause. The bandmaster turned and bowed. Behind him, the SA men had already begun half walking, half running back to their bus. The motorcycle cop waited until the Platz was clear, then blew a short blast on his whistle. With a white-gloved hand he waved them through the gate.

Unter den Linden gaped ahead of them. It had lost its lime trees in '36—cut down in an act of official vandalism at the time of the Berlin Olympics. In their place, on either side of the boulevard, the city's *Gauleiter,* Josef Goebbels, had erected an avenue of ten-meter-high stone columns, on each of which perched a Party eagle, wings outstretched. Water dripped from their beaks and wingtips. It was like driving through a Red Indian burial ground.

March slowed for the lights at the Friedrich-Strasse intersection and turned right. Two minutes later they were parking in a space opposite the Kripo building in Werderscher-Markt.

It was an ugly place—a heavy, soot-streaked, Wilhelmine monstrosity six stories high on the south side of the Markt. March had been coming here nearly seven days of the week for ten years. As his ex-wife had frequently complained, it had become more familiar to him than home. Inside, beyond the SS sentries and the creaky revolving door, a board announced the current state of terrorist alert. There were four codes, in ascending order of seriousness: green, blue, black and red. Today, as always, the alert was red.

A pair of guards in a glass booth scrutinized them as they entered the foyer. March showed his identity card and signed in Jost.

The Markt was busier than usual. The workload always tripled in the week before the *Führertag.* Secretaries with boxes of files clattered on high heels across the marble floor. The air smelled thickly of wet overcoats and floor polish. Groups of officers in Orpo green and Kripo black stood whispering of crime. Above their heads, from opposite ends of the lobby, garlanded busts of the Führer and the head of the Reich Main Security Office, Reinhard Heydrich, stared at each other with blank eyes.

March pulled back the metal grille of the elevator and ushered Jost inside.

The security forces Heydrich controlled were divided into three. At the bottom of the pecking order were the Orpo, the ordinary cops. They picked up the drunks, cruised the *Autobahnen,* issued the speeding tickets, made the arrests, fought the fires, patrolled the railways and the airports, answered the emergency calls, fished the bodies out of the lakes.

At the top were the Sipo, the Security Police. The Sipo embraced both the Gestapo and the Party's own security force, the SD. Their headquarters was in a grim complex around Prinz-Albrecht-Strasse, a kilometer southwest of the Markt. They dealt with terrorism, subversion, counterespionage and "crimes against the state." They had their ears in every factory and school, hospital and mess; in every town, in every village, in every street. A body in a lake would concern the Sipo only if it belonged to a terrorist or a traitor.

And somewhere between the other two, and blurring into both, came the Kripo—Department V of the Reich Main Security Office. They investigated straightforward crime, from burglary through bank robbery, violent assault, rape and mixed marriage, all the way up to murder. Bodies in lakes—who they were and how they had gotten there—they were Kripo business.

The elevator stopped at the second floor. The corridor was lit like an aquarium. Weak neon bounced off green linoleum and green-washed walls. There was the same smell of polish as in the lobby, but here it was spiced with lavatory disinfectant and stale cigarette smoke. Twenty doors of frosted glass, some half open, lined the hallway. These were the investigators' offices. From one came the sound of a solitary finger picking at a typewriter; in another, a telephone rang unanswered.

" 'The nerve center in the ceaseless war against the criminal enemies of National Socialism,' " said March, quoting a recent headline in the Party newspaper, the *Völkischer Beobachter.* He paused, and when Jost continued to look blank he explained, "A joke."

"Sorry?"

"Forget it."

He pushed open a door and switched on the light. His office was little more than a gloomy cupboard, a cell, its solitary window opening on to a courtyard of blackened brick. One wall was shelved: tattered, leather-bound volumes of statutes and decrees, a handbook on forensic science, a dictionary, an atlas, a Berlin street guide, telephone directories, box files with labels gummed to them—"Braune," "Hundt," "Stark," "Zadek"—every one a bureaucratic tombstone memorializing some long-forgotten victim. Another side of the office was taken up by four filing cabinets. On top of one was a spider plant, placed there by a middle-aged secretary two years before at the height of an unspoken and unrequited passion for Xavier March. It was now dead. That was all the furniture, apart from two wooden desks pushed together beneath the window. One was March's; the other belonged to Max Jaeger.

March hung his overcoat on a peg by the door. He preferred not to wear a uniform when he could avoid it, and this morning he had used the rainstorm on the Havel as an excuse to dress in gray trousers and a thick blue sweater. He pushed Jaeger's chair toward Jost. "Sit down. Coffee?"

"Please."

There was a machine in the corridor. "We've got fucking *photographs.* Can you believe it? Look at that." Along the passage March could hear the voice of Fiebes of VB3—the sexual crimes division—boasting of his latest success. "Her maid took them. Look, you can see every *hair.* The girl should turn professional."

What would this be? March thumped the side of the coffee machine and it ejected a plastic cup. Some officer's wife, he guessed, and a Polish laborer shipped in from the General Government to work in the garden. It was usually a Pole—a dreamy, soulful Pole plucking at the heart of a wife whose husband was away at the front. It sounded as if they had been photographed in flagrante by some jealous girl from the *Bund deutscher Mädel,* anxious to please the authorities. This was a sexual crime, as defined in the 1935 Race Defilement Act.

He gave the machine another thump.

There would be a hearing in the People's Court, salaciously recorded in *Der Stürmer* as a warning to others. Two years in Ravensbrück for the wife. Demotion and disgrace for the husband. Twenty-five years for the Pole, if he was lucky; death if he was not.

"Fuck!" A male voice muttered something, and Fiebes, a weasel inspector in his mid-fifties whose wife had run off with an SS ski instructor ten years before, gave a shout of laughter. March, a cup of black coffee in either hand, retreated to his office and slammed the door behind him as loudly as he could with his foot.

*Reichskriminalpolizei* *Werderscher-markt 5-6*
*Berlin*

*Statement of Witness*

My name is Hermann Friedrich Jost. I was born on 2-23-45 in Dresden. I am a cadet at the Sepp Dietrich Academy, Berlin. At 0530 this morning, I left for my regular training run. I prefer to run alone. My normal route takes me west through the Grunewald Forest to the Havel, north along the lakeshore to the Lindwerder Restaurant, then south to the barracks in Schlachtensee. Three hundred meters north of the Schwanenwerder causeway, I saw an object lying in the water at the edge of the lake. It was the body of a male. I ran to a telephone half a kilometer along the lake path and informed the police. I returned to the body and waited for the arrival of the authorities. During all this time it was raining hard and I saw nobody.

I am making this statement of my own free will in the presence of Kripo investigator Xavier March.

SS-Schütze H. F. Jost.
0824 hours
4/14/64

March leaned back in his chair and studied the young man as he signed his statement. There were no hard lines to his face. It was as pink and soft as a baby's, with a clamor of acne around the mouth, a whisper of blond hair on the upper lip. March doubted if he shaved.

"Why do you run alone?"

Jost handed back his statement. "It gives me a chance to think. It is good to be alone once in the day. One is not often alone in a barracks."

"How long have you been a cadet?"

"Three months."

"Do you enjoy it?"

"Enjoy it!" Jost turned his face to the window. "I'd just begun studying at the university at Göttingen when my call-up came through. Let us say it was not the happiest day of my life."

"What were you studying?"

"Literature."

"German?"

"What other sort is there?" Jost gave one of his watery smiles. "I hope to go back to the university when I have served my three years. I want to be a teacher; a writer. Not a soldier."

March scanned his statement. "If you're so antimilitary, what are you doing in the SS?" He could guess the answer.

"My father. He was a founder member of the *Leibstandarte Adolf Hitler.* You know how it is: I'm his only son; it was his dearest wish."

"You must hate it."

Jost shrugged. "I survive. And I've been told—unofficially, naturally—that I will not have to go to the front. They need an assistant at the officers' school in Bad Tölz to teach a course on the degeneracy of American literature. That sounds more like my kind of thing: degeneracy." He risked another smile. "Perhaps I shall become an expert in the field."

March laughed and glanced again at the statement. Something was not right here, and now he saw it. "No doubt you will." He put the statement to one side and stood up. "I wish you luck with your teaching."

"Am I free to go?"

"Of course."

With a look of relief, Jost got to his feet. March grasped the door handle. "One thing." He turned and stared into the SS cadet's eyes. "Why are you lying to me?"

Jost jerked his head back. "What?"

"You say you left the barracks at five-thirty. You called the cops at five past six. Schwanenwerder is three kilometers from the barracks. You're fit: you run every day. You do not dawdle: it is raining hard. Unless you suddenly developed a limp, you must have arrived at the lake quite some time before six. So there are—what?—twenty minutes out of thirty-five unaccounted for in your statement. What were you doing, Jost?"

The young man looked stricken. "Maybe I left the barracks later. Or maybe I did a couple of circuits of the running track there first—"

" 'Maybe, maybe.' " March shook his head sadly. "These are facts that can be checked, and I warn you: it will go hard for you if I have to find out the truth and bring it to you, rather than the other way around. You are a homosexual, yes?"

"Herr Sturmbannführer! For God's sake—"

March put his hands on Jost's shoulders. "I don't care. Perhaps you run alone every morning so you can meet some fellow in the Grunewald for twenty minutes. That's your business. It's no crime in my book. All I'm interested in is the body. Did you see something? What did you really do?"

Jost shook his head. "Nothing. I swear." Tears were welling in his wide, pale eyes.

"Very well." March released him. "Wait downstairs. I'll arrange transport to take you back to Schlachtensee." He opened the door. "Remember what I said: better you tell me the truth now than I find it out for myself later."

Jost hesitated, and for a moment March thought he might say something, but then he walked out into the corridor and was gone.

March phoned the basement garage and ordered a car. He hung up and stared out of the grimy window at the wall opposite. The black brick glistened under the film of rainwater pouring down from the upper stories. Had he been too hard on the boy? Probably. But sometimes the truth could only be ambushed, taken unguarded in a surprise attack. Was Jost lying? Certainly. But then if he were a homosexual, he could scarcely afford not to lie: anyone found guilty of "anticommunity acts" went straight to a labor camp. SS men arrested for homosexuality were attached to punishment battalions on the eastern front; few returned.

March had seen a score of young men like Jost in the past year. There were more of them every day. Rebelling against their parents. Questioning the state. Listening to American radio stations. Circulating their crudely printed copies of proscribed books—Günter Grass and Graham Greene, George Orwell and J. D. Salinger. Chiefly, they protested against the war—the seemingly endless struggle against the American-backed Soviet guerrillas, which had been grinding on east of the Urals for twenty years.

He felt suddenly ashamed of his treatment of Jost and considered going down to apologize to him. But then he decided, as he always did, that his duty to the dead came first. His penance for his morning's bullying would be to put a name to the body in the lake.

The duty room of the Berlin Kriminalpolizei occupies most of Werderscher-Markt's third floor. March mounted the stairs two at a time. Outside the entrance, a guard armed with a machine gun demanded his pass. The door opened with a thud of electronic bolts.

An illuminated map of Berlin takes up half the far wall. A galaxy of stars, orange in the semidarkness, marks the capital's 122 police stations. To its left is a second map, even larger, depicting the entire Reich. Red lights pinpoint those towns big enough to warrant their own Kripo divisions. The center of Europe glows crimson. Further east, the lights gradually thin until, beyond Moscow, there are only a few isolated sparks, winking like camp fires in the blackness. It is a planetarium of crime.

Krause, the duty officer for the Berlin *Gau*, sat on a raised platform beneath the display. He was on the telephone as March approached and raised his hand in greeting. Before him, a dozen women in starched white shirts sat in glass partitions, each wearing a headset with a microphone attached. What they must hear! A sergeant from a Panzer division comes home from a tour in the East. After a family supper, he takes out his pistol, shoots his wife and each of his three children in turn. Then he splatters his skull across the ceiling. A hysterical neighbor calls the cops. And the news comes here—is controlled, evaluated, reduced—before being passed downstairs to that corridor with cracked green linoleum, stale with cigarette smoke.

Behind the duty officer, a uniformed secretary with a sour face was making entries on the night incident board. There were four columns: crime (serious), crime (violent), incidents, fatalities. Each category was further quartered: time reported, source of information, detail of report, action taken. An average night of mayhem in the world's largest city, with its population of ten million, was reduced to hieroglyphics on a few square meters of white plastic.

There had been eighteen deaths since ten the previous night. The worst incident—*1H 2D 4K*—was three adults and four children killed in a car crash in Pankow just after eleven. No action taken; that could be left to the Orpo. A family burned to death in a house fire in Kreuzberg, a stabbing outside a bar in Wedding, a woman beaten to death in Spandau. The record of March's own disrupted morning was last on the list: *0607 hours (O)* (that meant notification had come from the Orpo) *1H Havel/March.* The secretary stepped back and recapped her pen with a sharp click.

Krause had finished his telephone call and was looking defensive. "I've already apologized, March."

"Forget it. I want the missing list. Berlin area. Say, the past forty-eight hours."

"No problem." Krause looked relieved and swiveled around in his chair to the sour-faced woman. "You heard the investigator, Helga. Check whether anything's come in in the past hour." He spun back to face March, red-eyed with lack of sleep. "I'd have left it an hour. But any trouble around that place—you know how it is."

March looked up at the Berlin map. Most of it was a gray cobweb of streets. But over to the left were two splashes of color: the green of the Grunewald Forest and, running alongside it, the blue ribbon of the Havel. Curling into the lake, in the shape of a fetus, was an island linked to the shore by a thin umbilical causeway.

Schwanenwerder.

"Does Goebbels still have a place there?"

Krause nodded. "And the rest."

It was one of the most fashionable addresses in Berlin, practically a government compound. A few dozen large houses screened from the road. A sentry at the entrance to the causeway. A good place for privacy, for security, for forest views and private moorings; a bad place to discover a body. The corpse had been washed up fewer than three hundred meters away.

Krause said, "The local Orpo call it 'the pheasant run.' "

March smiled: "golden pheasants" was street slang for the Party leadership.

"It's not good to leave a mess for too long on *that* doorstep."

Helga had returned. "Persons reported missing since Sunday morning," she announced, "and still unaccounted for." She gave a long roll of printed-out names to Krause, who glanced at it and passed it on to March. "Plenty to keep you busy there." He seemed to find this amusing. "You should give it to that fat friend of yours, Jaeger. He's the one who should be looking after this business, remember?"

"Thanks. I'll make a start, at least."

Krause shook his head. "You put in twice the hours of the others. You get no promotions. You're on shitty pay. Are you crazy or what?"

March had rolled the list of missing persons into a tube. He leaned forward and tapped Krause lightly on the chest with it. "You forget yourself, comrade," he said. *"Arbeit macht frei."* The slogan of the labor camps: Work makes you free.

He turned and made his way back through the ranks of telephonists. Behind him he could hear Krause appealing to Helga. "See what I mean? What the hell kind of a joke is that?"

March arrived back in his office just as Max Jaeger was hanging up his coat. "Zavi!" Jaeger spread his arms wide. "I got a message from the duty room. What can I say?" He wore the uniform of an SS-Sturmbannführer. The black tunic still bore traces of his breakfast.

"Put it down to my soft old heart," said March. "And don't get too excited. There was nothing on the corpse to identify it and there are a hundred people missing in Berlin since Sunday. It'll take hours just to go through the list. And I've promised to take my boy out this afternoon, so you'll be on your own with it."

He lit a cigarette and explained the details: the location, the missing foot, his suspicions about Jost. Jaeger took it in with a series of grunts. He was a shambling, untidy hulk of a man, two meters tall, with clumsy hands and feet. He was fifty, nearly ten years older than March, but they had shared an office since 1959 and sometimes worked as a team. Colleagues in Werderscher-Markt joked about them behind their backs: the Fox and the Bear. And maybe there was something of the old married couple about them, in the way they bickered with and covered for each other.

"This is the 'missing' list." March sat down at his desk and unrolled the printout: names, dates of birth, times of disappearance, addresses of informants. Jaeger leaned over his shoulder. He smoked stubby fat cigars, and his uniform reeked of them. "According to the good doctor Eisler, our man probably died some time after six last night, so the chances are nobody missed him until seven or eight at the earliest. They may even be waiting to see if he shows up this morning. So he may not be on the list. But we have to consider two other possibilities, do we not? One: he went missing some time *before* he died. Two—and we know from hard experience this is not impossible—Eisler has screwed up the time of death."

"The guy isn't fit to be a vet," said Jaeger.

March counted swiftly. "One hundred two names. I'd put the age of our man at sixty."

"Better say fifty, to be safe. Twelve hours in the drink and nobody looks his best."

"True. So we exclude everyone on the list born after 1914. That should bring it down to a dozen names. Identification couldn't be much easier: was Grandpa missing a foot?" March folded the sheet, tore it in two and handed one half to Jaeger. "What are the Orpo stations around the Havel?"

"Nikolassee," said Max. "Wannsee. Kladow. Gatow. Pichelsdorf—but that's probably too far north."

Over the next half hour, March called each of them in turn, including Pichelsdorf, to see if any clothing had been handed in or if some local derelict matched the description of the man in the lake. Nothing. He turned his attention to his half of the list. By 11:30 he had exhausted every likely name. He stood up and stretched.

"Mr. Nobody."

Jaeger had finished calling ten minutes earlier and was staring out of the window, smoking. "Popular fellow, isn't he? Makes even you look loved." He removed his cigar and picked some shreds of loose tobacco from his tongue. "I'll see if the duty room has received any more names. Leave it to me. Have a good time with Pili."

The late-morning service had just ended in the ugly church opposite Kripo headquarters. March stood on the other side of the street and watched the priest, a shabby raincoat over his vestments, locking the door. Religion was officially discouraged in Germany. How many worshippers, March wondered, had braved the Gestapo's spies to attend. Half a dozen? The priest slipped the heavy iron key into his pocket and turned around. He saw March looking at him, and immediately scuttled away, eyes cast down, like a man caught in the middle of an illegal transaction. March buttoned his trench coat and followed him into the filthy Berlin morning.

"Construction of the Arch of Triumph was commenced in 1946 and work was completed in time for the Day of National Reawakening in 1950. The inspiration for the design came from the Führer and is based upon original drawings made by him during the Years of Struggle."

The passengers on the tour bus—at least those who could understand—digested this information. They raised themselves out of their seats or leaned into the aisle to get a better view. Xavier March, halfway down the bus, lifted his son onto his lap. Their guide, a middle-aged woman clad in the dark green of the Reich Tourist Ministry, stood at the front, feet planted wide apart, back to the windshield. Her voice over the address system was thick with cold.

"The arch is constructed of granite and has a capacity of two million, three hundred and sixty-five thousand, six hundred and eighty-five cubic meters." She sneezed. "The Arc de Triomphe in Paris will fit into it forty-nine times."

For a moment, the arch loomed over them. Then, suddenly, they were passing through it—an immense stone-ribbed tunnel longer than a football pitch, higher than a fifteen-story building, with the vaulted, shadowed roof of a cathedral. The headlights and taillights of eight lanes of traffic danced in the afternoon gloom.

"The arch has a height of one hundred and eighteen meters. It is one hundred and sixty-eight meters wide and has a depth of one hundred and nineteen meters. On the inner walls are carved the names of the three million soldiers who fell in defence of the Fatherland in the wars of 1914 to 1918 and 1939 to 1946."

She sneezed again. The passengers dutifully craned their necks to peer at the Roll of the Fallen. They were a mixed party. A group of Japanese, draped with cameras; an American couple with a little girl Pili's age; some German settlers, from Ostland or the Ukraine, in Berlin for the *Führertag.* March looked away as they passed the Roll of the Fallen. Somewhere on it were the names of his father and both his grandfathers. He kept his eyes on the guide. When she thought no one was looking, she turned away and quickly wiped her nose on her sleeve. The coach reemerged into the drizzle.

"Leaving the arch, we enter the central section of the Avenue of Victory. The avenue was designed by *Reichsminister* Albert Speer and was completed in 1957. It is one hundred and twenty-three meters wide and five-point-six kilometers in length. It is both wider, and two and a half times longer, than the Champs Elysées in Paris."

Higher, longer, bigger, wider, more expensive . . . even in victory, thought March, Germany has a parvenu's inferiority complex. Nothing stands on its own. Everything has to be compared with what the foreigners have . . .

"The view from this point northward along the Avenue of Victory is considered one of the wonders of the world."

"One of the wonders of the world," repeated Pili in a whisper.

And it was, even on a day like this. Dense with traffic, the avenue stretched before them, flanked on either side by the glass-and-granite walls of Speer's new buildings:

ministries, offices, big stores, cinemas, apartment blocks. At the far end of this river of light, rising as gray as a battleship through the spray, was the Great Hall of the Reich, its dome half hidden in the low clouds.

There were appreciative murmurs from the settlers. "It's like a mountain," said the woman sitting behind March. She was with her husband and four boys. They had probably been planning this trip all winter. A Tourist Ministry brochure and a dream of April in Berlin: comforts to warm them in the snowbound, moonless nights of Minsk or Kiev, a thousand kilometers from home. How had they gotten here? A package tour organized by Strength-Through-Joy, perhaps: two hours in a Junkers jet with a stopoff in Warsaw. Or a three-day drive in the family Volkswagen on the Berlin-Moscow autobahn.

Pili wriggled out of his father's grasp and walked unsteadily to the front of the coach. March pinched the bridge of his nose between thumb and forefinger, a nervous habit he had picked up—when?—in the U-boat service, he supposed, when the screws of the British warships sounded so close the hull shook and you never knew if their next depth charge would be your last. He had been invalided out of the navy in 1948 with suspected TB and spent a year convalescing. Then, for want of anything better to do, he had joined the *Marineküstenpolizei,* the Coastal Police, in Wilhelmshaven as a lieutenant. That year he had married Klara Eckart, a nurse he had met at the TB clinic. In 1952, he had joined the Hamburg Kripo. In 1954, with Klara pregnant and the marriage already failing, he had been promoted to Berlin. Paul—Pili—had been born exactly ten years and one month ago.

What had gone wrong? He did not blame Klara. She had not changed. She had always been a strong woman who wanted certain simple things from life: home, family, friends, acceptance. But March: he *had* changed. After ten years in the navy and twelve months in virtual isolation, he had stepped ashore into a world he barely recognized. As he went to work, watched television, ate with friends, even—God help him—slept beside his wife, he sometimes imagined himself aboard a U-boat still: cruising beneath the surface of everyday life; solitary, watchful.

He had picked Pili up at noon from Klara's place—a bungalow on a dreary postwar housing estate in Lichtenrade, in the southern suburbs. Park in the street, sound the horn twice, watch for the twitch in the parlor curtain. This was the routine that had evolved, unspoken, since their divorce five years ago—a means of avoiding embarrassing encounters; a ritual to be endured one Sunday in four, work permitting, under the strict provisions of the Reich Marriages Act. It was rare for him to see his son on a Tuesday, but this was a school vacation: since 1959, children had been given a week off for the Führer's birthday, rather than for Easter.

The door had opened and Pili had appeared, like a shy child actor being pushed out onto a stage against his will. Wearing his new *Pimpf* uniform—crisp black shirt and dark blue shorts—he had climbed wordlessly into the car. March had given him an awkward hug.

"You look smart. How's school?"

"All right."

"And your mother?"

The boy shrugged.

"What would you like to do?"

He shrugged again.

They had lunch in Budapester-Strasse, opposite the zoo, in a modern place with vinyl seats and a plastic-topped table: father and son, one with beer and sausages, the other with apple juice and a hamburger. They talked about the *Pimpfen* and Pili brightened. Until you were a Pimpf you were nothing, "a nonuniformed creature who has never participated in a group meeting or a route march." You were allowed to join when you were ten and stayed until you were fourteen, when you passed into the full Hitler Youth.

"I was top in the initiation test."

"Good lad."

"You have to run sixty meters in twelve seconds," said Pili. "Do the long jump and the shot put. There's a route march—a day and a half. Written stuff. Party philosophy. And you have to recite the 'Horst Wessel Lied.' "

For a moment, March thought he was about to break into song. He cut in hurriedly, "And your dagger?"

Pili fumbled in his pocket, a crease of concentration on his forehead. How like his mother he is, thought March. The same wide cheekbones and full mouth, the same serious brown eyes set far apart. Pili laid the dagger carefully on the table before him. He picked it up. It reminded him of the day he had gotten his own—when was it? '34? The excitement of a boy who believes he's been admitted to the company of men. He turned it over and the swastika on the hilt glinted in the light. He felt the weight of it in his hand, then gave it back.

"I'm proud of you," he lied. "What do you want to do? We can go to the cinema. Or the zoo."

"I want to go on the bus."

"But we did that last time. And the time before."

"Don't care. I want to go on the bus."

"The Great Hall of the Reich is the largest building in the world. It rises to a height of more than a quarter of a kilometer, and on certain days—observe today—the top of its dome is lost from view. The dome itself is one hundred and forty meters in diameter, and St. Peter's in Rome will fit into it sixteen times."

They had reached the top of the Avenue of Victory and were entering Adolf-Hitler-Platz. To the left, the square was bounded by the headquarters of the Wehrmacht High Command, to the right by the new Reich Chancellery and Palace of the Führer. Ahead was the hall. Its grayness had dissolved as their distance from it had diminished. Now they could see what the guide was telling them: that the pillars supporting the frontage were of red granite, mined in Sweden, flanked at either end by golden statues of Atlas and Tellus, bearing on their shoulders spheres depicting the heavens and the earth.

The building was as crystal white as a wedding cake, its dome of beaten copper a dull green. Pili was still at the front of the coach.

"The Great Hall is used only for the most solemn ceremonies of the German Reich and has a capacity of one hundred and eighty thousand people. One interesting and unforeseen phenomenon: the breath from this number of humans rises into the cupola and forms clouds, which condense and fall as light rain. The Great Hall is the only building in the world that generates its own climate . . ."

March had heard it all before. He looked out of the window and saw the body in the mud. Swimming trunks! What had the old man been thinking of, swimming on Monday night? Berlin had been blanketed by black clouds from late afternoon. When the storm had finally broken, the rain had descended in steel rods, drilling the streets and roofs, drowning the thunder. Suicide, perhaps? Think of it. Wade into the cold lake, strike out for the center, tread water in the darkness, watch the lightning over the trees, wait for tiredness to do the rest . . .

Pili had returned to his seat and was bouncing up and down in excitement. "Are we going to see the Führer, Papa?"

The vision evaporated and March felt guilty. This daydreaming was what Klara used to complain of: *"Even when you're here, you're not really here. . . ."*

He said, "I don't think so."

The guide again: "On the right is the Reich Chancellery and residence of the Führer. Its total façade measures exactly seven hundred meters, exceeding by one hundred meters the façade of Louis XIV's palace at Versailles."

The Chancellery slowly uncoiled as the bus drove by: marble pillars and red mosaics, bronze lions, gilded silhouettes, Gothic script—a Chinese dragon of a building, asleep at the side of the square. A four-man SS honor guard stood at attention beneath a billowing swastika banner. There were no windows, but set into the wall, five stories above the ground, was the balcony on which the Führer showed himself on those occasions when a million people gathered in the Platz. There were a few dozen sightseers even now, gazing up at the tightly drawn shutters, faces pale with expectation, hoping . . .

March glanced at his son. Pili was transfixed, his little dagger clutched tightly in his hand like a crucifix.

The coach dropped them back at its pickup point outside the Gotenland railway station. It was after five as they descended from the bus, and the last vestiges of natural light were fading. The day was giving up on itself in disgust.

The entrance to the station was disgorging people—soldiers with kit bags walking with girlfriends and wives, foreign workers with cardboard suitcases and shabby bundles tied with string, settlers emerging after two days' traveling from the steppes, staring in shock at the lights and the crowds. Uniforms were everywhere. Dark blue, green, brown, black, gray, khaki. It was like a factory at the end of a shift. There was a factory sound of shunting metal and shrill whistles, and a factory smell of heat and oil, stale air and steel dust. Exclamation marks clamored from the walls. "Be vigilant at all times!" "Attention! Report suspicious packages at once!" "Terrorist alert!"

From here, trains as high as houses, with a gauge of four meters, left for the outposts of the German Empire—for Gotenland (formerly the Crimea) and Theodorichshafen (formerly Sevastopol); for the *Generalkommissariat* of Taurida and its capital, Melitopol; for Volhynia-Podolia, Zhitomir, Kiev, Nikolayev, Dnepropetrovsk, Kharkov, Rostov, Saratov . . . it was the terminus of a new world. Announcements of arrivals and departures punctuated the "Coriolan Overture" on the public address system. March tried to take Pili's hand as they wove through the crowd, but the boy shook him away.

It took fifteen minutes to retrieve the car from the underground car park and another fifteen to get clear of the clogged streets around the station. They drove in silence. It was not until they were almost back at Lichtenrade that Pili suddenly blurted out, "You're an asocial, aren't you?"

It was such an odd word to hear on the lips of a ten-year-old, and so carefully pronounced, that March almost laughed out loud. An asocial: one step down from traitor in the Party's lexicon of crime. A noncontributor to Winter Relief. A nonjoiner of the endless National Socialist associations. The NS Skiing Federation. The Association of NS Ramblers. The Greater German NS Motoring Club. The NS Criminal Police Officers' Society. He had even one afternoon come across a parade in the Lustgarten organized by the NS League of Wearers of the Lifesaving Medal.

"That's nonsense."

"Uncle Erich says it's true."

Erich Helfferich. So he had become "Uncle" Erich now, had he? A zealot of the worst sort, a full-time bureaucrat at the Party's Berlin headquarters. An officious, bespectacled scoutmaster . . . March felt his hands tightening on the steering wheel. Helfferich had started seeing Klara a year ago.

"He says you don't give the Führer salute and you make jokes about the Party."

"And how does he know all this?"

"He says there's a file on you at Party headquarters and it's only a matter of time before you're picked up." The boy was almost in tears with the shame of it. "I think he's right."

"Pili!"

They were drawing up outside the house.

"I hate you." This was delivered in a calm, flat voice. He got out of the car. March opened his door, ran around and followed him up the path. He could hear a dog barking inside the house.

"Pili!" he shouted once more.

The door opened. Klara stood there in the uniform of the *NS-Frauenschaft.* Lurking behind her, March glimpsed the brown-clad figure of Helfferich. The dog, a young German shepherd, came running out and leapt up at Pili, who pushed his way past his mother and disappeared into the house. March wanted to follow him, but Klara blocked his path.

"Leave the boy alone. Get out of here. Leave us all alone."

She caught the dog and dragged it back by its collar. The door slammed on its yelping.

Later, as he drove back toward the center of Berlin, March kept thinking about that dog. It was the only living creature in the house, he realized, that was not wearing a uniform.

Had he not felt so miserable, he would have laughed.

"What a pig of a day," said Max Jaeger. It was 7:30 in the evening and he was pulling on his coat in Werderscher-Markt. "No possessions handed in; no clothing. I've gone back on the missing list to Thursday. Nothing. So that's more than twenty-four hours since estimated time of death and not a soul has missed him. You sure he's not just some derelict?"

March gave a brief shake of the head. "Too well fed. And derelicts don't own swimming trunks. As a rule."

"To cap it all off—" Max took a last puff on his cigar and stubbed it out "—I've got to go to a Party meeting tonight. 'The German Mother: Warrior of the *Volk* on the Home Front.' "

Like all Kripo investigators, including March, Jaeger had the SS rank of Sturmbannführer. Unlike March, he had joined the Party the previous year. Not that March blamed him: you had to be a Party member to gain promotion.

"Is Hannelore going?"

"Hannelore? Holder of the Honor Cross of the German Mother, Bronze Class? Naturally she's going." Max looked at his watch. "Just time for a beer. What do you say?"

"Not tonight, thanks. I'll walk down with you."

They parted on the steps of the Kripo building. With a wave, Jaeger turned left toward the bar in Oberwall-Strasse, while March turned right, toward the river. He walked quickly. The rain had stopped, but the air was still damp and misty. The prewar street lights gleamed on the black pavement. From the Spree came the low note of a foghorn, muffled by the buildings.

He turned a corner and walked alongside the river, enjoying the sensation of the cold night air against his face. A barge was chugging upstream, a single light at its prow, a cauldron of dark water boiling at its stern. Apart from that, there was silence. There were no cars here; no people. The city might have vaporized in the darkness. He left the river with reluctance, crossing Spittel-Markt to Seydel-Strasse. A few minutes later he entered the Berlin city morgue.

Dr. Eisler had gone home. No surprise there. "I love you," breathed a woman's voice in the deserted reception, "and I want to bear your children." An attendant in a stained white tunic reluctantly turned away from his portable television and checked March's ID. He made a note in his register, picked up a bunch of keys and gestured to the detective to follow him. Behind them, the theme tune of the Reichsrundfunk's nightly soap opera began to play.

Swing doors led on to a corridor identical to a dozen others back in Werderscher-Markt. Somewhere, thought March, there must be a *Reichsdirektor* for green linoleum. He followed the attendant into an elevator. The metal grille closed with a crash and they descended into the basement.

At the entrance to the storeroom, beneath a NO SMOKING sign, they both lit cigarettes—two professionals taking the same precaution, not against the smell of the bodies (the room was refrigerated; there was no stink of corruption) but to blot out the stinging fumes of the disinfectant.

"You want the old fellow? Came in just after eight?"

"Right," said March.

The attendant pulled a large handle and swung open the heavy door. There was a *whoosh* of cold air as they stepped inside. Harsh neon strips lit a floor of white tiles, slightly sloping on either side down to a narrow gutter in the center. Heavy metal drawers like filing cabinets were set into the walls. The attendant took a clipboard from a hook by the light switch and walked along them, checking the numbers.

"This one."

He tucked the clipboard under his arm and gave the drawer a hard tug. It slid open. March stepped over and pulled back the white sheet.

"You can go now, if you like," he said, without looking around. "I'll call when I've finished."

"Not allowed. Regulations."

"In case I tamper with the evidence? Do me a favor."

The body did not improve on second acquaintance. A hard, fleshy face, small eyes and a cruel mouth. The scalp was almost entirely bald, apart from the odd strand of white hair. The nose was sharp, with two deep indentations on either side of the bridge. He must have worn spectacles for years. The face itself was unmarked, but there were symmetrical bruises on either cheek. March inserted his fingers into the mouth and encountered only soft gums. At some point a complete set of false teeth must have been knocked loose.

March pulled the sheet back. The shoulders were broad, the torso that of a powerful man, just beginning to run to fat. He folded the cloth neatly a few centimeters above the stump. He was always respectful of the dead. No society doctor on the Kurfürstendamm was more tender with his clients than Xavier March.

He breathed warmth onto his hands and reached into the inside pocket of his overcoat. He pulled out a small tin case, which he opened, and two white cards. The cigarette smoke tasted bitter in his mouth. He grasped the corpse's left wrist—so *cold;* it never ceased to shock him—and pried open the fingers. Carefully, he pressed each tip onto the pad of black ink in the tin. Then he put the tin down, picked up one of the cards and pressed each finger onto that. When he was satisfied, he repeated the process on the old man's right hand. The attendant watched him, fascinated.

The smears of black on the white hands looked shocking; a desecration.

"Clean him up," said March.

The headquarters of the Reich Kripo are in Werderscher-Markt, but the actual hardware of police business—the forensic laboratories, criminal records, armory, workshops, detention cells—are in the Berlin Police Presidium building in the Alexander-Platz. It was to this sprawling Prussian fortress, opposite the busiest U-bahn station in the city, that March went next. It took him fifteen minutes, walking briskly.

"You want *what*?"

The voice, edged high with incredulity, belonged to Otto Koth, deputy head of the fingerprint section.

"Priority," repeated March. He took another draw on his cigarette. He knew Koth well. Two years ago they had trapped a gang of armed robbers who had killed a policeman in Lankwitz. Koth had gained a promotion on the strength of it. "I know you've got a backlog from here to the Führer's hundredth birthday. I know you've got the Sipo on your back for terrorists and God knows what. But do this for me."

Koth leaned back in his chair. In the bookcase behind him, March could see Artur Nebe's book on criminology, published thirty years ago but still the standard text. Nebe had been head of the Kripo since 1933.

"Let me see what you've got," said Koth.

March handed over the cards. Koth glanced at them, nodding.

"Male," said March. "About sixty. Dead for a day."

"I know how he feels." Koth took off his glasses and rubbed his eyes. "All right. They'll go to the top of the pile."

"How long?"

"Should have an answer by morning." Koth put his glasses back on. "What I don't understand is how you know this man, whoever he was, had a criminal record."

March did not know, but he was not going to hand Koth an excuse to wriggle out of his promise. "Trust me," he said.

March arrived back at his flat at eleven. The ancient cage elevator was out of order. The stairs, with their threadbare brown carpet, smelled of other people's old meals, of boiled cabbage and burned meat. As he passed the second floor he could hear the young couple who lived beneath him quarreling.

"How can you say that?"

"You've done nothing! Nothing!"

A door slammed. A baby cried. Elsewhere, someone turned up the volume of their radio in response. The symphony of apartment life. Once this had been a fashionable block. Now, like many of its tenants, it had fallen on harder times. He continued on up to the next floor and let himself in.

The rooms were cold, the heating having failed to come on, as usual. He had five rooms: a living room with a good high ceiling, looking out onto Ansbacher-Strasse; a bedroom with an iron bedstead; a small bathroom and an even smaller kitchen; a spare room filled with salvage from his marriage, still packed in boxes five years later. Home. It was bigger than the forty-four square meters that was the standard size of a *Volkswohnung*—a People's Flat—but not much.

Before March had moved in it had been occupied by the widow of a Luftwaffe general. She had lived in it since the war and had let it go to ruin. On his second weekend, redecorating the bedroom, he had stripped off the mildewed wallpaper and found tucked behind it a photograph, folded up very small. A sepia portrait, all misty browns and creams, dated 1929, taken by a Berlin studio. A family stood before a painted backdrop of trees and fields. A dark-haired woman gazed at a baby in her arms. Her husband stood proudly behind her, his hand resting on her shoulder. Next to him, a little boy. He had kept it on the mantelpiece ever since.

The boy was Pili's age, would be March's age today.

Who were these people? What had happened to the child? For years he had wondered, but hesitated—he always had plenty at the Markt to stretch his mind without finding fresh mysteries to unravel. Then, just before last Christmas, for no reason he could properly define—a vague and growing uneasiness that had happened to coincide with his birthday, no more than that—he had started to seek an answer.

The landlord's records showed that the apartment had been rented between 1928 and 1942 to one Weiss, Jakob. But there was no police file on any Jakob Weiss. He was not registered as having moved, or fallen sick, or died. Calls to the records bureaus of the army, navy and Luftwaffe confirmed he had not been conscripted to fight. The photographer's studio had become a television rental shop, its records lost. None of the young people in the landlord's office remembered the Weisses. They had vanished. *Weiss. White. A blank.* By now, in his heart, March knew the truth—perhaps had always known it—but he went around one evening with the photograph even so, like a policeman, seeking witnesses, and the other tenants in the house had looked at him as if he were crazy even for asking. Except one.

"They were Jews," the crone in the attic had said as she closed the door in his face.

Of course. The Jews had all been evacuated to the east during the war. Everyone knew that. What had happened to them since was not a question anyone asked in public—or in private either, if they had any sense, not even an SS-Sturmbannführer.

And that, he could see now, was when his relationship with Pili had started to go bad; the time when he had started to wake up before it was light and to volunteer for every case that came along.

March stood for a few minutes without switching on the lights, looking down at the traffic heading south to Wittenberg-Platz. Then he went into the kitchen and poured himself a large whisky. Monday's *Berliner Tageblatt* was lying by the sink. He carried it back with him into the sitting room.

March had a routine for reading the paper. He started at the back, which held the truth. If Leipzig was said to have beaten Cologne 4–0 at football, the chances were it was true: even the Party had yet to devise a means of rewriting the sports results. The sports news was a different matter. COUNTDOWN TO TOKYO OLYMPICS. U.S. MAY COMPETE FOR FIRST TIME IN 28 YEARS. GERMAN ATHLETES STILL LEAD WORLD. Then the advertisements: GERMAN FAMILIES! PLEASURE BECKONS IN GOTENLAND, RIVIERA OF THE REICH! French perfume, Italian silks, Scandinavian furs, Dutch cigars, Belgian coffee, Russian caviar, British televisions—the cornucopia of Empire spilled across the pages. Births, marriages and deaths: TEBBE, Ernst and Ingrid; a son for the Führer. WENZEL, Hans, aged 71; a true National Socialist, sadly missed.

And the lonely hearts:

> FIFTY years old. Pure Aryan doctor, veteran of the Battle of Moscow, who intends to settle on the land, desires male progeny through marriage with healthy, Aryan, virginal, young, unassuming, thrifty woman, adapted to hard work; broad-hipped, flat-heeled and earringless essential.

WIDOWER aged sixty once again wishes to have Nordic mate prepared to present him with children so that old family should not die out in male line.

Arts pages: Zarah Leander, still going strong, in *Woman of Odessa,* now showing at the Gloria-Palast: the epic story of the resettlement of the South Tyrolese. A piece by the music critic attacking the "pernicious Negroid wailings" of a group of young Englishmen from Liverpool who were playing to packed audiences of German youths in Hamburg. Herbert von Karajan to conduct a special performance of Beethoven's Ninth Symphony—the European anthem—at the Royal Albert Hall in London on the Führer's birthday.

Editorial on the student antiwar demonstrations in Heidelberg: TRAITORS MUST BE SMASHED BY FORCE! The *Tageblatt* always took a firm line.

Obituary: some old *Bonze* from the Ministry of the Interior. "A lifetime's service to the Reich . . ."

Reich news: SPRING THAW BRINGS FRESH FIGHTING ON SIBERIAN FRONT! GERMAN TROOPS SMASH IVAN TERROR GROUPS! In Rovno, capital of the *Reichskommissariat* Ukraine, five terrorist leaders had been executed for organizing the massacre of a family of German settlers. There was a photograph of the Reich's latest nuclear submarine, the *Grossadmiral Dönitz,* at its new base in Trondheim.

World news. In London it had been announced that King Edward and Queen Wallis were to pay a state visit to the Reich in July "further to strengthen the deep bonds of respect and affection between the peoples of Great Britain and the German Reich." In Washington, it was believed that President Kennedy's latest victory in the U.S. primaries had strengthened his chances of winning a second term . . .

The paper slipped from March's fingers and onto the floor.

Half an hour later, the telephone rang.

"*So* sorry to wake you." Koth was sarcastic. "I had the

impression this was supposed to be priority. Shall I call back tomorrow?"

"No, no." March was wide awake.

"This you will love. This is beautiful." For the first time in his life, March heard Koth chuckle. "Now, you're not playing a joke on me? This is not some little trick you and Jaeger have worked out between you?"

"Who is it?"

"The background first." Koth was enjoying himself too much to be hurried. "We had to go back a long way to get a match. A very long way. But we got one. Perfect. No mistake. Your man has a record, all right. He was arrested just once in his life. By our colleagues in Munich, forty years ago. To be precise, on November 9, 1923."

There was a silence. Five, six, seven seconds elapsed.

"Ah! I can tell that even you appreciate the significance of the date."

"An *alter Kämpfer.*" March reached down beside his chair for his cigarettes. "His name?"

"Indeed. An old comrade. Arrested with the Führer after the Bürgerbräukeller putsch. You have fished out of the lake one of the glorious pioneers of the National Socialist Revolution." Koth laughed again. "A wiser man might have left him where he was."

*"What is his name?"*

After Koth had hung up, March paced around the apartment for five minutes, smoking furiously. Then he made three calls. The first was to Max Jaeger. The second was to the duty officer at Werderscher-Markt. The third was to a Berlin number. A man's voice, slurred with sleep, answered just as March was about to give up.

"Rudi? It's Xavier March."

"Zavi? Are you crazy? It's midnight."

"Not quite." March patrolled the faded carpet, the body of the telephone in one hand, the receiver tucked beneath his chin. "I need your help."

"For God's sake!"

"What can you tell me about a man named Josef Buhler?"

That night, March had a dream. He was at the lakeshore again in the rain and there was the body, facedown in the mud. He pulled at the shoulder—pulled hard—but he could not move it. The body was gray-white lead. But when he turned to leave, it grabbed his leg and began pulling him toward the surface of the lake. He scrabbled at the earth, trying to dig his fingers into the soft mud, but there was nothing to hold on to. The corpse's grip was immensely strong. And as they went under, its face became Pili's, contorted with rage, grotesque in its shame, screaming "I hate you . . . I hate you . . . I hate you . . ."

# WEDNESDAY, APRIL 15

*détente,* n.f. 1 (a) Relaxation, loosening, slackening (of something that is taut); relaxing (of muscles). (b) Easing (of political situation).

Yesterday's rain was a bad memory, already half faded from the streets. The sun—the miraculous, impartial sun—bounced and glittered on the shopfronts and apartment windows.

In the bathroom, the rusted pipes clanked and groaned, the shower dangled a thread of cold water. March shaved with his father's old cutthroat razor. Through the open bathroom window, he could hear the sounds of the city waking up: the whine and clatter of the first tram; the distant hum of the traffic on Tauentzien-Strasse; the footsteps of the early risers hurrying to the big Wittenberg-Platz U-bahn station; the rattle of shutters going up in the bakery across the street. It was not quite seven and Berlin was alive with possibilities the day had yet to dull.

His uniform was laid out in the bedroom: the body armor of authority.

Brown shirt, with black leather buttons. Black tie. Black breeches. Black jackboots (the rich smell of polished leather).

Black tunic: four silver buttons; three parallel silvered threads on the collar tabs; on the left sleeve, a red-white-

and-black swastika armband; on the right, a diamond enclosing the Gothic letter "K," for Kriminalpolizei.

Black Sam Browne belt. Black cap with silver death's head and Party eagle. Black leather gloves.

March stared at himself in the mirror, and a Sturmbannführer of the SS stared back. He picked up his service pistol, a 9mm Luger, from the dressing table, checked the action and slotted it into his holster. Then he stepped out into the morning.

"Sure you have enough?"

Rudolf Halder grinned at March's sarcasm and unloaded his tray: cheese, ham, salami, three hard-boiled eggs, a pile of black bread, milk, a cup of steaming coffee. He arranged the dishes in a neat row on the white linen tablecloth.

"I understand that breakfasts provided by the Reich Main Security Office are not normally so lavish."

They were in the dining room of the Prinz Friedrich Karl Hotel in Dorotheen-Strasse, midway between Kripo headquarters and Halder's office in the Reichsarchiv. March used it regularly. The Friedrich Karl was a cheap stopover for tourists and salesmen, but it did a good breakfast. Dangling limply from a pole over the entrance was a European flag—the twelve gold stars of the European Community nations on a dark blue background. March guessed that the manager, Herr Brecker, had bought it secondhand and hung it there in an effort to drum up some foreign custom. It did not appear to have worked. A glance around the restaurant's shabby clientele and bored staff suggested little danger of being overheard.

As usual, people gave March's uniform a wide berth. Every few minutes, the walls shook as a train pulled into the Friedrich-Strasse station.

"Is that all you're having?" asked Halder. "Coffee?" He shook his head. "Black coffee, cigarettes and whisky. As a diet: not good. Now I think of it, I haven't seen you eat a decent meal since you and Klara split." He cracked one of his eggs and began removing pieces of shell.

March thought, Of all of us, Halder has changed the least. Beneath the layer of fat, behind the slackened muscle of incipient middle age, there lurked still the ghost of the gangling recruit, straight from university, who had joined the U-174 more than twenty years before. He had been a wireless operator—a bad one, rushed through training and into service at the start of 1942, when losses were at their height and Dönitz was ransacking Germany for replacements. Then as now, he had worn wire-framed glasses and had thin red hair, which stuck out at the back in a duck's tail. During a voyage, while the rest of the men had grown beards, Halder had sprouted orange tufts on his cheeks and chin, like a molting cat. The fact that he was in the U-boat service at all was a ghastly mistake, a joke. He was clumsy, barely capable of changing a fuse. He had been designed by nature to be an academic, not a submariner, and he passed each voyage in a sweat of fear and seasickness.

Yet he was popular. U-boat crews were superstitious, and somehow the word got around that Rudi Halder brought good luck. So they looked after him, covering his mistakes, letting him have an extra half hour to groan and thrash around on his bunk. He became a sort of mascot. When peace came, astonished to find that he had survived, Halder resumed his studies at the history faculty of Berlin University. In 1958 he had joined the team of academics working at the Reichsarchiv on the official history of the war. He had come full circle, spending his days hunched in a subterranean chamber in Berlin, piecing together the same grand strategy of which he had once been a tiny, frightened component. *The U-boat Service: Operations and Tactics, 1939–46* had been published in 1963. Now Halder was helping to compile the third volume of the history of the German Army on the eastern front.

"It's like working at the Volkswagen works in Fallersleben," said Halder. He took a bite out of his egg and chewed for a while. "I do the wheels, Jaeckel does the doors, Schmidt drops in the engine."

"How long is it going to take?"

"Oh, forever, I should think. Resources no object. This is the Arch of Triumph in words, remember? Every shot, every skirmish, every snowflake, every sneeze. Someone is even going to write the Official History of the Official Histories. Me, I'll do another five years."

"And then?"

Halder brushed egg crumbs from his tie. "A chair in a small university somewhere in the south. A house in the country with Ilse and the kids. A couple of books, respectfully reviewed. My ambitions are modest. If nothing else, this kind of work gives you a sense of perspective about your own mortality. Speaking of which—" From his inside pocket he pulled a sheet of paper. "With the compliments of the Reichsarchiv."

It was a photocopy of a page from an old Party directory. Four passport-sized portraits of uniformed officials, each accompanied by a brief biography. Brün. Brunner. Buch. And Buhler.

Halder said, "*Guide to the Personalities of the NSDAP.* 1951 edition."

"I know it well."

"A pretty bunch, you'll agree."

The body in the Havel had been Buhler's, no question of it. He stared up at March through his rimless spectacles, prim and humorless, his lips pursed. It was a bureaucrat's face, a lawyer's face; a face you might see a thousand times and never be able to describe; sharp in the flesh, fudged in memory; the face of a machine man.

"As you will see," resumed Halder, "a pillar of National Socialist respectability. Joined the Party in '22—that's as respectable as they come. Worked as a lawyer with Hans Frank, the Führer's own attorney. Deputy president of the Academy of German Law."

" 'State secretary, General Government, 1939,' " read

March. " 'SS-Brigadeführer.' " *Brigadeführer*, by God. He took out a notebook and began to write.

"Honorary rank," said Halder, his mouth full of food. "I doubt if he ever fired a shot in anger. He was strictly a desk man. When Frank was sent out as governor in '39 to run what was left of Poland, he must have taken his old legal partner, Buhler, with him, to be chief bureaucrat. You should try some of this ham. Very good."

March was scribbling quickly. "How long was Buhler in the East?"

"Twelve years, I guess. I checked the *Guide* for 1952. There's no entry for Buhler. So '51 must have been his last year."

March stopped writing and tapped his teeth with his pen. "Will you excuse me for a couple of minutes?"

There was a telephone booth in the foyer. He rang the Kripo switchboard and asked for his own extension. A voice growled "Jaeger."

"Listen, Max." March repeated what Halder had told him. "The *Guide* mentions a wife." He held up the sheet of paper to the booth's dim electric light and squinted at it. "Edith Tulard. Can you find her? To get the body positively identified."

"She's dead."

"What?"

"She died more than ten years ago. I checked with the SS records bureau—even honorary ranks have to give next of kin. Buhler had no kids, but I've traced his sister. She's a widow, seventy-two years old, named Elisabeth Trinkl. Lives in Fürstenwalde." March knew it: a small town about forty-five minutes' drive southeast of Berlin. "The local cops are bringing her straight to the morgue."

"I'll meet you there."

"Another thing. Buhler had a house on Schwanenwerder."

So that explained the location of the body. "Good work, Max." March hung up and made his way back to the dining room.

Halder had finished his breakfast. He threw down his napkin as March returned and leaned back in his chair. "Excellent. Now I can almost tolerate the prospect of sorting through fifteen hundred signals from Kleist's First Panzer Army." He began picking his teeth. "We should meet up more often. Ilse is always saying, 'When are you going to bring Zavi around?' " He leaned forward. "Listen: there's a woman at the archives working on the history of the *Bund deutscher Mädel* in Bavaria, 1935 to 1950. A stunner. Husband disappeared on the eastern front last year, poor devil. Anyway: you and she. What about it? We could have you both around, say, next week?"

March smiled. "You're very kind."

"That's not an answer."

"True." He tapped the photocopy. "Can I keep this?"

Halder shrugged. "Why not?"

"One last thing."

"Go ahead."

"State secretary to the General Government. What would he have done, exactly?"

Halder spread his hands. The backs were thick with freckles, wisps of reddish-gold hair curled from his cuffs. "He and Frank had absolute authority. They did whatever they liked. At that time, the main priority would have been resettlement."

March wrote "Resettlement" in his notebook and circled it. "How did that happen?"

"What is this? A seminar?" Halder arranged a triangle of plates in front of him—two smaller ones to the left, a larger one to the right. He pushed them together so they touched. "All this is Poland before the war. After '39, the western provinces"—he tapped the small plates—"were brought into Germany. Reichsgau Danzig–West Prussia and Reichsgau Wartheland." He detached the large plate. "And this became the General Government. The rump state. The two western provinces were Germanized. It's not my field, you understand, but I've seen some figures.

In 1940, they set a target density of one hundred Germans per square kilometer. And they managed it in the first three years. An incredible operation, considering the war was still on."

"How many people were involved?"

"One million. The SS eugenics bureau found Germans in places you'd never have dreamed of—Romania, Bulgaria, Serbia, Croatia. If your skull had the proper measurements and you came from the right village—you were just given a ticket."

"And Buhler?"

"Ah. Well. To make room for a million Germans in the new Reichsgaue, they had to move out a million Poles."

"And they went to the General Government?"

Halder turned his head and glanced around furtively to make sure he was not overheard—"the German look," people called it. "They also had to cope with the Jews being expelled from Germany and the western territories—France, Holland, Belgium."

"Jews?"

"Yes, yes. Keep your voice down." Halder was speaking so quietly, March had to lean across the table to hear. "You can imagine—it was chaos. Overcrowding. Starvation. Disease. From what one can gather, the place is still a shithole, despite what they say."

Every week the newspapers and television carried appeals from the East Ministry for settlers willing to move to the General Government. "Germans! Claim your birthright! A farmstead—free! Income guaranteed for the first five years." The advertisements showed happy colonists living in luxury. But word of the real story had filtered back—an existence conditioned by poor soil, backbreaking work, and drab satellite towns to which the Germans had to return at dusk for fear of attack from local partisans. The General Government was worse than the Ukraine; worse than Ostland; worse, even, than Muscovy.

A waiter came over to offer more coffee. March waved him away. When the man was out of earshot, Halder continued in the same low tone, "Frank ran everything from Wawel Castle in Krakau. That would have been where Buhler was based. I have a friend who works in the official archives there. God, he has some stories. . . . Apparently the luxury was incredible. Like something out of the Roman Empire. Paintings, tapestries, looted treasures from the church, jewelry. Bribes in cash and bribes in kind, if you know what I mean." Halder's blue eyes shone at the thought, his eyebrows danced.

"And Buhler was involved in this?"

"Who knows? If not, he must have been about the only one who wasn't."

"That would explain why he had a house on Schwanenwerder."

Halder whistled softly. "There you are, then. We had the wrong sort of war, my friend. Cooped up in a stinking metal coffin two hundred meters under the Atlantic, when we could have been in a Silesian castle sleeping on silk with a couple of Polish girls for company."

There was more March would have liked to ask him, but he had no time. As they were leaving, Halder said, "So you'll come to dinner with my BdM woman?"

"I'll think about it."

"Maybe we can persuade her to wear her uniform." Standing outside the hotel with his hands thrust deep into his pockets and his long scarf wrapped twice around his neck, Halder looked even more like a student. Suddenly he struck his forehead with the flat of his hand. "I clean forgot! I meant to tell you. My memory . . . A couple of Sipo guys were around at the archive last week asking about you."

March felt his smile shrink. "The Gestapo? What did they want?" He managed to keep his tone light, offhand.

"Oh, the usual sort of stuff. 'What was he like during the war? Does he have any strong political views? Who are his friends?' What's going on, Zavi? You up for promotion or something?"

"I must be." He told himself to relax. It was probably only a routine check. He must remember to ask Max if he had heard anything about a new screening.

"Well, when they've made you head of the Kripo, don't forget your old friends."

March laughed. "I won't." They shook hands. As they parted, March said, "I wonder if Buhler had any enemies."

"Oh, yes," said Halder. "Of course."

"Who were they, then?"

Halder shrugged. "Thirty million Poles, for a start."

The only person on the second floor at Werderscher-Markt was a Polish cleaning woman. Her back was to March as he came out of the lift. All he could see was a large rump resting on the soles of a pair of black rubber boots and the red scarf tied around her hair bobbing as she scrubbed the floor. She was singing softly to herself in her native language. As she heard him approach she stopped and turned her head to the wall. He squeezed past her and went into his office. When the door had closed he heard her begin singing again.

It was not yet nine. He hung his cap by the door and unbuttoned his tunic. There was a large brown envelope on his desk. He opened it and shook out the contents, the scene-of-crime photographs. Glossy color pictures of Buhler's body, sprawled like a sunbather's at the side of the lake.

He lifted the ancient typewriter from the top of the filing cabinet and carried it across to his desk. From a wire basket he took two pieces of much-used carbon paper, two flimsy sheets and one standard report form, arranged them in order and wound them into the machine. Then he lit a cigarette and stared at the dead plant for a few minutes.

He began to type.

TO: Chief, VB3(a)
SUBJECT: Unidentified body (male)
FROM: X. March, SS-Sturmbannführer 4/15/64

I beg to report the following.

1. At 0628 yesterday, I was ordered to attend the recovery of a body from the Havel. The body had been discovered by SS-Schütze Hermann Jost at 0602 and reported to the Ordnungspolizei (statement attached).
2. No male of the correct description having been reported missing, I arranged for the fingerprints of the subject to be checked against records.
3. This has enabled the subject to be identified as Doctor Josef Buhler, a Party member with the honorary rank of SS-Brigadeführer. The subject served as state secretary in the General Government, 1939–51.
4. A preliminary investigation at the scene by SS-Sturmbannführer Doctor August Eisler indicated the likely cause of death as drowning and the likely time of death as sometime on the night of 13 April.
5. The subject lived on Schwanenwerder, close to where the body was found.
6. There were no obvious suspicious circumstances.
7. A full autopsy examination will be carried out following formal identification of the subject by next of kin.

March pulled the report out of the typewriter, signed it and left it with a messenger in the foyer on his way out.

The old woman was sitting erect on a hard wooden bench in the Seydel-Strasse mortuary. She wore a brown tweed suit, brown hat with a drooping feather, sturdy brown shoes and gray woolen stockings. She was staring straight ahead, a handbag clasped in her lap, oblivious to the medical orderlies, the policemen, the grieving relatives passing in the corridor. Max Jaeger sat beside her, arms folded, legs outstretched, looking bored. As March arrived, he took him to one side.

"Been here ten minutes. Hardly spoken."

"In shock?"

"I suppose."

"Let's get it over with."

The old woman did not look up as March sat on the bench beside her. He said softly, "Frau Trinkl, my name is March. I am an investigator with the Berlin Kriminalpolizei. We have to complete a report on your brother's death, and we need you to identify his body. Then we'll take you home. Do you understand?"

Frau Trinkl turned to face him. She had a thin face, thin nose (her brother's nose), thin lips. A cameo brooch gathered a blouse of frilly purple at her bony throat.

"Do you understand?" he repeated.

She gazed at him with clear gray eyes, unreddened by crying. Her voice was clipped and dry: "Perfectly."

They moved across the corridor into a small, windowless reception room. The floor was made of wood blocks. The walls were lime green. In an effort to lighten the gloom, someone had stuck up tourist posters given away by the *Deutsche Reichsbahngesellschaft*: a nighttime view of the Great Hall, the Führer Museum at Linz, the Starnberger See in Bavaria. The poster that had hung on the fourth wall had been torn down, leaving pockmarks in the plaster, like bullet holes.

A clatter outside signaled the arrival of the body. It was wheeled in, covered by a sheet, on a metal trolley. Two attendants in white tunics parked it in the center of the floor—a buffet lunch awaiting its guests. They left and Jaeger closed the door.

"Are you ready?" asked March. She nodded. He turned back the sheet and Frau Trinkl stationed herself at his shoulder. As she leaned forward, a strong smell—of peppermint lozenges, of perfume mingled with camphor, an old lady's smell—washed across his face. She stared at the corpse for a long time, then opened her mouth as if to say something, but all that emerged was a sigh. Her eyes closed. March caught her as she fell.

"It's him," she said. "I haven't set eyes on him for ten years, and he's fatter, and I've never seen him before without his spectacles, not since he was a child. But it's him." She was on a chair under the poster of Linz, leaning forward with her head between her knees. Her hat had fallen off. Thin strands of white hair hung down over her face. The body had been wheeled away.

The door opened and Jaeger returned carrying a glass of water, which he pressed into her skinny hand. "Drink this." She held it for a moment, then raised it to her lips and took a sip. "I never faint," she said. "Never." Behind her, Jaeger made a face.

"Of course," said March. "I need to ask some questions. Are you well enough? Stop me if I tire you." He took out his notebook. "Why had you not seen your brother for ten years?"

"After Edith died—his wife—we had nothing in common. We were never close in any case. Even as children. I was eight years older than him."

"His wife died some time ago?"

She thought for a moment. "In '53, I think. Winter. She had cancer."

"And in all the time since then you never heard from him? Were there any other brothers and sisters?"

"No. Just the two of us. He did write occasionally. I had a letter from him on my birthday two weeks ago." She fumbled in her handbag and produced a single sheet of notepaper—good quality, creamy and thick, with an engraving of the Schwanenwerder house as a letterhead. The writing was copperplate, the message as formal as an official receipt: "My dear sister! Heil Hitler! I send you greetings on your birthday. I earnestly hope that you are in good health, as I am. Josef." March refolded it and handed it back. No wonder nobody missed him.

"In his other letters, did he ever mention anything worrying him?"

"What had he to be worried about?" She spat out the words. "Edith inherited a fortune in the war. They had money. He lived in fine style, I can tell you."

"There were no children?"

"He was sterile." She said this without emphasis, as if describing his hair color. "Edith was so unhappy. I think that was what killed her. She sat alone in that big house—it was cancer of the soul. She used to love music—she played the piano beautifully. A Bechstein, I remember. And he—he was such a cold man."

From the other side of the room Jaeger grunted, "So you didn't think much of him?"

"No, I did not. Not many people did." She turned back to March. "I have been a widow for twenty-four years. My husband was a navigator in the Luftwaffe, shot down over France. I was not left destitute—nothing like that. But the pension . . . *very* small for one who was used to something a little better. Not once in all that time did Josef offer to help me."

"What about his leg?" It was Jaeger again, his tone antagonistic. He had clearly decided to take Buhler's side in this family dispute. "What happened to that?" His manner suggested he thought she might have stolen it.

The old lady ignored him and gave her answer to March. "He would never speak of it himself, but Edith told me the story. It happened in 1951, when he was still in the General Government. He was traveling with an escort on the road from Krakau to Kattowitz when his car was ambushed by Polish partisans. A land mine, she said. His driver was killed. Josef was lucky only to lose a foot. After that, he retired from government service."

"And yet he still swam?" March looked up from his notebook. "You know that we discovered him wearing swimming trunks?"

She gave a tight smile. "My brother was a fanatic about everything, Herr March, whether it was politics or health.

He did not smoke, he never touched alcohol and he took exercise every day, despite his . . . disability. So, no: I am not in the least surprised that he should have been swimming." She set down her glass and picked up her hat. "I would like to go home now, if I may."

March stood up and held out his hand, helping her to her feet. "What did Doctor Buhler do after 1951? He was only—what?—in his early fifties?"

"That's the strange thing." She opened her handbag and took out a small mirror. She checked that her hat was on straight, tucking stray hairs out of sight with nervous, jerky movements of her fingers. "Before the war, he was so ambitious. He would work eighteen hours a day, every day of the week. But when he left Krakau, he gave up. He never even returned to the law. For more than ten years after poor Edith died, he just sat alone in that big house all day and did nothing."

Two floors below, in the basement of the morgue, SS-Surgeon August Eisler of Kriminalpolizei Department $VD_2$ (Pathology) was going about his business with his customary clumsy relish. Buhler's chest had been opened in the standard fashion: a *Y* incision, a cut from each shoulder to the pit of the stomach, a straight line down to the pubic bone. Now Eisler had his hands deep inside the stomach, green gloves sheened with red, twisting, cutting, pulling. March and Jaeger leaned against the wall by the open doorway, smoking a couple of Jaeger's cigars.

"Have you seen what your man had for lunch?" said Eisler. "Show them, Eck."

Eisler's assistant wiped his hands on his apron and held up a transparent plastic bag. There was something small and green in the bottom.

"Lettuce. Digests slowly. Stays in the intestinal tract for hours."

March had worked with Eisler before. Two winters ago, with snow blocking Unter den Linden and ice-skating competitions on the Tegelersee, a bargemaster named Kempf had been pulled out of the Spree, almost dead with cold. He had expired in the ambulance on the way to the hospital. Accident or murder? The time at which he had fallen into the water was crucial. Looking at the ice extending two meters out from the banks, March had estimated fifteen minutes as the maximum time he could have survived in the water. Eisler had said forty-five, and his view had prevailed with the prosecutor. It was enough to destroy the alibi of the barge's second mate and hang him.

Afterward, the prosecutor—a decent, old-fashioned sort—had called March into his office and locked the door. Then he'd shown him Eisler's "evidence": copies of documents stamped *Geheime Reichssache*—Top Secret State Document—and dated Dachau, 1942. There were reports of freezing experiments carried out on condemned prisoners, restricted to the department of the SS surgeon general. The men had been handcuffed and dumped into tanks of icy water, retrieved at intervals to have their temperatures taken, right up to the point at which they died. There were photographs of heads bobbing between floating chunks of ice, and charts showing heat loss, projected and actual. The experiments had lasted two years and been conducted, among others, by a young *Untersturmführer,* August Eisler. That night, March and the prosecutor had gone to a bar in Kreuzberg and gotten blind drunk. Next day, neither of them mentioned what had happened. They never spoke to each other again.

"If you expect me to come out with some fancy theory, March, forget it."

"I'd never expect that."

Jaeger laughed. "Nor would I."

Eisler ignored their mirth. "It was a drowning, no question about it. Lungs full of water, so he must have been breathing when he went into the lake."

"No cuts?" asked March. "Bruises?"

"Do you want to come over here and do this job? No?

Then believe me: he drowned. There are no contusions to the head to indicate he was hit or held under."

"A heart attack? Some kind of seizure?"

"Possible," admitted Eisler. Eck handed him a scalpel. "I won't know until I've completed a full examination of the internal organs."

"How long will that take?"

"As long as it takes."

Eisler positioned himself behind Buhler's head. Tenderly, he stroked the hair toward him, off the corpse's forehead, as if soothing a fever. Then he hunched down low and jabbed the scalpel through the left temple. He drew it in an arc across the top of the face, just below the hairline. There was a scrape of metal and bone. Eck grinned at them. March sucked a lungful of smoke from his cigar.

Eisler put the scalpel into a metal dish. Then he bent down once more and worked his forefingers into the deep cut. Gradually, he began peeling back the scalp. March turned his head away and closed his eyes. He prayed that no one he loved, or liked, or even vaguely knew, ever had to be desecrated by the butcher's work of an autopsy.

Jaeger said, "So what do you think?"

Eisler had picked up a small, hand-sized circular saw. He switched it on. It whined like a dentist's drill.

March took a final puff on his cigar. "I think we should get out of here."

They made their way down the corridor. Behind them, from the autopsy room, they heard the saw's note deepen as it bit into the bone.

Half an hour later, Xavier March was at the wheel of one of the Kripo's Volkswagens, following the curving path of the Havel-Chaussee, high above the lake. Sometimes the view was hidden by trees. Then he would round a bend, or the forest would thin, and he would see the water again, sparkling in the April sun like a tray of diamonds. Two yachts skimmed the surface—children's cut-outs, white triangles brilliant against the blue.

He had the window wound down, his arm resting on the sill, the breeze plucking at his sleeve. On either side, the bare branches of the trees were flecked with the green of late spring. In another month, the road would be nose to tail with cars: Berliners escaping from the city to sail or swim or picnic, or simply to lie in the sun on one of the big public beaches. But today there was still enough of a chill in the air, and winter was still close enough, for March to have the road to himself. He passed the red brick sentinel of the Kaiser Wilhelm Tower and the road began to drop to lake level.

Within ten minutes he was at the spot where the body had been discovered. In the fine weather it looked utterly different. This was a tourist spot, a vantage point known as the *Grosses Fenster*: the Picture Window. What had been a mass of gray yesterday was now a gloriously clear view across eight kilometers of water, right up to Spandau.

He parked and retraced the route Jost had been running when he discovered the body—down the woodland track, a sharp right turn and along the side of the lake. He did it a second time, and a third. Satisfied, he got back into the car and drove over the low bridge onto Schwanenwerder. A red-and-white pole blocked the road. A sentry emerged from a small hut, a clipboard in his hand, a rifle slung across his shoulder.

"Your identification, please."

March handed his Kripo ID through the open window. The sentry studied it and returned it. He saluted. "That's fine, Herr Sturmbannführer."

"What's the procedure here?"

"Stop every car. Check the papers and ask where they're going. If they look suspicious, we phone the house, see if they're expected. Sometimes we search the car. It depends on whether the Reichsminister is in residence."

"Do you keep a record?"

"Yes, sir."

"Do me a favor. Look and see if Doctor Josef Buhler had any visitors on Monday night."

The sentry hitched his rifle and went back into his hut. March could see him turning the pages of a ledger. When he returned he shook his head. "Nobody for Doctor Buhler all day."

"Did he leave the island at all?"

"We don't keep a record of residents, sir, only visitors. And we don't check people going, only coming."

"Right." March looked past the guard, across the lake. A scattering of seagulls swooped low over the water, crying. Some yachts were moored to a jetty. He could hear the clink of their masts in the wind.

"What about the shore? Is that watched at all?"

The guard nodded. "The river police have a patrol every couple of hours. But most of those houses have enough sirens and dogs to guard a KZ. We just keep the sightseers away."

*KZ*: pronounced *kah-tsett.* Less of a mouthful than *Konzentrationslager.* Concentration camp.

There was a sound of powerful engines gunning in the distance. The guard turned to look up the road behind him, toward the island.

"One moment, sir."

Around the bend, at high speed, came a gray BMW with its headlights on, followed by a long black Mercedes limousine and then another BMW. The sentry stepped back and pressed a switch, the barrier rose and he saluted. As the convoy swept by, March had a glimpse of the Mercedes' passengers—a young woman, beautiful, an actress perhaps, or a model, with short blond hair; and next to her, staring straight ahead, a wizened old man, his rodentlike profile instantly recognizable. The cars roared off toward the city.

"Does he always travel that quickly?" asked March.

The sentry gave him a knowing look. "The Reichsminister has been screen-testing, sir. Frau Goebbels is due back at lunchtime."

"Ah. All is clear." March turned the key in the ignition and the Volkswagen came to life. "Did you know that Doctor Buhler is dead?"

"No, sir." The sentry gave no sign of interest. "When did that happen?"

"Monday night. He was washed up a few hundred meters from here."

"I heard they'd found a body."

"What was he like?"

"I hardly noticed him, sir. He didn't go out much. No visitors. Never spoke. But then, a lot of them end up like that out here."

"Which was his house?"

"You can't miss it. It's on the east side of the island. Two large towers. It's one of the biggest."

"Thanks."

As he drove down the causeway, March checked in his mirror. The sentry stood looking after him for a few seconds, then hitched his rifle again, turned and walked slowly back to his hut.

Schwanenwerder was small, less than a kilometer long and half a kilometer wide, with a single loop of road running one-way clockwise. To reach Buhler's property, March had to travel three quarters of the way around the island. He drove cautiously, slowing almost to a halt each time he glimpsed one of the houses off to his left.

The place had been named after the famous colonies of swans that lived at the southern end of the Havel. It had become fashionable toward the end of the last century. Most of its buildings dated from then: large villas, steep roofed and stone fronted in the French style, with long drives and lawns, protected from prying eyes by high walls and trees. A piece of the ruined Tuileries Palace stood incongruously by the roadside—a pillar and a section of arch carted back from Paris by some long-dead Wilhelmine businessman. No one stirred. Occasionally, through the bars of a gate, he saw a guard dog, and—once—a gardener raking leaves. The owners were at work in the city, or away, or lying low.

March knew the identities of a few of them: party bosses; a motor industry tycoon, grown fat on the profits of slave labor immediately after the war; the managing director of Wertheim's, the great department store on Potsdamer-Platz, which had been confiscated from its Jewish owners more than thirty years before; an armaments manufacturer; the head of an engineering conglomerate building the great *Autobahnen* into the eastern territories. He wondered how Buhler could have afforded to keep such wealthy company. Then he remembered Halder's description: luxury like the Roman Empire . . .

"KP17, this is KHQ. KP17, answer, please!" A

woman's urgent voice filled the car. March picked up the radio handset concealed under the dashboard.

"This is $KP_{17}$. Go ahead."

"$KP_{17}$, I have Sturmbannführer Jaeger for you."

He had arrived outside the gates to Buhler's villa. Through the metalwork, March could see a yellow curve of drive and the towers, exactly as the sentry had described.

"You said trouble," boomed Jaeger. "And we've got it."

"Now what?"

"I hadn't been back here ten minutes when two of our esteemed colleagues from the Gestapo arrived. 'In view of Party Comrade Buhler's prominent position, blah blah blah, the case has been redesignated a security matter.' "

March thumped his hand against the steering wheel. "Shit!"

" 'All documents to be handed over to the Security Police forthwith, reports required from investigating officers on current status of inquiry, Kripo inquiry to be closed, effective immediately.' "

"When did this happen?"

"It's happening now. They're sitting in our office."

"Did you tell them where I am?"

"Of course not. I just left them to it and said I'd try to find you. I've come straight to the control room." Jaeger's voice dropped. March could imagine him turning his back on the woman operator. "Listen, Zavi, I wouldn't recommend any heroics. They mean serious business, believe me. The Gestapo will be swarming over Schwanenwerder any minute."

March stared at the house. It was utterly still, deserted. Damn the Gestapo.

He made up his mind at that moment. He said, "I can't hear you, Max. I'm sorry. The line is breaking up. I haven't been able to understand anything you've said. Request you report radio fault. Out." He switched off the receiver.

About fifty meters before the house, on the right side

of the road, March had passed a gated track leading into the woods that covered the center of the island. Now he put the Volkswagen into reverse gear, rapidly backed up to it and parked. He trotted back to Buhler's gates. He did not have much time.

They were locked. That was to be expected. The lock itself was a solid metal block a meter and a half off the ground. He wedged the toe of his boot into it and stepped up. There was a row of iron spikes, thirty centimeters apart, running along the top of the gate, just above his head. Gripping one in either hand, he hauled himself up until he was in a position to swing his left leg over. A hazardous business. For a moment he sat astride the gate, recovering his breath. Then he dropped down to the gravel driveway on the other side.

The house was large and of a curious design. It had three stories capped by a steep roof of blue slate. To the left were the two stone towers the sentry had described. These were attached to the main body of the house, which had a balcony with a stone balustrade running the entire length of the first floor. The balcony was supported by pillars. Behind these, half hidden in the shadows, was the main entrance. March started toward it. Beech trees and firs grew in untended profusion along the sides of the drive. The borders were neglected. Dead leaves, unswept since the winter, blew across the lawn.

He stepped between the pillars. The first surprise. The front door was unlocked.

March stood in the hall and looked around. There was an oak staircase to the right, two doors to the left and a gloomy passage straight ahead, which he guessed led to the kitchen.

He tried the first door. Behind it was a paneled dining room: a long table and twelve high-backed carved chairs, cold and musty from disuse.

The next door led to the drawing room. He continued his mental inventory. Rugs on a polished wooden floor. Heavy furniture upholstered in rich brocade. Tapestries on the wall—good ones, too, if March was any judge, which he wasn't. By the window was a grand piano on which stood two large photographs. March tilted one toward the light, which shone weakly through the dusty leaded panes. The frame was heavy silver, with a swastika motif. The picture showed Buhler and his wife on their wedding day, coming down a flight of steps between an honor guard of SA men holding oak boughs over the happy couple. Buhler was also in SA uniform. His wife had flowers woven into her hair and was—to use a favorite expression of Max Jaeger—as ugly as a box of frogs. Neither was smiling.

March picked up the other photograph and immediately felt his stomach lurch. There was Buhler again, slightly bowing this time and shaking hands. The man who was the object of this obeisance had his face half turned to the camera, as if distracted in midgreeting by something behind the photographer's shoulder. There was an inscription. March smeared his finger through the grime on the glass to decipher the crabbed writing. "To Party Comrade Buhler," it read. "From Adolf Hitler. May 17, 1945."

Suddenly, March heard a noise: a sound like a door being kicked, followed by a whimper. He replaced the photograph and went back into the hall. The noise was coming from the end of the passage.

He drew his pistol and edged down the corridor. As he had suspected, it gave on to the kitchen. The noise came again: a cry of terror and a drumming of feet. There was a smell, too—of something filthy.

At the far end of the kitchen was a door. He reached out and grasped the handle and then, with a jerk, pulled the door open. Something huge leapt out of the darkness. A dog, muzzled, eyes wide in terror, went crashing across the floor, down the passage, into the hall and out through the open front door. The larder floor was stinking, thick with feces and urine and food that the dog had pulled down from the shelves but been unable to eat.

After that, March would have liked to have stopped for a few minutes to steady himself. But he had no time. He put the Luger away and quickly examined the kitchen. A few greasy plates in the sink. On the table, a bottle of vodka, nearly empty, with a glass next to it. There was a door to a cellar, but it was locked; he decided not to break it down. He went upstairs. Bedrooms, bathrooms—everywhere had the same atmosphere of shabby luxury, of a grand life-style gone to seed. And everywhere, he noticed, there were paintings—landscapes, religious allegories, portraits—most of them thick with dust. The place had not been properly cleaned for months, maybe years.

The room that must have been Buhler's study was on the top floor of one of the towers. Shelves of legal textbooks, case studies, decrees. A big desk with a swivel chair next to a window overlooking the back lawn of the house. A long sofa with blankets draped beside it, which appeared to have been regularly slept on. And more photographs. Buhler in his lawyer's robes. Buhler in his SS uniform. Buhler with a group of Nazi bigwigs, one of whom March vaguely recognized as Hans Frank, in the front row of what might have been a concert. All the pictures seemed to be at least twenty years old.

March sat at the desk and looked out of the window. The lawn led down to the Havel's edge. There was a small jetty with a cabin cruiser moored to it and, beyond that, a clear view of the lake, right across to the opposite shore. Far in the distance, the Kladow–Wannsee ferry chugged by.

He turned his attention to the desk itself. A blotter. A heavy brass inkstand. A telephone. He stretched his hand toward it.

It began to ring.

His hand hung motionless. One ring. Two. Three. The stillness of the house magnified the sound; the dusty air vibrated. Four. Five. He flexed his fingers over the receiver. Six. Seven. He picked it up.

"Buhler?" The voice of an old man more dead than

alive; a whisper from another world. "Buhler? Speak to me. Who is that?"

March said, "A friend."

Pause. *Click.*

Whoever it was had hung up. March replaced the receiver. Quickly he began opening the desk drawers at random. A few pencils, some notepaper, a dictionary. He pulled the bottom drawers out, one after the other, and put his hand into the space.

There was nothing.

There was something.

At the very back, his fingers brushed against an object small and smooth. He pulled it out. A small notebook bound in black leather, an eagle and swastika in gold lettering on the cover. He flicked through it. The Party diary for 1964. He slipped it into his pocket and replaced the drawers.

Outside, Buhler's dog was going crazy, running from side to side along the water's edge, staring across the Havel, whinnying like a horse. Every few seconds it would get down on its hind legs before resuming its desperate patrol. He could see now that almost the whole of its right side was matted with dried blood. It paid no attention to March as he walked down to the lake.

The heels of his boots rang on the planks of the wooden jetty. Through the gaps between the rickety boards he could see the muddy water a meter below, lapping in the shallows. At the end of the jetty he stepped down into the boat. It rocked with his weight. There were several centimeters of rainwater on the aft deck, clogged with dirt and leaves, a rainbow of oil on the surface. The whole boat stank of fuel. There must be a leak. He stopped and tried the small door to the cabin. It was locked. Cupping his hands, he peered through the window, but it was too dark to see.

He jumped out of the boat and began retracing his steps. The wood of the jetty was weathered gray, except in one place, along the edge opposite the boat. Here there were orange splinters, a scrape of white paint. March was bending to examine the marks when his eye was caught by something pale gleaming in the water, close to the place where the jetty left the shore. He walked back and knelt, and by holding on with his left hand and stretching down as far as he could with his right, he was just able to retrieve it. Pink and chipped like an ancient china doll, with leather straps and steel buckles, it was an artificial foot.

The dog heard them first. It cocked its head, turned and trotted up the lawn toward the house. At once, March dropped his discovery back into the water and ran after the wounded animal. Cursing his stupidity, he worked his way around the side of the house until he stood in the shadow of the towers and could see the gate. The dog was leaping up at the ironwork, grunting through its muzzle. On the other side, March could make out two figures standing looking at the house. Then a third appeared with a large pair of bolt cutters, which he clamped onto the lock. After ten seconds of pressure, it gave way with a loud crack.

The dog backed away as the three men filed onto the grounds. Like March, they wore the black uniforms of the SS. One seemed to take something from his pocket and walked toward the dog, hand outstretched, as if offering it a treat. The animal cringed. A single shot exploded the silence, echoing around the grounds and sending a flock of rooks cawing into the air above the woods. The man holstered his revolver and gestured at the corpse to one of his companions, who seized it by the hind legs and dragged it into the bushes.

All three men strode toward the house. March stayed behind the pillar, slowly edging around it as they came up the drive, keeping himself out of sight. It occurred to him that he had no reason to hide. He could tell the Gestapo men that he had been searching the property, that he had not received Jaeger's message. But something in their manner, in the casual ruthlessness with which they had disposed of the dog, warned him against it. *They had been here before.*

As they came closer, he could make out their ranks. Two Sturmbannführer and an *Obergruppenführer*—a brace of majors and a general. What matter of state security could demand the personal attention of a full Gestapo general? The Obergruppenführer was in his late fifties, built like an ox, with the battered face of an ex-boxer. March recognized him from the television, from newspaper photographs.

Who was he?

Then he remembered. Odilo Globocnik. Familiarly known throughout the SS as Globus. Years ago he had been *Gauleiter* of Vienna. It was Globus who had shot the dog.

"You—the ground floor," said Globus. "You—check the back."

They drew their guns and disappeared into the house. March waited half a minute, then set off for the gate. He skirted the perimeter of the garden, avoiding the drive, picking his way instead, almost bent double, through the tangled shrubbery. Five meters from the gate, he paused for breath. Built into the right-hand gatepost, so discreet it was scarcely noticeable, was a rusty metal container—a mailbox—in which rested a large brown package.

This is madness, he thought. Absolute madness.

He did not run to the gate: nothing, he knew, attracts the human eye like sudden movement. Instead he made himself stroll from the bushes as if it were the most natural thing in the world, tugged the package from the mailbox and sauntered out of the open gate.

He expected to hear a shout from behind him, or a shot. But the only sound was the rustle of the wind in the trees. When he reached his car, he found his hands were shaking.

"Why do we believe in Germany and the Führer?"

"Because we believe in God, we believe in Germany, which He created, in His world and in the Führer, Adolf Hitler, whom He has sent us."

"Whom must we primarily serve?"

"Our people and our Führer, Adolf Hitler."

"Why do we obey?"

"From inner conviction, from belief in Germany, in the Führer, in the Movement and in the SS, and from loyalty."

"Good!" The instructor nodded. "Good. Reassemble in thirty-five minutes on the south sports field. Jost: stay behind. The rest of you: dismissed!"

With their cropped hair and their loose-fitting light gray drill uniforms, the class of SS cadets looked like convicts. They filed out noisily, with a scraping of chairs and a stamping of boots on the rough wooden floor. A large portrait of the late Heinrich Himmler smiled down on them benevolently. Jost looked forlorn standing at attention, alone in the center of the classroom. Some of the other cadets gave him curious glances as they left. It had to be Jost, you could see them thinking. Jost: the queer, the loner, always the odd one out. He might well be due another beating in the barracks tonight.

The instructor nodded toward the back of the classroom. "You have a visitor."

March was leaning against a radiator, arms folded, watching. "Hello again, Jost," he said.

They walked across the vast parade ground. In one corner, a batch of new recruits was being harangued by an *SS-Hauptscharführer.* In another, a hundred youths in black tracksuits stretched, twisted and touched their toes in perfect obedience to shouted commands. Meeting Jost here reminded March of visiting prisoners in jail. The same institutionalized smell of polish and disinfectant and boiled food. The same ugly concrete blocks of buildings. The same high walls and patrols of guards. Like a KZ, the Sepp Dietrich Academy was both huge and claustrophobic; an entirely self-enclosed world.

"Can we go somewhere private?" asked March.

Jost gave him a contemptuous look. "There is no privacy here. That's the point." They took a few more paces. "I suppose we could try the barracks. Everyone else is eating."

They turned, and Jost led the way into a low, gray-painted building. Inside it was gloomy, with a strong smell of male sweat. There must have been a hundred beds, laid out in four rows. Jost had guessed correctly: it was deserted. His bed was two thirds of the way down, in the center. March sat on the coarse brown blanket and offered Jost a cigarette.

"It's not allowed in here."

March waved the packet at him. "Go ahead. Say I ordered you."

Jost took it gratefully. He knelt, opened the metal locker beside the bed and began searching for something to use as an ashtray. As the door hung open, March could see inside: a pile of paperbacks, magazines, a framed photograph.

"May I?"

Jost shrugged. "Sure."

March picked up the photograph. A family group, it reminded him of the picture of the Weisses. Father in an SS uniform. Shy-looking mother in a hat. Daughter: a pretty girl with blond plaits; fourteen, maybe. And Jost himself: fat cheeked and smiling, barely recognizable as the harrowed, cropped figure now kneeling on the stone barracks floor.

Jost said, "Changed, haven't I?"

March was shocked and tried to hide it. "Your sister?" he asked.

"She's still at school."

"And your father?"

"He runs an engineering business in Dresden now. He was one of the first into Russia in '41. Hence the uniform."

March peered closely at the stern figure. "Isn't he wearing the Knight's Cross?" It was the highest decoration for bravery.

"Oh, yes," said Jost. "An authentic war hero." He took the photograph and replaced it in the locker. "What about your father?"

"He was in the Imperial Navy," said March. "He was wounded in the First War. Never properly recovered."

"How old were you when he died?"

"Seven."

"Do you still think about him?"

"Every day."

"Did you go into the navy?"

"I was in the U-boat service."

Jost shook his head slowly. His pale face had flushed pink. "We all follow our fathers, don't we?"

"Most of us, maybe. Not all."

They smoked in silence for a while. Outside, March could hear the physical training session still in progress. "One, two, three . . . One, two, three . . ."

"These people," said Jost, and shook his head again.

"There's a poem by Erich Kästner—'Marschliedchen.' "
He closed his eyes and recited:

> "You love hatred and want to measure the world
> against it.
> You throw food to the beast in man,
> That it may grow, the beast deep within you!
> Let the beast in man devour man."

The young man's sudden passion made March uncomfortable. "When was that written?"

"1932."

"I don't know it."

"You wouldn't. It's banned."

There was a silence, then March said, "We now know the identity of the body you discovered. Doctor Josef Buhler. An official of the General Government. An SS-Brigadeführer."

"Oh, God." Jost rested his head in his hands.

"It has become a more serious matter, you see. Before coming to you, I checked with the sentries' office at the main gate. They have a record that you left the barracks at five-thirty yesterday morning, as usual. So the times in your statement make no sense."

Jost kept his face covered. The cigarette was burning down between his fingers. March leaned forward, took it and stubbed it out. He stood.

"Watch," he said. Jost looked up and March began jogging on the spot.

"This is you yesterday, right?" March made a show of exhaustion, puffing out his cheeks, wiping his brow with his forearms. Despite himself, Jost smiled. "Good," said March. He continued jogging. "Now, you're thinking about some book, or how awful your life is, when you come through the woods and onto the path by the lake. It's pissing with rain and the light's not good, but off to your left you see something . . ."

March turned his head. Jost was watching him intently.

"Whatever it is, it's not the body . . ."

"But—"

March stopped and pointed at Jost. "Don't dig yourself any deeper into the shit, is my advice. Two hours ago I went back and checked the place where the corpse was found—there's no way you could have seen it from the road."

He resumed jogging. "So: you see something, but you don't stop. You run past. But being a conscientious fellow, five minutes up the road you decide you had better go back for a second look. And then you discover the body. And only then do you call the cops."

He grasped Jost's hands and pulled him to his feet. "Run with me," he commanded.

"I can't—"

"Run!"

Jost broke into an unwilling shuffle. Their feet clattered on the flagstones.

"Now describe what you can see. You're coming out of the woods and you're on the lake path—"

"Please—"

"Tell me!"

"I . . . I see . . . a car . . ." Jost's eyes were closed. "Then three men . . . It's raining fast, they have coats, hoods—like monks. . . . Their heads are down. . . . Coming up the slope from the lake . . . I . . . I'm scared. . . . I cross the road and run up into the trees so they don't see me . . ."

"Go on."

"They get into the car and drive off. . . . I wait, and then I come out of the woods and I find the body . . ."

"You've missed something."

"No, I swear—"

"You see a face. When they get into the car, you see a face."

"No . . ."

"Tell me whose face it is, Jost. You can see it. You know who it is. Tell me."

"Globus!" shouted Jost. "I see Globus!"

The package he had taken from Buhler's mailbox lay unopened on the front seat next to him. Perhaps it's a bomb, thought March as he started the Volkswagen. There had been a blitz of parcel bombs over the past few months, blowing off the hands and faces of half a dozen government officials. He might just make page three of the *Tageblatt*: INVESTIGATOR DIES IN MYSTERIOUS BLAST OUTSIDE BARRACKS.

He drove around Schlachtensee until he found a delicatessen, where he bought a loaf of black bread, some Westphalian ham and a quarter bottle of Scotch whisky. The sun still shone; the air was fresh. He pointed the car westward, back toward the lakes. He was going to do something he had not done for years. He was going to have a picnic.

After Göring had been made Chief Reich Huntsman in 1934, there had been some attempt to lighten the Grunewald. Chestnut and linden, beech, birch and oak, had all been planted. But the heart of it—as it had been a thousand years ago, when the plains of northern Europe were still forest—the heart remained the hilly woods of melancholy pine. From these forests, five centuries before Christ, the warring German tribes had emerged; and to these forests, twenty-five centuries later, mostly on weekends, in their campers and their trailers, the victorious German tribes returned. The Germans were a race of forest dwellers. You could make a clearing in your mind, if you liked; the trees just waited to reclaim it.

March parked, took his provisions and Buhler's mail bomb, or whatever it was, and walked carefully up a steep path into the forest. Five minutes' climb brought him to a spot that commanded a clear view of the Havel and of the smoky blue slopes of trees receding into the distance. The pines smelled strong and sweet in the warmth. Above his head, a large jet rumbled across the sky, making its approach to the Berlin airport. As it disappeared, the noise died, until at last the only sound was birdsong.

March did not want to open the parcel yet. It made him uneasy. So he sat on a large stone—no doubt casually deposited here by the municipal authorities for this very purpose—took a swig of whisky and began to eat.

Of Odilo Globocnik—Globus—March knew little, and that only by reputation. His fortunes had swung like a weathercock over the past thirty years. An Austrian by birth, a builder by profession, he had become Party leader in Carinthia in the mid-1930s, and ruler of Vienna. Then there had been a period of disgrace connected with illegal currency speculation, followed by a restoration, as a police chief in the General Government when the war started—he must have known Buhler there, thought March. At the end of the war, there had been a second fall to—where was it?—Trieste, he seemed to remember. But with Himmler's death Globus had come back to Berlin, and now he held some unspecified position within the Gestapo, reporting directly to Heydrich.

That smashed and brutal face was unmistakable, and despite the rain and the poor light, Jost had recognized it at once. A portrait of Globus hung in the Academy's Hall of Fame, and Globus himself had delivered a lecture to the awestruck cadets—on the police structures of the Reich—only a few weeks earlier. No wonder Jost had been so frightened. He should have called the Orpo anonymously and cleared out before they arrived. Better still, from his point of view, he should not have called them at all.

March finished his ham. He took the remains of the bread, broke it into pieces and scattered the crumbs across the forest floor. Two blackbirds that had watched him eat emerged cautiously from the undergrowth and began pecking at them.

He took out the pocket diary. Standard issue to Party members, available in any stationer's. Useful information at the beginning. The names of the Party hierarchy: government ministers, *Kommissariat* bosses, Gauleiters.

Public holidays: Day of National Reawakening, January 30; Potsdam Day, March 21; Führer's birthday, April 20; National Festival of the German People, May 1, . . .

Map of the Empire with railway journey times: Berlin-Rovno, sixteen hours; Berlin-Tiflis, twenty-seven hours; Berlin-Ufa, four days . . .

The diary itself was a week to two pages, the entries so sparse that at first March thought it was blank. He went through it carefully. There was a tiny cross on March 7. For April 1, Buhler had written "My sister's birthday." There was another cross on April 9. On April 11, he had noted "Stuckart/Luther, 10 A.M." Finally, on April 13, the day before his death, Buhler had drawn another small cross. That was all.

March wrote down the dates in his notebook. He began a new page. The death of Josef Buhler. Solutions. One: the death was accidental, the Gestapo had learned of it some hours before the Kripo was informed and Globus was merely inspecting the body when Jost passed by. Absurd.

Very well. Two: Buhler had been murdered by the Gestapo, and Globus had carried out the execution. Absurd again. The "Night and Fog" order of 1941 was still in effect. Buhler could have been bundled away quite legally to some secret death in a Gestapo cell, his property confiscated by the state. Who would have mourned him? Or questioned his disappearance?

And so, three: Buhler had been murdered by Globus, who had covered his tracks by declaring the death a matter of state security and by taking over the investigation himself. But why had the Kripo been allowed to get involved at all? What was Globus's motive? Why had Buhler's body been left in a public place?

March leaned back against the stone and closed his eyes. The sun on his face made the darkness bloodred. A warm haze of whisky enveloped him.

He could not have been asleep more than half an hour when he heard a rustle in the undergrowth beside him and felt something touch his sleeve. He was awake in an instant, in time to see the white tail and hindquarters of a deer darting into the trees. A rural idyll ten kilometers from the heart of the Reich! Either that, or the whisky. He shook his head and picked up the package.

Thick brown paper, neatly wrapped and taped. Indeed, *professionally* wrapped and taped. Crisp lines and sharp creases, an economy of materials used and effort expended. A paradigm of a package. No man March had ever met could have produced such an object—it must have been wrapped by a woman. Next, the postmark. Three Swiss stamps showing tiny yellow flowers on a green background. Posted in Zürich at 1600 hours on 4/13/64. The day before yesterday.

He felt his palms begin to sweat as he unwrapped the package with exaggerated care, first peeling off the tape and then slowly, centimeter by centimeter, folding back the paper. He lifted it fractionally. Inside was a box of chocolates.

Its lid showed flaxen-haired girls in red-checked dresses dancing around a maypole in a flowery meadow. Behind them, white-peaked against a fluorescent-blue sky, rose the Alps. Overprinted in black Gothic script was the legend, "Birthday Greetings to Our Beloved Führer,

1964." But there was something odd about it. The box was too heavy to contain just chocolates.

He took out a penknife and cut round the cellophane cover. He set the box gently on the log. With his face turned away and his arm fully extended, he lifted the lid with the point of the blade. Inside, a mechanism began to whir. Then this:

> Love unspoken
> Faith unbroken
> All life through
> Strings are playing
> Hear them saying
> "I love you."
> Now the echo answers
> "Say you'll want me too."
> All the world's in love with love
> And I love you.

Only the tune, of course, not the words; but he knew them well enough. Standing alone on a hill in the Grunewald Forest, March listened as the box played the waltz duet from Act Three of *The Merry Widow.*

The streets on the way back into central Berlin seemed unnaturally quiet, and when March reached Werderscher-Markt he discovered the reason. A large notice board in the foyer announced there would be a government statement at 4:30. Personnel were to assemble in the staff canteen. Attendance: compulsory. He was just in time.

They had developed a new theory at the Propaganda Ministry that the best time to make big announcements was at the end of the working day. News was thus received communally, in a comradely spirit: there was no opportunity for private skepticism or defeatism. Also, the broadcasts were always timed so that the workers could go home slightly early—at 4:50, say, rather than 5:00—fostering a sense of contentment, subliminally associating the regime with good feelings. That was how it was these days. The snow-white propaganda palace on Wilhelmstrasse employed more psychologists than journalists.

The Werderscher-Markt staff were filing into the canteen: officers and clerks, typists and drivers, shoulder to shoulder in a living embodiment of the National Socialist ideal. The four television screens, one in each corner, were showing a map of the Reich with a swastika superimposed, accompanied by selections from Beethoven. Occasionally, a male announcer would break in excitedly: "People of Germany, prepare yourselves for an important statement!" In the old days, on the radio, you got only the music. Progress again.

How many of these events could March remember? They stretched away behind him, islands in time. In '38, he had been called out of his classroom to hear that German troops were entering Vienna and that Austria had returned to the Fatherland. The headmaster, who had been gassed in the First War, had wept on the stage of the little gymnasium, watched by a gaggle of uncomprehending boys.

In '39, he had been at home with his mother in Hamburg—a Friday morning, eleven o'clock, the Führer's speech relayed live from the Reichstag: *"I am from now on just the first soldier of the German Reich. I have once more put on that uniform that was most sacred and dear to me. I will not take it off until victory is secured, or I will not survive the outcome."* A thunder of applause. This time his mother had wept—a hum of misery as her body rocked backward and forward. March, seventeen, had looked away in shame, sought out the photograph of his father—splendid in the uniform of the Imperial German Navy—and had thought, Thank God. War at last. Maybe now I will be able to live up to what you wanted.

He had been at sea for the next few broadcasts. Victory over Russia in the spring of '43—a triumph for the Führer's strategic genius! The Wehrmacht summer offensive of the year before had cut Moscow off from the Caucasus, separating the Red armies from the Baku oilfields. Stalin's war machine had simply ground to a halt for want of fuel.

Peace with the British in '44—a triumph for the Führer's counterintelligence genius! March remembered how all U-boats had been recalled to their bases on the Atlantic coast to be equipped with a new cipher system:

the treacherous British, they were told, had been reading the Fatherland's codes. Picking off merchant shipping had been easy after that. England was starved into submission. Churchill and his gang of warmongers had fled to Canada.

Peace with the Americans in '46—a triumph for the Führer's scientific genius! When America had defeated Japan by detonating an atomic bomb, the Führer had sent a V-3 rocket to explode in the skies over New York to prove he could retaliate in kind if struck. After that, the war had dwindled to a series of bloody guerrilla conflicts at the fringes of the new German Empire: a nuclear stalemate the diplomats called the Cold War.

But still the broadcasts had gone on. When Göring had died in '51, there had been a whole day of solemn music before the announcement was made. Himmler had received similar treatment when he had been killed in an aircraft explosion in '62. Deaths, victories, wars, exhortations for sacrifice and revenge, the dull struggle with the Reds on the Urals Front with its unpronounceable battlefields and offensives—Oktyabrskoye, Polunochoye, Alapayevsk . . .

March looked at the faces around him. Forced humor, resignation, apprehension. People with brothers and sons and husbands in the East. They kept glancing at the screens.

"People of Germany, prepare yourselves for an important statement!"

What was coming now?

The canteen was almost full. March was pressed up against a pillar. He could see Max Jaeger a few meters away, joking with a bosomy secretary from $VA_1$, the legal department. Max spotted him over her shoulder and gave him a grin. There was a roll of drums. The room became still. A newsreader said, "We are now going live to the Foreign Ministry in Berlin."

A bronze relief glittered in the television lights. A Nazi eagle clutching the globe shot off rays of illumination like a child's drawing of a sunrise. Before it, with his thick black eyebrows and shaded jowls, stood the Foreign Ministry spokesman, Drexler. March suppressed a laugh: you would have thought that in the whole of Germany, Goebbels could have found one spokesman who did not look like a convicted criminal.

"Ladies and gentleman, I have a brief statement for you from the Reich Ministry for Foreign Affairs." Drexler was addressing an audience of journalists, who were off camera. He put on a pair of glasses and began to read.

"In accordance with the long-standing and well-documented desire of the Führer and People of the Greater German Reich to live in peace and security with the countries of the world, and following extensive consultations with our allies in the European Community, the Reich Ministry for Foreign Affairs, on behalf of the Führer, has today issued an invitation to the president of the United States of America to visit the Greater German Reich for personal discussions aimed at promoting greater understanding between our two peoples. This invitation has been accepted. We understand that the American administration has indicated this morning that Herr Kennedy intends to meet the Führer in Berlin in September. Heil Hitler! Long live Germany!"

The picture faded to black and another drumroll signaled the start of the national anthem. The men and women in the canteen began to sing. March pictured them at that moment all over Germany—in shipyards and steelworks and offices and schools—the hard voices and the high merged together in one great bellow of acclamation rising to the heavens.

*Deutschland, Deutschland über Alles!*
*Über Alles in der Welt!*

His own lips moved in conformity with the rest, but no sound emerged.

♦

"More fucking work for us," said Jaeger. They were back in their office. He had his feet on the desk and was puffing at a cigar. "If you think the *Führertag* is a security nightmare—forget it. Can you imagine what it'll be like with Kennedy in town as well?"

March smiled. "I think, Max, you're missing the historic dimension of the occasion."

"Screw the historic dimension of the occasion. I'm thinking about my sleep. The bombs are already going off like firecrackers. Look at this."

Jaeger swung his legs off the desk and rummaged through a pile of folders. "While you were playing around by the Havel, some of us were having to do some work."

He picked up an envelope and tipped out the contents. It was a PPD file: Personal Possessions of the Deceased. From a mound of papers he pulled out two passports and handed them to March. One belonged to an SS officer, Paul Hahn; the other to a young woman, Magda Voss.

Jaeger said, "Pretty thing, isn't she? They'd just married. Were leaving the reception in Spandau. On their way to their honeymoon. He's driving. They turn into Nawener-Strasse. A lorry pulls out in front of them. Guy jumps out the back with a gun. Our man panics. Goes into reverse. Wham! Up the curb, straight into a lamppost. While he's trying to get back into first gear—bang!—shot in the head. End of groom. Little Magda gets out of the car, tries to make a run for it. Bang! End of bride. End of honeymoon. End of every fucking thing. Except it isn't, because the families are still back at the reception toasting the newlyweds and nobody bothers to tell them what's happened for another two hours."

Jaeger blew his nose on a grimy handkerchief. March looked again at the girl's passport. She was pretty: blond and dark eyed; now dead in the gutter at twenty-four.

"Who did it?" He handed the passports back.

Jaeger counted off on his fingers. "Poles. Latvians. Estonians. Ukranians. Czechs. Croats. Caucasians. Georgians. Reds. Anarchists. Who knows? Nowadays it could be anybody. The poor idiot stuck up an open invitation to the reception on his barracks notice board. The Gestapo figures a cleaner, a cook, someone like that, saw it and passed on the word. Most of these barracks ancillaries are foreigners. They were all taken away this afternoon, poor bastards."

He put the passports and identity cards back into the envelope and tossed it into a desk drawer.

"How did it go with you?"

"Have a chocolate." March handed the box to Jaeger, who opened it. The tinny music filled the office.

"Very tasteful."

"What do you know about it?"

"What? *The Merry Widow*? The Führer's favorite operetta. My mother was mad about it."

"So was mine."

Every German mother was mad about it. *The Merry Widow* by Franz Lehár. First performed in Vienna in 1905: as sugary as one of the city's cream cakes. Lehár had died in 1948, and Hitler had sent a personal representative to his funeral.

"What else is there to say?" Jaeger took a chocolate in one of his great paws and popped it into his mouth. "Who are these from? A secret admirer?"

"I took them from Buhler's mailbox." March bit into a chocolate and winced at the sickly taste of liquid cherry. "Consider: you have no friends, yet someone sends you an expensive box of chocolates from Switzerland. With no message. A box that plays the Führer's favorite tune. Who would do that?" He swallowed the other half of the chocolate. "A poisoner, perhaps?"

"Oh, Christ!" Jaeger spat the contents of his mouth into his hand, pulled out his handkerchief and began wiping the brown smears of saliva from his fingers and lips. "Sometimes I have my doubts about your sanity."

"I am systematically destroying state evidence," said

March. He forced himself to eat another chocolate. "No, worse than that: I am *consuming* state evidence, thereby committing a double offense. Tampering with justice while enriching myself."

"Take some leave, man. I'm serious. You need a rest. My advice is to go down and dump those fucking chocolates in the trash as fast as possible. Then come home and have supper with me and Hannelore. You look as if you haven't had a decent meal in weeks. The Gestapo has taken the file. The autopsy report is going straight to Prinz-Albrecht-Strasse. It's over. Done. Forget it."

"Listen, Max." March told him about Jost's confession, about how Jost had seen Globus with the body. He pulled out Buhler's diary. "These names written here. Who are Stuckart and Luther?"

"I don't know." Jaeger's face was suddenly drawn and hard. "What's more, I don't want to know."

A steep flight of stone steps led down to the semidarkness. At the bottom, March hesitated, the chocolates in his hand. A doorway to the left led out to the cobbled center courtyard, where the rubbish was collected from large, rusty bins. To the right, a dimly lit passage led to the Registry.

He tucked the chocolates under his arm and turned right.

The Kripo Registry was housed in what had once been a warren of rooms next to the boilerhouse. The closeness of the boilers and the web of hot water pipes crisscrossing the ceiling kept the place permanently hot. There was a reassuring smell of warm dust and dry paper, and in the poor light, between the pillars, the wire racks of files and reports seemed to stretch to infinity.

The registrar, a fat woman in a greasy tunic who had once been a wardress at the prison in Plötzensee, demanded his ID. He handed it to her as he had done more than once a week for the past ten years. She looked at it as she always did, as if she had never seen it before, then at his face, then back, then returned it and gave an upward tilt of her chin, something between an acknowledgment and a sneer. She wagged her finger. "And no smoking," she said, for the five hundredth time.

From the shelf of reference books next to her desk he selected *Wer Ist's?,* the German *Who's Who*—a red-bound directory a thousand pages thick. He also took down the smaller Party publication, *Guide to the Personalities of the NSDAP,* which included passport-sized photographs of each entrant. This was the book Halder had used to identify Buhler that morning. He lugged both volumes across to a table and switched on the reading light. In the distance the boilers hummed. The Registry was deserted.

Of the two books, March preferred the Party's *Guide.* This had been published more or less annually since the mid-1930s. Often, during the dark, quiet afternoons of the winter, he had come down to the warmth to browse through old editions. It intrigued him to trace how the faces had changed. The early volumes were dominated by the grizzled ex-*Freikorps* Red-baiters, men with necks wider than their foreheads. They stared into the camera, scrubbed and ill at ease, like nineteenth-century farmhands in their Sunday best. But by the 1950s, the beer-hall brawlers had given way to the smooth technocrats of the Speer type—well-groomed university men with bland smiles and hard eyes.

There was one Luther. Christian name: Martin. Now here, comrades, is a historic name to play with. But this Luther looked nothing like his famous namesake. He was pudding-faced with black hair and thick horn-rimmed glasses. March took out his notebook.

> Born: December 16, 1895, Berlin. Served in the German Army transport division, 1914–18. Profession: furniture remover. Joined the NSDAP and the SA on March 1, 1933. Sat on the Berlin City Council for the Dahlem dis-

trict. Entered the Foreign Office, 1936. Head of *Abteilung Deutschland*—the "German Division"—of the Foreign Office until retirement in 1955. Promoted to under state secretary, July 1941.

The details were sparse but clear enough for March to guess his type. Chippy and aggressive, a rough-and-tumble street politician. And an opportunist. Like thousands of others, Luther had rushed to join the Party a few weeks after Hitler had come to power.

He flicked through the pages to Stuckart, Wilhelm, Doctor of Law. The photograph was a professional studio portrait, the face cast in a film star's brooding half shadow. A vain man, and a curious mixture: curly gray hair, intense eyes, straight jawline—yet a flabby, almost voluptuous mouth. He took more notes.

Born November 16, 1902, Wiesbaden. Studied law and economics at Munich and Frankfurt-am-Main universities. Graduated magna cum laude, June 1928. Joined the Party in Munich, 1922. Various SA and SS positions. Mayor of Stettin, 1933. State secretary, Ministry of the Interior, 1935–53. Publication: *A Commentary on the German Racial Laws* (1936). Promoted to honorary SS-Obergruppenführer, 1944. Returned to private legal practice, 1953.

Here was a character quite different from Luther. An intellectual; an alter Kämpfer, like Buhler; a high flyer. To be mayor of Stettin, a port city of nearly 300,000, at the age of thirty-one . . . Suddenly March realized he had read all this before, very recently. But where? He could not remember. He closed his eyes. *Come on.*

*Wer Ist's?* added nothing new except that Stuckart was unmarried whereas Luther was on his third wife. He found a clean double page in his notebook and drew three columns; headed them *Buhler, Luther* and *Stuckart;* and began making lists of dates. Compiling a chronology was a favorite tool of his, a method of finding a pattern in what seemed otherwise to be a fog of random facts.

They had all been born in roughly the same period. Buhler was sixty-four; Luther, sixty-eight; Stuckart, sixty-one. They had all become civil servants in the 1930s—Buhler in 1939, Luther in 1936, Stuckart in 1935. They had all held roughly similar ranks—Buhler and Stuckart had been state secretaries; Luther, an under state secretary. They had all retired in the 1950s—Buhler in 1951, Luther in 1955, Stuckart in 1953. They must all have known one another. They had all met at 10 A.M. the previous Friday. Where was the pattern?

March tilted back in his chair and stared up at the tangle of pipes chasing one another like snakes across the ceiling.

And then he remembered.

He pitched himself forward onto his feet.

Next to the entrance were loosely bound volumes of the *Berliner Tageblatt,* the *Völkischer Beobachter* and the SS paper, *Das Schwarze Korps.* He wrenched back the pages of the *Tageblatt,* back to yesterday's issue, back to the obituaries. There it was. He had seen it last night.

> Party Comrade Wilhelm Stuckart, formerly state secretary of the Ministry of the Interior, who died suddenly of heart failure on Sunday, April 13, will be remembered as a dedicated servant of the National Socialist cause . . .

The ground seemed to shift beneath his feet. He was aware of the registrar staring at him.

"Are you ill, Herr Sturmbannführer?"

"No. I'm fine. Do me a favor, will you?" He picked up a file requisition slip and wrote out Stuckart's full name and date of birth. "Will you see if there's a file on this person?"

She looked at the slip and held out a hand. "ID."

He gave her his identity card. She licked her pencil and entered the twelve digits of March's service number onto the requisition form. By this means a record was kept of which Kripo investigator had requested which file, and at what time. His interest would be there for the Gestapo to see, a full eight hours after he had been ordered off the Buhler case. Further evidence of his lack of National Socialist discipline. It could not be helped.

The registrar had pulled out a long wooden drawer of index cards and was marching her square-tipped fingers along the tops of them. "Stroop," she murmured. "Strunck. Struss. Stülpnagel . . ."

March said, "You've gone past it."

She grunted and pulled out a slip of pink paper. " 'Stuckart, Wilhelm.' " She looked at him. "There is a file. It's out."

"Who has it?"

"See for yourself."

March leaned forward. Stuckart's file was with Sturmbannführer Fiebes of Kripo Department VB3: the sexual crimes division.

The whisky and the dry air had given him a thirst. In the corridor outside the Registry was a water cooler. He poured himself a drink and considered what to do.

What would a sensible man have done? That was easy. A sensible man would have done what Max Jaeger did every day. He would have put on his hat and coat and gone home to his wife and children. But for March that was not an option. The empty apartment in Ansbacher-Strasse, the quarreling neighbors and yesterday's newspaper, these held no attractions for him. He had narrowed his life to such a point that the only thing left was his work. If he betrayed that, what else was there?

And there was something else, the instinct that propelled him out of bed every morning into each unwelcoming day, and that was the desire to *know*. In police work, there was always another junction to reach, another corner to peer around. Who were the Weiss family, and what had happened to them? Whose was the body in the lake? What linked the deaths of Buhler and Stuckart? It kept him going, his blessing or his curse, this compulsion to *know.* And so, in the end, there was no choice.

He tossed the paper cup into the trash can and went upstairs.

Walter Fiebes was in his office drinking schnapps. Watching him from a table beneath the window was a row of five human heads—white plaster casts with hinged scalps, all raised like lavatory seats, displaying their brains in red and gray sections—the five strains that made up the German Empire.

Placards announced them from left to right, in descending order of acceptability to the authorities. Category One: Pure Nordic. Category Two: Predominantly Nordic or Phalic. Category Three: Harmonious Bastard with Slight Alpine Dinaric or Mediterranean Characteristics. These groups qualified for membership in the SS. The others could hold no public office and stared reproachfully at Fiebes. Category Four: Bastard of Predominantly East Baltic or Alpine Origin. Category Five: Bastard of Extra-European Origin.

March was a One/Two; Fiebes, ironically, a borderline Three. But then, the racial fanatics were seldom the blue-eyed Aryan supermen—they, in the words of *Das Schwarzes Korps,* were "too inclined to take their membership in the *Volk* for granted." Instead, the swampy frontiers of the German race were patrolled by those less confident of their bloodworthiness. Insecurity breeds good border guards. The knock-kneed Franconian schoolmaster, ridiculous in his *Lederhosen;* the Bavarian shopkeeper with his pebble glasses; the red-haired Thuringian accountant with a nervous tic and a predilection for the younger members of the Hitler Youth; the lame and the ugly, the runts of the national litter—these were the loudest defenders of the *Volk.*

So it was with Fiebes—the myopic, stooping, bucktoothed, cuckolded Fiebes—whom the Reich had blessed with the one job he really wanted. Homosexuality and miscegenation had replaced rape and incest as capital offenses. Abortion, "an act of sabotage against Germany's racial future," was punishable by death. The permissive 1960s were showing a strong increase in such sex crimes. Fiebes, a sheet sniffer by temperament, worked all the hours the Führer sent and was as happy, in Max Jaeger's words, as a pig in horseshit.

But not today. Now, he was drinking in the office, his eyes were moist and his bat-wing toupee hung slightly askew.

March said, "According to the newspapers, Stuckart died of heart failure."

Fiebes blinked.

"But according to the Registry, the file on Stuckart is out to you."

"I cannot comment."

"Of course you can. We are colleagues." March sat down and lit a cigarette. "I take it we're in the familiar business of 'sparing the family embarrassment.' "

Fiebes muttered, "Not just the family." He hesitated. "Could I have one of those?"

"Sure." March gave him a cigarette and flicked his lighter. Fiebes took an experimental draw, like a schoolboy.

"This affair has left me pretty well shaken, March, I don't mind admitting. The man was a hero to me."

"You knew him?"

"By reputation, naturally. I never actually *met* him. Why? What is your interest?"

"State security. That is all I can say. You know how it is."

"Ah. Now I understand." Fiebes poured himself another large helping of schnapps. "We're very much alike, March, you and I."

"We are?"

"Sure. You're the only investigator who's in this place as often as I am. We've got rid of our wives, our children—all that shit. We live for the job. When it goes well, we're well. When it goes badly . . ." His head fell forward. Presently he said, "Do you know Stuckart's book?"

"Unfortunately, no."

Fiebes opened a desk drawer and handed March a battered, leather-bound volume: *A Commentary on the German Racial Laws.* March leafed through it. There were chapters on each of the three Nuremberg Laws of 1935: the Reich Citizenship Law, the Law for the Protection of German Blood and German Honor, the Law for the Protection of the Genetic Health of the German People. Some passages were underlined in red ink, with exclamation marks beside them. "For the avoidance of racial damage, it is necessary for couples to submit to medical examination before marriage." "Marriage between persons suffering from venereal disease, feeblemindedness, epilepsy or genetic infirmities (see 1933 Sterilization Law) will be permitted only after production of a sterilization certificate." There were charts: "An Overview of the Admissibility of Marriage Between Aryans and Non-Aryans," "The Prevalence of *Mischlinge* of the First Degree."

It was all gobbledygook to Xavier March.

Fiebes said, "Most of it is out of date now. A lot of it refers to Jews, and the Jews, as we know"—he gave a wink—"have all gone east. But Stuckart is still the bible of my calling. This is the foundation stone."

March handed him the book. Fiebes cradled it like a

baby. "Now what I really need to see," said March, "is the file on Stuckart's death."

He was braced for an argument. Instead, Fiebes merely made an expansive gesture with his bottle of schnapps. "Go ahead."

The Kripo file was an ancient one. It went back more than a quarter of a century. In 1936, Stuckart had become a member of the Interior Ministry's Committee for the Protection of German Blood—a tribunal of civil servants, lawyers and doctors who considered applications for marriage between Aryans and non-Aryans. Shortly afterward, the police had started receiving anonymous allegations that Stuckart was providing marriage licenses in exchange for cash bribes. He had also apparently demanded sexual favors from some of the women involved.

The first named complainant was a Dortmund tailor, a Herr Maser, who had protested to his local Party office that his fiancée had been assaulted. His statement had been passed to the Kripo. There was no record of any investigation. Instead, Maser and his girlfriend had been dispatched to concentration camps. Various other stories from informants, including one from Stuckart's wartime *Blockwart,* were included in the file. No action had ever been taken.

In 1953, Stuckart had begun a liaison with an eighteen-year-old Warsaw girl, Maria Dymarski. She had claimed German ancestry back to 1720 in order to marry a Wehrmacht captain. The conclusion of the Interior Ministry's experts was that the documents had been forged. The following year, Dymarski had been given a permit to work as a domestic servant in Berlin. Her employer's name was listed as Wilhelm Stuckart.

March looked up. "How did he get away with it for ten years?"

"He was an Obergruppenführer, March. You don't make complaints about a man like that. Remember what happened to Maser when he complained? Besides, nobody had any evidence—then."

"And there is evidence now?"

"Look in the envelope."

Inside the file, in a manila envelope, were a dozen color photographs of startlingly good quality, showing Stuckart and Dymarski in bed. White bodies against red satin sheets. The faces—contorted in some shots, relaxed in others—were easy to identify. They were all taken from the same position, alongside the bed. The girl's body, pale and undernourished, looked fragile beneath the man's. In one shot she sat astride him—thin white arms clasped behind her head, face tilted toward the camera. Her features were broad, Slavic. But with her shoulder-length hair dyed blond she could have passed as a German.

"These weren't taken recently?"

"About ten years ago. He turned grayer. She put on a bit of weight. She looked like more of a tart as she got older."

"Do we have any idea where they are?" The background was a blur of colors. A brown wooden bedhead, red-and-white-striped wallpaper, a lamp with a yellow shade; it could have been anywhere.

"It's not his apartment—at least, not the way it's decorated now. A hotel, maybe a whorehouse. The camera is behind a two-way mirror. See the way they sometimes seem to be staring into the camera? I've seen that look a hundred times. They're checking themselves in the mirror."

March examined each of the pictures again. They were glossy and unscratched—new prints from old negatives. The sort of pictures a pimp might try to sell you in a back street in Kreuzberg.

"Where did you find them?"

"Next to the bodies."

Stuckart had shot his mistress first. According to the autopsy report, she had lain, fully clothed, facedown on the bed in Stuckart's apartment in Fritz-Todt-Platz. He had put a bullet into the back of her head with his SS Luger (if that was so, thought March, it was probably the first time the old pen pusher had ever used it). Traces of impacted cotton and down in the wound suggested he had fired the bullet through a pillow. Then he had sat on the edge of the bed and apparently shot himself through the roof of his mouth. In the scene-of-crime photographs neither body was recognizable. The pistol was still clutched in Stuckart's hand.

"He left a note," said Fiebes, "on the dining room table. 'By this action I hope to spare embarrassment to my family, the Reich and the Führer. Heil Hitler! Long live Germany! Wilhelm Stuckart.' "

"Blackmail?"

"Presumably."

"Who found the bodies?"

"This is the best part." Fiebes spat out each word as if it were poison: "An American woman journalist."

Her statement was in the file: Charlotte Maguire, age 25, Berlin representative of an American news agency, World European Features.

"A real little bitch. Started shrieking about her rights the moment she was brought in. Rights!" Fiebes took another swig of schnapps. "Shit, I suppose we have to be *nice* to the Americans now, do we?"

March made a note of her address. The only other witness questioned had been the porter who worked in Stuckart's apartment block. The American woman claimed to have seen two men on the stairs immediately before the discovery of the bodies, but the porter insisted there had been no one.

March looked up suddenly. Fiebes jumped. "What is it?"

"Nothing. A shadow at your door, perhaps."

"My God, this place—" Fiebes flung open the frosted-glass door and peered both ways along the corridor. While his back was turned, March detached the envelope pinned to the back of the file and slipped it into his pocket.

"Nobody." He shut the door. "You're losing your nerve, March."

"An overactive imagination has always been my curse." He closed the folder and stood up.

Fiebes swayed, squinting. "Don't you want to take it with you? Aren't you working on this with the Gestapo?"

"No. A separate matter."

"Oh." He sat down heavily. "When you said 'state security,' I assumed . . . Doesn't matter. Out of my hands. The Gestapo has taken it over, thank God. Obergruppenführer Globus has assumed responsibility. You must have heard of him? A thug, it's true, but he'll sort it out."

The information bureau at Alexander-Platz had Luther's address. According to police records, he still lived in Dahlem. March lit another cigarette, then dialed the number. The telephone rang for a long time—a bleak, unfriendly echo somewhere in the city. Just as he was about to hang up, a woman answered.

"Yes?"

"Frau Luther?"

"Yes." She sounded younger than he had expected. Her voice was thick, as if she had been crying.

"My name is Xavier March. I am an investigator with the Berlin Kriminalpolizei. May I speak to your husband?"

"I'm sorry . . . I don't understand. If you're from the police, surely you know—"

"Know? Know what?"

"That he's missing. He disappeared on Sunday." She started to cry.

"I'm sorry to hear that." March balanced his cigarette on the edge of the ashtray.

*God in heaven, another one.*

"He said he was going on a business trip to Munich and would be back on Monday." She blew her nose. "But I have already explained all this. Surely you know that this matter is being dealt with at the *very highest* level. What—?"

She broke off. March could hear a conversation at the other end. There was a man's voice in the background, harsh and questioning. She said something he could not hear, then came back on the line.

"Obergruppenführer Globocnik is with me now. He would like to talk to you. What did you say your name was?"

March replaced the receiver.

On his way out, he thought of the call at Buhler's place that morning. An old man's voice:

*"Buhler? Speak to me. Who is that?"*

*"A friend."*

*Click.*

Bülow-Strasse runs west to east for about a kilometer through one of the busiest quarters of Berlin, close to the Gotenland railway station. The American woman's address proved to be an apartment block midway down.

It was seedier than March had expected: five stories high, black with a century of traffic fumes, streaked with bird shit. A drunk sat on the pavement next to the entrance, turning his head to follow each passerby. On the opposite side of the street was an elevated section of the U-bahn. As he parked, a train was pulling out of the Bülow-Strasse station, its red and yellow carriages riding blue-white flashes of electricity, vivid in the gathering dark.

Her apartment was on the fourth floor. She was not in. "Henry," read a note written in English and pinned to her door, "I'm in the bar on Potsdamer-Strasse. Love, Charlie."

March knew only a few words of English—but enough to grasp the sense of the message. Wearily he descended the stairs. Potsdamer-Strasse was a long street with many bars.

"I'm looking for Fräulein Maguire," he said to the concierge in the hall. "Any idea where I might find her?"

It was like throwing a switch. "She went out an hour ago, Sturmbannführer. You're the second man to ask. Fifteen minutes after she went out, a young chap came looking for her. Another foreigner—smartly dressed, short hair. She won't be back until after midnight, that much I can promise you."

March wondered how many of her other tenants the old lady had informed on to the Gestapo.

"Is there a bar she goes to regularly?"

"Heini's, around the corner. That's where all the damned foreigners go."

"Your powers of observation do you credit, madam."

By the time he left her to her knitting, five minutes later, March was laden with information about "Charlie" Maguire. He knew she had dark hair, cut short; that she was small and slim; that she was wearing a raincoat of shiny blue plastic "and high heels, like a tart"; that she had lived here six months; that she stayed out till all hours and often got up at noon; that she was behind with the rent; that he should see the bottles of liquor the hussy threw out . . . No, thank you, madam, I have no desire to inspect them, that will not be necessary, you have been most helpful . . .

He turned right along Bülow-Strasse. Another right took him to Potsdamer-Strasse. Heini's was fifty meters up on the left. A painted sign showed a landlord with an apron and a handlebar mustache carrying a foaming stein of beer. Beneath it, part of the red neon lettering had burned out: HEI      S.

The bar was quiet except for one corner, where a group of six sat around a table talking loudly in English accents. She was the only woman. She was laughing and ruffling an older man's hair. He was laughing, too. Then he saw March and said something and the laughter stopped. They watched him as he approached. He was conscious of his uniform, of the noise of his jackboots on the polished wooden floor.

"Fräulein Maguire, my name is Xavier March of the Berlin Kriminalpolizei." He showed her his ID. "I would like to speak with you, please."

She had large dark eyes, glittering in the bar lights.

"Go ahead."

"In private, please."

"I've nothing more to say." She turned to the man whose hair she had ruffled and murmured something March did not understand. They all laughed. March did not move. Eventually, a younger man in a sport jacket and a button-down shirt stood up. He pulled a card from his breast pocket and held it out.

"Henry Nightingale. Second secretary at the United States Embassy. I'm sorry, Herr March, but Miss Maguire has said all she has to say to your colleagues."

March ignored the card.

The woman said, "If you're not going to go, why don't you join us? This is Howard Thompson of *The New York Times*." The older man raised his glass. "This is Bruce Fallon of United Press. Peter Kent, CBS. Arthur Haines, Reuters. Henry, you've met. Me, you know, apparently. We're just having a little drink to celebrate the *great news.* Come on. The Americans and the SS—we're all friends now."

"Careful, Charlie," said the young man from the embassy.

"Shut up, Henry. Oh, Christ, if this man doesn't move soon, I'll go and talk to him out of sheer boredom. Look—" There was a crumpled sheet of paper on the table in front of her. She tossed it to March. "That's what I got for getting mixed up in this. My visa's withdrawn for 'fraternizing with a German citizen without official permission.' I was supposed to leave today, but my friends here had a word with the Propaganda Ministry and got me a week's extension. Wouldn't have looked good, would it? Throwing me out on the day of the *great news.*"

March said, "It's important."

She stared at him, a cool look. The embassy man put his hand on her arm. "You don't have to go."

That seemed to make up her mind. "Will you shut up, Henry?" She shook herself free and pulled her coat over her shoulders. "He looks respectable enough. For a Nazi. Thanks for the drink." She downed the contents of her glass—whisky and water, by the look of it—and stood up. "Let's go."

The man called Thompson said something in English.

"I will, Howard. Don't worry."

Outside, she said, "Where are we going?"

"My car."

"Then where?"

"Dr. Stuckart's apartment."

"What fun."

She *was* small. Even clattering on her high heels, she was several centimeters short of March's shoulder. He opened the door of the Volkswagen for her. As she bent to get in, he smelled the whisky on her breath, and also cigarettes—French, not German—and perfume: something expensive, he thought.

The Volkswagen's 1300cc engine rattled behind them. March drove carefully: west along Bülow-Strasse, around the Berlin-Gotenland station, north up the Avenue of Victory. The captured artillery from the Barbarossa campaign lined the boulevard, barrels tilted toward the stars. Normally this section of the capital was quiet at night, Berliners preferring the noisy cafés behind the Ku'damm or the jumbled streets of Kreuzberg. But on this evening, people were everywhere—standing in groups, admiring the guns and the floodlit buildings, strolling and window-shopping.

"What kind of person wants to go out at night and look at guns?" She shook her head in wonderment.

"Tourists," said March. "By the twentieth, there'll be more than three million of them."

It was risky, taking the American woman back to

Stuckart's place, especially now that Globus knew someone from the Kripo was looking for Luther. But he needed to see the apartment, to hear the woman's story. He had no plan, no real idea of what he might find. He recalled the Führer's words—"I go the way that Providence dictates with the assurance of a sleepwalker"—and he smiled.

Ahead of them, searchlights picked out the eagle on top of the Great Hall. It seemed to hang in the sky, a golden bird of prey hovering over the capital.

She noticed his grin. "What's funny?"

"Nothing." He turned right at the European Parliament. The flags of the twelve member nations were lit by spots. The swastika that flew above them was twice the size of the other standards. "Tell me about Stuckart. How well did you know him?"

"Hardly at all. I met him through my parents. My father was at the embassy here before the war. He married a German, an actress. She's my mother. Monika Koch, did you ever hear of her?"

"No. I don't believe so." Her German was flawless. She must have spoken it since childhood; her mother's doing, no doubt.

"She'd be sorry to hear that. She seems to think she was a big star over here. Anyway, they both knew Stuckart slightly. When I arrived in Berlin last year, they gave me a list of people to go and talk to—contacts. Half of them turned out to be dead, one way or another. Most of the rest didn't want to meet me. American journalists don't make healthy company, if you know what I mean. Do you mind if I smoke?"

"Go ahead. What was Stuckart like?"

"Awful." Her lighter flared in the darkness; she inhaled deeply. "He made a grab at me, even though this woman of his was in the apartment at the same time. That was just before Christmas. I kept away from him after that. Then last week I got a message from my office in New York. They wanted a piece for Hitler's seventy-fifth birthday, talking to some of the people who knew him from the old days."

"So you called Stuckart?"

"Right."

"And arranged to meet him on Sunday, and when you got there, he was dead?"

"If you know it all," she said irritably, "why do you need to talk to me again?"

"I don't know it all, Fräulein. That's the point."

After that, they drove in silence.

Fritz-Todt-Platz was a couple of blocks from the Avenue of Victory. Laid out in the mid-1950s as part of Speer's redevelopment of the city, it was a square of expensive-looking apartment buildings erected around a small memorial garden. In the center stood an absurdly heroic statue of Todt, the creator of the *Autobahnen,* by Professor Thorak.

"Which one was Stuckart's?"

She pointed to a building on the other side of the square. March drove around and parked outside it.

"Which floor?"

"Fourth."

He looked up. The fourth floor was in darkness. Good.

Todt's statue was floodlit. In the reflected light, her face was white. She looked as if she was about to be sick. Then he remembered the photographs Fiebes had shown him of the corpses—Stuckart's skull had been a crater, like a guttered candle—and he understood.

She said, "I don't have to do this, do I?"

"No. But you will."

"Why?"

"Because you want to know what happened as much as I do. That's why you've come this far."

She stared at him again, then stubbed out her cigarette, twisting it and breaking it in the ashtray. "Let's do it quickly. I'd like to get back to my friends."

The keys to the apartment were still in the envelope March had removed from Stuckart's file. There were five in all. He found the one that fitted the front door and let them into the foyer. It was vulgarly luxurious, in the new Imperial style—white marble floor, crystal chandeliers, nineteenth-century gilt chairs with red plush upholstery, the air scented with dried flowers. No porter, thankfully: he must have gone off duty. Indeed, the entire building seemed deserted. Perhaps the tenants had left for their second homes in the country. Berlin could be unbearably crowded in the week before the *Führertag.* The smart set always fled the capital.

"Now what?"

"Just tell me what happened."

"The porter was at the desk, here," she said. "I asked for Stuckart. He directed me to the fourth floor. I couldn't take the elevator, it was being repaired. There was a man working on it. So I walked."

"What time was this?"

"Noon. Exactly."

They climbed the stairs.

She went on, "I had just reached the second floor when two men came running toward me."

"Describe them, please."

"It all happened too quickly for me to get a very good look. Both in their thirties. One had a brown suit, the other had a green anorak. Short hair. That's about it."

"What did they do when they saw you?"

"They just pushed past me. The one in the anorak said something to the other, but I couldn't hear what it was. There was a lot of drilling going on in the elevator shaft. After that, I went on up to Stuckart's apartment and rang the bell. There was no reply."

"So what did you do?"

"I walked down to the porter and asked him to open Stuckart's door, to check if he was okay."

"Why?"

She hesitated. "There was something about those two men. I had a hunch. You know: that feeling when you knock on a door and nobody answers but you're sure someone's in."

"And you persuaded the porter to open the door?"

"I told him I'd call the police if he didn't. I said he would have to answer to the authorities if anything had happened to Dr. Stuckart."

Shrewd psychology, thought March. After thirty years of being told what to do, the average German was careful not to take final responsibility for anything, even for not opening a door. "And then you found the bodies?"

She nodded. "The porter saw them first. He screamed and I came running."

"Did you mention the two men you'd seen on the stairs? What did the porter say?"

"He was too busy throwing up to talk at first. Then he insisted he'd seen nobody. He said I must have imagined it."

"Do you think he was lying?"

She considered this. "No, I don't. I think he genuinely didn't see them. On the other hand, I don't see how he could have missed them."

They were still on the second-floor landing, at the point at which she said the men had passed her. March walked back down the flight of stairs. She waited for a moment, then followed him. At the foot of the steps a door led off to the first-floor corridor.

He said, half to himself, "They could have hidden along here, I suppose. Where else?"

They continued down to the ground floor. Here there were two more doors. One led to the foyer. March tried the other. It was unlocked. "Or they could have slipped out down here."

Bare concrete steps, neon lit, led down to the basement. At the bottom was a long passage with doors off it. March opened each in turn. A lavatory. A storeroom. A generator room. A bomb shelter.

Under the 1948 Reich Civil Defense Law, every new building had to be equipped with a bomb shelter; those beneath offices and apartment buildings were also required to have their own generators and air-filtration systems. This one was particularly well appointed: bunk beds, a storage cupboard, a separate cubicle with toilet facilities. March carried a metal chair across to the air vent, set into the wall two and a half meters above the ground. He grasped the metal cover. It came away easily in his hands. All the screws had been removed.

"The Ministry of Construction specifies an aperture with a diameter of half a meter," said March. He unbuckled his belt and hung it and his pistol over the back of the chair. "If only they appreciated the difficulties that gives us. Would you mind?"

He took off his jacket and handed it to the woman, then mounted the chair. Reaching into the shaft, he found something hard to hold on to and pulled himself in. The filters and the fan had both been removed. By working his shoulders against the metal casing he was able to move slowly forward. The darkness was complete. He choked on the dust. His hands, stretched out in front of him, touched metal, and he pushed. The outside cover yielded and crashed to the ground. The night air rushed in. For a moment, he felt an almost overpowering urge to crawl out into it, but instead he wriggled backward and lowered himself into the basement shelter. He landed, dusty and grease smeared.

The woman was pointing his pistol at him.

"Bang, bang," she said. "You're dead." She smiled at his alarm. "American joke."

"Not funny." He took the Luger and put it back into his holster.

"Okay," she said. "Here's a better one. Two murderers are seen by a witness leaving a building and it takes the police four days to work out how they did it. I'd say that was funny, wouldn't you?"

"It depends on the circumstances." He brushed the dust off his shirt. "If the police found a note beside one of the victims in his own handwriting saying it was suicide,

I could understand why they wouldn't bother looking any further."

"But then you come along and you do look further."

"I'm the curious type."

"Clearly." She smiled again. "So Stuckart was shot and the murderers tried to make it look like suicide?"

He hesitated. "It's a possibility."

He regretted the words the moment he uttered them. She had led him into disclosing more than was wise about Stuckart's death. Now a faint light of mockery played in her eyes. He cursed himself for underrating her. She had the cunning of a professional criminal. He considered taking her back to the bar and going on alone but dismissed the idea. It was no good. To know what had happened, he needed to see it through her eyes.

He buttoned his tunic. "Now we must inspect Party Comrade Stuckart's apartment."

That, he was pleased to see, knocked the smile off her face. But she did not refuse to go with him. They climbed the stairs and it struck him again that she was almost as anxious to see Stuckart's flat as he was.

They took the elevator to the fourth floor. As they stepped out, he heard, along the corridor to their left, a door being opened. He grabbed the American's arm and steered her around the corner, out of sight. When he looked back, he could see a middle-aged woman in a fur coat heading for the elevator. She was carrying a small dog.

"You're hurting my arm."

"Sorry."

He was hiding from shadows. The woman talked quietly to the dog and disappeared into the lift. March wondered whether Globus had retrieved the file from Fiebes yet, whether he had discovered that the keys were missing. They would have to hurry.

The door to Stuckart's apartment had been sealed that day, close to the handle, with red wax. A note informed the curious that these premises were now under the jurisdiction of the *Geheime Staatspolizei,* the Gestapo, and that entry was forbidden. March pulled on a pair of thin leather gloves and broke the seal. The key turned easily in the lock.

He said, "Don't touch anything."

More luxury, to match the building: elaborate gilt mirrors, antique tables and chairs with fluted legs and ivory damask upholstery, a carpet of royal blue with Persian rugs. The spoils of war, the fruits of Empire.

"Tell me again what happened."

"The porter opened the door. We came into the hall." Her voice had risen. She was trembling. "He shouted and there was no reply, so we both came right in. I opened that door first."

It was the sort of bathroom March had seen only in glossy magazines. White marble and brown smoky mirrors, a sunken bathtub, twin basins with gold taps . . . Here, he thought, was the hand of Maria Dymarski, leafing through German *Vogue* at the Ku'damm hairdresser's while her Polish roots were bleached Aryan white.

"Then I came into the sitting room."

March switched on the light. One wall consisted of tall windows looking out over the square. The other three had large mirrors. Wherever he turned, he could see images of himself and the girl: the black uniform and the shiny blue coat incongruous among the antiques. Nymphs were the decorative conceit. Fashioned in gilt, they draped themselves around the mirrors; cast in bronze, they supported table lamps and clocks. There were paintings of nymphs and statues of nymphs; wood nymphs and water nymphs; Amphitrite and Thetis.

"I heard the porter scream. I went to help."

March opened the door of the bedroom. She turned away. Blood in half light looks black. Dark shapes, twisted and grotesque, leaped up the walls and across the ceiling like the shadows of trees.

"They were on the bed?"

She nodded.

"What did you do?"

"Called the police."

"Where was the porter?"

"In the bathroom."

"Did you look at them again?"

"What do you think?" She brushed her sleeve angrily across her eyes.

"All right, Fräulein. It's enough. Wait in the sitting room."

The human body contains six liters of blood: sufficient to paint a large apartment. March tried to avoid looking at the bed and the walls as he worked—opening the cupboard doors, feeling the lining of every item of clothing, skimming every pocket with his gloved hands. He moved on to the bedside cabinets. These had been unlocked and searched before. The contents of the drawers had been emptied out for inspection, then stuffed back haphazardly—a typical clumsy Orpo job, destroying more clues than it uncovered.

Nothing, nothing. Had he risked everything for this?

He was on his knees with his arm stretched beneath the bed when he heard it. It took a second for the sound to register.

*Love unspoken*
*Faith unbroken*
*All life through . . .*

"I'm sorry," she said when he rushed in. "I shouldn't have touched it."

He took the chocolate box from her, carefully, and closed the lid on its tune.

"Where was it?"

"On that table."

Someone had collected Stuckart's mail for the past three days and had inspected it, neatly slicing open the envelopes, pulling out the letters. They were heaped up next to the telephone. He had not noticed them when he came in. How had he missed them? The chocolates, he could see, had been wrapped exactly as Buhler's had been, postmarked Zürich, 1600 hours, Monday afternoon.

Then he saw that she was holding a paper knife.

"I told you not to touch anything."

"I said I'm sorry."

"Do you think this is a game?" *She's crazier than I am.* "You're going to have to leave." He tried to grab her, but she twisted free.

"No way." She backed away, pointing the knife at him. "I have as much right to be here as you do. You try and throw me out and I'll scream so loud I'll have every Gestapo man in Berlin hammering on that door."

"You have a knife, but I have a gun."

"Ah, but you daren't use it."

March ran his hand through his hair. He thought, You imagined you were so clever, finding her, persuading her to come back. And all the time, she wanted to come. She's looking for something. . . . He had been an idiot.

He said, "You've been lying to me."

She said, "*You've* been lying to *me.* That makes us even."

"This is dangerous. I beg you, you have no idea—"

"What I do know is this: my career could have ended because of what happened in this apartment. I could be fired when I get back to New York. I'm being thrown out of this lousy country, and I want to find out why."

"How do I know I can trust you?"

"How do I know I can trust *you*?"

They stood like that for perhaps half a minute: he with his hand to his hair, she with the silver paper knife still pointed at him. Outside, across the Platz, a clock began to chime. March looked at his watch. It was already ten.

"We have no time for this." He spoke quickly. "Here are the keys to the apartment. This one opens the door downstairs. This one is for the main door up here. This fits the bedside cabinet. That's a desk key. This one"—he held it up—"this, I think, is the key to a safe. Where is it?"

"I don't know." Seeing his look of disbelief, she added, "I swear."

They searched in silence for ten minutes, shifting furniture, pulling up rugs, looking behind paintings. Suddenly she said, "This mirror is loose."

It was a small antique looking glass, maybe thirty centimeters square, above the table on which she had opened the letters. March grasped the ormolu frame. It gave a little but would not come away from the wall.

"Try this." She gave him the knife.

She was right. Two thirds down the left-hand side, behind the lip of the frame, was a tiny lever. March pressed it with the tip of the paper knife and felt something yield. The mirror was on a hinge. It swung open to reveal a safe.

He inspected it and swore. The key was not enough. There was also a combination lock.

"Too much for you?" she asked.

" 'In adversity,' " quoted March, " 'the resourceful officer will always discover opportunity.' " He picked up the telephone.

Across a distance of five thousand kilometers, President Kennedy flashed his famous smile. He stood behind a cluster of microphones, addressing a crowd in a football stadium. Banners of red, white and blue streamed behind him—"Reelect Kennedy!" "Four More in Sixty-four!" He shouted something March did not understand and the crowd cheered back.

"What's he talking about?"

The television cast a blue glow in the darkness of Stuckart's apartment. The woman translated: " 'The Germans have their system and we have ours. But we are all citizens of one planet. And as long as our two nations remember that, I sincerely believe: we can have peace.' Cue loud applause from dumb audience."

She had kicked off her shoes and was lying full length on her stomach in front of the set.

"Ah. Here's the serious bit." She waited until he finished speaking, then translated again: "He says he plans to raise human rights questions during his visit in the fall." She laughed and shook her head. "God, Kennedy is so full of shit. The only thing he really wants to raise is his vote in November."

" 'Human rights'?"

"The thousands of dissidents you people lock up in camps. The millions of Jews who vanished in the war. The torture. The killing. Sorry to mention them, but we have this bourgeois notion that human beings have rights. Where have you been the last twenty years?"

The contempt in her voice jolted him. He had never properly spoken to an American before, had only encountered the occasional tourist—and those few had been chaperoned around the capital, shown only what the Propaganda Ministry wanted them to see, like Red Cross officials on a KZ inspection. Listening to her now, it occurred to him that she probably knew more about his country's recent history than he did. He felt he should make some sort of defense but did not know what to say.

"You talk like a politician" was all he could manage. She did not bother to reply.

He looked again at the figure on the screen. Kennedy projected an image of youthful vigor, despite his spectacles and balding head.

"Will he win?" he asked.

She was silent. For a moment he thought she had decided not to speak to him. Then she said, "He will now. He's in good shape for a man of seventy-five, wouldn't you say?"

"Indeed." March was standing a meter back from the window, smoking a cigarette, alternately watching the television and watching the square. Traffic was sparse—mostly people returning from dinner or the cinema. A young couple held hands under the statue of Todt. They might be Gestapo; it was hard to tell.

*"The millions of Jews who vanished in the war . . ."* He was risking court-martial simply by talking to her. Yet her mind must be a treasure house, full of ill-considered objects that meant nothing to her but would be gold to him. If he could somehow overcome her furious resentment, pick his way around the propaganda . . .

No. A ridiculous thought. He had problems enough as it was.

A solemn blond newsreader filled the screen; behind her, a composite picture of Kennedy and the Führer and the single word DÉTENTE.

Charlotte Maguire had helped herself to a glass of Scotch from Stuckart's liquor cabinet. Now she raised it to the television in mock salute. "To Joseph P. Kennedy: President of the United States—appeaser, anti-Semite, gangster and sonofabitch. May you roast in hell."

The clock outside struck ten-thirty, ten forty-five, eleven.

She said, "Maybe this friend of yours had second thoughts."

March shook his head. "He'll come."

A few moments later, a battered blue Skoda entered the square. It made one slow circuit of the Platz, then came around again and parked opposite the apartment block. Max Jaeger emerged from the driver's side; from the other came a small man in a shabby sport jacket and trilby, carrying a doctor's bag. He squinted up at the fourth floor and backed away, but Jaeger took his arm and propelled him toward the entrance.

In the stillness of the apartment, a buzzer sounded.

"It would be best," said March, "if you didn't speak."

She shrugged. "As you like."

He went into the hall and picked up the intercom.

"Hello, Max."

He pressed a switch and unlocked the door. The corridor was empty. After a minute, a soft *ping* signaled the arrival of the elevator and the little man appeared. He scuttled down the hallway and into Stuckart's foyer without uttering a word. He was in his fifties and carried with him, like bad breath, the reek of the back streets—of furtive deals and triple-entry accounting, of card tables folded away at the sound of a tread on the stairs. Jaeger followed close behind.

When the man saw March was not alone, he shrank back into the corner.

"Who's the woman?" He appealed to Jaeger. "You never said anything about a woman. Who's the woman?"

"Shut up, Willi," said Max. He gave him a gentle push into the living room.

March said, "Never mind her, Willi. Look at this."

He switched on the lamp, angling it upward.

Willi Stiefel took in the safe at a glance. "English," he said. "Casing: one and a half centimeters, high-tensile steel. Fine mechanism. Eight-figure code. Six, if you're lucky." He appealed to March: "I beg you, Herr Sturmbannführer. It's the guillotine for me next time."

"It'll be the guillotine for you this time," said Jaeger, "if you don't get on with it."

"Fifteen minutes, Herr Sturmbannführer. Then I'm out of here. Agreed?"

March nodded. "Agreed."

Stiefel gave the woman a last, nervous look. Then he removed his hat and jacket, opened his case and took out a pair of thin rubber gloves and a stethoscope.

March took Jaeger over to the window and whispered, "Did he take much persuading?"

"What do you think? But then I told him he was still covered by Forty-two. He saw the light."

Paragraph forty-two of the Reich Criminal Code stated that all "habitual criminals and offenders against morality" could be arrested on suspicion that they *might* commit an offense. National Socialism taught that criminality was in the blood—something you were born with, like musical talent or blond hair. Thus the character of the criminal rather than his crime determined the sentence. A gangster stealing a few marks after a fistfight could be sentenced to death, on the grounds that he "displayed an inclination toward criminality so deep rooted that it precluded his ever becoming a useful member of the folk community." But the next day, in the same court, a loyal

Party member who had shot his wife for an insulting remark might merely be bound over to keep the peace.

Stiefel could not afford another arrest. He had recently served nine years in Spandau for a bank robbery. He had no choice but to cooperate with the Polizei, whatever they asked him to be—informant, agent provocateur or safe-breaker. These days, he ran a watch repair business in Wedding and swore he was going straight: a protestation of innocence that was hard to believe, watching him now. He had placed the stethoscope against the safe door and was twisting the dial a digit at a time. His eyes were closed as he listened for the click of the lock's tumblers falling into place.

*Come on, Willi.* March rubbed his hands. His fingers were numb with apprehension.

"Jesus Christ," said Jaeger under his breath. "I hope you know what you're doing."

"I'll explain later."

"No, thanks. I told you: I don't want to know."

Stiefel straightened and let out a long sigh. "One," he said. One was the first digit of the combination.

Like Stiefel, Jaeger kept glancing at the woman. She was sitting demurely on one of the gilt chairs, her hands folded in her lap. "A foreign *woman,* for God's sake!"

"Six."

So it went on, one digit every few minutes, until, at 11:35, Stiefel said to March, "The owner: when was he born?"

"Why?"

"It would save time. I think he's set this with the date of his birth. So far, I've got one-one-one-six-one-nine. The eleventh month, sixteenth day, nineteen . . ."

March checked his notes from Stuckart's *Wer Ist's?* entry.

"Nineteen hundred two."

"Zero-two." Stiefel tried the combination, then smiled. "It's usually the owner's birthday," he said, "or the Führer's birthday or the Day of National Reawakening." He pulled open the door.

The safe was small: a twenty-centimeter cube containing no bank notes or jewelery, just paper—old paper, most of it. March piled it onto the table and began rifling through it.

"I'd like to leave now, Herr Sturmbannführer."

March ignored him. Tied up in red ribbon were the title deeds to a property in Wiesbaden—the family home, by the look of it. There were stock certificates. Hoesch, Siemens, Thyssen: the companies were standard, but the sums invested looked astronomical. Insurance papers. One human touch: a photograph of Maria Dymarski in a 1950s cheesecake pose.

Suddenly, from the window, Jaeger gave a shout of warning: "Here they come, you fucking, *fucking* fool!"

An unmarked gray BMW was driving around the square, fast, followed by an army truck. The vehicles swerved to a halt outside, blocking the street. A man in a belted leather coat leaped out of the car. The tailgate of the truck was kicked down and SS troops carrying automatic rifles began jumping out.

"Move! Move!" yelled Jaeger. He began pushing Charlie and Stiefel toward the door.

With shaking fingers, March worked his way through the remaining papers. A blue envelope, unmarked. Something heavy in it. The flap of the envelope was open. He saw a letterhead in copperplate—Zaugg & Cie., Bankiers—and stuffed it into his pocket.

The buzzer from the door downstairs began sounding in long urgent bursts.

"They must know we're up here!"

Jaeger said, "Now what?" Stiefel had turned gray. The woman stood like a statue. She did not seem to know what was going on.

"The basement!" shouted March. "They might just miss us. Get the elevator!"

The other three ran out into the corridor. He began

stuffing the papers back into the safe, slammed it shut, twirled the dial, pushed the mirror back into place. There was no time to do anything about the broken seal on the apartment door. They were holding the lift for him. He squeezed in and they began their descent.

Third floor, second floor . . .

March prayed it would not stop at the ground floor. It did not. It opened on to the empty basement. Above their heads they could hear the heels of the storm troopers on the marble slabs.

"This way!" He led them into the bomb shelter. The grating from the air vent was where he had left it, leaning against the wall.

Stiefel needed no telling. He ran to the air shaft, lifted his bag above his head and tossed it in. He grabbed at the brickwork, tried to haul himself after it, his feet scrabbling for a purchase on the smooth wall. He was yelling over his shoulder, "Help me!" March and Jaeger seized his legs and heaved. The little man wriggled headfirst into the hole and was gone.

Coming closer—the ring and scrape of boots on concrete. The SS had found the entrance to the basement. A man was shouting.

March to Charlie: "You next."

"I'll tell you something," she said, pointing at Jaeger. "He'll never make it."

Jaeger's hands went to his waist. It was true. He was too fat. "I'll stay. I'll think of something. You two get out."

"No." This was turning into a farce. March took the envelope from his pocket and pressed it into Charlie's hand. "Take this. We may be searched."

"And you?" She had her stupid shoes in one hand, was already mounting the chair.

"Wait till you hear from me. Tell nobody." He grabbed her, locked his hands just below her knees and threw. She was so light, he could have wept.

The SS were in the basement. Along the passage—the crash of doors flung open.

March swung the grating back into place and kicked away the chair.

# THURSDAY, APRIL 16

♦

When National Socialism has ruled long enough, it will no longer be possible to conceive of a form of life different from ours.

ADOLF HITLER, July 11, 1941

The gray BMW drove south down Saarland-Strasse, past the slumbering hotels and deserted shops of central Berlin. At the dark mass of the Museum für Völkerkunde it turned left, into Prinz-Albrecht-Strasse, toward the headquarters of the Gestapo.

There was a hierarchy in cars, as in everything. The Orpo was stuck with tinny Opels. The Kripo had Volkswagens—four-door versions of the original KdF-wagen, the round-backed workers' car that had been stamped out by the million at the Fallersleben works. But the Gestapo was smarter. They drove BMW 1800s—sinister boxes with growling, souped-up engines and dull gray bodywork.

Sitting in the backseat next to Max Jaeger, March kept his eyes on the man who had arrested them, the commander of the raid on Stuckart's apartment. When they had been led up from the basement into the foyer, he had given them an immaculate Führer salute. "Sturmbannführer Karl Krebs, Gestapo!" That had meant nothing to March. It was only now, in the BMW, in profile, that he recognized him. Krebs was one of the two SS officers who had been with Globus at Buhler's villa.

He was about thirty years old with an angular, intelligent face, and without the uniform he could have been anything—a lawyer, a banker, a eugenicist, an executioner. That was how it was with young men of his age. They had come off an assembly line of Pimpf, Hitler Youth, National Service and Strength-Through-Joy. They had heard the same speeches, read the same slogans, eaten the same one-pot meals in aid of Winter Relief. They were the regime's workhorses, had known no authority but the Party and were as reliable and commonplace as the Kripo's Volkswagens.

The car drew up and almost at once Krebs was on the pavement, opening the door. "This way, gentlemen. Please."

March hauled himself out and looked down the street. Krebs might be as polite as a scoutmaster, but ten meters back, the doors of a second BMW were opening even before it stopped and armed plainclothesmen were emerging. That was how it had been since their discovery at Fritz-Todt-Platz. No rifle butts in the belly, no oaths, no handcuffs. Just a telephone call to headquarters, followed by a quiet request to "discuss these matters further." Krebs had also asked them to surrender their weapons. Polite, but behind the politeness, always the threat.

Gestapo headquarters was in a grand five-story Wilhelmine construction that faced north and never saw the sun. Years ago, in the days of the Weimar Republic, the museumlike building had housed the Berlin School of Arts. When the secret police had taken over, the students had been forced to burn their modernist paintings in the courtyard. Tonight, the high windows were shielded by thick net curtains, a precaution against terrorist attack. Behind the gauze, as if in fog, chandeliers burned.

March had made it a policy in life never to cross the threshold of this building, and until this night he had succeeded. Three stone steps ran up into an entrance hall. More steps, and then a large, vaulted foyer: a red carpet on a stone floor, the hollow resonance of a cathedral. It was busy. The early hours of the morning were always busy for the Gestapo. From the depths of the building came the muffled echo of bells ringing, footsteps, a whistle, a shout. A fat man in the uniform of an *Obersturmführer* picked his nose and regarded them without interest.

They walked on, down a corridor lined with swastikas and marble busts of the Party leadership—Göring, Goebbels, Bormann, Frank, Ley and the rest—modeled after Roman senators. March could hear the plainclothes guards following. He glanced at Jaeger, but Max was staring fixedly ahead, jaw clenched.

More stairs, another hallway. The carpet had given way to linoleum. The walls were dingy. March guessed they were somewhere near the back of the building, on the second floor.

"If you would wait here," said Krebs. He opened a stout wooden door. Fluorescent tubes stuttered into life. He stood aside to allow them to file in. "Coffee?"

"Thank you."

And he was gone. As the door closed, March saw one of the guards, arms folded, take up station in the corridor outside. He half expected to hear a key turn in the lock, but there was no sound.

They had been put into some sort of interview room. A rough wooden table stood in the center of the floor, one chair on either side of it, half a dozen others pushed up against the walls. There was a small window. Opposite it was a reproduction of Josef Vietze's portrait of Reinhard Heydrich in a cheap plastic frame. On the floor were small brown stains that looked to March like dried blood.

Prinz-Albrecht-Strasse was Germany's black heart, as famous as the Avenue of Victory and the Great Hall, but without the tourist coaches. At number eight: the Gestapo. At number nine: Heydrich's personal headquarters. Around the corner: the Prinz-Albrecht Palace itself, headquarters of the SD, the Party's intelligence service. A complex of underground passages linked the three.

Jaeger muttered something and collapsed into a chair. March could think of nothing adequate to say, so he looked out of the window. It commanded a clear view of the palace grounds running behind the Gestapo building—the dark clumps of the bushes, the inkpool of the lawn, the skeletal branches of the limes raised in claws against the sky. Away to the right, lit up through the bare trees, was the concrete-and-glass cube of the Europa-Haus, built in the 1920s by the Jewish architect Mendelsohn. The Party had allowed it to stand as a monument to his "pygmy imagination." Dropped among Speer's granite monoliths, it was just a toy. March could remember a Sunday afternoon tea with Pili in its roof-garden restaurant. Ginger beer and *Obsttorte mit Sahne,* the little brass band playing—what else?—selections from *The Merry Widow,* the elderly women with their elaborate Sunday hats, their little fingers crooked over the bone china.

Most were careful not to look at the black buildings beyond the trees. For others, the proximity of Prinz-Albrecht-Strasse seemed to provide a frisson of excitement, like picnicking next to a prison. Down in the cellar the Gestapo was licensed to practice what the Ministry of Justice called "heightened interrogation." The rules had been drawn up by civilized men in warm offices, and they stipulated the presence of a doctor. There had been a conversation in Werderscher-Markt a few weeks ago. Someone had heard a rumor about the torturers' latest trick: a thin glass catheter inserted into the suspect's penis, then snapped.

*Strings are playing*
*Hear them saying*
*"I love you." . . .*

He shook his head, pinched the bridge of his nose, tried to clear his mind.

*Think.*

He had left a paper trail of clues, any one of which would have been enough to lead the Gestapo to Stuckart's apartment. He had requested Stuckart's file. He had discussed the case with Fiebes. He had rung Luther's home. He had gone looking for Charlotte Maguire.

He worried about the American woman. Even if she had managed to get clear of Fritz-Todt-Platz, the Gestapo could pull her in tomorrow. *"Routine questions, Fräulein . . . What is this envelope, please? . . . How did you come by it? . . . Describe the man who opened the safe . . ."* She was tough, with an actressy self-confidence, but in their hands she would not last five minutes.

March rested his forehead against the cold pane of glass. The window was bolted shut. There was a sheer drop of fifteen meters to the ground.

Behind him, the door opened. A swarthy man in shirtsleeves, stinking of sweat, came in and set two mugs of coffee on the table.

Jaeger, who had been sitting with his arms folded looking at his boots, asked, "How much longer?"

The man shrugged—*an hour? a night? a week?*—and left. Jaeger tasted the coffee and pulled a face. "Pig's piss." He lit a cigar, swilling the smoke around his mouth before sending it billowing across the room.

He and March stared at each other. After a while, Max said, "You know, you could have escaped."

"And left you to it? Hardly fair." March tried the coffee. It was lukewarm. The fluorescent light was flickering, fizzing, making his head throb. This was what they did to you. Left you until two or three in the morning, until your body was at its weakest, your defenses at their most vulnerable. He knew this part of the game as well as they did.

He swallowed the filthy coffee and lit a cigarette. Anything to stay awake. Guilt about the woman, guilt about his friend.

"I'm a fool. I shouldn't have involved you. I'm sorry."

"Forget it." Jaeger waved away the smoke. He leaned forward and spoke softly. "You have to let me carry my share of the blame, Zavi. Good Party Comrade Jaeger, here. Brownshirt. Blackshirt. Every goddamn shirt. Twenty years dedicated to the sacred cause of keeping my backside clean." He grasped March's knee. "I have favors to call in. I'm owed."

His head was bent. He was whispering. "They have you marked down, my friend. A loner. Divorced. They'll flay you alive. Me, on the other hand? The great conformer Jaeger. Married to a holder of the Cross of German Motherhood. Bronze Class, no less. Not so good at the job, maybe—"

"That's not true."

"—but *safe.* Suppose I didn't tell you yesterday morning that the Gestapo had taken over the Buhler case. Then when you got back *I* said let's check out Stuckart. They look at my record. They might buy that, coming from me."

"It's good of you."

"Christ, man—forget that."

"But it won't work."

"Why not?"

"Because this is beyond favors and clean sheets, don't you see? What about Buhler and Stuckart? They were in the Party before we were even born. And where were the favors when they needed them?"

"You really think the Gestapo killed them?" Jaeger looked scared.

March put his fingers to his lips and gestured to the picture. "Say nothing to me you wouldn't say to Heydrich," he whispered.

The night dragged by in silence. At about three o'clock, Jaeger pushed some of the chairs together, lay down awkwardly and closed his eyes. Within minutes he was snoring. March returned to his post at the window.

He could feel Heydrich's eyes drilling into his back. He tried to ignore it, failed, and turned to confront the picture. A black uniform, a gaunt white face, silver hair—not a human countenance at all but a photographic negative of a skull; an X ray. The only color was in the center of that death-mask face: those tiny pale blue eyes like splinters of winter sky. March had never met Heydrich or seen him; had only heard the stories. The press portrayed him as Nietzsche's Superman sprung to life. Heydrich in his pilot's uniform (he had flown combat missions on the eastern front). Heydrich in his fencing gear (he had fenced for Germany in the Olympics). Heydrich with his violin (he could reduce audiences to tears by the pathos of his playing). When the aircraft carrying Heinrich Himmler had blown up in midair two years ago, Heydrich had taken over as *Reichsführer-SS.* Now he was said to be in line to succeed the Führer. The whisper around the Kripo was that the Reich's chief policeman liked beating up prostitutes.

March sat down. A numbing tiredness was seeping through him, a paralysis: the legs first, then the body, at last the mind. Despite himself, he drifted into a shallow sleep. Once, far away, he thought he heard a cry—human and forlorn—but it might have been a dream. Footsteps echoed in his mind. Keys turned. Cell doors clanged.

He was jerked awake by a rough hand.

"Good morning, gentlemen. I hope you had some rest?"

It was Krebs.

March felt raw. His eyes were gritty in the sickly fluorescent light. Through the window the sky was pearl gray with the approaching morning.

Jaeger grunted and swung his legs to the floor. "Now what?"

"Now we talk," said Krebs. "Come."

"Who is this kid," grumbled Jaeger to March under his breath, "to push us about?" But he was wary enough to keep his voice low.

They filed into the corridor, and March wondered again what game was being played. Interrogation is a nighttime art. Why leave it until the morning? Why give them a chance to regain their strength, to concoct a story?

Krebs had recently shaved. His skin was studded with pinpricks of blood. He said, "Washroom on the right. You will wish to clean yourselves." It was an instruction rather than a question.

In the mirror, red eyed and unshaven, March looked more convict than policeman. He filled the basin, rolled up his sleeves and loosened his tie, splashed icy water on his face, his forearms, the nape of his neck, let it trickle down his back. The cold sting brought him back to life.

Jaeger stood alongside him. "Remember what I said."

March quickly turned the taps back on. "Be careful."

"You think they wire the toilet?"

"They wire everything."

Krebs conducted them downstairs. The guards fell in behind them. *To the cellar?* They clattered across the vestibule—quieter now than when they had arrived—and out into the grudging light.

*Not the cellar.*

Waiting in the BMW was the driver who had brought them from Stuckart's apartment. The convoy moved off, north into the rush hour traffic that was already building up around Potsdamer-Platz. In the big shops, the windows piously displayed large gilt-framed photographs of the Führer—the official portrait from the mid-1950s by the English photographer Cecil Beaton. The frames were garlanded with twigs and flowers, the traditional decoration heralding the Führer's birthday. Four days to go, each of which would see a fresh sprouting of swastika banners. Soon the city would be a forest of red, white and black.

Jaeger was gripping the armrest, looking sick. "Come

on, Krebs," he said in a wheedling voice. "We're all the same rank. You can tell us where we're going."

Krebs made no reply. The dome of the Great Hall loomed ahead. Ten minutes later, when the BMW turned left onto the East-West Axis, March guessed their destination.

It was almost eight by the time they arrived. The iron gates of Buhler's villa had been swung wide open. The grounds were filled with vehicles, dotted with black uniforms. One SS trooper was sweeping the lawn with a proton magnetometer. Behind him, jammed into the ground, was a trail of red flags. Three more soldiers were digging holes. Drawn up on the gravel were Gestapo BMWs, a lorry and a large armored security van of the sort used for transporting gold bullion.

March felt Jaeger nudge him. Parked in the shadows beside the house, its driver leaning against the bodywork, was a bulletproof Mercedes limousine. A metal pennant hung above the radiator grille: silver SS lightning flashes on a black background; in one corner, like a cabalistic symbol, the Gothic letter K.

The head of the Reich Kriminalpolizei was an old man. His name was Artur Nebe, and he was a legend.

Nebe had been head of the Berlin detective force even before the Party had come to power. He had a small head and the sallow, scaly skin of a tortoise. In 1954, to mark his sixtieth birthday, the Reichstag had voted him a large estate, including four villages, near Minsk in the Ostland, but he had never even been to look at it. He lived alone with his bedridden wife in Charlottenburg, in a large house marked by the smell of disinfectant and the whisper of pure oxygen. It was sometimes said that Heydrich wanted to get rid of him, to put his own man in charge of the Kripo, but dared not. "Onkel Artur" they called him in Werderscher-Markt: Uncle Artur. He knew everything.

March had seen Nebe from a distance but had never met him. Now he was sitting at Buhler's grand piano, picking at a high note with a single yellowish claw. The instrument was untuned, the sound discordant in the dusty air.

At the window, his broad back to the room, stood Odilo Globocnik.

Krebs brought his heels together and saluted. "Heil Hitler! Investigators March and Jaeger."

Nebe continued to tap the piano key.

"Ah!" Globus turned around. "The great detectives."

Close up, he was a bull in uniform. His neck strained at his collar. His hands hung at his sides, bunched in angry red fists. There was a mass of scar tissue on his left cheek, mottled crimson. Violence crackled around him in the dry air like static electricity. Every time Nebe struck a note, he winced. He wants to punch the old man, thought March, but he can't. Nebe outranks him.

"If the Herr Oberstgruppenführer has finished his recital," said Globus through his teeth, "we can begin."

Nebe's hand froze over the keyboard. "Why would anyone have a Bechstein and leave it untuned?" He looked at March. "Why would he do that?"

"His wife was the musician, sir," said March. "She died eleven years ago."

"And nobody played in all that time?" Nebe closed the lid quietly over the keys and drew his finger through the dust. "Curious."

Globus said, "We have much to do. Early this morning I reported certain matters to the Reichsführer. As you know, Herr Oberstgruppenführer, it is on his orders that this meeting is taking place. Krebs will state the position of the Gestapo."

March exchanged glances with Jaeger. So: it had gone up as far as Heydrich.

Krebs had a typed memorandum. In his precise, expressionless voice he began to read.

"Notification of Doctor Josef Buhler's death was received by teleprinter message at Gestapo Headquarters from the night duty officer of the Berlin Kriminalpolizei at two-fifteen yesterday morning, April fifteenth.

"At eight-thirty, in view of Party Comrade Buhler's honorary SS rank of Brigadeführer, the Reichsführer was personally informed of his demise."

March had his hands clasped behind his back, his nails

digging into his palms. In Jaeger's cheek, a muscle fluttered.

"At the time of his death, the Gestapo was completing an investigation into the activities of Party Comrade Buhler. In view of this, and in view of the deceased's former position in the General Government, the case was redesignated a matter of state security, and operational control was passed to the Gestapo.

"However, due to an apparent breakdown in liaison procedures, this redesignation was not communicated to Kripo Investigator Xavier March, who effected an illegal entry into the deceased's home."

*The Gestapo was investigating Buhler?* March struggled to keep his gaze fixed on Krebs, his expression impassive.

"Next: the death of Party Comrade Wilhelm Stuckart. Inquiries by the Gestapo indicated that the cases of Stuckart and Buhler were linked. Once again, the Reichsführer was informed. Once again, investigation of the matter was transferred to the Gestapo. And once again, Investigator March, this time accompanied by Investigator Max Jaeger, conducted his own inquiries at the home of the deceased.

"At zero-zero-twelve on April 16, Investigators March and Jaeger were apprehended by myself at Party Comrade Stuckart's apartment. They agreed to accompany me to Gestapo Headquarters, pending clarification of this matter at a higher level.

"Signed, Karl Krebs, Sturmbannführer.

"I have dated it and timed it at six this morning."

Krebs folded the memorandum and handed it to the head of the Kripo. Outside, a spade rang on gravel.

Nebe slipped the paper into his inside pocket. "So much for the record. Naturally, we shall prepare a report of our own. Now, Globus: what is this really about? You are desperate to tell us, I know."

"Heydrich wanted you to see for yourself."

"See what?"

"What your man here missed on his little free-lance excursion yesterday. Follow me, please."

It was in the cellar, although even if March had smashed the padlock on the entrance and forced his way down, he doubted if he would have found it. Past the usual household rubbish—broken furniture, discarded tools, rolls of filthy carpet bound with rope—was a wood-paneled wall. One of the panels was false.

"We knew what we were looking for, you see." Globus rubbed his hands together. "Gentlemen, I guarantee you will never have clapped eyes on the likes of this in your entire lives."

Beyond the panel was a chamber. When Globus turned on the lights, it was indeed dazzling: a sacristy; a jewel-box. Angels and saints; clouds and temples; high-cheeked noblemen in white furs and red damask; sprawling pink flesh on perfumed yellow silk; flowers and sunrises and Venetian canals . . .

"Go in," said Globus. "The Reichsführer is anxious that you should see it properly."

It was a small room—four meters square, March guessed—with a bank of spotlights built into the ceiling, directed onto the paintings that covered every wall. In the center was an old-fashioned swivel chair, of the sort a nineteenth-century clerk might have had in a counting house. Globus placed a gleaming jackboot on the arm and kicked, sending it spinning.

"Imagine him, sitting here. Door locked. Like a dirty old man in a brothel. We found it yesterday afternoon. Krebs?"

Krebs took the floor. "An expert is on his way this morning from the Führermuseum in Linz. We had Professor Braun of the Kaiser Friedrich, here in Berlin, give us a preliminary assessment last night."

He consulted his sheaf of notes.

"At the moment, we know we have *Portrait of a Young*

*Man* by Raphael, *Portrait of a Young Man* by Rembrandt, *Christ Carrying the Cross* by Rubens, Guardi's *Venetian Palace, Krakau Suburbs* by Bellotto, eight Canalettos, at least thirty-five engravings by Dürer and Kulmbach, a Gobelin. The rest he could only guess at."

Krebs reeled them off as if they were dishes in a restaurant. He rested his pale fingers on an altarpiece of gorgeous colors, raised on planks at the end of the room.

"This is the work of the Nuremberg artist Veit Stoss, commissioned by the King of Poland in 1477. It took ten years to complete. The center of the triptych shows the Virgin asleep, surrounded by angels. The side panels show scenes from the lives of Jesus and Mary. The predella—" he pointed to the base of the altarpiece—"shows the genealogy of Christ."

Globus said, "Sturmbannführer Krebs knows about these things. He is one of our brightest officers."

"I'm sure," said Nebe. "Most interesting. And where did it all come from?"

Krebs began, "The Veit Stoss was removed from the Church of Our Lady in Krakau in November 1939—"

Globus interrupted, "It came from the General Government. Warsaw, mainly, we think. Buhler recorded it as either lost or destroyed. God alone knows how much else the corrupt swine got away with. Think what he must have sold just to buy this place!"

Nebe reached out and touched one of the canvases: the martyred Saint Sebastian bound to a Doric pillar, arrows jutting from his golden skin. The varnish was cracked, like a dried riverbed, but the colors beneath—red, white, purple, blue—were bright still. The painting gave off a faint smell of must and incense—the scent of prewar Poland, of a nation vanished from the map. Some of the panels, March saw, had powdery lumps of masonry attached to their edges—traces of the monastery and castle walls from which they had been wrenched.

Nebe was rapt before the saint. "Something in his expression reminds me of you, March." He traced the body's outline with his fingertips and gave a wheezing laugh. " 'The willing martyr.' What do you say, Globus?"

Globus grunted. "I don't believe in saints. Or martyrs." He glared at March.

"Extraordinary," murmured Nebe, "to think of Buhler, of all people, with these—"

"You knew him?" March blurted out the question.

"Slightly, before the war. A committed National Socialist and a dedicated lawyer. Quite a combination. A fanatic for detail. Like our Gestapo colleague here."

Krebs gave a slight bow. "The Herr Oberstgruppenführer is kind."

"The point is this," said Globus irritably. "We have known about Party Comrade Buhler for some time. Known about his activities in the General Government. Known about his associates. Unfortunately, at some point last week, the bastard found out we were on to him."

"And killed himself?" Nebe asked. "And Stuckart?"

"The same. Stuckart was a complete degenerate. He not only helped himself to beauty on canvas, he liked to taste it in the flesh. Buhler had the pick of what he wanted in the East. What were those figures, Krebs?"

"A secret inventory was compiled in 1940 by the Polish museum authorities. We now have it. Art treasures removed from Warsaw alone: two thousand seven hundred paintings of the European school; ten thousand seven hundred paintings by Polish artists; fourteen hundred sculptures."

Globus again: "We're digging up some of the sculptures in the garden right now. Most of this stuff went where it was intended: the Führermuseum, Reichsmarschall Göring's museum at Carinhall, galleries in Vienna, Berlin. But there's a big discrepancy between the Polish lists of what was taken and our lists of what we got. It worked like this. As state secretary, Buhler had access to everything. He would ship the stuff under escort to Stuckart at the Interior Ministry. Everything legal looking.

Stuckart would arrange for it to be stored, or smuggled out of the Reich to be exchanged for cash, jewels, gold—anything portable and nontraceable."

March could see that Nebe was impressed despite himself. His little eyes were drinking in the art. "Was anyone else of high rank involved?"

"You're familiar with the former under secretary of state at the Foreign Ministry, Martin Luther?"

"Of course."

"He is the man we seek."

"Seek? He is missing?"

"He failed to return from a business trip three days ago."

"I take it you are certain of Luther's involvement in this affair?"

"During the war, Luther was head of the Foreign Ministry's German Department."

"I remember. He was responsible for Foreign Ministry liaison with the SS, and with us at the Kripo." Nebe turned to Krebs. "Another fanatical National Socialist. You would have appreciated his—ah—enthusiasm. A rough fellow, though. Incidentally, at this point, I should like to state, for the record, my astonishment at his involvement in anything criminal."

Krebs produced his pen. Globus went on, "Buhler stole the art. Stuckart received it. Luther's position at the Foreign Ministry gave him the opportunity to travel freely abroad. We believe he smuggled certain items out of the Reich and sold them."

"Where?"

"Switzerland, mainly. Also Spain. Possibly Hungary."

"And when Buhler came back from the General Government—when was that?"

He looked at March, and March said, "In 1951."

"In 1951 this became their treasure chamber."

Nebe lowered himself into the swivel chair and spun around slowly, inspecting each wall in turn. "Extraordinary. This must have been one of the best collections of art in private hands anywhere in the world."

"One of the best collections in *criminal* hands," cut in Globus.

"Ach." Nebe closed his eyes. "So much perfection in one space deadens the senses. I need air. Give me your arm, March."

As he stood up, March could hear the ancient bones cracking. But the grip on his forearm was of steel.

Nebe walked with a stick—*tap, tap, tap*—along the veranda at the back of the villa.

"Buhler drowned himself. Stuckart shot himself. Your case seems to be resolving itself rather conclusively, Globus, without requiring anything so embarrassing as a trial. Statistically, I should say Luther's chances of survival look rather poor."

"As it happens, Herr Luther *does* have a heart condition. Brought on by nervous strain during the war, according to his wife."

"You surprise me."

"According to his wife, he needs rest, drugs, quiet—none of which will he be getting at the moment, wherever he is."

"This business trip—"

"He was supposed to return from Munich on Monday. We've checked with Lufthansa. There was nobody called Luther on any Munich flights that day."

"Maybe he's fled abroad."

"Maybe. I doubt it. We'll hunt him down eventually, wherever he is."

*Tap, tap.* March admired Nebe's nimbleness of mind. As police commissioner for Berlin in the 1920s, he had written a treatise on criminology. He remembered seeing it on Koth's shelves in the fingerprint section on Tuesday night. It was still a standard text.

"And you, March." Nebe halted and swung around. "What is your view of Buhler's death?"

Jaeger, who had been silent since their arrival at the villa, butted in anxiously, "Sir, if I might say, we were merely collecting data—"

Nebe rapped the stone with his stick. "The question was not addressed to you."

March wanted a cigarette badly. "I have only preliminary observations," he began. He ran his hand through his hair. He was out of his depth here; a long way out. It was not where to start, he thought, but where to end. Globus had folded his arms and was staring at him.

"Party Comrade Buhler," he began, "died sometime between six o'clock on Monday evening and six o'clock the following morning. We are awaiting the autopsy report, but cause of death was almost certainly drowning—his lungs were full of fluid, indicating he was breathing when he entered the water. We also know, from the sentry on the causeway, that Buhler received no visitors during those crucial twelve hours."

Globus nodded. "Thus: suicide."

"Not necessarily, Herr Obergruppenführer. Buhler received no visitors *by land.* But the woodwork on the jetty was recently scraped, suggesting that a boat may have moored there."

"Buhler's boat," said Globus.

"Buhler's boat has not been used for months, maybe years."

Now that he held the attention of his small audience, March felt a rush of exhilaration, a sense of release. He was starting to talk quickly. Slow down, he told himself, be careful.

"When I inspected the villa yesterday morning, Buhler's guard dog was locked in the pantry, muzzled. The whole of one side of its head was bleeding. I ask myself: why would a man intending to commit suicide do that to his dog?"

"Where is this animal now?" asked Nebe.

"My men had to shoot it," said Globus. "The creature was deranged."

"Ah. Of course. Go on, March."

"I think Buhler's assailants landed late at night, in darkness. If you recall, there was a storm on Monday night. The lake would have been choppy—that explains the damage to the jetty. I think the dog was alerted and they clubbed it senseless, muzzled it, took Buhler unawares."

"And threw him into the lake?"

"Not immediately. Despite his disability, according to his sister, Buhler was a strong swimmer. You could see that by the look of him: his shoulders were well developed. But after he had been cleaned up, I inspected his body in the morgue. There was bruising here"—March touched his cheeks—"and on the gums at the front of his mouth. On the kitchen table yesterday was a bottle of vodka, most of it gone. I think the autopsy report will show alcohol in Buhler's bloodstream. I think they forced him to drink, stripped him, took him out on their boat and dumped him over the side."

"Intellectual pigshit," said Globus. "Buhler probably drank the vodka to give him the guts to kill himself."

"According to his sister, Party Comrade Buhler was a teetotaler."

There was a long silence. March could hear Jaeger breathing heavily. Nebe was gazing out across the lake. Eventually Globus muttered, "What this fancy theory doesn't explain is why these mysterious killers didn't just put a bullet into Buhler's brain and have done with it."

"I would have thought that was obvious," said March. "They wanted to make it look like suicide. But they bungled it."

"Interesting," murmured Nebe. "If Buhler's suicide was faked, then it is logical to suppose that Stuckart's was also."

Because Nebe was still staring at the Havel, March did

not realize at first that the remark was a question, addressed to him.

"That was my conclusion. That was why I visited Stuckart's apartment last night. Stuckart's murder, I think, was a three-man operation: two in the flat; one in the foyer, pretending to repair the elevator. The noise from his electric drill was supposed to mask the sound of the shot, giving the killers time to get away before the body was discovered."

"And the suicide note?"

"Forged, perhaps. Or written under duress. Or—"

He stopped himself. He was thinking aloud, he realized—a potentially fatal activity. Krebs was staring at him.

"Is that it?" asked Globus. "Are the Grimms' fairy stories over for the day? Excellent. Some of us have work to do. Luther is the key to this mystery, gentlemen. Once we have him, all will be explained."

Nebe said, "If his heart condition is as bad as you say, we need to move quickly. I'll arrange with the Propaganda Ministry for Luther's picture to be carried in the press and on television."

"No, no. Absolutely not." Globus sounded alarmed. "The Reichsführer has expressly forbidden any publicity. The last thing we need is a scandal involving the Party leadership, especially now, with Kennedy coming. God in heaven, can you imagine what the foreign press would make of this? No. I assure you, we can catch him without alerting the media. What we need is a confidential flash to all Orpo patrols; a watch on the main railway stations, ports, airports, border crossings . . . Krebs can handle that."

"Then I suggest he do so."

"At once, Herr Oberstgruppenführer." Krebs gave a slight bow to Nebe and trotted off along the veranda, into the house.

"I have business to attend to in Berlin," said Nebe.

"March here will act as Kripo liaison officer until Luther is caught."

Globus sneered. "That will not be necessary."

"Oh, but it will. Use him wisely, Globus. He has a brain. Keep him informed. Jaeger, you can return to your normal duties."

Jaeger looked relieved. Globus seemed about to say something, but thought better of it.

"Walk me to my car, March. Good day to you, Globus."

When they were around the corner, Nebe said, "You're not telling the truth, are you? Or at least, not all of it. That's good. Get in the car. We need to talk."

The driver saluted and opened the rear door. Nebe maneuvered himself painfully into the backseat. March got in on the other side.

"At six this morning, this arrived at my house by courier." Nebe unlocked his briefcase and pulled out a file a couple of centimeters thick. "It's all about you, Sturmbannführer. Flattering, isn't it, to merit such attention?"

The windows of the Mercedes were tinted green. In the half light, Nebe looked like a lizard in a reptile house.

"Born, Hamburg, 1922; father died of wounds, 1929; mother killed in a British air raid, 1942; joined the navy, 1939; transferred to the U-boat service, 1940; decorated for bravery and promoted, 1943; given command of your own boat, 1946—one of the youngest U-boat commanders in the Reich. A glittering career. And then it all starts going wrong."

Nebe leafed through the file. March stared at the green lawn, the green sky.

"No police promotions for *ten years.* Divorced, 1957. And then the reports start. *Blockwart*: persistent refusal to contribute to Winter Relief. Party officials at Werderscher-Markt: persistent refusal to join the NSDAP. Overheard in the canteen making disparaging comments about Himmler. Overheard in bars, overheard in restaurants, overheard in corridors . . ."

Nebe was pulling pages out.

"Christmas 1963—you start asking around about some Jews who used to live in your apartment. Jews! Are you mad? There's a complaint here from your ex-wife; even one from your son . . ."

"My son? My son is ten years old."

"Quite old enough to form a judgment, and be listened to—as you know."

"May I ask what it is I am supposed to have done to him?"

" 'Shown insufficient enthusiasm for his Party activities.' The point is, Sturmbannführer, that this file has been ten years maturing in the Gestapo Registry—a little here, a little there, year in, year out, growing like a tumor in the dark. And now you've made a powerful enemy, and he wants to use it."

Nebe put the folder back into his briefcase.

"Globus?"

"Globus, yes. Who else? He asked to have you transferred to Colombia House last night, pending court-martial by the SS." Colombia House was the private SS prison in General-Pape-Strasse. "I have to tell you, March, there's easily enough here to send you to a KZ. After that, you're beyond help—from me or anybody else."

"What stopped him?"

"To start court-martial proceedings against a serving Kripo officer, he first had to get permission from Heydrich. And Heydrich referred it to me. So what I said to our beloved Reichsführer was this: 'This fellow Globus,' I said, 'is obviously terrified that March has something on him, so he wants him done away with.' 'I see,' says the Reichsführer. 'So what do you suggest?' 'Why not,' say I, 'give him until the *Führertag* to prove his case against Globus? That's four days.' 'All right,' says Heydrich. 'But if he hasn't come up with anything by then, Globus can have him.' " Nebe gave a smile of contentment. "Thus are the affairs of the Reich arranged between colleagues of long standing."

"I suppose I must thank the Herr Oberstgruppenführer."

"Oh, no, don't thank me." Nebe was cheerful. "Heydrich genuinely wonders if you do have something on Globus. He would like to know. So would I. Perhaps for a different reason." He seized March's arm again—the same fierce grip—and hissed, "These bastards are up to something, March. What is it? You find out. You tell me. Don't trust anyone. That's how your Uncle Artur has lasted as long as he has. Do you know why some of the old-timers call Globus 'the Submarine'?"

"No, sir."

"Because he had a submarine engine hooked up to a Polish basement during the war and used the exhaust fumes to kill people. Globus likes killing people. He'd like to kill you. You should remember that." Nebe released March's arm. "Now we must say good-bye."

He rapped on the glass partition with the top of his cane. The driver came around and opened March's door.

"I'd offer you a lift into central Berlin, but I prefer traveling alone. Keep me informed. Find Luther, March. Find him before Globus gets to him."

The door slammed. The engine whispered. As the limousine crunched across the gravel, March could barely make out Nebe—just a green silhouette behind the bulletproof glass.

He turned to find Globus watching him.

The SS general started walking toward him, holding a Luger outstretched.

He's crazy, thought March. He is just about crazy enough to shoot me on the spot, like Buhler's dog.

But all Globus did was hand him the gun. "Your pistol, Sturmbannführer. You will need it." And then he came very close—close enough for March to smell the sour odor of garlic sausage on his hot breath. "You have no witness" was all he whispered. "You have no witness. Not anymore."

March ran.

He ran out of the grounds, across the causeway and off, up, into the woods—right through them, until he came to the autobahn that formed the Grunewald's eastern boundary.

There he stopped, his hands clutching his knees, his breath coming in sobs, as beneath him the traffic hurtled toward Berlin.

Then he was off again, despite the pain in his side, more of a trot now, over the bridge, past the Nikolassee S-bahn station, down Spanische-Allee toward the barracks.

His Kripo ID got him past the sentries, his appearance—red eyed, breathless, with more than a day's growth of beard—suggestive of some terrible emergency that brooked no discussion. He found the dormitory block. He found Jost's bed. The pillow was gone, the blankets had been stripped. All that remained was the ironwork and a hard brown mattress. The locker was bare.

A solitary cadet, polishing his boots a few beds away, explained what had happened. They had come for Jost in the night. There were two of them. He was to be sent east, they said, for "special training." He had gone without a word—seemed to have been expecting it. The cadet shook his head in amazement: Jost, of all people. The cadet was jealous. They all were. He'd see some *real* fighting.

The telephone booth stank of urine and ancient cigarette smoke; a used condom had been trodden into the dirt.

"Come on, come on," whispered March. He rapped a one-Reichsmark piece against the cloudy glass and listened to the electronic purr of her telephone ringing, unanswered. He let it ring for a long time before he hung up.

Across the street a grocery store was opening. He crossed and bought a bottle of milk and some warm bread, which he gulped down beside the road, conscious all the time of the shop's owner watching him from the window. It occurred to him that he was living like a fugitive already—stopping to grab food only when he happened across it, devouring it in the open, always on the move. Milk trickled down his chin. He brushed it away with the back of his hand. His skin felt like sandpaper.

He checked again to see if he was being followed. On this side of the street, a uniformed nanny pushed a baby carriage. On the other, an old woman had gone into the telephone booth. A schoolboy hurried toward the Havel, carrying a toy yacht. Normal, normal . . .

March, the good citizen, dropped the milk bottle into a wastebin and set off down the suburban road.

*"You have no witness. Not anymore . . ."*

He felt a great rage against Globus, the greater for being fueled by guilt. The Gestapo must have seen Jost's statement in the file on Buhler's death. They would have checked with the SS Academy and discovered that March had been back to reinterrogate him yesterday afternoon. That would have set them scurrying in Prinz-Albrecht-Strasse. So his visit to the barracks had been Jost's death warrant. He had indulged his curiosity—and killed a man.

And now the American girl was not answering her telephone. What might they do to her? An army truck overtook him, the draft sucked at him and a vision of Charlotte Maguire lying broken in the gutter bubbled in his mind. *"The Berlin authorities deeply regret this tragic accident. . . . The driver of the vehicle concerned is still being sought . . ."* He felt like the carrier of a dangerous disease. He should carry a placard: keep clear of this man, he is contagious.

Circulating endlessly in his head, fragments of conversation . . .

Artur Nebe: *"Find Luther, March. Find him before Globus gets to him."*

Rudi Halder: *"A couple of Sipo guys were around at the archive last week asking about you."*

Nebe again: *"There's a complaint here from your ex-wife; even one from your son."*

He walked for half an hour along the blossoming streets, past the high hedges and picket fences of prosperous suburban Berlin. When he reached Dahlem, he stopped a student to ask directions. At the sight of March's uniform, the young man bowed his head. Dahlem was a student quarter. The male undergraduates, like this one, let their hair grow a few centimeters over their collars; some of the women wore jeans—God only knew where they got them. White Rose, the student resistance movement that had flowered briefly in the 1940s until its leaders were executed, was suddenly alive again. *"Ihr Geist lebt weiter"* said the graffiti: Their spirit lives on. Members of White Rose grumbled about conscription, listened to banned music, circulated seditious magazines, were harassed by the Gestapo.

The student, his arms laden with books, gestured vaguely in response to March's question and was glad to be on his way.

Luther's house was close to the Botanischer Garten, set back from the road—a nineteenth-century country mansion at the end of a sickle of white gravel. Two men sat in an unmarked gray BMW, parked opposite the drive. The car and its color branded them at once. There would be two more watching the back, and at least one cruising the neighborhood streets. March walked past and saw one of the Gestapo watchers turn to the other and speak.

Somewhere a lawn mower was whining; the smell of freshly cut grass hung over the drive. The house and grounds must have cost a fortune—not as much as Buhler's villa, perhaps, but not far off. The red box of a newly installed burglar alarm jutted beneath the eaves.

He rang the bell and felt himself come under inspection through the spy hole in the center of the heavy door. After half a minute the door opened to reveal an English maid in a black-and-white uniform. He gave her his ID and she disappeared to check with her mistress, her feet flapping on the polished wooden floor. She returned to show March into the darkened drawing room. A sweet-smelling smog of eau de cologne lay over the scene. Frau Marthe Luther sat on a sofa, clutching a handkerchief. She looked up at him—glassy blue eyes cracked by minute veins.

"What news?"

"None, madam, I'm sorry to say. But you may be sure that no effort is being spared to find your husband." Truer than you know, he thought.

She was a woman fast losing her attractiveness, but

gamely staging a fighting retreat. Her tactics, though, were ill advised: unnaturally blond hair, a tight skirt, a silk blouse undone just a button too far to display fat, milky white cleavage. She looked every centimeter a third wife. A romantic novel lay open, facedown, on the embroidered cushion next to her: *The Kaiser's Ball* by Barbara Cartland.

She returned his identity card and blew her nose. "Will you sit down? You look exhausted. Not even time to shave! Some coffee? Sherry, perhaps? No? Rose, bring coffee for the Herr Sturmbannführer. And perhaps I might fortify myself with just the *smallest* sherry."

Perched uneasily on the edge of a deep chintz-covered armchair, his notebook open on his knee, March listened to Frau Luther's woeful tale. Her husband? A very good man, short tempered—yes, maybe, but that was his nerves, poor thing. Poor, poor thing—he had weepy eyes, did March know that?

She showed him a photograph: Luther at some Mediterranean resort, absurd in a pair of shorts, scowling, his eyes swollen behind the thick glasses.

On she went: a man of that age—he would be sixty-nine in December, they were going to Spain for his birthday. Martin was a friend of General Franco—a dear little man, had March ever met him?

No: a pleasure denied.

Ah, well. She couldn't bear to think what might have happened, always so careful about telling her where he was going, he had never done anything like this. It was such a help to talk, so sympathetic . . .

There was a sigh of silk as she crossed her legs, the skirt rising provocatively above a plump knee. The maid reappeared and set down a coffee cup, cream jug and sugar bowl in front of March. Her mistress was provided with a glass of sherry and a crystal decanter, three quarters empty.

"Did you ever hear him mention the name Josef Buhler or Wilhelm Stuckart?"

A little crack of concentration appeared in the cake of makeup: "No, I don't recall. . . . No, definitely not."

"Did he go out at all last Friday?"

"Last Friday? I think—yes. He went out early in the morning." She sipped her sherry. March made a note.

"And when did he tell you he had to go away?"

"That afternoon. He returned about two, said something had happened, that he had to spend Monday in Munich. He flew on Sunday afternoon so he could stay overnight and be up early."

"And he didn't tell you what it was about?"

"He was old-fashioned about that sort of thing. His business was his business, if you see what I mean."

"Before the trip, how did he seem?"

"Oh, irritable, as usual." She laughed—a girlish giggle. "Yes, perhaps he *was* a little more preoccupied than normal. The television news always depressed him—the terrorism, the fighting in the East. I told him to pay no attention—no good will come of worrying, I said—but things . . . yes, they preyed on his mind." She lowered her voice. "He had a breakdown during the war, poor thing. The strain . . ."

She was about to cry again. March cut in: "What year was his breakdown?"

"I believe it was in '43. That was before I knew him, of course."

"Of course." March smiled and bowed his head. "You must have been at school."

"Perhaps not quite at *school*. . . ." The skirt rose a little higher.

"When did you start to become alarmed for his safety?"

"When he didn't come home on Monday. I was awake all night."

"So you reported him missing on Tuesday morning?"

"I was about to when Obergruppenführer Globocnik arrived."

March tried to keep the surprise out of his voice. "He

arrived *before* you even told the Polizei? What time was that?"

"Soon after nine. He said he needed to speak to my husband. I told him the situation. The Obergruppenführer took it very seriously."

"I'm sure he did. Did he tell you why he needed to speak to Herr Luther?"

"No. I assumed it was a Party matter. Why?" Suddenly her voice had a harder edge. "Are you suggesting my husband did something wrong?"

"No, no . . ."

She straightened her skirt over her knees, smoothed it out with ring-encrusted fingers. There was a pause and then she said, "Herr Sturmbannführer, what is the purpose of this conversation?"

"Did your husband ever visit Switzerland?"

"He used to, occasionally, some years ago. He had business there. Why?"

"Where is his passport?"

"It is not in his study. I checked. But I have been over this with the Obergruppenführer. Martin always carried his passport with him. He said he never knew when he might need it. That was his Foreign Ministry training. Really, there's nothing unusual about that, really . . ."

"Forgive me, madam." He pressed on. "The burglar alarm. I noticed it on my way in. It looks new."

She glanced down at her lap. "Martin had it installed last year. We had intruders."

"Two men?"

She looked up at him with surprise. "How did you know?"

That was a mistake. He said, "I must have read the report in your husband's file."

"Impossible." Surprise had been replaced in her voice by suspicion. "He never reported it."

"Why not?"

She was on the point of making a blustering reply—"What business is it of yours?" or something of the sort—

but then she saw the expression in March's eyes and changed her mind. She said in a resigned voice, "I pleaded with him, Herr Sturmbannführer. But he wouldn't. And he wouldn't tell me why."

"What happened?"

"It was last winter. We were planning to stay in for the evening. Some friends called at the last minute and we went out to dinner, at Horcher's. When we got back, there were two men *in this room.*" She looked around as if they might still be hiding somewhere. "Thank God our friends came in with us. If we'd been alone . . . When they saw there were four of us, they jumped out of that window." She pointed behind March's shoulder.

"So he put in an alarm system. Did he take any other precautions?"

"He hired a security guard. Four of them, in fact. They worked shifts. He kept them on until after Christmas. Then he decided he didn't trust them any more. He was so *frightened,* Herr Sturmbannführer."

"Of what?"

"He wouldn't tell me."

Out came the handkerchief. Another helping of sherry was sloshed from the decanter. Her lipstick had left thick pink smears around the rim of her glass. She was sliding toward the edge of tears again. March had misjudged her. She was frightened for her husband, true. But she was more frightened now that he might have been deceiving her. The shadows were chasing one another across her mind, and in her eyes they left their trails. Was it another woman? A crime? A secret? Had he fled the country? Gone for good? March felt sorry for her, and for a moment considered warning her of the Gestapo's case against her husband. But why add to her misery? She would know soon enough. He hoped the state would not confiscate the house.

"Madam, I have intruded too long." He closed his notebook and stood up. She clutched his hand, peered up at him.

"I'm never going to see him again, am I?"
"Yes," he said.
*No,* he thought.

It was a relief to leave the dark and sickly room and escape into the fresh air. The Gestapo men were still sitting in the BMW. They watched him leave. He hesitated for a second, and then turned right, toward the Botanischer Garten railway station.

*Four security guards!*

He could begin to see it now. A meeting at Buhler's villa on Friday morning, attended by Buhler, Stuckart and Luther. A panicky meeting, old men in a sweat of fear—and with good reason. Perhaps they had each been given a separate task. At any rate, on Sunday, Luther had flown to Zürich. March was sure it was he who must have sent the chocolates from Zürich airport on Monday afternoon, perhaps just as he was about to board another aircraft. What were they? Not a present: a signal. Was their arrival meant to be taken as a sign that his task had been completed successfully? Or that he had failed?

March checked over his shoulder. Yes, now he was being followed, he was almost certain. They would have had time to organize while he was in Luther's house. Which were their agents? The woman in the green coat? The student on his bicycle? Hopeless. The Gestapo were too good for him to spot. There would be three or four of them, at least. He lengthened his stride. He was nearing the station.

Question: had Luther returned to Berlin from Zürich on Monday afternoon, or had he stayed out of the country? On balance, March inclined toward the view that he had returned. That call to Buhler's villa yesterday morning—*"Buhler? Speak to me. Who is that?"*—that had been Luther, he was sure. So: assume Luther posted the packages just before he boarded his flight, say around five o'clock. He would have landed in Berlin about seven that evening. And disappeared.

The Botanischer Garten station was on the suburban electric line. March bought a one-Mark ticket and lingered around the barrier until the train approached. He boarded it and then, just as the doors sighed shut, jumped off and sprinted over the metal footbridge to the other platform. Two minutes later he got on the southbound train, only to leap out at Lichterfelde and recross the tracks. The station was deserted. He let the first northbound train go by, caught the second and settled into his seat. The only other occupant of the carriage was a pregnant woman. He gave her a smile; she looked away. Good.

Luther. Luther. March lit a cigarette. Nearing seventy with a nervous heart and rheumy eyes. Too paranoid to trust even your wife. They came for you six months earlier, and by luck you escaped. Why did you make a run for it from Berlin airport? Did you come through customs and decide to call your confederates? In Stuckart's apartment, the telephone would have rung unanswered, next to the silent blood-washed bedroom. In Schwanenwerder, if Eisler's estimate of the time of death was accurate, Buhler must already have been surprised by his killers. Had they let the telephone ring? Or had one of them answered it while the others held Buhler down?

Luther, Luther: something happened to make you run for your life—out into the freezing rain of that Monday night.

He got out at Gotenland station. It was yet another piece of architectural fantasy come true—mosaic floors, polished stone, stained-glass windows thirty meters high. The regime closed churches and compensated by building railway termini to look like cathedrals.

Gazing down from the overhead walkway on to the thousands of hurrying passengers, March almost gave in to despair. Myriad lives—each with its own secrets and plans and dreams, its individual luggage of guilt—criss-crossed beneath him, not one touching the other, separate and distinct. To think that he alone could possibly track down one old man among so many—for the first time, the idea struck him as fantastic, absurd.

But Globus could do it. Already, March could see, the police patrols had been increased in strength. That must have happened in the last half hour. The Orpo men were scrutinizing every male over sixty. A derelict without papers was being led away, complaining.

Globus! March turned away from the handrail and stepped onto the descending escalator, in search of the one person in Berlin who might be able to save his life.

To travel on the central U-bahn line is, in the words of the Reich Ministry for Propaganda and Cultural Enlightenment, to take a trip through German history. Berlin-Gotenland, Bülow-Strasse, Nollendorf-Platz, Wittenberg-Platz, Nürnberger-Platz, Hohenzollern-Platz—the stations succeed one another like pearls on a string.

The carriages that work this line are prewar. Red cars for smokers, yellow for nonsmokers. Hard wooden seats have been rubbed shiny by three decades of Berlin backsides. Most passengers stand, holding on to the worn leather hand grips, swaying with the rhythm of the train. Signs urge them to turn informer. "The fare dodger's profit is the Berliner's loss! Notify the authorities of all wrongdoing!" "Has he given up his seat to a woman or veteran? Penalty for failure: 25 Reichsmarks!"

March had bought a copy of the *Berliner Tageblatt* from a platform newsstand and was leaning next to the doors, skimming through it. Kennedy and the Führer, the Führer and Kennedy—that was all there was to read. The regime was clearly investing heavily in the success of the talks. That could only mean that things in the East were even worse than everyone thought. "A permanent state of war on the eastern front will help to form a sound race of men," the Führer had once said, "and will prevent us from relapsing into the softness of a Europe thrown back upon itself." But people *had* grown soft. What else was the point of victory? They had Poles to dig their gardens and Ukrainians to sweep their streets, French chefs to cook their food and English maids to serve it. Having tasted the comforts of peace, they had lost their appetite for war.

Way down on an inside page, in type so small it was barely readable, was Buhler's obituary. He was reported as having died in a "bathing accident."

March stuffed the paper into his pocket and got out at Bülow-Strasse. From the open platform he could see across to Charlotte Maguire's apartment. A shape moved against the curtain. She was at home. Or rather, someone was at home.

The concierge was not in her chair, and when he knocked on the apartment door there was no reply. He knocked again, more loudly.

Nothing.

He walked away from the door and clattered down the first flight of steps. Then he stopped, counted to ten and crept back up again, sideways, with his back pressed to the wall—one step, pause; another step, pause—wincing whenever he made a noise, until he stood once more outside the door. He drew his pistol.

Minutes passed. Dogs barked, cars and trains and planes went by, babies cried, birds sang: the cacophony of silence. And at one point, inside the apartment, loud above it all, a floorboard creaked.

The door opened a fraction.

March spun, rammed into it with his shoulder. Whoever was on the other side was knocked back by the force of the blow. And then March was in and on him, pushing him through the tiny hall and into the sitting room. A lamp fell to the floor. He tried to bring up the gun, but the man had grabbed his arms. And now it was he who was being pushed backward. The back of his legs made contact with a low table and he toppled over, cracking his head on something, the Luger skittering across the floor.

Well, now, this was quite funny, and in other circumstances March might have laughed. He had never been very good at this sort of thing, and now—having started with the advantage of surprise—he was on his back, unarmed, with his head in the fireplace and his legs still resting on top of the coffee table, in the position of a pregnant woman undergoing an internal examination.

His assailant fell on top of him, winding him. One gloved hand clawed at his face, the other seized his throat. March could neither see nor breathe. He twisted his head from side to side, chewed on the leather hand. He flailed at the other man's head with his fists but could put no force behind his blows. What was on him was not human. It had the remorseless power of machinery. It was grinding him. Steel fingers had found that artery—the one March could never remember, let alone locate—and he felt himself surrendering to the force, the rushing blackness obliterating the pain. *So,* he thought, *I have walked the earth and come to this.*

A crash. The hands slackened, withdrew. March came swimming back into the fight, at least as a spectator. The man had been knocked sideways, hit on the head by a chair of tubular steel. Blood masked his face, pulsing from a cut above his eye. Crash. The chair again. With one arm, the man tried to ward off the blows, with the other he wiped frantically at his blinded eyes. He began shuffling on his knees for the door, a devil on his back—a hissing, spitting fury, claws scrabbling to find his eyes. Slowly, as if carrying an immense weight, he raised himself onto one leg, then the other. All he wanted now was to get away. He blundered into the door frame, turned and hammered his tormentor against it—once, twice.

Only then did Charlie Maguire let the man go.

♦

Clusters of pain, bursting like fireworks: his head, the backs of his legs, his ribs, his throat.

"Where did you learn to fight?"

He was in the tiny kitchen, bent over the sink. She was mopping blood from the cut on the back of his head.

"Try growing up as the only girl in a family with three brothers. You learn to fight. Hold still."

"I pity the brothers. Ah." March's head hurt the most. The bloody water dripping into the greasy plates a few centimeters from his face made him feel sick. "In Hollywood, I think, it is traditional for the man to rescue the girl."

"Hollywood is full of shit." She applied a fresh cloth. "This is deep. Are you sure you don't want to go to the hospital?"

"No time."

"Will that man come back?"

"No. At least, not for a while. Supposedly this is still a clandestine operation. Thank you."

He held the cloth to the back of his head and straightened. As he did so, he discovered a new pain, at the base of his spine.

" 'A clandestine operation?' " she repeated. "You don't think he could have been an ordinary thief?"

"No. He was a professional. An authentic, Gestapo-trained professional."

"And I beat him!" The adrenaline had given luster to her skin; her eyes sparkled. Her only injury was a bruise on her shoulder. She was more attractive than he remembered. Delicate cheekbones, a strong nose, full lips, large brown eyes. She had brown hair, cut to the nape of her neck, which she wore swept back behind her ears.

"If his orders had been to kill you, he would have done so."

"Really? Then why didn't he?" Suddenly she sounded angry.

"You're an American. A protected species, especially at the moment." He inspected the cloth. The flow of blood had stopped. "Don't underrate the enemy, Fräulein."

"Don't underrate *me.* If I hadn't come home, he'd have killed you."

He decided to say nothing. She clearly kept her temper on a hair trigger.

The apartment had been thoroughly ransacked. Her clothes hung out of their drawers, papers had been spilled across the desk and onto the floor, suitcases had been upended. Not, he thought, that it could have been very neat before: the dirty dishes in the sink, the profusion of bottles (most of them empty) in the bathroom, the yellowing copies of *The New York Times* and *Time,* their pages sliced to ribbons by the German censors, stacked haphazardly around the walls. Searching it must have been a nightmare. Weak light filtered in through dirty net curtains. Every few minutes the walls shook as a train passed.

"This is yours, I take it?" She pulled out the Luger from beneath a chair and held it up between finger and thumb.

"Yes. Thank you." He took it. She had a gift for making him feel stupid. "Is anything missing?"

"I doubt it." She glanced around. "I'm not sure I'd know if there was."

"The item I gave you last night . . . ?"

"Oh, that? It was here on the mantelpiece." She ran her hand along it, frowning. "It *was* here . . ."

He closed his eyes. When he opened them, she was grinning.

"Don't worry, Sturmbannführer. It's stayed close to my heart. Like a love letter."

She turned her back to him, unbuttoning her shirt. When she turned around, she had the envelope in her hand. He took it over to the window. It was warm to the touch.

It was long and slim, made of thick paper—a rich creamy blue with brown specks of age, like liver spots. It was luxurious, handmade, redolent of another age. There was no name or address.

Inside the envelope was a small brass key and a letter on matching blue paper, as thick as cardboard. Printed in the top right-hand corner, in flowery copperplate, was: Zaugg & Cie., Bankiers, Bahnhof-Strasse 44, Zürich. A single sentence, typed beneath, identified the bearer as a joint holder of account number 2402. The letter was dated July 8, 1942. It was signed Hermann Zaugg, Director.

March read it through again. He was not surprised that Stuckart had kept it locked in his safe: it was illegal for a German citizen to possess a foreign bank account without the permission of the Reichsbank. The penalty for non-compliance was death.

He said, "I was worried about you. I tried to call you a couple of hours ago, but there was no answer."

"I was out doing research."

"Research?"

She grinned again.

At March's suggestion, they went for a walk in the Tiergarten, the traditional rendezvous for Berliners with secrets to discuss. Even the Gestapo had yet to devise a means of bugging a park. Daffodils poked through the rough grass at the foot of the trees. Children fed the ducks on the Neuersee.

Getting out of Stuckart's apartment building had been easy, she said. The air shaft had emerged into the alley almost at ground level. There had been no SS men; they had all been at the front. So she had simply walked down the side of the building to the street at the rear and caught a taxi home. She had stayed up half the night waiting for him to call, rereading the letter until she knew it by heart. When by nine o'clock she had still heard nothing, she had decided not to wait.

She wanted to know what had happened to him and

Jaeger. He told her only that they had been taken to Gestapo headquarters and released that morning.

"Are you in trouble?"

"Yes. Now tell me what you discovered."

She had gone first to the public library in Nollendorf-Platz—she had nothing better to do now that her press accreditation had been withdrawn. In the library was a directory of European banks. Zaugg & Cie. still existed. The bank's premises remained in Bahnhof-Strasse. From the library she had gone to the U.S. Embassy to see Henry Nightingale.

"Nightingale?"

"You met him last night."

March remembered: the young man in the sport jacket and the button-down shirt, with his hand on her arm. "You didn't tell him anything?"

"Of course not. Anyway, he's discreet. We can trust him."

"I prefer to make my own judgments about whom I can trust." He felt disappointed in her. "Is he your lover?"

She stopped in her tracks. "What kind of a question is that?"

"I have more at stake in this than you have, Fräulein. Much more. I have a right to know."

"You have no right to know *at all.*" She was furious.

"All right." He held up his hands. The woman was impossible. "Your business."

They resumed walking.

Nightingale, she explained, was an expert in Swiss commercial matters, having dealt with the affairs of several German refugees in the United States trying to extract their money from banks in Zürich and Geneva.

It was almost impossible.

In 1934, a Gestapo agent named Georg Hannes Thomae had been sent to Switzerland by Reinhard Heydrich to find out the names of as many German account holders as possible. Thomae had set up house in Zürich, begun affairs with several lonely female cashiers, befriended minor bank officials. When the Gestapo had suspicions that a certain individual had an illegal account, Thomae would visit the bank posing as an intermediary and try to deposit money. The moment any cash was accepted, Heydrich knew an account existed. Its holder was arrested and tortured into revealing the details, and soon the bank would receive a detailed cable requesting, in proper form, the repatriation of all assets.

The Gestapo's war against the Swiss banks had become increasingly sophisticated and extensive. Telephone calls, cables and letters between Germany and Switzerland were intercepted as a matter of routine. Clients were executed or sent to concentration camps. In Switzerland, there was an outcry. Finally, the Swiss National Assembly rushed through a new banking code making it illegal for banks to disclose any details of their clients' holdings, on pain of imprisonment. Georg Thomae was exposed and expelled.

Swiss banks had come to regard doing business with German citizens as too dangerous and time consuming to countenance. Communication with clients was virtually impossible. Hundreds of accounts had simply been abandoned by their terrified owners. In any case, respectable bankers had no desire to become involved in these life-and-death transactions. The publicity was damaging. By 1939 the once lucrative German numbered-account business had collapsed.

"Then came the war," said Charlie. They had reached the end of the Neuersee and were walking back. From beyond the trees came the hum of the traffic on the East-West Axis. The dome of the Great Hall rose above the trees. Berliners joked that the only way to avoid seeing it was to live inside it.

"After 1939, the demand for Swiss accounts increased dramatically, for obvious reasons. People were desperate to get their property out of Germany. So banks like Zaugg devised a new kind of deposit account. For a fee of 200 francs, you received a box and a number, a key and a letter of authorization."

"Exactly like Stuckart."

"Right. You simply needed to show up with the letter and the key, and it was all yours. No questions. Each account could have as many keys and letters of authorization as the holder was prepared to pay for. The beauty of it was, the banks were no longer involved. One day, if she could get the travel permit, some little old lady might turn up with her life savings. Ten years later, her son could turn up with a letter and a key and walk off with his inheritance."

"Or the Gestapo might turn up—"

"—and if they had the letter and the key, the bank could give them everything. No embarrassment. No publicity. No breaking the banking code."

"These accounts—they still exist?"

"The Swiss government banned them at the end of the war, under pressure from Berlin, and no new ones have been allowed since. But the old ones—they still exist, because the terms of the original agreement have to be honored. They've become valuable in their own right. People sell them to one another. According to Henry, Zaugg developed quite a specialty in them. God knows what he's got locked in those boxes."

"Did you mention Stuckart's name to this Mr. Nightingale?"

"Of course not. I told him I was writing a piece for *Fortune* about 'the lost legacies of the war.' "

"Just as you told me you were going to interview Stuckart for an article about 'the Führer's early years'?"

She hesitated and said quietly, "What's that supposed to mean?"

His head was throbbing, his ribs still ached. What did he mean? He lit a cigarette to give himself time to think.

"People who encounter violent death—they try to forget it, run away. Not you. Last night: your eagerness to go back to Stuckart's apartment, the way you opened his letters. This morning: turning up information about Swiss banks . . ."

He stopped speaking. An elderly couple passed on the footpath, staring at them. He realized they must look like an odd pair: an SS Sturmbannführer, unshaven and slightly bashed around, and a woman who was clearly a foreigner. Her accent might be perfect, but there was something about her, in her expression, her clothes, her stance—something that betrayed that she was not German.

"Let's walk this way." He led her off the path toward the trees.

"Can I have one of those?"

In the shadows, as he lit her a cigarette, she cupped the flame. Reflections of the fire danced in her eyes.

"All right." She stepped back a pace, hugging herself as if she were cold. "It's true my parents knew Stuckart before the war. It's true I went to see him before Christmas. But I didn't call him. He called me."

"When?"

"On Saturday. Late."

"What did he say?"

She laughed. "Oh, no, Sturmbannführer. In my business information is a commodity, exchangeable on the open market. But I'm willing to trade."

"What do you want to know?"

"Everything. Why you had to break into that apartment last night. Why you're keeping secrets from your own people. Why the Gestapo almost killed you an hour ago."

"Oh, *that.*" He smiled. He felt weary. He leaned back against the rough bark of the tree and stared across the park. It seemed to him he had nothing to lose.

"Two days ago," he began, "I fished a body out of the Havel."

He told her everything. He told her about Buhler's death and Luther's disappearance. He told her what Jost had seen, and what had happened to him. He told her about Nebe and Globus, about the art treasures and the

Gestapo file. He even told her about Pili's statement. And—something he had noticed about criminals confessing, even those who knew that their confessions would one day hang them—when he finished, he felt better.

She was silent a long time. "That's fair," she said. "I don't know how this helps, but this is what happened to me."

She had gone to bed early on Saturday night. The weather had been foul—the start of that great bank of rain that had washed over the city for three days. She was not feeling sociable, had not for weeks. You know how it is, Berlin can get to you like that: make you feel small and hopeless in the shade of those vast gray buildings; the endless uniforms; the unsmiling bureaucrats.

The phone rang about eleven-thirty, just as she was drifting off to sleep. A man's voice. Taut. Precise. "There is a telephone booth opposite your apartment. Go to it. I shall call you there in five minutes. If the booth is occupied, please wait."

She had not recognized who it was, but something in the man's tone had told her it was not a joke. She had dressed, grabbed her coat, hobbled down the stairs and into the street, trying to pull on her shoes and walk at the same time. The rain had hit her like a slap across the face. Across the street, outside the station, was an old wooden telephone booth—empty, thank God.

It was while she was waiting for the call that she remembered where she had first heard the voice.

"Go back a bit," said March. "Your first meeting with Stuckart. Describe it."

That was before Christmas. She had called him cold. Explained who she was. He seemed reluctant, but she had persisted, so he had invited her over for tea. He had a shock of white curly hair and one of those orangey tans, as if he had spent a long time in the sun or under an ultraviolet lamp. The woman, Maria, was also in the apartment but behaved like a maid. She served some tea, then left them to it. Usual chat: how is your mother? Very well, thank you.

Ha, that was a joke.

She flicked ash from the end of her cigarette.

"My mother's career died when she left Berlin. My arrival buried it. As you can imagine, there wasn't a great demand for German actresses in Hollywood during the war."

And then he had asked about her father, in a gritted-teeth kind of way. And she had been able to take great pleasure in saying: very well, thank you. He had retired in '61, when Kennedy had taken over. Deputy Under Secretary of State Michael Maguire. God bless the United States of America. Stuckart had met him through Mom, had known him when he was at the embassy here.

March interrupted, "When was that?"

" 'Thirty-seven to 'thirty-nine."

"Go on."

Well, then he had wanted to know about the job and she had told him. World European Features: he had never heard of them. Not surprising, she said: nobody had. That sort of thing. Polite interest, you know. So when she left she had given him her card and he had bent to kiss her hand, had lingered over it, made a meal of it, made her feel sick. He had patted her bottom on the way out. And that had been that, she was glad to say. Five months: nothing.

"Until Saturday night?"

Until Saturday night. She had been in the telephone booth no more than thirty seconds when he called. Now all the arrogance was gone from his voice.

"Charlotte?" He had placed heavy emphasis on the second syllable. Shar-*lot*-te. "Forgive this melodrama. Your telephone is tapped."

"They say every foreigner's line is tapped."

"This is true. When I was in the ministry, I used to see transcripts. But phone booths are safe. I am in a phone booth now. I came on Thursday and took the number of the one you're in. It's serious, you see. I need to contact the authorities in your country."

"Why not talk to the embassy?"

"The embassy is not safe."

He had sounded terrified. And tight. He had definitely been drinking.

"Are you saying you want to defect?"

A long silence. Then there had been a noise behind her, a sound of metal tapping on glass. She had turned to discover, in the rain and the dark, a man with his hands cupped around his eyes, peering into the booth, looking like a deep-sea diver. She must have let out a cry or something, because Stuckart had become even more frightened.

"What was that? What is it?"

"Nothing. Just someone wanting to use the phone."

"We must be quick. I deal only with your father, not the embassy."

"What do you want me to do?"

"Come to me tomorrow and I will tell you everything. Shar-*lot*-te, I will make you the most famous reporter in the world."

"Where? What time?"

"My apartment. Noon."

"Is that safe?"

"Nowhere is safe."

And then he had hung up. Those were the last words she had heard Stuckart speak.

She finished her cigarette, ground it under foot.

The rest he knew, more or less. She had found the bodies, called the police. They had taken her to the big city station in Alexander-Platz, where she had sat in a blank-walled room for more than three hours, going crazy. Then she had been driven to another building to give a statement to some creepy SS man in a cheap wig, whose office had been more like that of a pathologist than a detective.

March smiled at the description of Fiebes.

She had already made up her mind not to tell the Polizei about Stuckart's call on Saturday night, for an obvious reason. If she had hinted that she had been preparing to help Stuckart defect, she would have been accused of "activities incompatible with her status as a journalist" and arrested. As it was, they had decided to deport her anyway. So it goes.

The authorities were planning a fireworks display in the Tiergarten, to commemorate the Führer's birthday. An area of the park had been fenced off, and pyrotechnicians in blue overalls were laying their surprises, watched by a curious crowd. Mortar tubes, sandbagged emplacements, dugouts, kilometers of cable: they looked more like the preparations for an artillery bombardment than for a celebration. Nobody paid any attention to the SS-Sturmbannführer and the woman in the blue plastic coat.

He scribbled on a page of his notebook.

"These are my telephone numbers—office and home. Also, here are the numbers of a friend of mine called Max Jaeger. If you can't get hold of me, call him." He tore out the page and gave it to her. "If anything suspicious happens, anything worries you—it doesn't matter what the time is—call."

"What about you? What are you going to do?"

"I'm going to try to get to Zürich tonight. Check out this bank account first thing tomorrow."

He knew what she would say even before she opened her mouth.

"I'll come with you."

"You'll be much safer here."

"But it's my story, too."

She sounded like a spoiled child. "It's not a story, for God's sake." He bit back his anger. "Look. A deal. Whatever I find out, I swear I'll tell you. You can have it all."

"It's not as good as being there."

"It's better than being dead."

"They wouldn't do anything like that abroad."

"On the contrary, that's exactly where they would do it. If something happens here, they're responsible. If something happens abroad . . ." He shrugged. "Prove it."

They parted in the center of the Tiergarten. He strode briskly across the grass, toward the humming city. As he walked, he took the envelope out of his pocket, squeezed it to check that the key was still in it and—on impulse—raised it to his nose. Her scent. He looked back over his shoulder. She was walking through the trees with her back to him. She disappeared for a moment, then reappeared; disappeared, reappeared—a tiny, birdlike figure—bright blue plumage against the dreary wood.

The door to March's apartment hung off its hinges like a broken jaw. He stood on the landing, listening, his pistol drawn. The place was silent, deserted.

Like Charlotte Maguire's, his apartment had been searched, but by hands of greater malevolence. Everything had been tipped into a heap in the center of the living room—clothes and books, shoes and old letters, photographs and crockery and furniture—the detritus of a life. It was as if someone had intended to make a bonfire but had been distracted at the last minute, before he could apply the torch.

Wedged upright on top of the pyre was a wooden-framed photograph of March, age twenty, shaking hands with the commander of the *U-Boot Waffe,* Admiral Dönitz. Why had it been left like that? What point was being made? He picked it up, carried it over to the window, blew dust off it. He had forgotten he even had it. Dönitz liked to come aboard every boat before it left Wilhelmshaven: an awesome figure, ramrod straight, iron-gripped, gruff. "Good hunting," he had barked at March. He growled the same to everyone. The picture showed five young crewmen lined up beneath the conning tower to meet him. Rudi Halder was to March's left. The other three had died later that year, trapped in the hull of U-175.

Good hunting.

He tossed the picture back onto the pile.

It had taken time to do all this. Time and anger and the certainty of not being disturbed. It must have happened while he was under guard in Prinz-Albrecht-Strasse. It could only have been the work of the Gestapo. He remembered a line of graffiti scrawled by the White Rose on a wall near Werderscher-Markt: "A police state is a country run by criminals."

They had opened his mail. A couple of bills, long overdue—they were welcome to *them*—and a letter from his ex-wife, dated Tuesday. He glanced through it. She had decided he was not to see Pili in the future. It upset the boy too much. She hoped he would agree that this was for the best. If necessary, she would be willing to swear a deposition before the Reich Family Court, giving her reasons. She trusted this would not be necessary, both for his sake and the boy's. It was signed "Klara Eckart." So she had gone back to her maiden name. He screwed the letter up and threw it next to the photograph with the rest of the rubbish.

The bathroom, at least, had been left intact. He showered and shaved, inspecting himself in the mirror for damage. It felt worse than it looked: a large bruise developing nicely on his chest, more on the backs of his legs and at the base of his spine; a livid mark at his throat. Nothing serious. What was it his father used to say—his paternal balm for all the batterings of childhood? "You'll live, boy." That was it. "You'll live!"

Naked, he went back into the living room and searched through the wreckage, pulling out clean clothes, a pair of shoes, a suitcase, a leather holdall. He feared they might have taken his passport, but it was there at the bottom of the mound. It had been issued in 1961, when March had gone to Italy to bring back a gangster being held in Milan. His younger self stared up at him, fatter cheeked, half smiling. My God, he thought, I've aged ten years in three.

He brushed his uniform and put it back on, together with a clean shirt, and packed his suitcase. As he bent to snap it shut, his eye was caught by something in the empty grate. The photograph of the Weiss family was lying face-down. He hesitated, picked it up, folded it into a small square—exactly as he had found it five years earlier—and slipped it into his wallet. If he were stopped and searched, he would say they were his family.

Then he took a last look around and left, closing the broken door behind him as best he could.

At the main branch of the Deutsche Bank in Wittenberg-Platz, he asked how much he had in his account.

"Four thousand two hundred seventy-seven marks and thirty-eight pfennigs."

"I'll take it."

"All of it, Herr Sturmbannführer?" The teller blinked at him through wire-framed spectacles. "You're closing the account?"

"All of it."

March watched him count out forty-two one-hundred-mark notes, then stuffed them into his wallet, next to the photograph. Not much in the way of life savings.

*This is what no promotions and seven years of alimony do to you.*

The teller was staring at him. "Did the Herr Sturmbannführer say something?"

He had given voice to his thoughts. He must be going mad. "No. Sorry. Thank you."

March picked up his suitcase, went out into the square and caught a taxi to Werderscher-Markt.

♦

Alone in his office, he did two things. He called the headquarters of Lufthansa and asked the head of security—a former Kripo investigator he knew named Friedman—to check if the airline had carried a passenger by the name of Martin Luther on any of its Berlin–Zürich flights on Sunday or Monday.

"Martin Luther, right?" Friedman was greatly amused. "Anyone else you want, March? Emporor Charlemagne? Herr von Goethe?"

"It's important."

"It's always important. Sure. I know." Friedman promised to find out the information at once. "Listen. When you get tired of chasing ambulances, there's always a job for you here if you want it."

"Thanks. I may well."

After he hung up, March took the dead plant down from the filing cabinet. He lifted the atrophied roots out of the pot, put the brass key in, replaced the plant and returned the pot to its old position.

Five minutes later, Friedman called him back.

Artur Nebe's suite of offices was on the fourth floor—all cream carpets and cream paint work, recessed lighting and black leather sofas. On the walls were prints of Thorak's sculptures: herculean figures with gargantuan torsos rolled boulders up steep hills in celebration of the building of the *Autobahnen;* Valkyries fought the triple demons Ignorance, Bolshevism and Slav. The immensity of Thorak's statuary was a whispered joke. "Thorax" they called him: "The Herr Professor is not receiving visitors today—he is working in the left ear of the horse."

Nebe's adjutant, Otto Beck, a smooth-faced graduate of Heidelberg and Oxford, looked up as March came into the outer office.

March said, "I need to speak with the Oberstgruppenführer."

"He is seeing nobody."

"He will see me."

"He will not."

March leaned very close to Beck's face, his fists on his desk. "Ask."

Behind him, he heard Nebe's secretary say, "Shall I call security?"

"One moment, Ingrid." It was fashionable among the graduates of the SS academy in Oxford to affect an English coolness. Beck flicked an invisible speck from the sleeve of his tunic. "And what name is it?"

"March."

"Ah. The famous *March.*" Beck picked up the telephone. "Sturmbannführer March is demanding to see you, Herr Oberstgruppenführer." He looked at March and nodded. "Very well."

Beck pressed a button concealed beneath the desk, releasing the electronic bolts. "Five minutes, March. He has an appointment with the Reichsführer."

The door to the inner office was solid oak, six centimeters thick. Inside, the blinds were tightly drawn against the day. Nebe was curled over his desk in a puddle of yellow light, studying a typed list through a magnifying glass. He turned one vast and blurry fish eye upon his visitor.

"What have we here?" He lowered the glass. "Sturmbannführer March. Empty-handed, I assume?"

"Unfortunately."

Nebe nodded. "I learn from the duty office that the police stations of the Reich are even now being filled to overflowing with elderly beggars, ancient drunkards who have lost their papers, absconding geriatrics . . . enough to keep Globus busy until Christmas." He leaned back in his chair. "If I know Luther, he's far too cunning to show himself yet. He'll wait a few days. That must be your hope."

"I have a favor to ask."

"Proceed."

"I wish to leave the country."

Nebe let out a shout of laughter. He pounded the desk with both hands. "Your file is compendious, March, but nowhere does it mention your sense of humor. Excellent! Who knows? You may yet survive. Some KZ commandant may adopt you as a pet."

"I wish to go to Switzerland."

"Of course. The scenery is spectacular."

"I've had a call from Lufthansa. Luther flew to Zürich on Sunday afternoon and returned to Berlin on the last flight on Monday night. I believe he had access to a numbered bank account."

Nebe's laughter had dwindled to an occasional snort. "On what evidence?"

March placed the envelope on Nebe's desk. "I removed this from Stuckart's apartment last night."

Nebe opened it and inspected the letter through the magnifying glass. He glanced up. "Should there not be a key with this?"

March was staring at the paintings behind Nebe's head—Schmutzler's *Farm Girls Returning from the Fields,* Padua's *The Führer Speaks*—ghastly orthodox muck.

"Ah. I see." Nebe sat back again, stroking his cheek with the glass. "If I don't allow you to go, I don't get the key. I could, of course, turn you over to the Gestapo, and they could persuade you to disgorge the key—probably quite quickly. But then it would be Globus and Heydrich who would learn the contents of the safe deposit box, rather than me."

He was silent for a while. Then he dragged himself to his feet and hobbled across to the blinds. He opened the slats a fraction and peered out. March could see his eyes moving slowly from side to side.

At last he said, "A tempting bargain. But why is it that I have this vision of myself waving you off with a white handkerchief from the tarmac of Hermann Göring Airport, and of you never coming back?"

"I suppose giving you my word that I would return would be of no use?"

"The suggestion demeans our intelligence."

Nebe went back to his desk and read the letter again. He pressed a switch on his desk. "Beck."

The adjutant appeared. "March—give him your passport. Now, Beck, get that to the Interior Ministry and have them issue an immediate twenty-four-hour exit visa, starting at six tonight and expiring at six tomorrow."

Beck glanced at March, then slid out of the office.

Nebe said, "This is my offer: the head of the Swiss Criminal Police, Herr Streuli, is a good friend of mine. From the moment you step off the aircraft until the moment you reboard it, his people will be watching you. Do not attempt to evade them. If you fail to return tomorrow, you will be arrested and deported. If you try to make a run to Bern, to enter a foreign embassy, you will be stopped. In any case, there is nowhere for you to go. After yesterday's happy announcement, the Americans will simply toss you back over the border to us. The British, French and Italians will do what we tell them. Australia and Canada will obey the Americans. There are the Chinese, I suppose, but if I were you I'd sooner take my chances in a KZ. And the moment you return to Berlin, you will tell me everything you have discovered. Right?"

March nodded.

"Good. The Führer calls the Swiss 'a nation of hotel keepers.' I recommend the Baur au Lac on Tal-Strasse, overlooking the See. Most luxurious. A fine place for a condemned man to spend a night."

Back in his office, a parody of a tourist, March booked his hotel room and reserved a plane seat. Within the hour, he had his passport back. The visa had been stamped inside: the ubiquitous eagle and garlanded swastika, the blank spaces for the dates filled in by a crabbed and bureaucratic hand.

The duration of an exit visa was in direct ratio to the applicant's political reliability. Party bosses got ten years; Party members, five; citizens with unblemished records, one; the dregs of the camps naturally got nothing at all. March had been given a day pass to the outside world. He was down there among the untouchables of society—the grumblers, the parasites, the work shy, the crypto-criminals.

He called the Kripo's economic investigation division and asked for the resident Swiss expert. When he mentioned Zaugg's name and asked if the division had any information, the man at the other end laughed. "How long do you have?"

"Start at the beginning."

"Hold, please." The man put down the phone and went to fetch the file.

Zaugg and Cie. had been founded in 1877 by a Franco-German financier, Louis Zaugg. Hermann Zaugg, the signatory of Stuckart's letter, was the founder's grandson. He was still listed as the bank's chief director. Berlin had followed his activities for more than two decades. During the 1940s, Zaugg had dealt extensively with German nationals of dubious reliability. He was currently suspected of harboring millions of Reichsmarks in cash, art, bullion, jewelry and precious stones—all of which rightfully should have been confiscated, but to none of which could the Finance Ministry gain access. They had been trying for years.

"What do we have on Zaugg personally?"

"Only the bare details. He's fifty-four, married, with one son. Has a mansion on the Zürichsee. Very respectable. Very private. Plenty of powerful friends in the Swiss government."

March lit a cigarette and grabbed a scrap of paper. "Give me that address again."

◆

Max Jaeger arrived as March was writing him a note. He pushed open the door with his backside and came in carrying a stack of files, looking sweaty. Nearly two days' growth of beard gave him a menacing air.

"Zavi, thank Christ!" He peered over the top of the paperwork. "I've been trying to reach you all day. Where have you been?"

"Around. What's this? Your memoirs?"

"The Spandau shootings. You heard Uncle Artur this morning." He mimicked Nebe's reedy voice. " 'Jaeger, you can return to normal duties.' "

He dropped the files on his desk. The window rattled. Dust shot across the office. "Statements of witnesses and wedding guests. Autopsy report—they dug fifteen bullets out of that poor bastard." He stretched, rubbed his eyes with his fists. "I could sleep for a week. I tell you: I'm too old for scares like last night. My heart won't stand it." He broke off. "Now what the hell are you doing?"

March had lifted the dead plant from its pot and was retrieving the key to the safe deposit box.

"I have a plane to catch in two hours."

Jaeger looked at his suitcase. "Don't tell me—a holiday! A little balalaika music on the shores of the Black Sea . . ." He folded his arms and kicked out his legs in a dance, Russian style.

March shook his head, smiling. "Do you feel like a beer?"

"Do I feel like a beer?" Jaeger had danced out of the door before March could turn around.

The little bar in Oberwall-Strasse was run by a retired Orpo man called Fischer. It smelled of smoke and sweat, stale beer and fried onions. Most of its clientele were policemen. Green and black uniforms clustered around the bar or lurked in the dimness of the wood-paneled booths.

The Fox and the Bear were greeted warmly.

"Taking a vacation, March?"

"Hey, Jaeger! Stand a little closer to the razor next time!"

Jaeger insisted on buying the drinks. March took a booth in the corner, stowed his suitcase under the table, lit a cigarette. There were men here he had known for a decade. The drivers from Rahnsdorf with their poker schools and dirty stories. The heavy drinkers from Serious Crimes in Worth-Strasse. He would not miss them. Walther Fiebes sat alone at the bar, moping over a bottle of schnapps.

Jaeger returned and raised his glass. *"Prost!"*

*"Prost."*

Max wiped the foam from his lips. "Good sausages, good engines, good beer—Germany's three gifts to the world." He always said this when they had a drink, and March always lacked the heart to point it out. "So. What's this about a *plane*?" For Jaeger, the word seemed to conjure images of all that was exotic in the world. The farthest he had ever traveled from Berlin was to a family camp on the Black Sea—a holiday last summer near Gotenburg organized by Strength-Through-Joy.

March turned his head slightly, glanced from side to side. The German look. The booths on either side were unoccupied. Shouts of laughter came from the bar.

"I have to go to Switzerland. Nebe's given me a twenty-four-hour visa. That key you saw just now in the office—I took it from Stuckart's safe last night. It opens a safety deposit box in Zürich."

Jaeger's eyes opened wide. "That must be where they keep the art stuff. Remember what Globus said this morning: they smuggled it out and sold it in Switzerland."

"There's more to it than that. I've been speaking to the American girl again. It seems Stuckart called her at home on Saturday night, wanting to defect."

*Defect.* The unmentionable act. It hung in the air between them.

Jaeger said, "But the Gestapo must know that already, Zavi. Surely her phone is tapped?"

March shook his head. "Stuckart was too clever for that. He used the phone booth opposite her apartment." He sipped his beer. "You see how it goes, Max? I feel like a man descending stairs in the dark. First the body in the lake turns out to be an alter Kämpfer. Then his death is linked to Stuckart's. Last night, my one witness to Globus's involvement—the cadet, Jost—was taken away by the SS, on Globus's orders. Now it turns out that Stuckart wanted to defect. What comes next?"

"You'll fall down those stairs and break your neck, my friend. That's what comes next."

"A fair prediction. And you don't know the worst of it."

March told him about the Gestapo dossier. Jaeger looked stricken. "Jesus Christ. What are you going to do?"

"I thought of trying to stay out of the Reich. I even withdrew all my money from the bank. But Nebe's right: no other country would touch me." March finished his drink. "Would you do something for me?"

"Name it."

"The American woman's apartment was broken into this morning. Could you ask the Orpo in Schöneberg to take a look occasionally—I've left the address on my desk. Also, I've given her your telephone number in case of trouble."

"No problem."

"And can you look after this for Pili?" He handed Jaeger an envelope containing half the cash he had withdrawn from the bank. "It's not much, but I may need the rest. Hang on to it until he's old enough to know what to do with it."

"Oh, come on, man!" Max leaned across and clapped him on the shoulder. "It's not as bad as that? Is it? Surely?"

March stared at him. After a second or two, Jaeger

grunted and looked away. "Yes. Well . . ." He tucked the envelope into his pocket. "My God," he said with sudden vehemence, "if a lad of mine denounced me to the Gestapo, I'd be giving him something, all right—and it wouldn't be money."

"It's not the boy's fault, Max."

Fault, thought March. How could you fault a ten-year-old? The boy needed a father figure. That was what the Party provided—stability, companionship, something to believe in—all the things March should have given him and hadn't. Besides, the Pimpf *expected* the young to transfer their allegiance from their family to the state. No, he would not—could not—blame his son.

Gloom had settled over Jaeger. "Another beer?"

"Sorry." March stood. "I have to go. I owe you."

Jaeger lurched to his feet as well. "When you get back, Zavi, come and stay with us for a couple of days. The younger girls are at a Bund deutscher Mädel camp for the week—you can have their room. We can work something out for the court-martial."

"Harboring an asocial—that won't go down well with your local Party."

"Fuck my local Party."

This was said with feeling. Jaeger stuck out his hand, and March shook it—a great, callused paw.

"Look after yourself, Zavi."

"Look after yourself, Max."

Drawn up on the runways of the Flughafen Hermann Göring, shimmering through the haze of fuel, was the new generation of passenger jets: the blue-and-white Boeings of Pan American, the red-white-and-black swastika-decked Junkers of Lufthansa.

Berlin has two airports. The old Tempelhof aerodrome near the city center handles short-haul, internal flights. International traffic passes through Hermann Göring in the northwestern suburbs. The new terminal buildings are long, low edifices of marble and glass, designed—of course—by Speer. Outside the arrivals hall stands a statue of Hanna Reitsch, Germany's leading aviatrix, made of melted-down Spitfires and Lancasters. She scans the sky for intruders. A sign behind her says WELCOME TO BERLIN, CAPITAL OF THE GREATER GERMAN REICH, in five languages.

March paid the taxi driver, tipped him and walked up the ramp toward the automatic doors. The air here was cold and man-made: drenched with aviation fuel, torn by the screams of throttling engines. Then the doors opened and hissed shut behind him, and suddenly he was in the soundproofed bubble of the departure terminal.

*"Lufthansa flight 401 to New York. Passengers are requested to make their way to gate number eight for boarding . . ."*

*"Final call for Lufthansa flight 014 to Theoderichshafen. Passengers . . ."*

March went first to the Lufthansa sales desk to pick up his ticket, then to the check-in, where his passport was scrutinized carefully by a blonde with "Gina" pinned to her left breast, a swastika badge on her lapel.

"Does the Herr Sturmbannführer wish to check in any luggage?"

"No, thank you. I have only this." He patted his small suitcase.

She returned his passport with his boarding card folded inside it. Accompanying this act was a smile as bright and cheerless as neon.

"Boarding in thirty minutes. Have a good flight, Herr Sturmbannführer."

"Thank you, Gina."

"You're welcome."

"Thank you."

They were bowing like a pair of Japanese businessmen. Air travel was a new world to March, a strange land with its own impenetrable rituals.

He followed the signs to the lavatory, selected the cubicle farthest from the washbasins, locked the door, opened the suitcase, took out the leather holdall. Then he sat down and tugged off his boots. White light gleamed on chrome and tile.

When he had stripped to his shorts, he put the boots and his uniform into the holdall, stuffed his Luger into the middle of the bag, zipped it up and locked it.

Five minutes later he emerged from the cubicle transformed. In a light gray suit, white shirt, pale blue tie and soft brown shoes, the Aryan Superman had turned back into a normal citizen. He could see the transformation reflected in people's eyes. No more frightened glances.

The attendant at the left-luggage area where he deposited the holdall was surly. He handed March the ticket.

"Don't lose it. If you do, don't bother coming back." He jerked his head to the sign behind him: WARNING! ITEMS RETURNED ON PRODUCTION OF TICKET ONLY!

At the passport control zone March lingered, noting the security. Barrier one: checking of boarding cards, unobtainable without the proper visa. Barrier two: rechecking of the visas themselves. Three members of the *Zollgrenzschutz,* the border protection police, were stationed on either side of the entrance, carrying submachine guns. The elderly man in front of March was scrutinized with particular care, the customs officer speaking to someone on the telephone before waving him through. They were still looking for Luther.

When March's turn came, he saw how his passport baffled the customs man. An SS-Sturmbannführer with only a twenty-four-hour visa? The normal signals of rank and privilege, usually so clear, were too confused to read. Curiosity and servility warred in the customs man's face. Servility, as usual, won.

"Enjoy your journey, Herr Sturmbannführer."

On the other side of the barrier, March resumed his study of airport security. All luggage was scanned by X ray. He was frisked, then asked to open his case. Each item was inspected—the sponge bag unzipped, the shaving foam uncapped and sniffed. The guards worked with the care of men who knew that if an aircraft were lost to hijackers or a terrorist bomb during their watch, they would spend the next five years in a KZ.

Finally he was clear of the checks. He patted his inside pocket to make sure Stuckart's letter was still there, turned the little brass key over in his other hand. Then he went to the bar and had a large whisky and a cigarette.

He boarded the Junkers ten minutes before takeoff.

It was the day's last flight from Berlin to Zürich and the

cabin was full of businessmen and bankers in dark three-piece suits, reading pink financial newspapers. March had a seat next to the window. The place beside his was empty. He stowed his suitcase in a compartment above his head, settled back and closed his eyes. Inside the plane, a Bach cantata was playing. Outside, the engines started. They climbed the scale from hum to brittle whine, one coming in after another like a chorus. The aircraft jolted slightly and began to move.

For thirty-three hours out of the past thirty-six March had been awake. Now the music bathed him, the vibrations lulled him. He slept.

He missed the safety demonstration. The takeoff barely penetrated his dreams. Nor did he notice a person slip into the seat beside him.

Not until they were cruising at ten thousand meters and the pilot was informing them that they were passing over Leipzig did he open his eyes. The stewardess was leaning toward him, asking him if he wanted a drink. He started to say "a whisky" but was too distracted to finish his reply. Sitting next to him, pretending to read a magazine, was Charlotte Maguire.

The Rhine slid by beneath them, a wide curve of molten metal in the dying sun. March had never seen it from the air. "Dear Fatherland, no danger thine: / Firm stands thy watch along the Rhine." Lines from his childhood, hammered out on an untuned piano in a drafty gymnasium. Who had written them? He could not remember.

Crossing the river was a signal that they had passed out of the Reich and into Switzerland. In the distance: mountains, gray-blue and misty; below: neat rectangular fields and dark clumps of pine forests, steep red roofs and little white churches.

When he had awakened she had laughed at the surprise on his face. You may be used to dealing with hardened criminals, she had said, and with the Gestapo and the SS.

But you've never come up against the good old American press.

He had sworn, to which she had responded with a wide-eyed look, mock innocent, like one of Max Jaeger's daughters. An act, deliberately done badly, which made it naturally an even better act, turning his anger against him, making him part of the play.

She had then insisted on explaining everything, whether he wanted to listen or not, gesturing with a plastic tumbler of whisky. It had been easy, she said. He had told her he was flying to Zürich that night. There was only one flight. At the airport she had informed the Lufthansa desk that she was supposed to be with Sturmbannführer March. She was late: could she please have the seat next to him? When they agreed, she knew he must be on board.

"And there you were, asleep," she concluded. "Like a babe."

"And if they had said they had no passenger called March?"

"I would have come anyway." She was impatient with his anger. "Listen, I already have most of the story. An art fraud. Two senior officials dead. A third on the run. An attempted defection. A secret Swiss bank account. At worst, alone, I'd have picked up some extra color in Zürich. At best I might have charmed Herr Zaugg into giving me an interview."

"I don't doubt it."

"Don't look so worried, Sturmbannführer—I'll keep your name out of it."

Zürich is only twenty kilometers south of the Rhine. They were descending quickly. March finished his Scotch and set the empty container on the stewardess's outstretched tray.

Charlotte Maguire drained her own glass and placed it next to his. "We have whisky in common, Herr March, at least." She smiled.

He turned to the window. This was her skill, he thought: to make him look stupid, a Teutonic flatfoot.

First she had failed to tell him about Stuckart's telephone call. Then she had maneuvered him into letting her join in his search of Stuckart's apartment. This morning, instead of waiting for him to contact her, she had talked to the American diplomat, Nightingale, about Swiss banks. Now this. It was like having a child forever at your heels—a persistent, intelligent, embarrassing, deceitful, dangerous child. Surreptitiously he felt his pockets again, to check that he still had the letter and key. She was not beyond stealing them while he was asleep.

The Junkers was coming in to land. Like a film gradually speeding up, the Swiss countryside began rushing past: a tractor in a field, a road with a few headlights in the smoky dusk, and then—one bounce, two—they were touching down.

Zürich airport was not how he had imagined it. Beyond the aircraft and hangars were wooded hillsides, with no evidence of a city. For a moment, he wondered if Globus had discovered his mission and had arranged for the plane to be diverted. Perhaps they had been set down in some remote air base in southern Germany? But then he saw ZÜRICH on the terminal building.

The instant the plane taxied to a halt, the passengers—professional commuters, most of them—rose as one. She was on her feet, too, pulling down her case and that ridiculous blue coat. He reached past her.

"Excuse me."

She shrugged on the coat. "Where to now?"

"I'm going to my hotel, Fräulein. What you do is your concern."

He managed to squeeze in front of a fat Swiss who was cramming documents into a leather attaché case. The maneuver left her trapped some way behind him. He did not look back as he shuffled down the aisle and off the aircraft.

He walked briskly through the arrivals hall to passport control, overtaking most of the other passengers to station himself near the head of the queue. Behind him, he heard a commotion as she tried to catch up.

The Swiss border official, a serious young man with a drooping mustache, leafed through his passport. "Business or pleasure, Herr March?"

"Business." Definitely business.

"One moment."

The young man picked up the telephone, dialed three digits, turned away from March and whispered something into the receiver. He said, "Yes. Yes. Of course." Then he hung up and returned the passport to March.

There were two of them waiting for him by the baggage carousel. He spotted them from fifty meters away: bulky figures with close-cropped hair, wearing stout black shoes and belted fawn raincoats. Policemen—they were the same the world over. He walked past them without a glance and sensed rather than saw them falling in behind him.

He went unchallenged through the green customs channel and out into the main concourse. Taxis. Where were taxis?

*Clip-clop, clip-clop.* Coming up behind him.

The air outside was several degrees colder than in Berlin. *Clip-clop, clip-clop.* He wheeled around. There she was, in her coat, clutching her case, balanced on her high heels.

"Go away, Fräulein. Do you understand me? Do you need it in writing? Go back to America and publish your stupid story. I have business to attend to."

Without waiting for her reply, he opened the rear door of the waiting taxi, threw in his case, climbed in after it. "Baur au Lac," he said to the driver.

They pulled out of the airport and onto the highway, heading south toward the city. The day was almost gone. Craning his neck to look out of the back window, March could see a taxi tucked in ten meters behind them, with an unmarked white Mercedes following it. Christ, what a comedy this was turning into. Globus was chasing Luther, he was chasing Globus, Charlie Maguire was chasing him and now the Swiss police were on the tails of both of them. He lit a cigarette.

"Can't you read?" said the driver. He pointed to a sign: THANK YOU FOR NOT SMOKING.

"Welcome to Switzerland," muttered March. He wound down the window a few centimeters, and the cloud of blue smoke was plucked into the chilly air.

Zürich was more beautiful than he had expected. Its center reminded him of Hamburg. Old buildings clustered around the edge of the wide lake. Trams in a livery of green and white rattled along the front, past well-lit shops and cafés. The driver was listening to the Voice of America. In Berlin it was a blur of static; here it was clear. "I wanna hold your hand," sang a youthful English voice. "I wanna hold your ha-a-and!" A thousand teenage girls screamed.

The Baur au Lac was a street's width from the lake. March paid the taxi driver in Reichsmarks—every country on the continent accepted Reichsmarks, it was Europe's common currency—and went inside. It was as luxurious as Nebe had promised. His room had cost him half a month's salary. *"A fine place for a condemned man to spend a night. . . ."* As he signed the register he glimpsed a flash of blue at the door, swiftly followed by the fawn raincoats. I'm like a movie star, thought March as he caught the elevator. Everywhere I go, I have two detectives and a brunette in tow.

He spread a map of the city on the bed and sat down beside it, sinking into the spongy mattress. He had so little time. The broad expanse of the Zürichsee thrust up into the complex of streets like a blue blade. According to his Kripo file, Hermann Zaugg had a place on See-Strasse. March found it. See-Strasse ran alongside the eastern shore of the lake, about four kilometers south of the hotel.

Someone tapped softly on the door. A man's voice called his name.

Now what? He strode across the room, flung open the door. A waiter was in the corridor, holding a tray. He looked startled.

"Sorry, sir. With the compliments of the lady in room 277, sir."

"Yes. Of course." March stood aside to let him through. The waiter came in hesitantly, as if he thought March might hit him. He set down the tray, lingered fractionally for a tip and then, when none was forthcoming, left. March locked the door behind him.

On the table was a bottle of Glenfiddich, with a one-word note: "Détente?"

He stood at the window, his tie loosened, sipping the malt whisky, looking out across the Zürichsee. Traceries of yellow lanterns were strung around the black water; on the surface, pinpricks of red, green and white bobbed and winked. He lit yet another cigarette, his millionth of the week.

People were laughing in the drive beneath his window. A light moved across the lake. No Great Hall, no marching bands, no uniforms. For the first time in—what was it?—a year, at least, he was away from the iron and granite of Berlin. So. He held up his glass and studied the pale liquid. There *were* other lives, other cities.

He noticed, along with the bottle, that she had ordered two glasses.

He sat down on the edge of the bed and looked at the telephone. He drummed his fingers on the little table.

Madness.

She had a habit of thrusting her hands deep into her pockets and standing with her head on one side, half smiling. On the plane, he remembered, she had been wearing a red wool dress with a leather belt. She had good legs, in black stockings. And when she was angry or amused, which was most of the time, she would flick at the hair behind her ear.

The laughter outside drifted away.

*"Where have you been the past twenty years?"* Her contemptuous question to him in Stuckart's apartment.

She knew so much. She danced around him.

*"The millions of Jews who vanished in the war . . ."*

He turned her note over in his fingers, poured himself another drink and lay back on the bed. Ten minutes later he lifted the receiver and spoke to the operator.

"Room 277."

Madness, *madness.*

They met in the lobby, beneath the fronds of a luxuriant palm. In the opposite corner a string quartet scraped its way through a selection from *Die Fledermaus.*

March said, "The Scotch is very good."

"A peace offering."

"Accepted. Thank you." He glanced across at the elderly cellist. Her stout legs were held wide apart, as if she were milking a cow. "God knows why I should trust you."

"God knows why I should trust *you.*"

"Ground rules," he said firmly. "One: no more lies. Two: we do what I say, whether you want to or not. Three: you show me what you plan to print, and if I ask you not to write something, you take it out. Agreed?"

"It's a deal." She smiled and offered him her hand. He took it. She had a cool, firm grip. For the first time he noticed she had a man's watch around her wrist.

"What changed your mind?" she asked.

He released her hand. "Are you ready to go out?" She was still wearing the red dress.

"Yes."

"Do you have a notebook?"

She tapped her coat pocket. "Never travel without one."

"Nor do I. Good. Let's go."

♦

Switzerland was a cluster of lights in a great darkness, enemies all around it: Italy to the south, France to the west, Germany north and east. Its survival was a source of wonder: "the Swiss miracle," they called it.

Luxembourg had become Moselland, Alsace-Lorraine was Westmark; Austria was Ostmark. As for Czechoslovakia—that bastard child of Versailles had dwindled to the Protectorate of Bohemia and Moravia. Poland, Latvia, Lithuania, Estonia—vanished from the map. In the East, the German Empire was carved four ways into the *Reichskommissariate* Ostland, Ukraine, Caucasus, Muscovy.

In the West, twelve nations—Portugal, Spain, France, Ireland, Great Britain, Belgium, Holland, Italy, Denmark, Norway, Sweden and Finland—had been corralled by Germany, under the Treaty of Rome, into a European trading bloc. German was the official second language in all schools. People drove German cars, listened to German radios, watched German televisions, worked in German-owned factories, moaned about the behavior of German tourists in German-dominated holiday resorts, while German teams won every international sporting competition except cricket, which only the English played.

In all this, Switzerland alone was neutral. That had not been the Führer's intention. But by the time the Wehrmacht's planners had designed a strategy to subdue the Swiss state, the stalemate of the Cold War had begun. It remained a patch of no-man's-land, increasingly useful to both sides as the years went by, a place to meet and deal in secret.

"There are only three classes of citizen in Switzerland," the Kripo's expert had told March. "American spies, German spies and Swiss bankers trying to get hold of their money."

Over the past century those bankers had settled around the northern rim of the Zürichsee like a rich crust; a tidemark of money. As on Schwanenwerder, their villas presented to the world a blank face of high walls and stout gates, backed by dense screens of trees.

March leaned forward and spoke to the driver. "Slow down here."

They were quite a cavalcade by now: March and Charlie in a taxi followed by two cars, each occupied by a Swiss policeman. Bellerive-Strasse turned into See-Strasse. March counted off the numbers.

"Pull over here."

The taxi swerved up onto the curb. The police cars passed them; a hundred meters down the road, their brake lights glowed.

Charlie looked around. "Now what?"

"Now we take a look at the home of Dr. Hermann Zaugg."

March paid the taxi driver, who promptly turned and set off back toward the city center. The road was quiet.

All the villas were well protected, but Zaugg's—the third they came to—was a fortress. The gates were solid metal, three meters high, flanked on either side by a stone wall. A security camera scanned the entrance. March took Charlie's arm and they strolled past like lovers taking the air. They crossed the road and waited in a driveway on the other side. March looked at his watch. It was just after nine. Five minutes passed. He was about to suggest they leave when, with a clank and a hum of machinery, the gates began to swing open.

Charlie whispered, "Someone's coming out."

"No." He nodded up the road. "Coming in."

The limousine was big and powerful: a British car, a Bentley, finished in black. It came from the direction of the city, traveling rapidly, and swerved and swung into the drive. A chauffeur and another man in the front; in the back, a flash of silver hair—Zaugg's, presumably. March just had time to notice how low the bodywork hung to the ground. Then, one after another, the tires were absorbing the impact as the Bentley bounced over the curb—*whump, whump, whump, whump*—and it was gone.

The gates started to close, then stopped halfway. Two men appeared from the direction of the house, walking fast.

"You!" one of them shouted. "Both of you! Stay where you are!" He strode into the road. March seized Charlie by the elbow. At that instant, one of the police cars began backing toward them, gearbox howling. The man glanced to his right, hesitated and retreated.

The car skidded to a halt. The window was wound down. A weary voice said, "For fuck's sake, get in."

March opened the back door and ushered in Charlie, then slipped in after her. The Swiss policeman executed a rapid three-point turn and accelerated away toward the city. Zaugg's bodyguards had already disappeared; the gates were banging shut behind them.

March twisted around to stare out of the rear window. "Are all your bankers as well protected as that?"

"Depends who they do business with." The policeman adjusted his mirror to look at them. He was in his late forties, with bloodshot eyes. "Are you planning any further adventures, Herr March? A brawl somewhere, perhaps? It would help if we had a little warning next time."

"I thought you were supposed to be following us, not guarding us."

" 'Follow and protect as necessary': those are our orders. That's my partner in the car behind, by the way. It's been a fucking long day. Excuse my language, Fräulein—they never said there'd be a woman involved."

"Can you drop us back at the hotel?" asked March.

The policeman grumbled. "So now I'm to add chauffeur to my list of duties?" He switched on his radio and spoke to his partner. "Panic over. We're going back to the Baur au Lac."

Charlie had her notebook open on her lap and was writing. "Who are these people?"

March hesitated but then thought: what does it matter?

"This officer and his partner are members of the Swiss police, here to ensure I don't attempt to defect while outside the borders of the Reich. And also to ensure that I return in one piece."

"Always a pleasure, assisting our German colleagues," grunted a voice from the front.

Charlie said, "There's a danger you might not?"

"Apparently."

"Jesus." She wrote something down. He looked away. Off to their left, a couple of kilometers across the See, the lights of Zürich formed a yellow ribbon on the dark water. His breath misted the window.

Zaugg must have been returning from his office. It was late, but the burghers of Zürich worked hard for their money—twelve or fourteen hours a day was common. The banker's house could be reached only by traveling this road, which ruled out the most effective security precaution: varying his route each night. And See-Strasse, bounded on one side by the lake and with several dozen streets leading off the other, was a security man's nightmare. That explained something.

"Did you notice his car?" he said to Charlie. "How heavy it was, the noise its tires made? You see those often in Berlin. That Bentley was armor plated." He ran his hand through his hair. "Two bodyguards, a pair of prison gates, remote cameras and a bombproof car. What kind of banker is that?"

He could not see her face properly in the shadows, but he could feel her excitement beside him. She said, "We've got the letter of authorization, remember? Whatever kind of banker he is—he's *our* banker now."

They ate at a restaurant in the old town—a place with thick linen napkins and heavy silver cutlery, where the waiters lined up behind them and whipped the covers from their plates like a troupe of conjurers performing a trick. If the hotel had cost him half a month's salary, this meal would cost him the other half, but March didn't care.

She was unlike any other woman he had met. She was not one of the homebodies of the Party's Women's League, all *"Kinder, Kirche und Küche"*—her husband's supper always ready on the table, his uniform freshly pressed, five children asleep upstairs. And while a good National Socialist girl abhorred cosmetics, nicotine and alcohol, Charlie Maguire made liberal use of all three. Her dark eyes soft in the candlelight, she talked almost without pause of New York, foreign reporting, her father's days in Berlin, the wickedness of Joseph Kennedy, politics, money, men, herself.

She had been born in Washington, D.C., in the spring of 1939 ("The last spring of peace, my parents called it—in all senses"). Her father had recently returned from Berlin to work at the State Department. Her mother had been trying to make a success as an actress, but after 1941 was lucky simply to escape internment. In the 1950s, after the war, Michael Maguire had gone to Omsk, capital of what was left of Russia, to serve in the U.S. Embassy. It was considered too dangerous a place to take four children. *Charlotte* had been left behind to be educated at expensive schools in Virginia; *Charlie* had dropped out at seventeen—spitting and swearing and rebelling against everything in sight.

"I went to New York. Tried to be an actress. That didn't work. Tried to be a journalist. That suited me better. Enrolled at Columbia—to my father's great relief. And then—what do you know?—I start an affair with Teacher." She shook her head. "How stupid can you get?" She blew out a jet of cigarette smoke. "Is there any more wine in there?"

He poured out the last of the bottle, ordered another. It seemed to be his turn to say something. "Why Berlin?"

"A chance to get away from New York. My mother being German made it easier to get a visa. I have to admit: World European Features is not quite as grand as it sounds. Two men in an office on the wrong side of town with a telex machine. To be honest, they were happy to take anyone who could get a visa out of Berlin. Even me." She looked at him with shining eyes. "I didn't know he was married, you see. The teacher." She snapped her fingers. "Basic failure of research there, wouldn't you say?"

"When did it end?"

"Last year. I came to Europe to show them all I could do it. Him especially. That's why I felt so sick about being expelled. God, the thought of facing them all again . . ." She sipped her wine. "Perhaps I've got a father fixation. How old are you?"

"Forty-two."

"Right in my age range." She smiled at him over the rim of her glass. "You'd better watch out. Are you married?"

"Divorced."

"Divorced! That's promising. Tell me about her."

Her frankness kept catching him off guard. "She was—" he began, and corrected himself. "She's—" He stopped. How did you summarize someone you had been married to for nine years, divorced from for seven, who had just denounced you to the authorities? "She's not like you" was all he could think to say.

"Meaning?"

"She doesn't have ideas of her own. She's concerned about what people think. She has no curiosity. She's bitter."

"About you?"

"Naturally."

"Is she seeing anyone else?"

"Yes. A Party bureaucrat. Much more suitable than me."

"And you? Do you have anyone?"

A klaxon sounded in March's mind. *Dive, dive, dive.* He had had two affairs since his divorce. A teacher who had lived in the apartment beneath his, and a young widow who taught history at the university—another friend of Rudi Halder's: he sometimes suspected Rudi had made it his mission in life to find him a new wife. The liaisons had drifted on for a few months, until both women had tired of the last-minute calls from Werderscher-Markt: "Something's come up, I'm sorry . . ."

Instead of answering her, March said, "So many questions. You should have been a detective."

She made a face at him. "So few answers. *You* should have been a reporter."

The waiter poured more wine. After he had moved away, she said, "You know, when I met you, I hated you on sight."

"Ah. The uniform. It blots out the man."

"*That* uniform does. When I looked for you on the plane this afternoon I barely recognized you."

It occurred to March that here was another reason for his good mood: he had not caught a glimpse of his black silhouette in a mirror, had not seen people shrinking away at his approach.

"Tell me," he said, "what do they say about the SS in America?"

She rolled her eyes. "Oh, come on, March. Please. Don't let's ruin a good evening."

"I mean it. I'd like to know." He had to coax her into answering.

"Well, murderers," she said eventually. "Sadists. Evil personified. All that. You asked for it. Nothing personal intended, you understand. Any other questions?"

"A million. A lifetime's worth."

"A lifetime! Well, go ahead. I have nothing planned."

He was momentarily dumbfounded, paralyzed by choice. Where to start?

"The war in the East," he said. "In Berlin we hear only of victories. Yet the Wehrmacht has to ship the coffins home from the Urals front at night on special trains, so nobody sees how many dead there are."

"I read somewhere that the Pentagon estimates a hundred thousand Germans killed since 1960. The Luftwaffe is bombing the Russian towns flat day after day, and still they keep coming back at you. You can't win because they don't have anywhere else to go. And you can't use nuclear weapons, in case we retaliate and the world blows up."

"What else?" He tried to think of recent headlines. "Goebbels says German space technology beats the Americans' every time."

"Actually, I think that's true. Peenemünde had satellites in orbit years ahead of ours."

"Is Winston Churchill still alive?"

"Yes. He's an old man now. In Canada. He lives there. So does the queen." She noticed his puzzlement. "Elizabeth claims the English throne from her uncle."

"And the Jews?" said March. "What do the Americans say we did to them?"

She was shaking her head. "Why are you doing this?"

"Please. The truth."

"The truth? How do I know what the truth is?" Suddenly she had raised her voice, was almost shouting. People at the next table were turning around. "We're brought up to think of Germans as something from outer space. Truth doesn't enter into it."

"Very well, then. Give me the propaganda."

She glanced away, exasperated, but then looked back with an intensity that made it difficult for him to meet her eyes. "All right. They say you scoured Europe for every living Jew—men, women, children, babies. They say you shipped them to ghettos in the East, where thousands died of malnutrition and disease. Then you forced the survivors farther east, and nobody knows what happened after that. A handful escaped over the Urals into Russia. I've seen them on TV. Funny old men, most of them a bit crazy. They talk about execution pits, medical experiments, camps that people went into but never came out of. They talk about millions of dead. But then the German ambassador comes along in his smart suit and tells everyone it's all just Communist propaganda. So nobody knows what's true and what isn't. And I'll tell you something else—most people don't care." She sat back in her chair. "Satisfied?"

"I'm sorry."

"So am I." She reached for her cigarettes, then stopped and looked at him again. "That's why you changed your mind at the hotel about bringing me along, isn't it? Nothing to do with whisky. You wanted to pick my brains." She started to laugh. "And I thought *I* was using *you.*"

After that, they got on better. Whatever poison there was between them had been drawn out. He told her about his father and how he had followed him into the navy, about how he had drifted into police work and found a taste for it—a vocation, even.

She said: "I still don't understand how you can wear it."

"What?"

"That uniform."

He poured himself another glass of wine. "Oh, there's a simple answer to that. In 1936, the Kriminalpolizei was merged into the SS; all officers had to accept honorary SS rank. So I have a choice: either I'm an investigator in that uniform, and try to do a little good; or I'm something else without that uniform, and do no good at all."

And the way things are going, I shall soon not have that choice, he thought.

She tilted her head to one side and nodded. "I can see that. That seems fair."

He felt impatient, sick of himself. "No, it's not. It's bullshit, Charlie." It was the first time he had called her that since she had insisted on it at the beginning of the dinner; using it sounded like a declaration. He hurried on, "That's the answer I've given everybody, including myself, for the past ten years. Unfortunately, even I have stopped believing it."

"But what happened—the worst of what happened—was during the war, and you weren't around. You told me: you were at sea."

He looked down at his plate, silent. She went on, "And anyway, wartime is different. All countries do wicked things in wartime. My country dropped an atom bomb on Japanese civilians—killed a quarter of a million people in an instant. And the Americans have been allies of the Russians for the past twenty years. Remember what the Russians did?"

There was truth in what she said. One by one, as they had advanced eastward, beginning with the bodies of ten thousand Polish officers in the Katyn forest, the Germans had discovered the mass graves of Stalin's victims. Millions had died in the famines, purges, deportations of the

1930s. Nobody knew the exact figure. The execution pits, the torture chambers, the gulags inside the Arctic Circle—all were now preserved by the Germans as memorials to the dead, museums of Bolshevik evil. Children were taken around to see them; ex-prisoners acted as guides. There was a whole school of historical studies devoted to investigating the crimes of Communism. Television showed documentaries on Stalin's holocaust—bleached skulls and walking skeletons, bulldozed corpses and the earth-caked rags of women and children bound with wire and shot in the back of the neck.

She put her hand over his. "The world is as it is. Even I can see that."

He spoke without looking at her. "Yes. Fine. But everything you've said, I've already heard. 'It was a long time ago.' 'That was war.' 'The Ivans were worst of all.' 'What can one man do?' I've listened to people whisper that for ten years. That's all they ever do, by the way. Whisper."

She withdrew her hand and lit another cigarette, turning the little gold lighter over and over in her fingers. "When I first came to Berlin and my parents gave me that list of people they knew in the old days, there were lots of theater people on it, artists—friends of my mother. I suppose quite a few of them, in the way of things, must have been Jews, or homosexuals. And I went looking for them. All of them had gone, of course. That didn't surprise me. But they hadn't just vanished. *It was as if they'd never existed.*"

She tapped the lighter gently against the tablecloth. He noticed her fingers—slim, unmanicured, unadorned.

"Of course, there were people living in the places my mother's friends used to live in. Old people, often. They must have known, mustn't they? But they just looked blank. They were watching television, having tea, listening to music. There was nothing left *at all.*"

March said, "Look at this."

He pulled out his wallet, took out the photograph. It looked incongruous amid the plushness of the restaurant—a relic from someone's attic, rubbish from a flea market stall.

He gave it to her. She studied it. A strand of hair fell over her face and she brushed it away. "Who are they?"

"When I moved into my apartment after Klara and I split up, it hadn't been decorated for years. I found that tucked behind the wallpaper in the bedroom. I tell you, I took that place to pieces, but that was all there was. Their surname was Weiss. But who are they? Where are they now? What happened to them?"

He took the photograph, folded it into quarters, put it back into his wallet.

"What do you do," he said, "if you devote your life to discovering criminals, and it gradually occurs to you that the real criminals are the people you work for? What do you do when everyone tells you not to worry, you can't do anything about it, it was a long time ago?"

She was looking at him in a different way. "I suppose you go crazy."

"Or worse. Sane."

Despite his protests, she insisted on paying half the bill. It was almost midnight by the time they left the restaurant. They walked in silence toward the hotel. Stars arched across the sky; at the bottom of the steep cobbled street, the lake waited.

She took his arm. "You asked me if that man at the embassy—Nightingale—if he was my lover."

"That was rude of me. I'm sorry."

"Would you have been disappointed if I'd said he was?"

He hesitated.

She went on, "Well, he isn't. He'd like to be. Sorry. That sounds like boasting."

"It doesn't at all. I'm sure many would like to be."

"I hadn't met anyone . . ."

*Hadn't . . .*

She stopped. "I'm twenty-five. I go where I like. I do what I like. I choose whom I like." She turned to him, touched him lightly on the cheek with a warm hand. "God, I hate getting this sort of thing out of the way, don't you?"

She drew his head to hers.

How odd it is, thought March afterward, to live your life in ignorance of the past, of your world, yourself. Yet how easy to do it! You go along from day to day, down paths other people prepare for you, never raising your head—enfolded in their logic, from swaddling clothes to shroud. It's a kind of fear.

Well, good-bye to that. And good to leave it behind—whatever happens now.

His feet danced on the cobblestones. He slipped his arm around her. He had so many questions.

"Wait, wait." She was laughing, holding on to him. "Enough. Stop. I'm starting to worry that you only want me for my *mind.*"

In his hotel room, she unknotted his tie and reined him to her once more, her mouth soft on his. Still kissing him, she smoothed the jacket from his shoulders, unbuttoned his shirt, parted it. Her hands skimmed over his chest, around his back, across his stomach.

She knelt and tugged at his belt.

He closed his eyes and coiled his fingers in her hair.

After a few moments he pulled away gently, and knelt to face her, lifted her dress. Freed from it, she threw back her head and shook her hair. He wanted to know her completely. He kissed her throat, her breasts, her stomach; inhaled her scent, felt the firm flesh stretching smooth and taut beneath his hands, her soft skin on his tongue.

Later she guided him onto the bed and settled herself above him. The only light was cast by the lake. Rippling shadows all around them. When he opened his mouth to say something, she put a finger to his lips.

# FRIDAY, APRIL 17

♦

The Gestapo, the Kriminalpolizei and the security services are enveloped in the mysterious aura of the political detective story.

REINHARD HEYDRICH

The Berlin stock exchange had opened for trading thirty minutes earlier. In the window display of the Union des Banques Suisses on Zürich's Bahnhof-Strasse, the Börse's numbers clicked like knitting needles. Bayer, Siemens, Thyssen, Daimler—up, up, up, up. The only stock falling on the news of détente was Krupp.

A small well-dressed crowd had gathered anxiously, as it did every morning, to watch this monitor of the Reich's economic health. Prices on the Börse had been falling for six months, and a mood close to panic had seized investors. But this week, thanks to old Joe Kennedy—he always knew a thing or two about markets, did old Joe: made half a billion dollars on Wall Street in his day—yes, thanks to Joe, the slide had stopped. Berlin was happy, so everyone was happy. Nobody paid attention to the couple walking up the street from the lake, not holding hands but close enough for their bodies to touch occasionally, followed by a weary-looking pair of gentlemen in fawn raincoats.

March had been given a short briefing on the customs and practices of Swiss banking the afternoon he had left Berlin.

"Bahnhof-Strasse is the financial center. It looks like the main shopping street, which it is. But it's the court-yards behind the shops and the offices above them that matter. That's where you'll find the banks. But you'll have to keep your eyes open. The Swiss say: the older the money, the harder to see it. In Zürich, the money's so old, it's invisible."

Beneath the paving stones and tramlines of Bahnhof-Strasse ran the catacomb of vaults in which three generations of Europe's rich had buried their wealth. March looked at the shoppers and tourists pouring along the street and wondered upon what ancient dreams and secrets, upon what bones they were treading.

These banks were small, family-run concerns: a dozen or two employees, a suite of offices, a small brass plate. Zaugg & Cie. was typical. The entrance was in a side street, behind a jewelers, scanned by a remote camera identical to the one outside Zaugg's villa. As March rang the bell beside the discreet door, he felt Charlie brush his hand.

A woman's voice over the intercom demanded his name and business. He looked up at the camera.

"My name is March. This is Fräulein Maguire. We wish to see Herr Zaugg."

"Do you have an appointment?"

"No."

"The Herr Direktor sees no one without an appointment."

"Tell him we have a letter of authorization for account number 2402."

"One moment, please."

The policemen were lounging at the entrance to the side street. March glanced at Charlie. It seemed to him her eyes were brighter, her skin more lustrous. He supposed he flattered himself. Everything looked heightened today—the trees greener, the blossoms whiter, the sky bluer, as if washed with gloss.

She was carrying a leather shoulder bag, from which

she now produced a camera, a Leica. "I think a shot for the family album."

"As you like. But leave me out of it."

"Such modesty."

She took a photograph of Zaugg's door and nameplate. The receptionist's voice snapped over the intercom, "Please come to the second floor." There was a buzz of bolts being released, and March pushed at the heavy door.

The building was an optical illusion. Small and nondescript from the outside, inside a staircase of glass and tubular chrome led to a wide reception area decorated with modern art. Hermann Zaugg was waiting to meet them. Behind him stood one of the bodyguards from last night.

"Herr March, is it?" Zaugg extended his hand. "And Fräulein Maguire?" He shook her hand, too, and gave a slight bow. "English?"

"American."

"Ah, good. Always a pleasure to meet our American friends." He was like a little doll: silver hair, shiny pink face, tiny hands and feet. He wore a suit of immaculate black, a white shirt, a pearl-gray tie. "I understand you have the necessary authorization?"

March produced the letter. Zaugg held the paper swiftly to the light and studied the signature. "Yes, indeed. The hand of my youth. I fear my script has deteriorated since those years. Come."

In his office, he directed them to a low sofa of white leather. He sat behind his desk. Now the advantage of height lay with him: the oldest trick.

March had decided to be frank. "We passed your home last night. Your privacy is well protected."

Zaugg had his hands folded on his desk. He made a noncommittal gesture with his tiny thumbs, as if to say, *You know how it is.* "I gather from my associates that you had protection of your own. Do I take it this visit is official, or private?"

"Both. That is to say, neither."

"I am familiar with the situation. Next you will tell me it is 'a delicate matter.' "

"It *is* a delicate matter."

"My speciality." He adjusted his cuffs. "Sometimes it seems to me that the whole history of twentieth-century Europe has flowed through this office. In the 1930s, it was Jewish refugees who sat where you now sit—often pathetic creatures, clutching whatever they had managed to salvage. They were usually followed closely by gentlemen from the Gestapo. In the 1940s, it was German officials of—how shall we say?—recently acquired wealth. Sometimes the very men who had once come to close the accounts of others returned to open new ones on their own behalf. In the 1950s, we dealt with the descendants of those who had vanished during the 1940s. Now, in the 1960s, I anticipate an increase in American custom, as your two great countries come together once more. The 1970s I shall leave to my son."

"This letter of authorization," said March. "How much access does it give us?"

"You have the key?"

March nodded.

"Then you have total access."

"We'd like to begin with the account records."

"Very well." Zaugg studied the letter, then picked up his telephone. "Fräulein Graf, bring in the file for 2402."

She appeared a minute later, a middle-aged woman carrying a thin sheaf of papers in a manila binding. Zaugg took it. "What do you wish to know?"

"When was the account opened?"

He looked through the papers. "July 1942. The eighth of that month."

"And who opened it?"

Zaugg hesitated. He was like a miser with his store of precious information: parting with each fact was agony. But under the terms of his own rules he had no choice.

He said at last, "Herr Martin Luther."

March was making notes. "And what were the arrangements for the account?"

"One box. Four keys."

"*Four* keys?" March's eyebrows rose in surprise. That was Luther himself, and Buhler and Stuckart, presumably. But who held the fourth key? "How were they distributed?"

"They were all issued to Herr Luther, along with four letters of authorization. Naturally, what he chose to do with them is not our concern. You appreciate that this was a special form of account—an emergency, wartime account—designed to protect anonymity, and also to allow ease of access for any heirs or beneficiaries, should anything happen to the original account holder."

"How did he pay for the account?"

"In cash. Swiss francs. Thirty years' rental. In advance. Don't worry, Herr March—there is nothing to pay until 1972."

Charlie said, "Do you have a record of transactions relating to the account?"

Zaugg turned to her. "Only the dates on which the box was opened."

"What are they?"

"July 8, 1942. December 17, 1942. August 9, 1943. April 13, 1964."

April 13! March barely suppressed a cry of triumph. His guess had been right. Luther *had* flown to Zürich at the start of the week. He scribbled the dates in his notebook. "Only four times?" he asked.

"Correct."

"And until last Monday, the box had not been opened for nearly twenty-one years?"

"That's what the dates indicate." Zaugg closed the file with a flick of annoyance. "I might add, there's nothing especially unusual about that. We have boxes here that have lain untouched for fifty years or more."

"You set up the account originally?"

"I did."

"Did Herr Luther say why he wanted to open it, or why he needed these particular arrangements?"

"Client privilege."

"I'm sorry?"

"That is privileged information between client and banker."

Charlie interrupted, "But we are your clients."

"No, Fräulein Maguire. You are beneficiaries of my client. An important distinction."

"Did Herr Luther open the box personally on each occasion?" asked March.

"Client privilege."

"Was it Luther who opened the box on Monday? What sort of mood was he in?"

"Client privilege, client privilege." Zaugg held up his hands. "We can go on all day, Herr March. Not only am I under no obligation to give you that information, it would be illegal under the Swiss Banking Code for me to do so. I have passed on all you are entitled to know. Is there anything else?"

"Yes." March closed his notebook and looked at Charlie. "We would like to inspect the box for ourselves."

A small elevator led down to the vault. There was just enough room for four passengers. March and Charlie, Zaugg and his bodyguard, stood awkwardly pressed together. Up close, the banker reeked of eau de cologne; his hair glistened beneath an oily pomade.

The vault was like a prison, or a mortuary: a white-tiled corridor that stretched ahead of them for thirty meters, with bars on either side. At the far end, next to the gate, a security guard sat at a desk. Zaugg pulled a heavy bunch of keys from his pocket, attached by a chain to his belt. He hummed as he searched for the right one.

The ceiling vibrated slightly as a tram passed overhead.

He let them into the cage. Steel walls gleamed in the neon light: banks of doors, each half a meter square.

Zaugg moved in front of them, unlocked one at waist height and stood back. The security guard pulled out a long box the size of a metal footlocker and carried it over to a table.

Zaugg said, "Your key fits the lock on that box. I shall wait outside."

"There's no need."

"Thank you, but I prefer to wait."

Zaugg left the cage and stood outside with his back to the bars. March looked at Charlie and gave her the key.

"You do it."

"I'm shaking . . ."

She inserted the key. It turned easily. The end of the box opened. She reached inside. There was a look of puzzlement on her face, then disappointment. "It's empty, I think." Her expression changed. "No . . ."

She smiled and pulled out a flat cardboard box about fifty centimeters square, five centimeters deep. The lid was sealed with red wax and had a typewritten label gummed on top: PROPERTY OF THE REICH FOREIGN MINISTRY TREATY ARCHIVE, BERLIN. And underneath, in Gothic lettering: *Geheime Reichssache.* Top Secret State Document.

*A treaty?*

March broke the seal, using the key. He lifted the lid. The interior released a scent of mingled must and incense.

Another tram passed. Zaugg was still humming, jingling his keys.

Inside the cardboard box was an object wrapped in an oilcloth. March lifted it out and laid it flat on the desk. He drew back the cloth: a panel of wood, scratched and ancient; one of the corners was broken off. He turned it over.

Charlie was next to him. She murmured, "It's beautiful."

The edges of the panel were splintered, as if it had been wrenched from its setting. But the portrait itself was perfectly preserved. A young woman, exquisite, with pale brown eyes, was glancing to the right, a string of black beads looped twice around her neck. In her lap, in long, aristocratic fingers, she held a small animal with white fur. Not a dog, exactly; more like a weasel.

Charlie was right. It *was* beautiful. It seemed to suck in the light from the vault and radiate it back. The girl's pale skin glowed—luminous, like an angel's.

"What does it mean?" whispered Charlie.

"God knows." March felt vaguely cheated. Was the deposit box no more than an extension of Buhler's treasure chamber? "How much do you know about art?"

"Not much. But there's something familiar about it. May I?" She took it, held it at arm's length. "It's Italian, I think. You see her costume—the way the neckline of her dress is cut square, the sleeves. I'd say Renaissance, very old—and very genuine."

"And very stolen. Put it back."

"Do we have to?"

"Of course. Unless you can think of a good story for the Zollgrenzschutz at Berlin airport."

Another painting: that was all! Cursing under his breath, March ran the oilcloth through his hands, checked the cardboard container. He turned the safety deposit box on its end and shook it. Nothing. The empty metal mocked him. What had he hoped for? He did not know. But something to give him a better clue than this.

"We must leave," he said.

"One minute."

Charlie propped the panel up against the box. She crouched and took half a dozen photographs. Then she rewrapped the picture, replaced it in its container and locked the box.

March called, "We've finished here, Herr Zaugg. Thank you."

Zaugg reappeared with the security guard—a fraction too quickly, March thought. He guessed the banker had been straining to overhear them.

Zaugg rubbed his hands together. "All is to your satisfaction, I trust?"

"Perfectly."

The guard slid the box back into the cavity, Zaugg locked the door and the girl with the weasel was reinterred in darkness. *"We have boxes here that have lain untouched for fifty years or more."* Was that how long it would be before she saw the light again?

They rode the elevator in silence. Zaugg shepherded them out at street level. "And so we say good-bye." He shook hands with each of them in turn.

March felt he had to say something more, should try one final tactic. "I feel I must warn you, Herr Zaugg, that two of the joint holders of this account have been murdered in the past week, and that Martin Luther himself has disappeared."

Zaugg did not even blink. "Dear me, dear me. Old clients pass away and new ones"—he gestured to them—"take their place. And so the world turns. The only thing you can be sure of, Herr March, is that whoever wins, still standing when the smoke of battle clears, will be the banks of the cantons of Switzerland. Good day to you."

They were out on the street and the door was closing when Charlie shouted, "Herr Zaugg!"

His face appeared, and before he could withdraw it, the camera clicked. His eyes were wide, his little mouth popped into a perfect *O* of outrage.

Zürich's lake was misty blue, like a picture from a fairy story—a landscape fit for sea monsters and heroes to do battle in. If only the world had been as we were promised, thought March, then castles with pointed turrets would have risen through that haze.

He was leaning against the damp stone balustrade outside the hotel, his suitcase at his feet, waiting for Charlie to settle her bill.

He wished he could have stayed longer—taken her out

on the water, explored the city, the hills; had dinner in the old town; returned to his room each night to make love to the sound of the lake . . . A dream. Fifty meters to his left, sitting in their cars, his guardians from the Swiss police yawned.

Many years ago, when March had been a young detective in the Hamburg Kripo, he had been ordered to escort a prisoner serving a life sentence for robbery, who had been given a special day pass. The man's trial had been in the papers; his childhood sweetheart had seen the publicity and written to him; had visited him in jail; had agreed to marry him. The affair had touched that streak of sentimentality that runs so strong in the German psyche. There had been a public campaign to let the ceremony go ahead. The authorities had relented. So March had taken him to his wedding, had stood handcuffed beside him throughout the service and even during the wedding pictures, like an unusually attentive best man.

The reception had been in a grim hall next to the church. Toward the end, the groom had whispered that there was a storeroom with a rug in it, that the priest had no objections . . . And March—young husband that he was—had checked the storeroom and seen that there were no windows and had left the man and his wife alone for twenty minutes. The priest—who had worked as a chaplain in Hamburg's docklands for thirty years and seen most things—had given March a grave wink.

On the way back to prison, as the high walls came into view, March had expected the man to be depressed, to plead for extra time, maybe even to dive for the door. Not at all. He had sat smiling, finishing his cigar. Standing by the Zürichsee, March realized how he had felt. It had been sufficient to know that the possibility of another life existed; one day of it had been enough.

He felt Charlie come up beside him. She kissed him lightly on the cheek.

♦

A shop at Zürich airport was piled high with brightly colored gifts—cuckoo clocks, toy skis, ashtrays glazed with pictures of the Matterhorn, chocolates. March picked out one of the musical boxes with "Birthday Greetings to Our Beloved Führer, 1964" written on the lid and took it to the counter, where a plump middle-aged woman was waiting.

"Could you wrap this and send it for me?"

"No problem, sir. Write down where you want it to go."

She gave him a form and a pencil and March wrote Hannelore Jaeger's name and address. Hannelore was even fatter than her husband, and a lover of chocolates. He hoped Max would see the joke.

The assistant wrapped the box swiftly in brown paper, with skilled fingers.

"Do you sell many of these?"

"Hundreds. You Germans certainly love your Führer."

"We do, it's true." He was looking at the parcel. It was wrapped exactly like the one he had taken from Buhler's mailbox. "You don't, I suppose, keep a record of the places to which you send these packages?"

"That would be impossible." She addressed it, stuck on a stamp and added it to the pile behind her.

"Of course. And you wouldn't remember serving an elderly German here, about four o'clock on Monday afternoon? He had thick glasses and runny eyes."

Her face was suddenly hard with suspicion. "What are you? A policeman?"

"It's of no importance." He paid for the chocolates, and also for a mug with I LOVE ZÜRICH printed on the side.

Luther would not have come all the way to Switzerland to *put* that painting in the bank vault, thought March. Even as a retired Foreign Ministry official, he could never have smuggled a package that size, stamped top secret, past the Zollgrenzschutz. He must have come here to *retrieve* something, to take it back to Germany. And as it was the first time he had visited the vault for twenty-one years, and as there were three other keys, and as he trusted nobody, he must have had doubts about whether *that other thing* would still be here.

He stood looking at the departure lounge and tried to imagine the elderly man hurrying into the terminal building, clutching his precious cargo, his weak heart beating sharply against his ribs. The chocolates must have been a message of success: so far, my old comrades, so good. What could he have been carrying? Not paintings or money, surely; they had plenty of both in Germany.

*"Paper."*

"What?" Charlie, who had been waiting for him in the concourse, turned around in surprise.

"That must have been the link. Paper. They were all civil servants. They lived their lives by paper, on paper."

He pictured them in wartime Berlin—sitting in their offices at night, circulating memos and minutes in a perpetual bureaucratic paper chase, building themselves a paper fortress. Millions of Germans had fought in the war: in the freezing mud of the steppes, in the Libyan desert, in the clear skies over southern England or—like March—at sea. But these old men had fought their war—had bled and expended their middle age—*on paper.*

Charlie was shaking her head. "You're not making any sense."

"I know. To myself, perhaps. I bought you this."

She unwrapped the mug and laughed, clasped it to her heart. "I'll treasure it."

They walked quickly through passport control. Beyond the barrier, March turned for a final look. The two Swiss policemen were watching from the ticket desk. One of them—the one who had rescued them outside Zaugg's villa—raised his hand. March waved in return.

Their flight number was being called for the last time:

*"Passengers for Lufthansa flight 227 to Berlin must report immediately . . ."*

He let his arm fall back and turned toward the departure gate.

No whisky on this flight, but coffee—plenty of it, strong and black. Charlie tried to read a newspaper but fell asleep. March was too excited to rest.

He had torn a dozen blank pages from his notebook, had ripped them in half and half again. Now he had them spread out on the plastic table in front of him. On each he had written a name, a date, an incident. He reshuffled them endlessly—the front to the back, the back to the middle, the middle to the beginning—a cigarette dangling from his lips, smoke billowing, his head in the clouds. To the other passengers, a few of whom stole curious glances, he must have looked like a man playing a particularly demented form of solitaire.

*July 1942. On the Eastern Front, the Wehrmacht has launched Operation "Blue": the offensive that will eventually win Germany the war. America is taking a hammering from the Japanese. The British are bombing the Ruhr, fighting in North Africa. In Prague, Reinhard Heydrich is recovering from an assassination attempt.*

*So: good days for the Germans, especially those in the conquered territories. Elegant apartments, girlfriends, bribes—packing cases of plunder to send back home. Corruption from high to low; from corporal to Kommissar; from alcohol to altarpieces. Buhler, Stuckart and Luther have an especially good racket in play. Buhler requisitions art treasures in the General Government, sends them under cover to Stuckart at the Interior Ministry—quite safe, for who would dare tamper with the mail of such powerful servants of the Reich? Luther smuggles the objects abroad to sell—safe again, for who would dare order the head of the Foreign Ministry's German Division to open his bags? All three retire in the 1950s, rich and honored men.*

*And then, in 1964: catastrophe.*

March shuffled his bits of paper, shuffled them again.

*On Friday, April 11, the three conspirators gather at Buhler's villa: the first piece of evidence that suggests a panic . . .*

No. That wasn't right. He leafed back through his notes to Charlie's account of her conversation with Stuckart. Of course.

*On Thursday, April 10, the day before the meeting, Stuckart stands in Bülow-Strasse and notes the number of the telephone in the booth opposite Charlotte Maguire's apartment. Armed with that, he goes to Buhler's villa on Friday. Something so terrible threatens to overwhelm them that the three men contemplate the unthinkable: defection to the United States of America. Stuckart lays out the procedure. They cannot trust the embassy, because Kennedy has stuffed it with appeasers. They need a direct link with Washington. Stuckart has it: Michael Maguire's daughter. It is agreed. On Saturday, Stuckart telephones the girl to arrange a meeting. On Sunday, Luther flies to Switzerland: not to fetch pictures or money, which they have in abundance in Berlin, but to collect something put there in the course of three visits between the summer of 1942 and the spring of 1943.*

*But already it is too late. By the time Luther has made the withdrawal, sent the signal from Zürich and landed in Berlin, Buhler and Stuckart are dead. And so he decides to disappear, taking with him whatever he removed from the vault in Zürich.*

March sat back and contemplated his half-finished puzzle. It was a version of events as valid as any other.

Charlie sighed and stirred in her sleep, twisted to rest her head on his shoulder. He kissed her hair. Today was Friday. The *Führertag* was Monday. He had only the weekend left. "Oh, my dear Fräulein Maguire," he murmured. "I fear we've been looking in the wrong place."

*"Ladies and gentlemen, we shall shortly be beginning our descent into Flughafen Hermann Göring. Please return your seats to the upright position and fold away the tables in front of you . . ."*

Carefully, so as not to wake her, March withdrew his shoulder from beneath Charlie's head, gathered up his pieces of paper and made his way, unsteadily, toward the back of the aircraft. A boy in the uniform of the Hitler Youth emerged from the lavatory and held the door open politely. March nodded, went inside and locked it behind him. A dim light flickered.

The tiny compartment stank of stale air, endlessly recycled; of cheap soap; of feces. He lifted the lid of the metal lavatory basin and dropped in the paper. The aircraft pitched and shook. A warning light pinged. ATTENTION! RETURN TO YOUR SEAT! The turbulence made his stomach lurch. Was this how Luther had felt as the aircraft dropped toward Berlin? The metal was clammy to the touch. He pulled a lever and the lavatory flushed, his notes sucked from sight in a whirlpool of blue water.

Lufthansa had stocked the toilet not with towels but with moist little paper handkerchiefs, impregnated with some sickly liquid. March wiped his face. He could feel the heat of his skin through the slippery fabric. Another vibration, like a U-boat being depth-charged. They were falling fast. He pressed his burning forehead to the cool mirror. *Dive, dive, dive . . .*

She was awake, dragging a comb through her thick hair. "I was beginning to think you had jumped."

"It's true, the thought did enter my mind." He fastened his seat belt. "But you may be my salvation."

"You say the nicest things."

"I said 'may be.' " He took her hand. "Listen. Are you sure Stuckart told you he came on *Thursday* to check out that telephone opposite your apartment?"

She thought about it for a moment. "Yes, I'm sure. I remember it made me realize: this man is serious, he's done his homework."

"That's what I think. The question is, was Stuckart acting on his own—trying to set up his own private escape route—or was calling you a course of action he had discussed with the others?"

"Does it matter?"

"Very much. Think about it. If he agreed on it with the others on Friday, it means Luther may know who you are and know the procedure for contacting you."

She pulled her hand back in surprise. "But that's crazy. He'd never trust me."

"You're right. It's crazy." They had dropped through one layer of cloud; beneath them was another. March could see the tip of the Great Hall poking through it like the top of a helmet. "But suppose Luther is still alive down there. What are his options? The airport is being watched. So are the docks, the railway stations, the border. He can't risk going directly to the American Embassy, not after what's happened about Kennedy's visit. He can't go home. What can he do?"

"I don't believe it. He could have called me Tuesday or Wednesday. Or Thursday morning. Why would he wait?"

But he could hear the doubt in her voice. He thought:

you don't *want* to believe it. You thought you were clever, looking for your story in Zürich, but all the time your story might actually have been looking for you—in Berlin.

She had turned away from him to stare through the window.

March suddenly felt deflated. He hardly knew her, despite everything. He said, "The reason he would have waited is to try to find something better to do, something safer. Who knows? Maybe he's found it."

She did not answer.

They landed in Berlin in a thin drizzle, just before two o'clock. At the end of the runway, as the Junkers turned, moisture scudded across the window, leaving threads of droplets. The swastika above the terminal building hung limp in the wet.

There were two lines at passport control: one for German and European Community nationals, one for the rest of the world.

"This is where we part," said March. He had persuaded her, with some difficulty, to let him carry her case. Now he handed it back. "What are you going to do?"

"Go back to my apartment, I guess, and wait for the telephone to ring. What about you?"

"I thought I'd arrange myself a history lesson." She looked at him, uncomprehending. He said, "I'll call you later."

"Be sure you do."

A vestige of the old mistrust had returned. He could see it in her eyes, felt her searching it out in his. He wanted to say something to reassure her. "Don't worry. A deal is a deal."

She nodded. There was an awkward silence. Then abruptly she stood on tiptoe and brushed her cheek against his. She was gone before he could think of a response.

♦

The line of returning Germans shuffled one at a time, in silence, into the Reich. March waited patiently with his hands clasped behind his back while his passport was scrutinized. In these last few days before the Führer's birthday, the border checks were always more stringent, the guards more jittery.

The eyes of the Zollgrenzschutz officer were hidden in the shade of his visor. "The Herr Sturmbannführer is back with three hours to spare." He drew a thick black line through the visa, scrawled "VOID" across it and handed the passport back. "Welcome home."

In the crowded customs hall March kept a look out for Charlie but could not see her. Perhaps they had refused to let her back into the country. He almost hoped they had: it would be safer for her.

The Zollgrenzschutz was opening every bag. Never had he seen such security. It was chaos. The passengers milling and arguing around the mounds of clothes made the hall look like an Indian bazaar. He waited his turn.

It was after three by the time March reached the left-luggage area and retrieved his case. In the toilet he changed back into his uniform, folded his civilian clothes and packed them away. He checked his Luger and slipped it into his holster. As he left, he glanced at himself in the mirror. A familiar black figure.

Welcome home.

When the sun shone the Party called it "Führer weather." The Party had no name for rain.

Nevertheless, it had been decreed, drizzle or not, that this afternoon was to be the start of the three-day holiday. And so, with National Socialist determination, the people set about their celebrations.

March was in a taxi heading south through Wedding. This was workers' Berlin, a Communist stronghold of the 1920s. In a festive gesture, the factory whistles had sounded an hour earlier than usual. Now the streets were dense with damp revelers. The *Blockwarte* had been active. From every second or third building a banner hung—mostly swastikas, but also the occasional slogan—between the iron balconies of the fortress-tenements. WORKERS OF BERLIN SALUTE THE FÜHRER ON HIS 75TH BIRTHDAY! LONG LIVE THE GLORIOUS NATIONAL SOCIALIST REVOLUTION! LONG LIVE OUR GUIDE AND FIRST COMRADE ADOLF HITLER! The back streets were a delirium of color, throbbing to the *oom-pah!* of the local SA bands. And this was only Friday. March wondered what the Wedding authorities had planned for the day itself.

During the night, on the corner of Wolff-Strasse, some rebellious spirit had added a piece of graffiti in white paint: ANYONE FOUND NOT ENJOYING THEMSELVES WILL BE SHOT. A couple of anxious-looking brownshirts were trying to clean it off.

March took the taxi as far as Fritz-Todt-Platz. His Volkswagen was still outside Stuckart's apartment, where he had parked it the night before last. He looked up at the fourth floor. Someone had drawn all the curtains.

At Werderscher-Markt, he stowed his suitcase in his office and rang the duty officer. Martin Luther had not been located.

Krause said, "Between you and me, March, Globus is driving us all fucking mad. In here every half hour, ranting and raving that someone will go to a KZ unless he gets results."

"The Herr Obergruppenführer is a very dedicated officer."

"Oh, he is, he is." Krause's voice was suddenly panicky. "I didn't mean to suggest—"

March hung up. That would give whoever was listening to his calls something to think about.

He lugged the typewriter across to his desk and inserted a single sheet of paper. He lit a cigarette.

TO: Artur Nebe, SS-Oberstgruppenführer, Reich Kriminalpolizei
FROM: X. March, SS-Sturmbannführer 4 17 64

1. I have the honor to inform you that at 10:00 this morning I attended the premises of Zaugg & Cie., Bankiers, Bahnhof-Strasse, Zurich.
2. The numbered account, whose existence we discussed yesterday, was opened by Foreign Ministry Under State Secretary Martin Luther on 7 8 42. Four keys were issued.
3. The box was subsequently opened on three occasions: 12 17 42, 8 9 43, 4 13 64.
4. On inspection by myself, the box was found to contain

March leaned back in his seat and blew a pair of neat smoke rings toward the ceiling. The thought of that painting in the hands of Nebe—dumped into his collection of bombastic, syrupy Schmutzlers and Kirchners—was repugnant, even sacrilegious. Better to leave her at peace in the darkness. He let his fingers rest on the typewriter keys for a moment, then typed:

nothing.

He wound the paper out of the typewriter, signed it and sealed it in an envelope. He called Nebe's office and was ordered to bring it up at once, personally. He hung up and stared out the window at the brickwork view.

*Why not?*

He stood and checked along the bookshelves until he found the Berlin area telephone directory. He took it down and looked up a number, which he dialed from the office next door so as not to be overheard.

A man's voice answered, "Reichsarchiv."

Ten minutes later his boots were sinking into the soft mire of Artur Nebe's office carpet.

"Do you believe in coincidences, March?"

"No, sir."

"No," said Nebe. "Good. Neither do I." He put down his magnifying glass and pushed away March's report. "I don't believe two retired public servants of the same age and rank *just happen* to choose to commit suicide rather than be exposed as corrupt. My God"—he gave a harsh little laugh—"if every government official in Berlin took that approach, the streets would be piled high with the dead. Nor do they *just happen* to be murdered in the week an American president announces he will grace us with a visit."

He pushed back his chair and hobbled across to a small bookcase lined with the sacred texts of National Socialism: *Mein Kampf*, Rosenberg's *Der Mythus des XX. Jahrhunderts*, Goebbels' *Tagebücher* . . . He pressed a switch and the front of the bookcase swung open to reveal a cocktail cabinet. The tomes, March saw now, were merely the spines of books, pasted onto the wood.

Nebe helped himself to a large vodka and returned to his desk. March continued to stand before him, neither fully at attention nor fully at ease.

"Globus works for Heydrich," said Nebe. "That's simple. Globus wouldn't wipe his own backside unless Heydrich told him it was time to do it."

March said nothing.

"And Heydrich works for the Führer most of the time, and all of the time he works for himself . . ."

Nebe held the heavy tumbler to his lips. His lizard's tongue darted into the vodka, playing with it. He was silent for a while. Then he said, "Do you know why we're greasing up to the Americans, March?"

"No, sir."

"Because we're in the shit. Here is something you won't read in the little doctor's newspapers. Twenty million settlers in the East by 1960, that was Himmler's plan. Ninety million by the end of the century. Fine. Well, we shipped them out all right. Trouble is, half of them want to come back. Consider that cosmic piece of irony, March: living space that no one wants to live in. Terrorism"—he gestured with his glass, the ice clinked—"I don't need to tell an officer of the Kripo how serious terrorism has become. The Americans supply money, weapons, training. They've kept the Reds going for twenty years. As for us: the young don't want to fight and the old don't want to work."

He shook his gray head at such follies, fished an ice cube out of his drink and sucked it noisily.

"Heydrich's mad for this American deal. He'd kill to keep it sweet. Is that what's happening here, March? Buhler, Stuckart, Luther—were they a threat to it somehow?"

Nebe's eyes searched his face. March stared straight ahead. "You're an irony yourself, March, in a way. Did you ever consider that?"

"No, sir."

" 'No, sir.' " Nebe mimicked him. "Well, consider it now. We set out to breed a generation of supermen to rule an empire, yes? We trained them to apply hard logic—pitilessly, even cruelly. Remember what the Führer once said? 'My greatest gift to the Germans is that I have taught them to think clearly.' And what happens? A few of you—perhaps the best of you—begin to turn this pitiless clear thinking onto *us*. I tell you, I'm glad I'm an old man. I fear the future." He was quiet for a minute, lost in his own thoughts. At length, disappointed, the old man picked up the magnifying glass. "Corruption it is, then." He read through March's report once more, then tore it up and dropped it into his wastebin.

Clio, the Muse of History, guarded the Reichsarchiv: an Amazonian nude designed by Adolf Ziegler, the "Reich Master of the Pubic Hair." She frowned across the Avenue of Victory toward the Soldiers' Hall, where a long queue of tourists waited to file past Frederick the Great's bones. Pigeons perched on the slopes of her immense bosom, like mountaineers on the face of a glacier. Behind her, a sign had been carved above the entrance to the archive, gold leaf inlaid on polished granite. A quotation from the Führer: FOR ANY NATION, THE RIGHT HISTORY IS WORTH 100 DIVISIONS.

Rudi Halder led March inside and up to the third floor. He pushed at the double doors and stood aside to let him walk through. A corridor with stone walls and a stone floor seemed to stretch forever.

"Impressive, yes?" In his place of work, Halder spoke in the tone of a professional historian, conveying pride and sarcasm simultaneously. "We call the style mock Teutonic. This, you will not be surprised to hear, is the largest archive building in the world. Above us: two floors of administration. On this floor: researchers' offices and reading rooms. Beneath us: *six floors* of documents. You are treading, my friend, on the history of the Fatherland. For my part, I tend Clio's lamp in here."

It was a monkish cell: small, windowless, the walls made of blocks of granite. Papers were stacked on a table in piles half a meter high; they spilled over onto the floor. Books were everywhere—several hundred of them—each sprouting a thicket of markers: multicolored bits of paper, tram tickets, pieces of cigarette carton, spent matches.

"The historian's mission: to bring out of chaos—more chaos." Halder lifted a stack of old army signals off the solitary chair, brushed the dust off the seat and gestured to March to sit.

"I need your help, Rudi—again."

Halder perched on the edge of his desk. "I don't hear from you for months, then suddenly it's twice in a week. I presume this also has to do with the Buhler business? I saw the obituary."

March nodded. "I should say now that you are talking to a pariah. You may be endangering yourself merely by meeting with me."

"That only makes it sound more fascinating." Halder put his long fingers together and cracked the joints. "Go on."

"This is a real challenge for you." March paused, took a breath. "Three men: Buhler, Wilhelm Stuckart and Martin Luther. The first two dead; the last, a fugitive. All three senior civil servants, as you know. In the summer of 1942, they opened a bank account in Zürich. At first I assumed they'd put away a hoard of money or art treasures—as you suspected, Buhler was up to his armpits in corruption—but now I think it's more likely to have been documents."

"What sort of documents?"

"Not sure."

"Sensitive?"

"Presumably."

"You've got one problem straight away. You're talking about three different ministries—Foreign, Interior and General Government, which isn't really a ministry at all. That's tons of documents. I mean it, Zavi, literally—tons."

"Do you have their records here?"

"Foreign and Interior, yes. General Government is in Krakau."

"Do you have access to them?"

"Officially—no. Unofficially . . ." He wobbled a bony hand. "Perhaps, if I'm lucky. But Zavi, it would take a lifetime simply to look through them. What are you suggesting we do?"

"There must be some clue in there. Perhaps there are papers missing."

"But this is an impossible task."

"I told you it was a challenge."

"And how soon does this 'clue' need to be discovered?"

"I need to find it tonight."

Halder made an explosive sound—of mingled incredulity, anger, scorn. March said quietly, "Rudi, in three days' time, they're threatening to put me in front of an SS Honor Court. You know what that means. *I have to find it now.*"

Halder looked at him for a moment, unwilling to believe what he was hearing, then turned away, muttering, "Let me think . . ."

March said, "Can I have a cigarette?"

"In the hallway. Not in here—this stuff is irreplaceable."

As March smoked he could hear Halder in his office, pacing up and down. He looked at his watch. Six o'clock. The long hallway was deserted. Most of the staff must have gone home to begin the holiday weekend. March tried a couple of office doors, but both were locked. The third was open. He picked up the telephone, listened to the tone and dialed nine. The tone changed: an outside line. He called Charlie's number. She answered at once.

"It's me. Are you all right?"

She said, "I'm fine. I've discovered something—just a tiny thing."

"Don't tell me over an open line. I'll talk to you later." He tried to think of something else to say, but she had replaced the receiver.

Now Halder was on the telephone, his cheerful voice echoing down the flagstone hall. "Eberhard? Good evening to you . . . Indeed, no rest for some of us. A quick question, if I may. The Interior Ministry series . . . Oh, they have been? Good. On an office basis? . . . I see. Excellent. And all that is done?"

March leaned against the wall with his eyes closed, trying not to think of the ocean of paper beneath his feet. Come on, Rudi. *Come on.*

He heard a bell tinkle as Halder hung up. A few seconds later Rudi appeared in the corridor, pulling on his jacket. A bunch of pen tops jutted from his breast pocket. "One small piece of luck. According to my colleague, the Interior Ministry files at least have been cataloged." He set off down the passage at a rapid pace. March strode beside him.

"What does that mean?"

"It means there should be a central index, showing us which papers actually crossed Stuckart's desk, and when." He hammered at the buttons beside the elevator. Nothing happened. "Looks as if they've turned this thing off for the night. We'll have to walk."

As they clattered down the wide spiral staircase, Halder shouted, "You appreciate this is completely against the rules? I'm cleared for Military, Eastern Front, not Administration, Internal. If we're stopped, you'll have to spin Security some yarn about Polizei business—something that'll take them a couple of hours to check. As for me, I'm just a poor sucker doing you a favor, right?"

"I appreciate it. How much farther?"

"All the way to the bottom." Halder was shaking his head. "An Honor Court! Dear God, Zavi, what's happened to you?"

Sixty meters beneath the ground the air circulated cool and dry and the lights were dimmed to protect the archives. "They say this place was built to withstand a direct hit from an American missile," said Halder.

"What's behind there?"

March pointed to a steel door covered with warning signs: ATTENTION! NO ADMITTANCE TO UNAUTHORIZED PERSONS! ENTRY FORBIDDEN! PASSES MUST BE SHOWN!

" 'The right history is worth a hundred divisions,' remember? That's the place where the wrong history goes. Shit. Look out."

Halder pulled March into a doorway. A security guard was coming toward them, bent like a miner in an underground shaft, pushing a metal cart. March thought he was certain to see them, but he went straight past, grunting with effort. He stopped at the metal barrier and unlocked it. There was a glimpse of a furnace, a roar of flames, before the door clanged shut behind him.

"Let's go."

As they walked, Halder explained the procedure. The archive worked on warehouse principles. Requisitions for files came down to a central handling area on each floor. Here, in ledgers a meter high and twenty centimeters thick, the main index was kept. Entered next to each file was a stack number. The stacks themselves were in fireproof storerooms leading off from the handling area. The secret, said Halder, was to know your way around the index. He paraded in front of the crimson leather spines, tapping each with his finger until he found the one he wanted, then lugged it over to the floor manager's desk.

March had once been below decks on the aircraft carrier *Grossadmiral Raeder.* The depths of the Reichsarchiv reminded him of that: low ceilings strung with lights, the sense of something vast pressing down from above. Next to the desk: a photocopier—a rare sight in Germany, where their distribution was strictly controlled to stop subversives' producing illegal literature. A dozen empty carts were drawn up by the lift shaft. He could see fifty meters in either direction. The place was deserted.

Halder gave a cry of triumph. "State Secretary: Office Files, 1939 to 1950! Oh, Christ: four hundred boxes. What years do you want to look at?"

"The Swiss bank account was opened in July '42, so let's say the first seven months of that year."

Halder turned the page, talking to himself. "Yes. I see what they've done. They've arranged the papers in four series: office correspondence, minutes and memoranda, statutes and decrees, ministry personnel . . ."

"What I'm looking for is something that connects Stuckart with Buhler and Luther."

"In that case, we'd better start with office correspondence. That should give us a feel for what was going on at the time." Halder was scribbling notes. "D/15/M/28–34. Okay. Here we go."

Storeroom D was twenty meters down on the left. Stack fifteen, section M was in the dead center of the room. Halder said, "Only six boxes, thank God. You take January to April, I'll do May to July."

The boxes, each the size of a large desk drawer, were made of cardboard. There was no table, so they sat on the floor. With his back pressed against the metal shelving, March opened the first box, pulled out a handful of papers and began to read.

You need a little luck in this life.

The first document was a letter dated January 2, from the under state secretary at the Air Ministry, regarding the distribution of gas masks to the *Reichsluftschutzbund,* the Air Raid Protection organization. The second, dated January 4, was from the Office of the Four-Year Plan and concerned the alleged unauthorized use of gasoline by senior government officials.

The third was from Reinhard Heydrich.

March saw the signature first—an angular, spidery scrawl. Then his eyes traveled to the letterhead—the Reich Main Security Office, Berlin SW 11, Prinz-Albrecht-Strasse 8—then to the date: January 6, 1942. And only then to the text:

> This is to confirm that the interagency discussion followed by luncheon originally scheduled for December 9, 1941, has now been postponed to January 20, 1942, in the office of the International Criminal Police Commission, Berlin, Am grossen Wannsee, No. 56–58.

March leafed through the other letters in the box: carbon flimsies and creamy originals; imposing letterheads—Reichschancellery, Economics Ministry, Organisation-Todt invitations to luncheons and meetings; pleas, demands, circulars. But there was nothing else from Heydrich.

March passed the letter to Halder. "What do you make of this?"

Halder frowned. "Unusual, I would say, for the Main Security Office to convene a meeting of government agencies."

"Can we find out what they discussed?"

"Should be able to. We can cross-reference it to the minutes and memoranda series. Let's see: January 20 . . ."

Halder looked at his notes, pulled himself to his feet and walked along the stack. He dragged out another box, returned with it and sat, cross-legged. March watched him flick through the contents. Suddenly, he stopped. He said slowly, "Oh my God . . ."

"What is it?"

Halder handed him a single sheet of paper on which was typed "In the interest of state security, the minutes of the interagency meeting of January 20, 1942, have been removed at the request of the Reichsführer-SS."

Halder said, "Look at the date."

March looked. It was April 6, 1964. The minutes had been extracted by Heydrich eleven days earlier.

"Can he do that—legally, I mean?"

"The Gestapo can weed out whatever it wants on the grounds of security. They usually transfer the papers to the vaults in Prinz-Albrecht-Strasse."

There was a noise in the hallway outside. Halder held up a warning finger. Both men were silent, motionless, as the guard clattered past, wheeling the empty cart back from the furnace room. They listened as the sounds faded toward the other end of the building.

March whispered, "Now what do we do?"

Halder scratched his head. "An interagency meeting at the level of state secretary . . ."

March saw what he was thinking. "Buhler and Luther would have been invited, as well?"

"It would seem logical. At that rank, they get fussy about protocol. You wouldn't have a state secretary from one ministry attending, and only a junior civil servant from another. What time is it?"

"Eight o'clock."

"They're an hour ahead in Krakau." Halder chewed his lip for a moment, then reached a decision. He stood up. "I'll telephone my friend who works at the archives in the General Government and ask if the SS has been sniffing around there in the past couple of weeks. If they haven't, maybe I can persuade him to go in tomorrow and see if the minutes are still in Buhler's papers."

"Couldn't we just check here, in the Foreign Ministry archives? In Luther's papers?"

"No. Too vast. It could take us weeks. This is the best way, believe me."

"Be careful what you say to him, Rudi."

"Don't worry. I'm aware of the dangers." Halder paused at the door. "And no smoking while I'm gone, for Christ's sake. This is the most inflammable building in the Reich."

*True enough,* thought March. He waited until Halder had gone and then began walking up and down between the stacks of boxes. He wanted a cigarette badly. His hands were trembling. He thrust them into his pockets.

What a monument to German bureaucracy this place was. Herr A, wishing to do something, asked permission of Doctor B. Doctor B. covered himself by referring it upward to Ministerialdirektor C. Then Ministerialdirektor C. shuffled it to Reichsminister D., who said he would leave it to the judgment of Herr A., who naturally went back to Doctor B. . . . The alliances and rivalries, traps and intrigues of three decades of Party rule wove in and out of these metal stacks; ten thousand webs, spun from paper threads, suspended in the cool air.

Halder was back within ten minutes. "The SS was in Krakau two weeks ago, all right." He was rubbing his hands uneasily. "Their memory is still vivid. A distinguished visitor. Obergruppenführer Globocnik himself."

"Everywhere I turn," said March, "Globocnik!"

"He flew in on a Gestapo jet from Berlin with special authorization from Heydrich, personally signed. He gave them all the shits, apparently. Shouting and swearing. Knew exactly what he was looking for: one file removed. He was out of there by lunchtime."

Globus, Heydrich, Nebe. March put his hand to his head. It was dizzying. "So here it ends?"

"Here it ends. Unless you think there might be something else in Stuckart's papers."

March looked down at the boxes. The contents seemed to him as dead as dust; dead men's bones. The thought of sifting through them anymore was repugnant to him. He needed to breathe some fresh air. "Forget it, Rudi. Thanks."

Halder stooped to pick up Heydrich's note. "Interesting that the conference was postponed, from December 9 to January 20."

"What's the significance of that?"

Halder gave him a pitying look. "Were you really so

completely cooped up in that fucking tin can we had to live in? Did the outside world never penetrate? On December 7, 1941, you blockhead, the forces of His Imperial Majesty Emperor Hirohito of Japan attacked the U.S. Pacific fleet at Pearl Harbor. On December 11, Germany declared war on the United States. Good reasons to postpone a conference, wouldn't you say?" Halder was grinning, but slowly the grin faded, to be replaced by a more thoughtful expression. "I wonder . . ."

"What?"

He tapped the paper. "There must have been an original invitation, before this one."

"So what?"

"It depends. Sometimes our friends from the Gestapo are not quite as efficient at weeding out embarrassing details as they like to think, especially if they're in a hurry . . ."

March was already standing in front of the stack of boxes, glancing up and down, his depression lifted. "Which one? Where do we start?"

"For a conference at that level, Heydrich would have had to have given the participants at least two weeks' notice." Halder looked at his notes. "That would mean Stuckart's office correspondence file for November 1941. Let me see. That should be box twenty-six, I think."

He joined March in front of the shelves and counted off the boxes until he found the one he wanted. He pulled it down, cradled it. "Don't snatch, Zavi. All in good time. History teaches us patience."

He knelt, placed the box in front of him, opened it, pulled out an armful of papers. He glanced at each in turn, placing them in a pile to his left. "Invitation to a reception given by the Italian ambassador: boring. Conference organized by Walther Darré at the Agriculture Ministry: *very* boring . . ."

He went on like that for perhaps two minutes, with March standing, watching, nervously grinding his fist into his palm. Then suddenly Halder froze. "Oh shit." He read it through again and looked up. "Invitation from Heydrich. Not boring at all, I'm afraid. Not boring at all."

The heavens were in chaos. Nebulae exploded. Comets and meteors rushed across the sky, disappeared for an instant, then detonated against green oceans of cloud.

Above the Tiergarten, the firework display was nearing its climax. Parachute flares lit up Berlin like an air raid.

As March waited in his car to turn left onto Unter den Linden, a gang of SA men lurched out in front of him. Two of them, their arms draped around each other, performed a drunken can-can in the beam of the headlights. The others banged on the Volkswagen's bodywork or pressed their faces against the windows—eyes bulging, tongues lolling; grotesque apes. March put the engine into first gear and skidded away. There was a thud as one of the dancers was sent spinning.

He drove back to Werderscher-Markt. All police leave had been canceled. Every window was ablaze with light. In the foyer, someone hailed him, but March ignored the cry. He clattered down the stairs to the basement.

Bank vaults and basements and underground storerooms . . . I am turning into a troglodyte, thought March; a cave dweller, a recluse; a robber of paper tombs.

The Gorgon of the Registry was still sitting in her lair. Did she never sleep? He showed her his ID. There were a couple of other detectives at the central desk, leafing in a languid manner through the ubiquitous manila files. March took a seat in the farthest corner of the room. He switched on an angle-poise lamp, bent its shade low over the table. From inside his tunic he drew the three sheets of paper he had taken from the Reichsarchiv.

They were poor-quality photocopies. The machine had been set too faint, the originals had been thrust into it hastily and skewed. He did not blame Rudi for that. Rudi had not wanted to make the copies at all. Rudi had been terrified. All his schoolboy bravado had vanished when he had read Heydrich's invitation. March had been obliged virtually to drag him to the photocopier. The moment the historian had finished, he had darted back into the storeroom, shoveled the papers back into the boxes, put the boxes back onto the shelves. At his insistence, they had left the archive building by a rear entrance.

"I think, Zavi, we should not see each other for a long time now."

"Of course."

"You know how it is . . ."

Halder had stood, miserable and helpless, while above their heads the fireworks had whooshed and banged. March had embraced him—"Don't feel bad. I know: your family comes first"—and quickly walked away.

Document one: Heydrich's original invitation, dated November 19, 1941:

> On 7/31/41, the Reichsmarschall of the Greater German Reich charged me, in cooperation with all the other relevant central agencies, to make all the necessary preparations with regard to organizational, technical and material measures for a complete solution of the Jewish question in Europe and to present him shortly with a complete draft proposal on this matter. I enclose a photocopy of this commission.

> In view of the extraordinary importance which must be accorded to these questions, and in the interest of securing a uniform view among the relevant central agencies of the further tasks concerned with the remaining work on this final solution, I propose to make these problems the subject of a general discussion. This is particularly necessary since from October 10 onward the Jews have been evacuated from Reich territory, including the Protectorate, to the East in a continuous series of transports.
>
> I therefore invite you to join me and others, whose names I enclose, at a discussion followed by luncheon on December 9, 1941, at 12:00 in the office of the International Criminal Police Commission, Berlin, Am grossen Wannsee, No. 56–58.

Document two: a photostat of a photostat, almost illegible in places, the words rubbed away like an ancient inscription on a tomb. Hermann Göering's directive to Heydrich, dated July 31, 1941:

> To supplement the task that was assigned to you on January 24, 1939, which dealt with the solution of the Jewish problem by emigration and evacuation in the most suitable way, I hereby charge you with making all necessary preparations with regard to organizational, technical and material matters for bringing about a complete solution of the Jewish question within the German sphere of influence in Europe.
>
> Wherever other governmental agencies are involved, these are to cooperate with you.
>
> I request you further to send me, in the near future, an overall plan covering the organizational, technical and material measures necessary for the accomplishment of the final solution of the Jewish question which we desire.

Document three: a list of the fourteen people Heydrich had invited to the conference. Stuckart was third on the list; Buhler, sixth; Luther, seventh. March recognized a couple of the other names.

He ripped a sheet from his notebook, wrote down eleven names and took it to the issuing desk. The two detectives had gone. The registrar was nowhere to be seen. He rapped on the counter and shouted, "Anyone at home?" From behind a row of filing cabinets came a guilty clink of glass on bottle. So that was her secret. She must have forgotten he was there. A moment later, she waddled into view.

"What do we have on these eleven men?"

He tried to hand her the list. She folded a pair of plump arms across a greasy tunic. "No more than three files at any one time without special authorization."

"Never mind that."

"It is not permitted."

"It is not permitted to drink alcohol on duty, either, yet you stink of it. Now get me these files."

To every man and woman, a number; to every number, a file. Not all files were held at Werderscher-Markt; only those whose lives had come into contact with the Reich Kriminalpolizei, for whatever reason, had left their spoor here. But by using the information bureau at Alexander-Platz and the obituaries of the *Völkischer Beobachter* (published annually as *The Roll Call of the Fallen*) March was able to fill in the gaps. He tracked down every name. It took him two hours.

The first man on the list was Dr. Alfred Meyer of the East Ministry. According to his Kripo file, Meyer had committed suicide in 1960 after undergoing treatment for various mental illnesses.

The second name: Dr. Georg Leibrandt, also of the East Ministry. He had died in an automobile accident in 1959, his car crushed by a truck on the autobahn between Stuttgart and Augsburg. The driver of the truck had never been found.

Erich Neumann, State Secretary in the Office of the Four-Year Plan, had shot himself in 1957.

Dr. Roland Freisler, State Secretary from the Justice Ministry: hacked to death by a maniac with a knife on the steps of the Berlin People's Court in the winter of 1954. An investigation into how his security guards had managed to let a criminal lunatic come so close had concluded that nobody was to blame. The assassin had been shot seconds after the attack on Freisler.

At this point, March had gone into the corridor for a cigarette. He drew the smoke deep into his lungs, tilted back his head and let it out slowly, as if taking a cure.

He returned to find a fresh heap of files on his desk.

SS-Oberführer Gerhard Klopfer, deputy head of the Party Chancellery, had been reported missing by his wife in May 1963; his body had been found by building site workers in southern Berlin, stuffed into a cement mixer.

Friedrich Kritzinger. That name was familiar. Of course. March remembered the scenes from the television news: the familiar taped-off street, the wrecked car, the widow supported by her sons. Kritzinger, the former Ministerialdirektor from the Reich Chancellery, had been blown up outside his home in Munich just over a month ago, on March 7. No terrorist group had yet claimed responsibility.

Two men were recorded by the *Völkischer Beobachter* as having died of natural causes. SS-Standartenführer Adolf Eichmann of the Reich Main Security Office had succumbed to a heart attack in 1961. SS-Sturmbannführer Dr. Rudolf Lange of KdS Latvia had died of a brain tumor in 1955.

Heinrich Müller. Here was another name March knew. The Bavarian policeman Müller, the former head of the Gestapo, had been on board Himmler's plane when it had crashed in 1962, killing everyone on board.

SS-Oberführer Dr. Karl Schöngarth, representing the security services of the General Government, had fallen beneath the wheels of a U-bahn train pulling into Zoo Station on April 9, 1964—barely more than a week ago. There had been no witnesses.

SS-Obergruppenführer Otto Hoffman of the Reich Security Office had been found hanging from a length of clothesline in his Spandau apartment on December 26, 1963.

That was all. Of the fourteen men who had attended the conference at Heydrich's invitation, thirteen were dead. The fourteenth—Luther—was missing.

As part of its campaign to raise public awareness about terrorism, the Propaganda Ministry had produced a series of children's cartoons. Someone had pinned one up on the notice board on the second floor. A little girl receives a parcel and begins opening it. In each succeeding picture she removes more layers of wrapping paper, until she is left holding an alarm clock with two sticks of dynamite attached to it. The last picture is of an explosion, with the caption "Warning! Do not open a parcel unless you know its contents!"

A good joke. A maxim for every German policemen. Do not open a parcel unless you know its contents. Do not ask a question unless you know the answer.

*Endlösung:* final solution. *Endlösung. Endlösung.* The word tolled in March's head as he half walked, half ran along the corridor and into his office.

*Endlösung.*

He wrenched open the drawers of Max Jaeger's desk and searched through the clutter. Max was notoriously inefficient about administrative matters, had often been reprimanded for his laxity. March prayed he had not taken the warnings to heart.

He had not.

Bless you, Max, you dumbhead.

He slammed the drawers shut.

Only then did he notice it. Someone had attached a yellow message slip to March's telephone: "Urgent. Contact the Duty Office immediately."

In the marshaling yards of the Gotenland railway station, arc lights had been set up around the body. From a distance the scene looked oddly glamorous, like a film set.

March stumbled toward it, up and down across the wooden sleepers and metal tracks, over the diesel-soaked stone.

Before it had been renamed Gotenland, this had been the Anhalter Bahnhof: the Reich's main eastern railway terminus. It was from here that the Führer had set out in his armored train *Amerika* for his wartime headquarters in East Prussia; from here, too, that Berlin's Jews—the Weisses among them—must have embarked on their journey east.

*" . . . from October 10 onward the Jews have been evacuated from Reich territory . . . to the East in a continuous series of transports . . ."*

In the air behind him, growing fainter: the platform announcements; somewhere ahead, the clank of wheels and couplings, a bleak whistle. The yard was vast—a dreamscape in the orange sodium lighting. At its center was the one patch of brilliant white. As March neared it, he could make out a dozen figures standing in front of a high-sided freight train: a couple of Orpo men, Krebs, SS surgeon Dr. Eisler, a photographer, a group of anxious officials of the Deutsche Reichsbahn—and Globus.

Globus saw him first and slowly clapped his gloved hands in muffled and mocking applause. "Gentlemen, we can relax. The heroic forces of the Kriminalpolizei have arrived to give us their theories."

One of the Orpo men sniggered.

The body, or what was left of it, was under a rough woolen blanket spread across the tracks, and also in a green plastic sack.

"May I see the corpse?"

"Of course. We haven't touched him yet. We've been waiting for you, the great detective." Globus nodded to Krebs, who pulled away the blanket.

A man's torso, neatly cropped at either end along the lines of the rails. He was belly down, slanted across the tracks. One hand had been severed, the head crushed. Both legs had also been run over, but the bloodied shards of clothing made it difficult to gauge the precise point of amputation. There was a strong smell of alcohol.

"And now you must look in here." Globus was holding the plastic sack up to the light. He opened it and brought it close to March's face. "The Gestapo does not wish to be accused of concealing evidence."

The stumps of feet, one of them still shod; a hand ending in ragged white bone and the gold band of a wristwatch. March did not close his eyes, which seemed to disappoint Globus. "Ach, well." He dropped the sack. "They're worse when they stink, when the rats have been at them. Check his pockets, Krebs."

In his flapping leather coat, Krebs squatted over the body like carrion. He reached beneath the corpse, feeling for the inside of the jacket. Over his shoulder, Krebs said, "We were informed two hours ago by the Reichsbahnpolizei that a man answering Luther's description had been seen here. But by the time we got here . . ."

"He had already suffered a fatal accident." March smiled bitterly. "How unexpected."

"Here we are, Herr Obergruppenführer." Krebs had retrieved a passport and wallet. He straightened and handed them to Globus.

"This is his passport, no question," said Globus, flicking through it. "And here are several thousand Reichsmarks in cash. Money enough for silk sheets at the Hotel Adlon. But of course the bastard couldn't show his face in civilized company. He had no choice but to sleep rough out here."

This thought appeared to give him satisfaction. He showed March the passport: Luther's ponderous face peered out from above his callused thumb. "Look at it, Sturmbannführer, then run along and tell Nebe it is all over. The Gestapo will handle everything from now on. You can clear off and get some rest." *And enjoy it,* his eyes said, *while you can.*

"The Herr Obergruppenführer is kind."

"You'll discover how kind I am, March, that much I promise you." He turned to Eisler. "Where's that fucking ambulance?"

The pathologist stood to attention. "On its way, Herr Obergruppenführer. Most definitely."

March gathered he had been dismissed. He moved toward the railway workers standing in a forlorn group about ten meters away. "Which one of you discovered the body?"

"I did, Herr Sturmbannführer." The man who stepped forward wore the dark blue tunic and soft cap of a locomotive engineer. His eyes were red, his voice raw. Was that because of the body, wondered March, or was it fear at the unexpected presence of an SS general?

"Cigarette?"

"God, yes, sir. Thanks."

The engineer took one, giving a furtive glance toward Globus, who was now talking to Krebs.

March offered him a light. "Relax. Take your time. Has this happened to you before?"

"Once." The man exhaled and looked gratefully at the cigarette. "It happens here every three or four months. The derelicts sleep under the wagons to keep out of the rain, poor devils. Then, when the engines start, instead of staying where they are, they try to get out of the way." He put his hand to his eyes. "I must have backed up over him, but I never heard a thing. When I looked back up the track, there he was—just a heap of rags."

"Do you get many derelicts in this yard?"

"Always a couple of dozen. The Reichsbahnpolizei try to keep them away, but the place is too big to patrol properly. Look over there. Some of them are making a run for it."

He pointed across the tracks. At first, March could make out nothing, except a line of cattle cars. Then, almost invisible in the shadow of the train, he spotted a movement—a shape, running jerkily, like a marionette; then another; then more. They ran along the sides of the wagons, darted into the gaps between the trucks, waited, then scampered out again toward the next patch of cover.

Globus had his back to them. Oblivious to their presence, he was still talking to Krebs, smacking his right fist into the palm of his left hand.

March watched as the stick figures worked their way to safety—then suddenly the rails were vibrating, there was a rush of wind and the view was cut off by the sleeper train to Rovno, accelerating out of Berlin. The wall of double-decker dining cars and sleeping compartments took half a minute to pass, and by the time it had cleared the little colony of drifters had vanished into the orangey dark.

# SATURDAY, APRIL 18

♦

Most of you know what it means when one hundred corpses are lying side by side. Or five hundred. Or one thousand. To have stuck it out and at the same time—apart from some exceptions caused by human weakness—to have remained decent fellows, that is what has made us hard. This is a page of glory in our history which has never to be written and is never to be written.

HEINRICH HIMMLER, *secret speech to senior SS officers, Poznan, October 4, 1943*

A crack of light showed beneath her door. Inside her apartment a radio was playing. Lovers' music—soft strings and low crooning, appropriate for the night. A party? Was this how Americans behaved in the presence of danger? He stood alone on the tiny landing and looked at his watch. It was almost two. He knocked, and after a few moments the volume was turned down. He heard her voice.

"Who is it?"

"The police."

A second or two elapsed, then there was a clatter of bolts and chains and the door opened. She said, "You're very funny," but her smile was a false one, pasted on for his benefit. In her dark eyes exhaustion showed, and also—was it?—fear? He bent to kiss her, his hands resting lightly on her waist, and immediately felt a pricking of desire. My God, he thought, she's turning me into a sixteen-year-old . . .

Somewhere in the apartment: a footstep. He looked up. Over her shoulder, a man loomed in the doorway of the bathroom. He was a couple of years younger than March:

brown brogues, sport jacket, a bowtie, a white sweater pulled on casually over a business shirt. Charlie stiffened in March's embrace and gently broke free of him. "You remember Henry Nightingale?"

He straightened, feeling awkward. "Of course. The bar in Potsdamer-Strasse."

Neither man made a move toward the other. The American's face was a mask.

March stared at Nightingale and said softly, "What's going on here, Charlie?"

She stood on tiptoe and whispered in his ear. "Don't say anything. Not here. Something's happened." Then, loudly, "Isn't this interesting, the three of us?" She took March's arm and guided him toward the bathroom. "I think you should come into my parlor."

In the bathroom, Nightingale assumed a proprietorial air. He turned on the cold water taps above the basin and the bath, increased the volume of the radio. The program had changed. Now the clapboard walls vibrated to the strains of "German jazz"—a watery syncopation, officially approved, from which all traces of "Negroid influences" had been erased. When he had arranged everything to his satisfaction, Nightingale perched on the edge of the bathtub. March sat next to him. Charlie squatted on the floor.

She opened the meeting. "I told Henry about my visitor the other morning. The one you had the fight with. He thinks the Gestapo may have planted a bug."

Nightingale gave an amiable grin. "Afraid that's the way your country works, Herr Sturmbannführer."

*Your* country . . .

"I'm sure—a wise precaution."

Perhaps he isn't younger than me, thought March. The American had thick blond hair, blond eyelashes, a ski tan. His teeth were absurdly regular—strips of enamel, gleaming white. Not many one-pot meals in *his* childhood, no watery potato soups or sawdust sausages in *that* complexion. His boyish looks embraced all ages from twenty-five to fifty.

For a few moments nobody spoke. Euro-pap filled the silence. Charlie said to March, "I know you told me not to speak to anyone. But I had to. Now you have to trust Henry and Henry has to trust you. Believe me, there's no other way."

"And naturally, we *both* have to trust you."

"Oh, come on . . ."

"All right." He held up his hands in a gesture of surrender.

Next to her, balanced on top of the lavatory, was the latest in American portable tape recorders. Trailing from one of its sockets was a cable, at the end of which, instead of a microphone, was a small suction cup.

"Listen," she said. "You'll understand." She leaned across and pressed a switch. The spools of tape began to revolve.

*"Fräulein Maguire?"*

*"Yes?"*

*"The same procedure as before, Fräulein, if you please."*

There was a click, followed by a buzz.

She pressed another switch, stopping the tape. "That was the first call. You said he'd call. I was waiting for him." She was triumphant. "It's Martin Luther."

This was a crazy business, the craziest he had ever known, like picking your way through a haunted house in the Tiergarten fun fair. No sooner did you plant your feet on solid ground than the floorboards gave way beneath you. You rounded a corner and a madman rushed out. Then you stepped back, and found that all the time you had been looking at yourself in a distorting mirror.

Luther.

March said, "What time was that?"

"Eleven forty-five."

Eleven forty-five: forty minutes after the discovery of the body on the railway tracks. He thought of the exultant look on Globus's face, and he smiled.

Nightingale said, "What's so funny?"

"Nothing. I'll explain. What happened next?"

"Exactly as before. I went over to the telephone booth and five minutes later he rang again."

March raised his hand to his brow. "Don't tell me you dragged that machine all the way across the street?"

"Damn it, I needed some proof!" She glared at him. "I knew what I was doing. Look." She stood to demonstrate. "The deck hangs from this shoulder strap. The whole thing fits under my coat. The wire runs down my sleeve. I attach the suction cup to the receiver, like this. Easy. It was dark. Nobody could have seen a thing."

Nightingale, the professional diplomat, cut in smoothly, "Never mind how you got the tape, Charlie, or whether you should have gotten it." He said to March, "May I suggest we simply let her play it?"

Charlie pushed a button. There was a fumbling noise, greatly magnified—the sound of her attaching the microphone to the telephone—and then:

*"We don't have much time. I'm a friend of Stuckart."*

An elderly voice, but not frail. A voice with the sarcastic, singsong quality of the native Berliner. He spoke exactly as March had expected. Then Charlie's voice, in her good German: *"Tell me what you want."*

*"Stuckart is dead."*

*"I know. I found him."*

A long pause. On the tape, in the background, March could hear a station announcement. Luther must have used the distraction caused by the discovery of the body to make a phone call from the Gotenland platform.

Charlie whispered, "He went so quiet, I thought I'd frightened him away."

March shook his head. "I told you. You're his only hope."

The conversation on the tape resumed.

*"You know who I am?"*

*"Yes."*

Wearily: *"You say: what do I want? What do you think I want? Asylum in your country."*

*"Tell me where you are."*

*"I can pay."*

*"That won't—"*

*"I have information. Certain facts."*

*"Tell me where you are. I'll come and get you. We'll go to the embassy."*

*"Too soon. Not yet."*

*"When?"*

*"Tomorrow morning. Listen to me. Nine o'clock. The Great Hall. Central steps. Have you got that?"*

*"Right."*

*"Bring someone from the embassy. But you must be there as well."*

*"How do we recognize you?"*

A laugh. *"No. I shall recognize* you, *show myself when* I *am satisfied."* Pause. *"Stuckart said you were young and pretty."* Pause. *"That was Stuckart all over."* Pause. *"Wear something that stands out."*

*"I have a coat. Bright blue."*

*"Pretty girl in blue. That's good. Until the morning, Fräulein."*

Click.

Purr.

The clatter of the tape machine being switched off.

"Play it again," said March.

She rewound the tape, stopped it, pressed PLAY. March looked away, watched the rusty water swirling down the plughole as Luther's voice mingled with the reedy sound of a single clarinet. *"Pretty girl in blue . . ."* When they had heard it through for the second time, Charlie reached over and turned off the machine.

"After he hung up, I came over here and dropped off the tape. Then I went back to the telephone booth and tried to call you. You weren't there. So I called Henry.

What else could I do? He says he wants someone from the embassy."

"Got me out of bed," said Nightingale. He yawned and stretched, revealing an expanse of pale, hairless leg. "What I don't understand is why he didn't just let Charlie pick him up and bring him straight to the embassy tonight."

"You heard him," said March. "Tonight is too soon. He daren't show himself. He has to wait until the morning. By then the Gestapo's search for him will probably have been called off."

Charlie frowned. "I don't understand . . ."

"The reason you couldn't reach me two hours ago was because I was on my way to the Gotenland marshaling yards, where our friends from the Gestapo were hugging themselves with joy that they had finally discovered Luther's body."

"That can't be."

"No, it can't." March pinched the bridge of his nose and shook his head. It was hard to keep his mind clear. "My guess is, Luther's been hiding in the rail yard for the past four days, ever since he got back from Switzerland, trying to work out some way of contacting you."

"But how did he survive all that time?"

March shrugged. "He had money, remember. Perhaps he picked out some drifter he thought he could trust, paid him to bring him food and drink; warm clothes, maybe. Until he had his plan."

Nightingale said, "And what was his plan, Sturmbannführer?"

"He needed someone to take his place, to convince the Gestapo he was dead." Was he talking too loudly? The Americans' paranoia was contagious. He leaned forward and said softly, "Yesterday, when it was dark, he must have killed a man. A man of roughly his age and build. Got him drunk, knocked him out—I don't know how he did it—dressed him in his clothes, gave him his wallet, his passport, his watch. Then he put him under a freight train with his hands and head on the rails. Stayed with him to make sure he didn't move until the wheels went over him. He's trying to buy himself some time. He's gambling that by nine o'clock this morning, the Berlin police will have stopped looking for him. A fair bet, I would say."

"Jesus Christ." Nightingale looked from March to Charlie and back again. "And this is the man I'm supposed to take in to the embassy?"

"Oh, it gets better than that." From the inside pocket of his tunic, March produced the documents from the archive. "On January 20, 1942, Martin Luther was one of fourteen men summoned to attend a special conference at the headquarters of Interpol in Wannsee. Since the end of the war, six of those men have been murdered, four have committed suicide, one has died in an accident, two have supposedly died of natural causes. Today only Luther is left alive. A freak of statistics, wouldn't you agree?" He handed Nightingale the papers. "As you will see, the conference was called by Reinhard Heydrich to discuss the final solution of the Jewish question in Europe. My guess is, Luther wants to make you an offer: a new life in America in exchange for documentary proof of what happened to the Jews."

The water ran. The music ended. An announcer's silky voice whispered in the bathroom, "And now, for you night lovers everywhere, Peter Kreuder and his orchestra with their version of 'Cheek to Cheek' . . ."

Without looking at him, Charlie held out her hand. March took it. She laced her fingers into his and squeezed, hard. Good, he thought, she should be afraid. Her grip tightened. Their hands were linked like parachutists' in free-fall. Nightingale had his head hunched over the documents and was murmuring "Jesus Christ, Jesus Christ" over and over again.

"We have a problem here," said Nightingale. "I'll be frank with you both. Charlie, this is off the record." He was talking so quietly they had to strain to hear. "Three days ago, the President of the United States, for whatever reason, announced he was going to visit this godforsaken country. At which point, twenty years of American foreign policy were turned upside down. Now this guy Luther, in theory—if what you say is true—could turn it upside down again, all in the space of seventy-two hours."

Charlie said, "Then at least it would end the week the right way up."

"That's a cheap crack."

He said it in English. March stared at him. "What are you saying?"

"I'm saying, Sturmbannführer, that I'm going to have to talk to Ambassador Lindbergh and Ambassador Lindbergh is going to have to talk to Washington. And my hunch is, they're both going to want a lot more proof than this"—he tossed the photocopies onto the floor—"before they open the embassy gates to a man you say is probably a common murderer."

"But Luther's offering you the proof."

"So *you* say. But I don't think Washington will want to risk all the progress that's been made on détente this week just because of your . . . theories."

Now Charlie was on her feet. "This is insane. If Luther doesn't go straight with you to the embassy, he'll be captured and killed."

"Sorry, Charlie. I can't do that." He appealed to her. "Come on! I can't take in every old Nazi who wants to defect. Not without authorization. Especially not with things as they are."

"I don't believe what I'm hearing." She had her hands on her hips and was staring at the floor, shaking her head.

"Just think it through for a minute." He was almost pleading. "This Luther character seeks asylum. The Germans say: hand him over, he's just killed a man. We say: no, because he's going to tell us what you bastards did to the Jews in the war. What will that do for the summit? No—Charlie, don't just look away. *Think.* Kennedy gained ten points in the polls *overnight* on Wednesday. How's the White House going to react if we drop this on them?" For a second time, Nightingale glimpsed the implications; for a second time he shuddered. "Jesus Christ, Charlie, what have you gotten yourself mixed up in here?"

The Americans argued back and forth for another ten minutes, then March said quietly, "Aren't you overlooking something, Mr. Nightingale?"

Reluctantly Nightingale switched his attention from Charlie to March. "Probably. You're the policeman. You tell me."

"It seems to me that all of us—you, me, the Gestapo—we all keep underestimating good Party Comrade Luther. Remember what he said to Charlie about the nine o'clock meeting: '*You must be there as well.*' "

"So what?"

"He knew this would be your reaction. Don't forget, he used to work at the Foreign Ministry. With a summit coming, he guessed the Americans might want to throw him straight back to the Gestapo. Otherwise, why did he not simply take a taxi from the airport to the embassy on Monday night? That's why he wanted to involve a journalist. As a witness." March stooped and picked up the documents. "Forgive me, as a mere *policeman* I do not understand the workings of the American press. But Charlie has her story now, does she not? She has Stuckart's death, the Swiss bank account, these papers, her tape recording of Luther . . ." He turned to her. "The fact that the American government chooses not to give Luther asylum but abandons him to the Gestapo—won't that just make it even more attractive to the degenerate U.S. media?"

Charlie said, "You bet."

Nightingale had started to look desperate again. "Hey, come on, Charlie. All that was off the record. I never said I agreed with any of it. There are plenty of us at the embassy who don't think Kennedy should come here. At all. Period." He fiddled with his bowtie. "But this situation—it's tricky as hell."

Eventually they reached an agreement. Nightingale would meet Charlie on the steps of the Great Hall at five minutes to nine. Assuming Luther turned up, they would hustle him quickly into a car, which March would drive. Nightingale would listen to Luther's story and decide on the basis of what he heard whether to take him to the embassy. He would not tell the ambassador, Washington or anyone else what he was planning to do. Once they were inside the embassy compound, it would be up to what he called "higher authorities" to decide Luther's fate—but they would have to act in the knowledge that Charlie had the whole story, and would print it. Charlie was confident the State Department would not dare turn Luther away.

Exactly how they would smuggle him out of Germany was another matter.

"We have methods," said Nightingale. "We *have* handled defectors before. But I'm not discussing it. Not in front of an SS officer. However trustworthy." It was Charlie, he said, whom he was most worried about. "You're going to come under a lot of pressure to keep your mouth shut."

"I can handle it."

"Don't be so sure. Kennedy's people—they fight dirty. All right. Let's suppose Luther *has* got something. Let's say it stirs everybody up—speeches in Congress, demonstrations, editorials—this is election year, remember? So suddenly the White House is in trouble over the summit. What do you think they're going to do?"

"I can handle it."

"They're going to tip a truckful of shit over your head, Charlie, and over this old Nazi of yours. They'll say: what's he got that's new? The same old story we've heard for twenty years, plus a few documents, probably forged by the Communists. Kennedy'll go on TV, and he'll say,

'My fellow Americans, ask yourselves: why has all this come up now? In whose interest is it to disrupt the summit?' " Nightingale leaned close to her, his face a few centimeters from hers. "First off, they'll put Hoover and the FBI on to it. Know any left-wingers, Charlie? Any Jewish militants? Slept with any? Because sure as hell, they'll find a few who say you have, whether you've ever met them or not."

"Screw you, Nightingale." She shoved him away with her fist. "Screw *you*!"

Nightingale really was in love with her, thought March. Lost in love, hopelessly in love. And she knew it, and she played on it. He remembered that first night he had seen them together in the bar: how she had shrugged off his restraining hand. Tonight: how he had looked at March when he saw him kissing her; how he had absorbed her temper, watching her with his moony eyes. In Zürich, her whisper: *"You asked if he was my lover . . . He'd like to be."*

And now, on her doorstep, in his raincoat: hovering, uncertain, reluctant to leave them behind together, then finally disappearing into the night.

He would be there to meet Luther tomorrow, thought March, if only to make sure she was safe.

After the American had gone they lay side by side on her narrow bed. For a long time neither spoke. The streetlights cast long shadows, the window frame slanted across the ceiling like cell bars. In the slight breeze the curtains trembled. Once there were the sounds of shouts and car doors slamming—revelers returning from watching the fireworks.

They listened to the voices fade along the street, then March whispered, "Last night on the telephone—you said you had found something."

She touched his hand, climbed off the bed. In the living room he could hear her rummaging among the heaps of papers. She returned half a minute later carrying a large coffee-table book. "I bought this on the way back from the airport." She sat on the edge of the bed, switched on the lamp, turned the pages. "There." She handed March the open book.

It was a reproduction, in black and white, of the painting in the Swiss bank vault. The monochrome did not do it justice. He marked the page with his finger and closed the book to read its title. *The Art of Leonardo da Vinci,* by Professor Arno Braun of the Kaiser Friedrich Museum, Berlin.

"My God."

"I know. I thought I recognized it. Read it."

"*Lady with an Ermine,*" the scholars called it. "One of the most mysterious of all Leonardo's works." It was believed to have been painted circa 1483–86, and "believed to show Cecilia Gallerani, the young mistress of Ludovico Sforza, ruler of Milan." There were two published references to it: one in a poem by Bernardino Bellincioni (died 1492); the other, an ambiguous remark about an "immature" portrait, written by Cecilia Gallerani herself in a letter dated 1498. "But sadly for the student of Leonardo, the real mystery today is the painting's whereabouts. It is known to have entered the collection of the Polish Prince Adam Czartoryski in the late eighteenth century, and was photographed in Krakau in 1932. Since then it has disappeared into what Karl von Clausewitz so eloquently called 'the fog of war.' All efforts by the Reich authorities to locate it have so far failed, and it must now be feared that this priceless flowering of the Italian Renaissance is lost to mankind forever."

He closed the book. "Another story for you, I think."

"And a good one. There are only nine undisputed Leonardos in the world." She smiled. "If I ever get out of here to write it."

"Don't worry. We'll get you out." He lay back and

closed his eyes. After a few moments he heard her put down the book, then she joined him on the bed, wriggling close to him.

"And you?" she breathed into his ear. "Will you come out with me?"

"We can't talk now. Not here."

"Sorry. I forgot." Her tongue tip touched his ear.

A jolt, like electricity.

Her hand rested lightly on his leg. With her fingers, she traced the inside of his thigh. He started to murmur something, but again, as in Zürich, she placed a finger to his lips.

"The object of the game is not to make a sound."

Later, unable to sleep, he listened to her: the sigh of her breath, the occasional mutter—far away and indistinct. In her dream, she turned toward him, groaning. Her arm was flung across the pillow, shielding her face. She seemed to be fighting some private battle. He stroked the tangle of her hair, waiting until whatever demon it was had released her. Then he slipped out from beneath the sheets.

The kitchen floor was cold to his naked feet. He opened a couple of cupboards. Dusty crockery and a few half-empty packages of food. The refrigerator was ancient, might have been borrowed from some institute of biology, its contents blue furred and mottled with exotic molds. Cooking, it was clear, was not a priority around here. He boiled a kettle, rinsed a mug and heaped in three spoonsful of instant coffee.

He wandered through the apartment sipping the bitter drink. In the living room he stood beside the window and pulled back the curtain a fraction. Bülow-Strasse was deserted. He could see the telephone booth, dimly illuminated, and the shadows of the station entrance behind it. He let the curtain fall back.

America. The prospect had never occurred to him before. When he thought of it, his brain reached automatically for the images Doctor Goebbels had planted there. Jews and Negroes. Top-hatted capitalists and smokestack factories. Beggars on the streets. Striptease bars. Gangsters shooting at one another from vast automobiles. Smoldering tenements and modern jazz bands, wailing across the ghettos like police sirens. Kennedy's toothy smile. Charlie's dark eyes and white limbs. *America.*

He went into the bathroom. The walls were stained by steam clouds and splashes of soap. Bottles everywhere, and tubes, and small pots. Mysterious feminine objects of glass and plastic. It was a long time since he had seen a woman's bathroom. It made him feel clumsy and foreign—the heavy-footed ambassador of some other species. He picked up a few things and sniffed at them, squeezed a drop of white cream onto his finger and rubbed at it with his thumb. This smell of her mingled with the others already on his hands.

He wrapped himself in a large towel and sat down on the floor to think. Three or four times before dawn he heard her shout out in her sleep.

Just before seven he went down into Bülow-Strasse. His Volkswagen was parked a hundred meters up the street, on the left, outside a butcher's shop. The owner was hanging plump carcasses in the window. A heaped tray of bloodred sausages at his feet reminded March of something.

Globus's fingers, that's what it was—those immense raw fists.

He bent over the backseat of the Volkswagen, tugging his suitcase toward him. As he straightened, he glanced quickly in either direction. There was nothing special to see—just the usual signs of Saturday morning. Most shops would open as normal but then close early in honor of the holiday.

Back in the apartment he made more coffee, set a mug on the bedside table beside Charlie and went into the bathroom to shave. After a couple of minutes he heard her come in behind him. She clasped her arms around his chest and squeezed, her breasts pressing into his bare back. Without turning around he kissed her hand and wrote in the steam on the mirror: PACK. NO RETURN. As he wiped away the message, he saw her clearly for the first time—hair tangled, eyes half closed, the lines of her face still soft with sleep. She nodded and ambled back into the bedroom.

He dressed in his civilian clothes as he had for Zürich, but with one difference. He slipped his Luger into the right-hand pocket of his trench coat. The coat—old surplus Wehrmacht issue, picked up cheaply long ago—was baggy enough for the weapon not to show. He could even hold the pistol and aim it surreptitiously through the material of the pocket, gangster-style: "Okay, buddy, let's go." He smiled to himself. America again.

The possible presence of a microphone cast a shadow over their preparations. They moved quietly around the apartment without speaking. At ten past eight she was ready. March got the radio from the bathroom, placed it on the table in the sitting room and turned up the volume. *"From the pictures sent in for exhibition, it is clear that the eye of some men shows them things other than as they are—that there really are men who on principle feel meadows to be blue, the heavens green, the clouds sulfur yellow . . ."* It was the custom at this time to rebroadcast the Führer's most historic speeches. They replayed this one every year—the attack on modern painters, delivered at the inauguration of the House of German Art in 1937.

Ignoring her silent protests, March picked up her suitcase as well as his own. She donned her blue coat. From one shoulder she hung a leather bag. Her camera dangled from the other. On the threshold, she turned for a final look.

*"Either these 'artists' do really see things in this way and believe in that which they represent—then one has but to ask how the defect in vision arose, and if it is hereditary the Minister of the Interior will have to see to it that so ghastly a defect shall not be allowed to perpetuate itself—or, if they do* not *believe in the reality of such impressions but seek on other grounds to impose them upon the nation, then it is a matter for a criminal court."*

They closed the door on a storm of laughter and applause.

As they went downstairs, Charlie whispered, "How long does this go on?"

"All weekend."

"That will please the neighbors."

"Ah, but will anyone dare ask you to turn it down?"

At the foot of the stairs, as still as a sentry, stood the concierge—a bottle of milk in one hand, a copy of the *Völkischer Beobachter* tucked under her arm. She spoke to Charlie but stared at March: "Good morning, Fräulein."

"Good morning, Frau Schustermann. This is my cousin from Aachen. We are going to record the images of spontaneous celebration on the streets." She patted her camera. "Come on, Harald, or we'll miss the beginning."

The old woman continued to scowl at March, and he wondered if she recognized him from the other night. He doubted it: she would remember only the uniform. After a few moments she grunted and waddled back into her apartment.

"You lie very plausibly," said March when they were out on the street.

"A journalist's training." They walked quickly toward the Volkswagen. "It was lucky you weren't wearing your uniform. Then she really would have had some questions."

"There's no possibility of Luther getting into a car driven by a man in the uniform of an SS-Sturmbannführer. Tell me: do I look like an embassy chauffeur?"

"Only a very distinguished one."

He stowed the suitcases in the trunk of the car. When he was settled in the front seat, before he switched on the engine, he said, "You can never go back, you realize that? Whether this works or not. Assisting a defector—they'll think you're a spy. It won't be a question of deporting you. It's much more serious than that."

She waved her hand dismissively. "I never cared for that place anyway."

He turned the key in the ignition and they pulled out into the morning traffic.

Driving carefully, checking every thirty seconds to make sure they were not being followed, they reached Adolf-Hitler-Platz at twenty to nine. March executed one circuit of the square. Reich Chancellery, Great Hall, Wehrmacht High Command building—all seemed as it should be: masonry gleaming, guards marching; everything was as crazily out of scale as ever.

A dozen tour buses were already disgorging their awed cargoes. A crocodile file of children made its way up the snowy steps of the Great Hall, toward the red granite pillars, like a line of ants. In the center of the Platz, beneath the great fountains, were piles of crush barriers, ready to be put into position on Monday morning, when the Führer was due to drive from the chancellery to the hall for the annual ceremony of thanksgiving. Afterward he would return to his residence to appear on the balcony. German television had erected a scaffolding tower directly opposite. Live broadcast vans clustered around its base.

March pulled into a parking space close to the tour buses. From here he had a clear view across the lanes of traffic to the center of the hall.

"Walk up the steps," he said. "Go inside, buy a guidebook, look as natural as you can. When Nightingale appears, bump into him: you're old friends, isn't it marvelous, you stop and talk for a while."

"What about you?"

"When I see you've made contact with Luther, I'll drive across and pick you up. The rear doors are unlocked. Keep to the lower steps, close to the road. And don't let him drag you into a long conversation—we need to get out of here fast."

She was gone before he could wish her luck.

Luther had chosen his ground well. There were vantage points all around the Platz: the old man would be able to watch the steps without showing himself. Nobody would pay any attention to three strangers meeting. And if something did go wrong, the throngs of visitors offered the ideal cover for escape.

March lit a cigarette. Twelve minutes to go. He watched as Charlie climbed the long flight of steps. She paused at the top for breath, then turned and disappeared inside.

Everywhere activity. White taxis and the long green Mercedeses of the Wehrmacht High Command circled the Platz. The television technicians checked their camera angles and shouted instructions at one another. Stallholders arranged their wares—coffee, sausages, postcards, newspapers, ice cream. A squadron of pigeons wheeled overhead in tight formation and fluttered in to land beside one of the fountains. A couple of young boys in Pimpf uniforms ran toward them, flapping their arms, and March thought of Pili—a stab—and closed his eyes for an instant, confining his guilt to the dark.

At five to nine exactly she came out of the shadows and began descending the steps. A man in a fawn raincoat strode toward her. Nightingale.

*Don't make it too obvious, idiot . . .*

She stopped and threw her arms wide—a perfect mime of surprise. They began talking.

Two minutes to nine.

Would Luther come? If so, from which direction? From the chancellery to the east? The High Command building to the west? Or directly north, from the center of the Platz?

Suddenly, at the window beside him, a gloved hand appeared. Attached to it: the body of an Orpo traffic cop in leather uniform.

March wound down the window.

The cop said, "Parking here suspended."

"Understood. Two minutes and I'm out of here."

"Not two minutes. Now." The man was a gorilla, escaped from the Berlin Zoo.

March tried to keep his eyes on the steps, maintain a conversation with the Orpo man, while pulling his Kripo ID out of his inside pocket.

"You're screwing up badly, friend," he hissed. "You're in the middle of a Sipo surveillance operation and, I have to tell you, you're blending into the background as well as a prick in a nunnery."

The cop grabbed the ID and held it close to his eyes. "Nobody told me about any operation, Sturmbannführer. What operation? Who's being watched?"

"Communists. Freemasons. Students. Slavs."

"Nobody told me about it. I'll have to check."

March clutched the steering wheel to steady his shaking hands. "We're observing radio silence. You break it and I guarantee you, Heydrich personally will have your balls for cuff links. Now: my ID."

Doubt clouded the Orpo man's face. For an instant he almost looked ready to drag March out of the car, but then he slowly returned the ID. "I don't know . . ."

"Thank you for your cooperation, Unterwachtmeister." March wound up his window, ending the discussion.

One minute past nine. Charlie and Nightingale were still talking. He glanced into his mirror. The cop had walked a few paces, had stopped and was staring back at the car. He looked thoughtful, then made up his mind, went over to his bike and picked up his radio.

March swore. He had two minutes at the outside.

Of Luther: no sign.

Then he saw him.

A man with thick-framed glasses, wearing a shabby overcoat, had emerged from the Great Hall. He stood, peering around him, his hand touching one of the granite pillars as if afraid to let go. Then, hesitantly, he began to make his way down the steps.

March switched on the engine.

Charlie and Nightingale still had their backs to him. He was heading toward them.

*Come on. Come on. Look around at him, for God's sake.*

At that moment Charlie did turn. She saw the old man and recognized him. Luther's arm came up, like that of an exhausted swimmer reaching for the shore.

*Something is going to go wrong,* thought March suddenly. *Something is not right. Something I haven't thought of . . .*

Luther had barely five meters to go when his head disappeared. It vanished in a puff of moist red sawdust and then his body was pitching forward, rolling down the steps, and Charlie was putting up her hand to shield her face from the sunburst of blood and brain.

A beat. A beat and a half. Then the crack of a high-velocity rifle howled around the Platz, scooping up the pigeons, scattering them like gray litter across the square.

People started to scream.

March threw the car into gear, flashed his indicator and cut sharply into the traffic, ignoring the outraged hooting—across one lane, and then another. He drove like a man who believed himself invulnerable, as if faith and willpower alone would protect him from collision. He could see a little group forming around the body, which was leaking blood and tissue down the steps. He could hear police whistles. Figures in black uniforms were converging from all directions—Globus and Krebs among them.

Nightingale had Charlie by the arm and was propelling her away from the scene, toward the road, to where March was braking to a halt. The diplomat wrenched open the door and threw her into the backseat, crammed himself in after her. The door slammed. The Volkswagen accelerated away.

*We were betrayed.*

*Fourteen men summoned; now fourteen dead.*

*Luther's hand outstretched, the fountain bursting from his neck, his trunk exploding, toppling forward. Globus and Krebs running. Secrets scattered in that shower of tissue; salvation gone . . .*

*Betrayed . . .*

He drove to an underground parking lot just off Rosen-Strasse, close to the Börse, where the Synagogue had once stood—a favorite spot of his for meeting informers. Was there anywhere more lonely? He took a ticket from the machine and pointed the car down the steep ramp. The tires cried out against the concrete; the headlights picked out ancient stains of oil and carbon on the floors and walls, like cave paintings.

Level two was empty—on Saturdays, the financial sector of Berlin was a desert. March parked in a central bay. When the engine died, the silence was complete.

Nobody said anything. Charlie was dabbing at her coat with a tissue. Nightingale was leaning back with his eyes closed. Suddenly March slammed his fists down on the top of the steering wheel.

"Whom did you tell?"

Nightingale opened his eyes. "Nobody."

"The ambassador? Washington? The resident spy master?"

"I told you: nobody." There was anger in his voice.

"This is no help," said Charlie.

"It's also insulting and absurd. Christ, you two—"

"Consider the possibilities." March counted them off on his fingers. "Luther betrayed *himself* to somebody—ridiculous. The telephone booth in Bülow-Strasse was tapped—impossible: even the Gestapo does not have the resources to bug every public telephone in Berlin. Very well. So was our discussion last night overheard? Unlikely, as we could hardly hear it ourselves!"

"Why does it have to be this big conspiracy? Maybe Luther was just followed."

"Then why not just pick him up? Why shoot him in public, at the very moment of contact?"

"He was looking straight at me." Charlie covered her face with her hands.

"It needn't have been me," said Nightingale. "The leak could have come from one of you two."

"How? We were together all night."

"I'm sure you were." He spat out the words and fumbled for the door. "I don't have to take this sort of shit from you. Charlie—you'd better come back to the embassy with me. Now. We'll get you on a flight out of Berlin tonight and just hope to Christ no one connects us with any of this." He waited. "Come on."

She shook her head.

"If not for your sake, then think of your father."

She was incredulous. "What's my father got to do with it?"

Nightingale hauled himself out of the Volkswagen. "I should never have let myself be talked into this insanity. You're a fool. As for him"—he nodded toward March—"he's a dead man."

He walked away from the car, his footsteps richocheting around the deserted lot—loud at first, but fast becoming fainter. There was the clang of a metal door banging shut, and he was gone.

March looked at Charlie in the mirror. She seemed very small, huddled up in the backseat.

Far away: another noise. The barrier at the top of the ramp was being raised. A car was coming. March felt suddenly panicky, claustrophobic. Their refuge could equally well serve as a trap.

"We can't stay here," he said. He switched on the engine. "We have to keep moving."

"In that case, I want to take more pictures."

"Do you have to?"

"You assemble your evidence, Sturmbannführer, and I'll assemble mine."

He glanced at her again. She had put aside her tissue and was staring at him with a fragile defiance. He took his foot off the brake. Crossing the city was risky, no question, but what else were they to do? Lie behind a locked door waiting to be caught?

He swung the car around in a circle and headed toward the exit as headlights flashed in the gloom behind them.

They parked beside the Havel and walked to the shore. March pointed to the spot where Buhler's body had been found. Her camera clicked as Spiedel's had four days before, but there was little left to record. A few footprints were just visible in the mud. The grass was flattened slightly where the corpse had been dragged from the water. In another day or two even these signs would disappear. She turned away from the water and drew her coat around her, shivering.

It was too dangerous to drive to Buhler's villa, so he stopped at the end of the causeway with the engine running. She leaned out to take a picture of the road leading to the island. The red-and-white pole was down. No sign of the sentry.

"Is that it?" she asked. "*Life* won't pay much for these."

He thought for a moment. "Perhaps there is another place."

No. 56–58 Am grossen Wannsee turned out to be a large nineteenth-century mansion with a pillared façade. It no longer housed the German headquarters of Interpol. At some point in the years since the war it had become a girls' school. March looked this way and that, up and down the leafy street, where the blossom was in full pink bloom, and tried the gate. It was unlocked. He gestured to Charlie to join him.

"We are Herr and Frau March," he said as he pushed open the gate. "We have a daughter—"

Charlie nodded. "Yes, of course. Heidi. She's seven. With braids—"

"She is unhappy at her present school. This one was recommended. We wanted to look around." They stepped into the grounds. March closed the gates behind them.

She said, "Naturally, if we're trespassing, we apologize . . ."

"But surely Frau March does not look old enough to have a seven-year-old daughter?"

"She was seduced at an impressionable age by a handsome investigator . . ."

"A likely story."

The gravel drive looped around a circular flower bed. March tried to picture it as it might have looked in January 1942. A dusting of snow on the ground, perhaps, or frost. Bare trees. A couple of guards shivering by the entrance. The government cars, one after the other, crunching over the icy gravel. An adjutant saluting and stepping forward to open the doors. Stuckart: handsome and elegant. Buhler: his lawyer's notes carefully arranged in his briefcase. Luther: blinking behind his thick spectacles. Did their breath hang in the air after them? And Heydrich. Would he have arrived first, as host? Or last, to demonstrate his power? Had the cold imparted color even to those pale cheeks?

The house was barred and deserted. While Charlie took a picture of the entrance, March picked his way through low shrubbery to peer through a window. Rows of dwarf-sized desks with dwarf-sized chairs upended and stacked on top. A pair of blackboards from which the pupils were being taught the Party's special grace. On one:

*Before meals—*
Führer, my Führer, bequeathed to me by the Lord,
Protect and preserve me as long as I live!
Thou hast rescued Germany from deepest distress,
I thank thee today for my daily bread.
Abideth thou long with me, forsaketh me not,
Führer, my Führer, my faith and my light!
*Heil, mien Führer!*

On the other:

*After meals—*
Thank thee for this bountiful meal,
Protector of youth and friend of the aged!
I know thou hast cares, but worry not,
I am with thee by day and by night.
Lay thy head in my lap,
Be assured, my Führer, that thou art great.
*Heil, mein Führer!*

Childish paintings decorated the walls—blue meadows, green skies, clouds of sulfur yellow. Children's art was perilously close to degenerate art; such perversity would have to be knocked out of them. . . . March could smell the school smell even from here: the familiar compound of chalk dust, wooden floors and stale institutional food. He turned away.

Someone in a neighboring garden had lit a bonfire. Pungent white smoke—wet wood and dead leaves—drifted across the lawn at the back of the house. A wide flight of steps flanked by stone lions with frozen snarls led down to the lawn. Beyond the grass, through the trees, lay the dull, glassy surface of the Havel. They were facing south. Schwanenwerder, less than half a kilometer away, would be just visible from the upstairs windows. When Buhler had bought his villa in the early 1950s, had the proximity of the two sites been a motive? Had he been the villain being drawn back to the scene of his crime? If so, what crime had it been, exactly?

March bent and dug up a handful of soil, sniffed at it, let it run through his fingers. The trail had gone cold years ago.

At the bottom of the garden were a couple of wooden barrels, green with age, used by the gardener to collect rainwater. March and Charlie sat on them side by side, legs dangling, looking across the lake. He was in no hurry to move on. Nobody would look for them here. There was something indescribably melancholy about it all—the silence, the dead leaves blowing across the lawn, the smell of the smoke—something that was the opposite of spring. It spoke of autumn, of the end of things.

He said, "Did I tell you that before I went away to sea, there were Jews in our town? When I got back, they were all gone. I asked about it. People said they had been evacuated to the East. For resettlement."

"Did they believe that?"

"In public, of course. Even in private it was wiser not to speculate. And easier. To pretend it was true."

"Did *you* believe it?"

"I didn't think about it." He was silent, then: "Who cares?" he said suddenly. "Suppose everyone knew all the details. Who would care? Would it really make any difference?"

"Someone thinks so," she reminded him. "That's why everyone who attended Heydrich's conference is dead. Except Heydrich."

He looked back at the house. His mother, a firm believer in ghosts, had used to tell him that brickwork and plaster soaked up history, stored what they had witnessed like a sponge. Since then March had seen his share of places in which evil had been done, and he did not believe it. There was nothing especially wicked about Am grossen Wannsee 56–58. It was just a businessman's large mansion, now converted into a girls' school. So what were the walls absorbing now? Teenage crushes? Geometry lessons? Exam nerves?

He pulled out Heydrich's invitation. "A discussion followed by luncheon." Starting at noon. Ending at—what?—three or four in the afternoon. It would have been growing dark by the time they left. Yellow lamps in the windows; mist from the lake. Fourteen men. Well fed; maybe some of them tipsy on the Gestapo's wine. Cars to take them back to central Berlin. Chauffeurs who had waited a long time outside, with cold feet and noses like icicles . . .

And then, less than five months later, in Zürich in the heat of midsummer, Martin Luther had marched into the offices of Hermann Zaugg, banker to the rich and frightened, and opened an account with four keys.

"I wonder why he was empty-handed."

"What?" She was distracted. He had interrupted her thoughts.

"I always imagined Luther carrying a small suitcase of some sort. Yet when he came down the steps to meet you, he was empty-handed."

"Perhaps he had stuffed everything into his pockets."

"Perhaps." The Havel looked solid; a lake of mercury. "But he must have landed from Zürich with luggage of some sort. He had spent a night out of the country. And he had picked up something at the bank."

The wind stirred in the trees. March looked around. "He was a suspicious old bastard, after all. It would have been in his character to have kept back the really valuable material. He wouldn't have risked giving the Americans everything at once—otherwise, how could he have bargained?"

A jet passed low overhead, dropping toward the airport, the pitch of its engines descending with it. Now *that* was a sound that had not existed in 1942 . . .

Suddenly he was on his feet, lifting her down to join him, and then he was striding up the lawn toward the house and she was following—stumbling, laughing, shouting at him to slow down.

He parked the Volkswagen beside the road in Schlachtensee and sprinted into the telephone booth. Max Jaeger was not replying, neither at Werderscher-Markt nor at his home. The lonely purr of the unanswered phone made March want to reach someone, anyone.

He tried Rudi Halder's number. Perhaps he could apologize, somehow hint that it had been worth the risk. Nobody was in. He looked at the receiver. What about Pili? Even the boy's hostility would be contact of a sort. But in the bungalow in Lichtenrade there was no response either.

The city had shut down on him.

He was halfway out of the booth when, on impulse, he turned back and dialed the number of his own apartment. On the second ring, a man answered.

"Yes?" It was the Gestapo: Krebs's voice. "March? I know it's you! Don't hang up!"

He dropped the receiver as if it had bitten him.

Half an hour later he was pushing through the scuffed wooden doors into the Berlin city morgue. Without his uniform he felt naked. A woman was crying softly in one corner, a female police auxiliary sitting stiffly beside her, embarrassed at this display of emotion in an official place. He showed the attendant his ID and asked about Martin Luther. The man consulted a set of dogeared notes.

"Male, mid-sixties, identified as Luther, Martin. Brought in just after midnight. Railway accident."

"What about the shooting this morning, the one in the Platz?"

The attendant sighed, licked a nicotined forefinger and turned a page. "Male, mid-sixties, identified as Stark, Alfred. Came in an hour ago."

"That's the one. How was he identified?"

"ID in his pocket."

"Right." March moved decisively toward the elevator, forestalling any objection. "I'll make my own way down."

It was his misfortune, when the elevator doors opened, to find himself confronted by SS surgeon August Eisler.

"March!" Eisler looked shocked and took a pace backward. "The word is, you've been arrested."

"The word is wrong. I'm working undercover."

Eisler was staring at his civilian suit. "What as? A pimp?" This amused the SS surgeon so much that he had to take off his spectacles and wipe his eyes. March joined in his laughter.

"No, a pathologist. I'm told the pay is good and the hours are nonexistent."

Eisler stopped smiling. "*You* can say that. *I've* been here since midnight." He dropped his voice. "A very senior man. Gestapo operation. Hush-hush." He tapped the side of his long nose. "I can say nothing."

"Relax, Eisler. I'm aware of the case. Did Frau Luther identify the remains?"

Eisler looked disappointed. "No," he muttered. "We spared her that."

"And Stark?"

"My, my, March—you *are* well informed. I'm on my way to deal with him now. Would you care to join me?"

In his mind March saw again the exploding head, the thick spurt of blood and brain. "No. Thank you."

"I thought not. What was he shot with? A Panzerfaust?"

"Have they caught the killer?"

"You're the investigator. You tell me. 'Don't probe too deeply' was what I heard."

"Stark's effects. Where are they?"

"Bagged and ready to go. In the property room."

"Where's that?"

"Follow the corridor. Fourth door on the left."

March set off. Eisler shouted after him, "Hey, March! Save me a couple of your best whores!" The pathologist's high-pitched laughter pursued him down the passage.

The fourth door on the left was unlocked. He checked to make sure he was unobserved, then let himself in.

It was a small storeroom, three meters wide, with just enough room for one person to walk down the center. On either side of the gangway were racks of dusty metal shelving heaped with bundles of clothing wrapped in thick polyurethane. There were suitcases, handbags, umbrellas, artificial legs, a wheelchair—grotesquely twisted—hats . . . From the morgue the deceased's belongings were usually collected by the next of kin. If the circumstances were suspicious, they would be taken away by the investigators or sent directly to the forensic laboratories in Schönweld. March began inspecting the plastic tags, each of which recorded the time and place of death and the name of the victim. Some of the stuff here went back years—pathetic bundles of rags and trinkets, the final bequests of corpses nobody cared about, not even the police.

How typical of Globus not to admit to his mistake. The infallibility of the Gestapo must be preserved at all costs! Thus Stark's body would continue to be treated as Luther's, while Luther's would go to a pauper's grave as that of the drifter Stark.

March tugged at the bundle closest to the door, turned the label to the light. *4/18/64. Adolf-Hitler-Pl. Stark, Alfred.*

So Luther had left the world like the lowest inmate of a KZ—violently, half starved, in someone else's filthy clothes, his body unhonored, with a stranger picking over his belongings after his death. Poetic justice—about the only sort of justice to be found.

He pulled out his pocketknife and slit the bulging plastic. The contents spilled over the floor like guts.

He did not care about Luther. All he cared about was how, in the hours between midnight and nine that morning, Globus had discovered that Luther was still alive.

Americans!

He tore away the last of the polyurethane.

The clothes stank of shit and piss, of vomit and sweat—of every odor the human body nurtures. God only knew what parasites the fabric harbored. He went through the pockets. They were empty. His hands itched. *Don't give up hope. A left-luggage ticket is a small thing—tightly rolled, no bigger than a matchstick; an incision in a coat collar would conceal it.* With his knife he hacked at the lining of the long brown overcoat matted with congealing blood, his fingers turning brown and slippery . . .

Nothing. All the usual scraps that in his experience tramps carry—the bits of string and paper, the buttons, the cigarette ends—had been removed already. The Gestapo had searched Luther's clothes with care. Naturally they had. He had been a fool to think they wouldn't. Furious, he slashed at the material—right to left, left to right, right to left . . .

He stood back from the heap of rags, panting like an assassin. Then he picked up a piece of rag and wiped his knife and hands.

"You know what I think?" said Charlie when he returned to the car empty-handed. "I think he never brought anything here from Zürich at all."

She was still in the backseat of the Volkswagen. March turned to look at her. "Yes, he did. Of course he did." He tried to hide his impatience; it was not her fault. "But he was too scared to keep it with him. So he stored it, received a ticket for it—either at the airport or at the station—and planned on collecting it later. I'm sure that's it. Now Globus has it, or it's lost for good."

"No. Listen. I was thinking. Yesterday, when I was coming through the airport, I thanked God you stopped me from trying to bring the painting back with us to Berlin. Remember the lines? They searched every bag. How could Luther have gotten *anything* past the Zollgrenzschutz?"

March considered this, massaging his temples. "A good question," he said eventually. "Maybe," he added a minute later, "the best question I ever heard."

At the Flughafen Hermann Göring the statue of Hanna Reitsch was steadily oxidizing in the rain. She stared across the concourse outside the departure terminal with corrosion-pitted eyes.

"You'd better stay with the car," said March. "Do you drive?"

She nodded. He dropped the keys into her lap. "If the Flughafenpolizei try to move you on, don't argue with them. Drive off and come around again. Keep circling. Give me twenty minutes."

"Then what?"

"I don't know." His hand fluttered in the air. "Improvise."

He strode into the airport terminal. The big digital clock above the passport control zone flicked over: 13:22. He glanced behind him. He could measure his freedom probably in minutes. Less than that if Globus had issued a general alert, for nowhere in the Reich was more heavily patrolled than the airport.

He kept thinking of Krebs in his apartment, and Eisler: *"The word is, you've been arrested."*

A man with a souvenir bag from the Soldiers' Hall looked familiar. A Gestapo watcher? March abruptly changed direction and headed into the toilets. He stood at the urinal, pissing air, his eyes fixed on the entrance. Nobody came in. When he emerged, the man was gone.

*"Last call for Lufthansa flight 270 to Tiflis . . ."*

He went to the central Lufthansa desk and showed his ID to one of the guards. "I need to speak to your head of security. Urgently."

"He may not be here, Herr Sturmbannführer."

"Look for him."

The guard was gone a long time. 13:27, said the clock. 13:28. Perhaps he was calling the Gestapo. 13:29. March put his hand into his pocket and felt the cold metal of the Luger. Better to make a stand here than crawl around the stone floor in Prinz-Albrecht-Strasse spitting teeth into your hand.

13:30.

The guard returned. "This way, Herr Sturmbannführer. If you please."

Friedman had joined the Berlin Kripo at the same time as March. He had left it five years later, one step ahead of a corruption investigation. Now he wore handmade English suits, smoked duty-free Swiss cigars and made five times his official salary by methods long suspected but never proved. He was a merchant prince, the airport his corrupt little kingdom.

When he realized March had come not to investigate him but to beg a favor, he was almost ecstatic. His excellent mood persisted as he led March along a passage away from the terminal building. "And how is Jaeger? Spreading chaos, I suppose? And Fiebes? Still jerking off over pictures of Aryan maidens and Ukrainian window cleaners? Oh, how I miss you all—I don't think! Here we are." Friedman transferred his cigar from his hand to his mouth and tugged at a large door. "Behold the cave of Aladdin!"

The metal slid open with a crash to reveal a small hangar stuffed with lost and abandoned property. "The things people leave behind," said Friedman. "You wouldn't believe it. We even had a leopard once."

"A leopard? A cat?"

"It died. Some idle bastard forgot to feed it. It made a

good coat." He laughed and snapped his fingers, and from the shadows an elderly, stoop-shouldered man appeared—a Slav, with wide-set, fearful eyes.

"Stand up straight, man. Show respect." Friedman gave him a shove that sent him staggering backward. "The Sturmbannführer here is a good friend of mine. He's looking for something. Tell him, March."

"A case, perhaps a bag," said March. "The last flight from Zürich on Monday night, the thirteenth. Left either on the aircraft or in the baggage claim area."

"Got that? Right?" The Slav nodded. "Well, go on, then!" He shuffled away and Friedman gestured to his mouth. "Dumb. Had his tongue cut out in the war. The ideal worker!" He laughed and clapped March on the shoulder. "So. How goes it?"

"Well enough."

"Civilian clothes. Working the weekend. Must be something big."

"It may be."

"This is the Martin Luther character, right?" March made no reply. "So you're dumb, too. I see." Friedman flicked cigar ash onto the clean floor. "Fair enough by me. A brown-pants job, possibly?"

"A what?"

"Zollgrenzschutz expression. Someone plans to bring in something they shouldn't. They get to the customs shed, see the security, start shitting themselves. Drop whatever it is and run."

"But this is special, yes? You don't open every case every day?"

"Just in the week before the *Führertag*."

"What about the lost property? Do you open that?"

"Only if it looks valuable!" Friedman laughed again. "No. A jest. We haven't the manpower. Anyway, it's been X-rayed, remember—no guns, no explosives. So we just leave it here, wait for someone to claim it. If no one's turned up in a year, then we open it, see what we've got."

"Pays for a few suits, I suppose."

"What?" Friedman plucked at his immaculate sleeve. "These poor rags?" There was a sound, and he turned around. "Looks like you're in luck, March."

The Slav was returning, carrying something. Friedman took it from him and weighed it in his hand. "Quite light. Can't be gold. What do you think it is, March? Drugs? Some dollars? Contraband silk from the East? A treasure map?"

"Are you going to open it?" March touched the gun in his pocket. He would use it if he had to.

Friedman appeared shocked. "This is a favor. One friend to another. Your business." He handed the case to March. "You'll remember that, Sturmbannführer, won't you? A favor? One day you'll do the same for me, comrade to comrade?"

The case was of the sort that doctors carry, with brass-reinforced corners and a stout brass lock, dull with age. The brown leather was scratched and faded, the heavy stitching dark, the hand grip worn smooth like a brown pebble by years of carrying until it felt like an extension of the hand. It proclaimed reliability and reassurance; professionalism; quiet wealth. It was certainly prewar, maybe even pre–Great War—built to last a generation or two. Solid. Worth a lot.

All this March absorbed on the walk back to the Volkswagen. The route avoided the Zollgrenzschutz—another favor from Friedman.

Charlie fell upon it like a child upon a birthday present and swore with disappointment when she found it locked. As March drove out of the airport perimeter she fished in her own bag and retrieved a pair of nail scissors. She picked desperately at the lock, the blades scrabbling ineffectively on the brass.

March said, "You're wasting your time. I'll have to break it open. Wait till we get there."

She shook the bag with frustration. "Get where?"

He ran a hand through his hair.
A good question.

Every room in the city was booked. The Eden with its roof-garden café, the Bristol on Unter den Linden, the Kaiserhof in Mohren-Strasse—all had stopped taking reservations months ago. The monster hotels with a thousand bedrooms and the little rooming houses dotted around the railway termini were filled with uniforms. Not just the SA and the SS, the Luftwaffe and the Wehrmacht, the Hitler Youth and the League of German Girls, but all the others besides: the National Socialist Empire War Association, the German Falconry Order, the National Socialist Leadership Schools . . .

Outside the most famous and luxurious of all Berlin's hotels—the Adlon, on the corner of Pariser-Platz and Wilhelm-Strasse—the crowds were straining at the metal barriers for a glimpse of a celebrity: a film star, a footballer, a Party satrap in town for the *Führertag.* As March and Charlie passed it, a Mercedes was drawing up, its black-uniformed passengers bathed in the light of a score of flashguns.

March drove straight over the Platz into Unter den Linden, turned left and then right into Dorotheen-Strasse. He parked among the dustbins at the back of the Prinz Friedrich Karl Hotel. It was here, over breakfast with Rudi Halder, that this business had really begun. When had that been? He could not remember.

The manager of the Friedrich Karl was habitually clad in an old-fashioned black jacket and a pair of striped pants, and he bore a striking resemblance to the late President von Hindenburg. He came bustling out to the front desk, smoothing a large pair of white whiskers as if they were pets.

"Sturmbannführer March, what a pleasure! What a pleasure, indeed! And dressed for relaxation!"

"Good afternoon, Herr Brecker. A difficult request. I must have a room."

Brecker threw up his hands in distress. "It's impossible! Even for so distinguished a customer as yourself."

"Come, Herr Brecker. You must have something. An attic would do, a broom closet. You would be rendering the Reichskriminalpolizei the greatest assistance . . ."

Brecker's elderly eye traveled over the luggage and came to rest on Charlie, at which point a gleam entered it. "And this is Frau March?"

"Unfortunately, no." March put his hand on Brecker's sleeve and guided him into a corner, where they were watched with suspicion by the elderly receptionist. "This young lady has information of a crucial character, but we wish to interrogate her . . . how shall I put it?"

"In an informal setting?" suggested the old man.

"Precisely!" March pulled out what was left of his life savings and began peeling off notes. "For this 'informal setting' the Kriminalpolizei naturally would wish to reimburse you handsomely."

"I see." Brecker looked at the money and licked his lips. "And since this is a matter of security, no doubt you would prefer it if certain formalities—registration, for example—were dispensed with?"

March stopped counting, pressed the entire roll of notes into the manager's moist hand and closed his fingers around it.

In return for bankrupting himself March was given a kitchen maid's room in the roof, reached from the third floor by a rickety back staircase. They had to wait in the reception for five minutes while the girl was turned out of her home and fresh linen was put on the bed. Herr Brecker's repeated offers to help with their luggage were turned down by March, who also ignored the lascivious looks the old man kept giving Charlie. He did, however, ask for some food—some bread, cheese, ham, fruit, a flask of black coffee—which the manager promised to bring up personally. March told him to leave it in the corridor.

"It's not the Adlon," said March when he and Charlie were alone. The little room was stifling. All the heat in the hotel seemed to have risen and become trapped beneath the tiles. He climbed on a chair to tug open the attic window and jumped down in a shower of dust.

"Who cares about the Adlon?" She flung her arms around him, kissed him hard on the mouth.

The manager set down the tray of food as instructed outside the door. Climbing the stairs had almost done him in. Through three centimeters of wood, March listened to his ragged breathing and then to his footsteps retreating along the passage. He waited until he was sure the old man had gone before retrieving the tray and setting it on the flimsy dressing table. There was no lock on the bedroom door, so he wedged a chair under the handle.

March laid Luther's case on the hard wooden bed and took out his pocket knife.

The lock had been fashioned to withstand exactly this sort of assault. It took five minutes of hacking and twisting, during which he snapped one short blade, before the fastener broke free. He pulled the bag open.

That papery smell again—the odor of a long-sealed filing cabinet or desk drawer, a whiff of typewriter oil. And behind that, something else: something antiseptic, medicinal . . .

Charlie was at his shoulder. He could feel her warm breath on his cheek. "Don't tell me. It's empty."

"No. It's not empty. It's full."

He pulled out his handkerchief and wiped the sweat from his hands. Then he turned the case upside down and shook the contents out onto the bedspread.

*Affidavit sworn by Wilhelm Stuckart, State Secretary, Interior Ministry:*
*[4 pages; typewritten]*
On Sunday, December 21, 1941, the Interior Ministry's Adviser on Jewish Affairs, Dr. Bernhard Losener, made an urgent request to see me in private. Dr. Losener arrived at my home in a state of extreme agitation. He informed me that his subordinate, the Assistant Adviser on Racial Affairs, Dr. Werner Feldscher, had heard "from a fully reliable source, a friend" that the one thousand Jews recently evacuated from Berlin had been massacred in the Rumbuli Forest in Poland. He further informed me that his feelings of outrage were sufficient to prevent him from continuing his present employment in the Ministry, and he therefore requested to be transferred to other duties. I replied that I would seek clarification on this matter.

The following day, at my request, I visited Obergruppenführer Reinhard Heydrich in his office in Prinz-Albrecht-Strasse. The Obergruppenführer confirmed that Dr. Feldscher's information was correct and pressed me to discover its source, as such breaches of security could not be tolerated. He then dismissed his adjutant from the room and said that he wished to speak to me on a private basis.

He informed me that in July he had been summoned to the Führer's headquarters in East Prussia. The Führer had spoken to him frankly in the following terms: He had decided to resolve the Jewish Question once and for all. The hour had arrived. He could not rely upon his successors having the necessary will or the military power he now commanded. He was not afraid of the consequences. People presently revered the French Revolution, but who now remembered the thousands of innocents who had died? Revolutionary times were governed by their own laws. When Germany had won the war, nobody would ask afterward how we did it. Should Germany lose the mortal struggle, at least those who had hoped to profit from the defeat of National Socialism would be wiped out. It was necessary to remove the biological bases of Judaism once and for all. Otherwise the problem would erupt to plague future generations. That was the lesson of history.

Obergruppenführer Heydrich stated further that the necessary powers to enable him to implement this Führer Order had been granted to him by Reichsmarschall Göring on 31.7.41. These matters would be discussed at the forthcoming interdepartmental conference. In the meantime, he urged me to use whatever means I considered necessary to discover the identity of Dr. Feldscher's source. This was a matter of the highest security classification.

I thereupon suggested that, in view of the grave issues involved, it would be appropriate, from a legal point of view, to have the Führer Order placed in writing. Obergruppenführer Heydrich stated that such a course was impossible, due to political considerations, but that if I had any reservations I should take them up with the Führer personally. Obergruppenführer Heydrich concluded our meeting by remarking in a jocular manner that we should have no cause for concern on legalistic grounds, considering that I was the Reich's chief legal draftsman and he was the Reich's chief policeman.

I hereby swear that this is a true record of our conversation, based upon notes taken by myself that same evening.

Signed, Wilhelm Stuckart (attorney)
Dated June 4, 1942, Berlin
Witnessed, Josef Buhler (attorney)

Across the city the day died. The sun dropped behind the dome of the Great Hall, gilding it like the cupola of a giant mosque. With a hum, the floodlights cut on along the Avenue of Victory and the East-West Axis. The afternoon crowds melted, dissolved, re-formed as nighttime queues outside the cinemas and restaurants, while above the Tiergarten, lost in the gloom, an airship droned.

*Reich Ministry for Foreign Affairs Secret State Document*

*Dispatch from German Ambassador in London, Herbert von Dirksen*

*Account of conversations with Ambassador Joseph P. Kennedy, United States Ambassador to Great Britain*

*[Extracts; two pages, printed]*

Received Berlin, June 13, 1938

Although he did not know Germany, [Ambassador Kennedy] had learned from the most varied sources that the present government had done great things for Germany and that the Germans were satisfied and enjoying good living conditions.

The ambassador then touched upon the Jewish question and stated that it was naturally of great importance to German-American relations. In this connection it was not so much the fact that we wanted to get rid of the Jews that was harmful to us, but rather the loud clamor with which we accompanied this purpose. He himself understood our Jewish policy completely; he was from Boston, and there, in one golf club and in other clubs, no Jews had been admitted for the past fifty years.

Received Berlin, October 18, 1938

Today, too, as during former conversations, Kennedy mentioned that very strong anti-Semitic tendencies existed in the United States and that a large portion of the population had an understanding of the German attitude toward the Jews. From his whole personality, I believe he would get on very well with the Führer.

"We can't do this alone."

"We must."

"Please. Let me take them to the embassy. They could smuggle them out through the diplomatic bag."

"No!"

"You can't be certain he betrayed us—"

"Who else could it be? And look at this. Do you really think American diplomats would want to touch it?"

"But if we're caught with it . . . it's a death warrant!"

"I have a plan."

"A good one?"

"It had better be."

*Central Construction Office, Auschwitz, to German Equipment Works, Auschwitz, March 31, 1943*

Re your letter of March 24, 1943

*[Excerpt]*

In reply to your letter, the three airtight towers are to be built in accordance with the order of January 18, 1943, for Bw 30B and 3C, in the same dimensions and in the same manner as the towers already delivered.

We take this occasion to refer to another order of March 6, 1943, for the delivery of a gas door 100/192 for corpse cellar I of crematory III, Bw 30A, which is to be built in the manner and according to the same measure as the cellar door of the opposite crematory II, with peephole of double 8-millimeter glass encased in rubber. This order is to be viewed as especially urgent . . .

Not far from the hotel, north of Unter den Linden, was an all-night pharmacy. It was owned, as all businesses were, by Germans, but it was run by Romanians—the only people poor enough and willing enough to work such hours. It was stocked like a bazaar, with cooking pans, paraffin heaters, stockings, baby food, greeting cards, stationery, toys, film . . . Among Berlin's swollen population of guest workers it did a brisk trade.

They entered separately. At one counter Charlie spoke to the elderly woman assistant, who promptly disappeared into a back room and returned with an assortment of bottles. At another March bought a school exercise book, two sheets of thick brown paper, two sheets of gift wrap paper and a roll of clear tape.

They left and walked two blocks to the Friedrich-Strasse station, where they caught the southbound U-bahn train. The carriage was packed with the usual Saturday night crowd—lovers holding hands, families off to the illuminations, young men on a drinking spree—and nobody, as far as March could tell, paid them the slightest attention. Nevertheless, he waited until the doors were about to slide shut before he dragged her out onto the platform of the Tempelhof station. A ten-minute journey on a number thirty-five tram brought them to the airport.

Throughout all this they sat in silence.

Krakau
7/18/43
*[Handwritten]*
My dear Kritzinger,
Here is the list.

| | | |
|---|---|---|
| Auschwitz | 50.02N | 19.11E |
| Kulmhof | 53.20N | 18.25E |
| Blezec | 50.12N | 23.28E |
| Treblinka | 52.48N | 22.20E |
| Majdanek | 51.18N | 22.31E |
| Sobibor | 51.33N | 23.31E |

Heil Hitler!
*[Signed]*
Buhler *[?]*

Tempelhof was older than the Flughafen Hermann Göring—shabbier, more primitive. The departure terminal had been built before the war and was decorated with pictures of the pioneering days of passenger flight—old Lufthansa Junkers with corrugated fuselages, dashing pilots with goggles and scarves, intrepid women travelers with stout ankles and cloche hats. Innocent days! March took up a position by the entrance to the terminal and pretended to study the photographs as Charlie approached the car rental desk.

Suddenly she was smiling, making apologetic gestures with her hands—playing to perfection the lady in distress. She had missed the flight, her family was waiting . . . The rental agent was charmed and consulted a typed sheet. For a moment, the issue hung in the balance—and then, yes, as it happened, Fräulein, he *did* have something. Something for someone with eyes as pretty as yours, of course . . . Your driver's license, please . . .

She handed it over. It had been issued the previous year in the name of Voss, Magda, age twenty-four, of Mariendorf, Berlin. It was the license of the girl murdered on her wedding day five days ago—the license Max Jaeger had left in his desk, along with all the other papers from the Spandau shootings.

March looked away, forcing himself to study an old aerial photograph of the Tempelhof airfield. BERLIN was painted in huge white letters along the runway. When he glanced back, the agent was entering details of the license on the rental form, laughing at some witticism of his own.

As a strategy it was not without risk. In the morning, a copy of the rental agreement would be forwarded automatically to the police, and even the Orpo would wonder why a murdered woman was hiring a car. But tomorrow was Sunday, Monday was the *Führertag,* and by Tuesday—the earliest the Orpo was likely to pull its finger out of its backside—March reckoned he and Charlie would either be safe or arrested—or dead.

Ten minutes later, with a final exchange of smiles, she was given the keys to a four-door black Opel with ten thousand kilometers on the odometer. Five minutes after that, March joined her in the parking lot. He navigated while she drove. It was the first time he had seen her behind the wheel: another side of her. In the busy traffic she displayed an exaggerated caution that he felt did not come naturally.

The lobby of the Prinz Friedrich Karl was deserted: the guests were out for the night. As they passed through it toward the stairs, the receptionist kept her head down. They were just another of Herr Brecker's little scams—best not to know too much.

Their room had not been searched. The cotton threads hung where March had wedged them between door and frame. Inside, when he pulled Luther's case out from beneath the bed, the single strand of hair was still laced through the lock.

♦

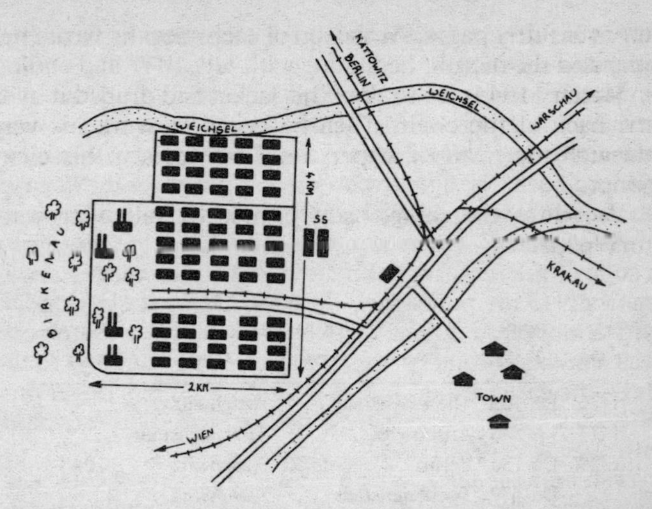


Charlie stepped out of her dress and wrapped a towel around her shoulders.

In the bathroom at the end of the hallway, a naked bulb lit a grimy sink. A bath stood on tiptoe, on iron claws.

March walked back to the bedroom, shut himself in and once more propped the chair up against the door. He piled the contents of the case onto the dressing table—the map, the various envelopes, the minutes and memoranda, the reports, including the one with the rows of statistics, typed on the machine with the extra large letters. Some of the paper crackled with age. He remembered how he and Charlie had sat during the sunlit afternoon with the rumble of traffic outside; how they had passed the evidence backward and forward to each other—at first with excitement, then stunned, disbelieving, silent, until at last they had come to the pouch with the photographs.

Now he needed to be more systematic. He pulled up a chair, cleared a space and opened the exercise book. He tore out thirty pages. At the top of each sheet he wrote the year and the month, beginning with July 1941 and ending in January 1944. He took off his jacket and draped it over the back of the chair. Then he began to work his way through the heap of papers, making notes in his clear script.

A railway timetable, badly printed on yellowing wartime paper:

| DATE | TRAIN NO. | DEPARTURE FROM | DEPARTURE TIME | ARRIVAL TO | ARRIVAL TIME |
|---|---|---|---|---|---|
| 1/26 | Da 105 | Theresienstadt | | Auschwitz | |
| 1/27 | Lp 106 | Auschwitz | | Theresienstadt | |
| 1/29 | Da 13 | Berlin | 1720 | Auschwitz | 1048 |
| | Da 107 | Theresienstadt | | Auschwitz | |
| 1/30 | Lp 108 | Auschwitz | | Theresienstadt | |
| 1/31 | Lp 14 | Auschwitz | | Zamocz | |
| 2/1 | Da 109 | Theresienstadt | | Auschwitz | |
| 2/2 | Da 15 | Berlin | 1720 | Auschwitz | 1048 |
| | Lp 110 | Auschwitz | | Myslowitz | |
| 2/3 | Po 65 | Zamocz | 1100 | Auschwitz | |
| 2/4 | Lp 16 | Auschwitz | | Litzmannstadt | |

And so on until, in the second week of February, a new destination appeared. Now almost all the times had been worked out to the minute:

| | | | | | |
|---|---|---|---|---|---|
| 2/11 | Pj 131 | Bialystok | 900 | Treblinka | 1210 |
| | Lp 132 | Treblinka | 2118 | Bialystok | 130 |
| 2/12 | Pj 133 | Bialystok | 900 | Treblinka | 1210 |
| | Lp 134 | Treblinka | 2118 | Grodno | |
| 2/13 | Pj 135 | Bialystok | 900 | Treblinka | 1210 |
| | Lp 136 | Treblinka | 2118 | Bialystok | 130 |
| 2/14 | Pj 163 | Grodno | 540 | Treblinka | 1210 |
| | Lp 164 | Treblinka | | Scharfenwiese | |

And so on again until the end of the month.

A rusty paper clip had mottled the edge of the timetable. Attached to it was a telegram from the General Management, Directorate East of the German Reich Railways, dated Berlin, January 13, 1943. First, a list of recipients:

Reich Railway Directorates
Berlin, Breslau, Dresden, Erfurt, Frankfurt, Halle (S), Karlsruhe, Königsberg (Pr), Linz, Mainz, Oppeln, East in Frankfurt (O), Posen, Vienna
General Directorate of East Railway in Krakau
Reichsprotektor, Group Railways in Prague
General Traffic Directorate Warsaw
Reich Traffic Directorate Minsk

Then, the main text:

Subject: Special trains for resettlers during the period from January 20 to February 28, 1943.
We enclose a compilation of the special trains (Vd, Rm, Po, Pj and Da) agreed upon in Berlin on January 15, 1943 for the period from January 20, 1943 to February 28, 1943 and a circulatory plan for cars to be used in these trains.

Train formation is noted for each recirculation and attention is to be paid to these instructions. After each full trip, cars are to be well cleaned, if necessary fumigated, and upon completion of the program prepared for further use. Number and kinds of cars are to be determined upon dispatch of the last train and are to be reported to me by telephone with confirmation on service cards.

[Signed] Dr. Jacobi

33 Bfp 5 Bfsv Minsk, February 9, 1943

March flicked back to the timetable and read it through again. Theresienstadt–Auschwitz, Auschwitz–Theresienstadt, Bialystok–Treblinka, Treblinka–Bialystok: the syllables drummed in his tired brain like the rhythm of wheels on a railway track.

He ran his finger down the columns of figures, trying to decipher the message behind them. So: a train would be loaded in the Polish town of Bialystok at breakfast time. By lunchtime it would be at this hell, Treblinka. (Not all the journeys were so brief—he shuddered at the thought of the *seventeen hours* from Berlin to Auschwitz.) In the afternoon, the cars would be unloaded at Treblinka and fumigated. At nine that evening they would return to Bialystok, arriving in the early hours, ready to be loaded up again at breakfast.

On February 12 the pattern broke. Instead of going back to Bialystok, the empty train was sent to Grodno. Two days in the sidings there, and then—in the dark, long before dawn—the train was once more heading back, fully laden, to Treblinka. It arrived at lunchtime. Was unloaded. And that night began rattling back westward again, this time to Scharfenweise.

What else could an investigator of the Berlin Kriminalpolizei deduce from this document?

Well, he could deduce numbers. Say: sixty persons per car, an average of sixty cars per train. Deduction: three thousand six hundred persons per transport.

By February, the transports were running at the rate of one per day. Deduction: twenty-five thousand persons per week; one hundred thousand persons per month; one and a quarter million persons per year. And this was the average achieved in the depths of the Central European winter, when the switches froze and drifts of snow blocked the tracks and partisans materialized from the woods like ghosts to plant their bombs.

Deduction: the numbers would be even greater in the spring and summer.

He stood at the bathroom door. Charlie, in a black slip, had her back to him and was bending over the washbasin.

With her hair wet she looked smaller, almost fragile. The muscles in her pale shoulders flexed as she massaged her scalp. She rinsed her hair a final time and stretched a hand out blindly behind her. He gave her a towel.

Along the edge of the bath she had set out various objects—a pair of green rubber gloves, a brush, a dish, a spoon, two bottles. March picked up the bottles and studied their labels. One contained a mixture of magnesium carbonate and sodium acetate, the other a twenty-volume solution of hydrogen peroxide. Next to the mirror above the basin she had propped open the girl's passport. Magda Voss regarded March with wide, untroubled eyes.

"Are you sure this is going to work?"

Charlie wound the towel around her head into a turban. "First I go red. Then orange. Then white blonde." She took the bottles from him. "I was a fifteen-year-old schoolgirl with a crush on Jean Harlow. My mother went crazy. Trust me."

She squeezed her hands into the rubber gloves and measured the chemicals into the dish. With the spoon she began to mix them into a thick blue paste.

> SECRET REICH MATTER. CONFERENCE MINUTES. 30 COPIES. COPY NUMBER . . .

(the figure had been scratched out)

> "The following participated in the conference of January 20, 1942, in Berlin, Am grossen Wannsee 56–58, on the final solution of the Jewish question.

March had read the minutes twice that afternoon. Nevertheless, he forced himself to wade through the pages again. "Around 11 million Jews are involved in this final solution of the European Jewish question. . . ." Not just German Jews. The minutes listed more than thirty European nationalities, including French Jews (865,000), Dutch Jews (160,000), Polish Jews (2,284,000), Ukrainian Jews (2,994,684); there were English, Spanish, Irish, Swedish and Finnish Jews; the conference even found room for the Albanian Jews (all 200 of them).

> In the course of the final solution, the Jews should be brought under appropriate direction in a suitable manner to the East for labor utilization. Separated by sex, the Jews capable of work will be led into these areas in large labor columns to build roads, whereby doubtless a large part will fall away through natural reduction.
>
> The inevitable final remainder, which doubtless constitutes the toughest element, will have to be dealt with appropriately, since it represents a natural selection which upon liberation is to be regarded as a germ cell of a new Jewish development. (See the lesson of history.)
>
> In the course of the practical implementation of the final solution, Europe will be combed from west to east.

"*. . . brought under appropriate direction in a suitable manner . . . the toughest element will have to be dealt with appropriately . . .*" Appropriate, appropriately. The favorite words in the bureaucrat's lexicon—the grease for sliding around unpleasantness, the funkhole for avoiding specifics.

March unfolded a set of rough photostats. These appeared to be copies of the original draft minutes of the Wannsee conference, compiled by *SS-Standartenführer* Eichmann of the Reich Main Security Office. It was a typewritten document full of amendments and angry crossings-out in a neat hand that March had come to recognize as belonging to Reinhard Heydrich.

For example, Eichmann had written:

> Finally, Obergruppenführer Heydrich was asked about the practical difficulties involved in the processing of such large numbers. The Obergruppenführer stated that various methods had been employed. Shooting was to be regarded as an inadequate solution for various reasons. The

> work was slow. Security was poor, with the consequent risk of panic among those awaiting special treatment. Also, this method had been observed to have a deleterious effect upon our men. He invited Sturmbannführer Dr. Rudolf Lange (KdS Latvia) to give an eyewitness report.
>
> Sturmbannführer Lange stated that three methods had been undertaken recently, providing an opportunity for comparison. On November 30, one thousand Berlin Jews had been shot in the forest near Riga. On December 8, his men had organized a special treatment at Kulmhof with gas trucks. In the meantime, commencing in October, experiments had been conducted at the Auschwitz camp on Russian prisoners and Polish Jews using Zyklon B. Results here were especially promising from the point of view of both capacity and security.

Against this, in the margin, Heydrich had written "No!" March checked the final version of the minutes. This entire section of the conference had been reduced to a single phrase:

> Finally, there was a discussion of the various types of solution possibilities.

Thus sanitized, the minutes were fit for the archives.

March scribbled more notes: October, November, December 1941. Slowly the blank sheets were being filled. In the dim light of the attic room, a picture was developing: connections, strategies, causes and effects . . . He looked up the contributions of Luther, Stuckart and Buhler to the Wannsee conference. Luther foresaw problems in "the Nordic states" but "no major difficulties in southeastern and western Europe." Stuckart, when asked about persons with one Jewish grandparent, "proposed to proceed with compulsory sterilization." Buhler, characteristically, toadied to Heydrich: "He had only one favor to ask—that the Jewish question in the General Government be solved as rapidly as possible."

♦

He broke off for five minutes to smoke a cigarette, pacing the corridor, shuffling his papers, an actor learning his lines. From the bathroom: the sound of running water. From the rest of the hotel: nothing except creaks in the darkness, like a galleon at anchor.

*Notes on a visit to Auschwitz-Birkenau by Martin Luther, Under State Secretary, Reich Ministry for Foreign Affairs* [*Handwritten; 11 pages*]

July 14, 1943

At last, after almost a year of repeated requests, I am given permission to undertake a full tour of inspection of the Auschwitz-Birkenau camp on behalf of the Foreign Ministry.

I land at Krakau airfield from Berlin shortly before sunset and spend the night with Governor-General Hans Frank, State Secretary Josef Buhler and their staff at Wawel Castle. Tomorrow morning at dawn I am to be picked up from the castle and driven to the camp (journey time: approximately one hour), where I am to be received by the commandant, Rudolf Hoess.

July 15, 1943

The camp. My first impression is of the sheer scale of the installation, which measures, according to Hoess, almost 2 km. X 4 km. The earth is of yellowish clay similar to that of eastern

Silesia—a desertlike landscape broken occasionally by green thickets of trees. Inside the camp, stretching far beyond the limits of my vision, are hundreds of wooden barracks, their roofs covered with green tar paper. In the distance, moving between them, I see small groups of prisoners in blue-and-white-striped clothing—some carrying planks, others shovels and picks; a few are loading large crates onto the backs of trucks. A smell hangs over the place.

I thank Hoess for receiving me. He explains the administrative setup. This camp is under the jurisdiction of the SS Economic Administration Main Office. The others, in the Lublin district, fall under the control of SS-Obergruppenführer Odilo Globocnik. Unfortunately, the pressure of his work prevents Hoess from conducting me around the camp personally, and he therefore entrusts me into the care of a young Untersturmführer, Weidemann. He orders Weidemann to ensure I am shown everything, and that all my questions are answered fully. We begin with breakfast in the SS barracks.

After breakfast: we drive into the southern sector of the camp. Here: a railway siding, approx 1.5 km. in length. On either side: wire fencing supported by concrete pylons, and also wooden observation towers with machine-gun nests. It is already hot. The smell is bad here, a million flies buzz. To the west, rising above trees: a square red-brick factory chimney, belching smoke.

7:40 A.M.: the area around the railway track begins to fill with SS troops, some with dogs, and also with special prisoners delegated to assist them. In the distance we hear the whistle of a train. A few minutes later: the locomotive pulls slowly through the entrance, its exhalations of steam throw up clouds of yellow dust. It draws to a halt in front of us. The gates close behind it. Weidemann: "This is a transport of Jews from France."

I reckon the length of the train to be some 60 freight cars, with high wooden sides. The troops and special prisoners crowd around. The doors are unbolted and slid open. All along the train the same words are shouted: "Everyone get out! Bring your hand baggage with you! Leave all heavy baggage in the cars!" The men come out first, dazed by the light, and jump to the ground—

1.5 meters—then turn to help their women and children and the elderly, and to receive their luggage.

The deportees' state: pitiful—filthy, dusty, holding out bowls and cups, gesturing to their mouths, crying with thirst. Behind them in the trucks lie the dead and those too sick to move—Weidemann says their journey began four nights ago. SS guards force those able to walk into two lines. As families separate, they shout to one another. With many gestures and calls the columns march off in different directions. The able-bodied men go toward the work camp. The rest head toward the screen of trees, with Weidemann and myself following. As I look back, I see the prisoners in their striped clothing clambering into the freight cars, dragging out the baggage and the bodies.

8:30 A.M.: Weidemann puts the size of the column at nearly 2,000: women carrying babies, children at their skirts; old men and women; adolescents; sick people; mad people. They walk five abreast down a cinder path for 300 meters, through a courtyard, along another path, at the end of which twelve concrete steps lead down to an immense underground chamber 100 meters long. A sign proclaims in several languages (German, French, Greek, Hungarian): "Baths and Disinfecting Room." It is well lit, with scores of benches, hundreds of numbered pegs.

The guards shout, "Everyone undress! You have ten minutes!" People hesitate, look at one another. The order is repeated more harshly, and this time, hesitantly but calmly, they comply. "Remember your peg number, so you can recover your clothes!" The camp trustees move among them, whispering encouragement, helping the feeble-bodied and the feebleminded to strip. Some mothers try to hide their babies in the piles of discarded clothing, but the infants are quickly discovered.

9:05 A.M.: Naked, the crowd shuffles through large oak doors flanked by troops into a second room, as large as the first but utterly bare, apart from four thick, square columns supporting the ceiling at twenty-meter intervals. At the bottom of each column is a metal grille. The chamber fills, the doors swing shut. Weidemann gestures. I follow him out through the empty changing room, up the concrete steps, into the air. I can hear the sound of an automobile engine.

Across the grass that covers the roof of the installation bounces a small van with Red Cross markings. It stops. An SS officer and a doctor emerge wearing gas masks and carrying four metal canisters. Four squat concrete pipes jut from the grass, twenty meters apart. The doctor and SS man lift the lids of the pipes and pour in a mauve granulated substance. They remove the masks, light cigarettes in the sunshine.

9:09 A.M.: Weidemann conducts me back downstairs. Only sound is a muffled drumming coming from the far end of the room, from beyond the suitcases and the piles of still-warm clothes. A small glass panel is set into the oak doors. I put my eye to it. A man's palm beats against the aperture and I jerk my head away.

Says one guard, "The water in the shower rooms must be very hot today, since they shout so loudly."

Outside, Weidemann says: now we must wait twenty minutes. Would I care to visit Canada? I say: What? He laughs: "Canada"—a section of the camp. Why Canada? He shrugs: nobody knows.

Canada. 1 km. north of gas chamber. Huge rectangular yard, watchtower in each corner and surrounded by barbed wire. Mountains of belongings—trunks, rucksacks, cases, kitbags, parcels; blankets; prams, wheelchairs, false limbs; brushes, combs. Weidemann: figures prepared for RF-SS on property recently sent to Reich—men's shirts: 132,000; women's coats: 155,000; women's hair: 3,000 kg. ("a freight car"); boys' jackets: 15,000; girls' dresses: 9,000; handkerchiefs: 135,000. I get doctor's bag, beautifully made, as souvenir—Weidemann insists.

9:31 A.M.: Return to underground installation. Loud electric humming fills the air—the patented "Exhator" system, for evacuation of gas. Doors open. The bodies are piled up at one end *[illegible]* legs smeared with excrement, menstrual blood; bite and claw marks. Jewish *Sonderkommando* detachment enters to hose down corpses, wearing rubber boots, aprons, gas masks (according to W., pockets of gas remain trapped at floor level for up to two hours). Corpses slippery. Straps around wrists used to haul them to four double-doored elevators. Capacity of each: 25 *[illegible]* bell rings, ascend one floor to . . .

10:02 A.M.: Incineration room. Stifling heat: 15 ovens operating full blast. Loud noise: diesel motors ventilating flames. Corpses from elevator loaded onto conveyor belt (metal rollers). Blood etc. into concrete gutter. Barbers either side shave heads. Hair collected in sacks. Rings, necklaces, bracelets, etc. dropped into metal box. Last: dental team—eight men with crowbars and pliers—gold removal (teeth, bridgework, fillings). W. gives me tin of gold to test weight: very heavy. Corpses tipped into furnaces from metal pushcarts.

Weidemann: four such gas chamber/crematorium installations in camp. Total capacity of each: 2,000 bodies per day = 8,000 overall. Operated by Jewish labor, changed every 2–3 months. The operation thus self-supporting; the secret self-sealing. Biggest security headache—stink from chimneys and flames at night, visible over many kilometers, especially to troop trains heading east on main line.

March checked the dates. Luther had visited Auschwitz on July 15. On July 17 Buhler had forwarded the map locations of the six camps to Kritzinger of the Reich Chancellery. On August 9 the last deposit had been made in Switzerland. That same year, according to his wife, Luther had suffered a breakdown.

He made a note. Kritzinger was the fourth man. His name was everywhere. He checked Buhler's pocket diary. Those dates tallied also. Another mystery solved.

His pen moved across the paper. He was almost finished.

A small thing, it had passed unnoticed during the afternoon; one of a dozen or so scraps of paper stuffed at random into a torn folder. It was a circular from SS-Gruppenführer Richard Glücks, Chief of Amtsgruppe D in the SS Economic Administration Main Office. It was dated August 6, 1942.

Re: the utilization of cut hair.

In response to a report, the Chief of the SS Economic Administration Main Office, SS-Obergruppenführer Pohl, has ordered that all human hair cut off in concentration camps should be utilized. Human hair will be processed for industrial felt and spun into thread. Female hair that has been cut and combed out will be used as thread to make socks for U-boat crews and felt stockings for the railways.

You are instructed, therefore, to store the hair of female prisoners after it has been disinfected. Cut hair from male prisoners can be utilized only if it is at least 20 mm. in length. . . .

The amounts of hair collected each month, separated into female and male hair, must be reported on the 5th of each month to this office, beginning with September 5, 1942.

He read it again: "*. . . for U-boat crews . . .*"

*One. Two. Three. Four. Five.* March was underwater, holding his breath, counting. He listened to the muffled noises, saw patterns like strings of algae float past him in the dark. *Fourteen. Fifteen. Sixteen.* With a roar he rose above the surface, sucking in air, streaming water. He filled his lungs a few more times, took an immense gulp of oxygen, then went down again. This time he made it to twenty-five before his breath exploded and he burst upward, slopping water onto the bathroom floor.

Would he ever be clean again?

Afterward, he lay with his arms dangling over the sides of the tub, his head tilted back, staring at the ceiling like a drowned man.

# SUNDAY, APRIL 19

♦

However this war may end, we have won the war against you; none of you will be left to bear witness, but even if someone were to survive, the world would not believe him. There will perhaps be suspicions, discussions, research by historians, but there will be no certainties, because we will destroy the evidence together with you. And even if some proof should remain and some of you survive, people will say that the events you describe are too monstrous to be believed: they will say that they are the exaggerations of Allied propaganda and will believe us, who will deny everything, and not you. We will be the ones to dictate the history of the Lagers.

SS OFFICER, quoted in *The Drowned and the Saved* by Primo Levi

In July 1953, not long after Xavier March had turned thirty and his work as yet consisted of little more than the arresting of whores and pimps around the docks of Hamburg, he and Klara had taken a holiday. They had started in Freiburg, in the foothills of the Black Forest, had driven south to the Rhine, then eastward in his battered KdF-wagen toward the Bodensee, and in one of the little riverside hotels, during a showery afternoon with a rainbow cast across the sky, they had planted the seed that had grown into Pili.

He could see the place still: the wrought-iron balcony, the Rhine valley beyond, the barges moving lazily in the wide water, the stone walls of the old town, the cool church; Klara's skirt, waist to ankle, sunflower yellow.

And there was something else he could still see: a kilometer downriver, spanning the gulf between Germany and Switzerland—the glint of a steel bridge.

Forget about trying to escape by way of the main air or sea ports: they were watched and guarded as tightly as the Reich Chancellery. Forget about crossing the border to France, Belgium, Holland, Denmark, Croatia, Yugoslavia,

Italy—that was to scale the wall of one prison merely to drop into the exercise yard of another. Forget about mailing the documents out of the Reich: too many packages were routinely opened by the postal service for that to be safe. Forget about giving the material to any of the other correspondents in Berlin: they would only face the same obstacles and were, in any case, according to Charlie, as trustworthy as rattlesnakes.

The Swiss border offered the best hope; the bridge beckoned.

Now hide it. Hide it all.

He knelt on the threadbare carpet and spread out a single sheet of brown paper. He made a neat stack of the documents, squaring off the edges. From his wallet he took the photograph of the Weiss family. He stared at it for a moment, then added it to the pile. He wrapped the entire collection tightly in the paper, binding cellophane tape around and around it until the package felt as solid as a block of wood.

He was left with an oblong parcel, ten centimeters thick, unyielding to the touch, anonymous to the eye.

He let out a breath. That was better.

He added another layer, this time of gift paper. Golden letters spelled GOOD LUCK! and HAPPINESS!, the words curling like streamers amid balloons and champagne corks behind a smiling bride and groom.

By autobahn from Berlin to Nuremberg: 500 kilometers. By autobahn from Nuremberg to Stuttgart: 150 kilometers. From Stuttgart the road then wound through the valleys and forests of Württemberg to Waldshut on the Rhine: 150 kilometers again. Eight hundred kilometers in all.

"What's that in miles?"

"Five hundred. Do you think you can manage it?"

"Of course. Twelve hours, maybe less." She was perched on the edge of the bed, leaning forward attentively. She wore two towels—one wrapped around her body, the other in a turban around her head.

"No need to rush it—you've got twenty-four. When you calculate you've put a safe distance between yourself and Berlin, telephone the Hotel Bellevue in Waldshut and reserve a room—it's out of season, there should be no difficulty."

"Hotel Bellevue. Waldshut." She nodded slowly as she memorized it. "And you?"

"I'll be following a couple of hours behind. I'll aim to join you at the hotel around midnight."

He could see she did not believe him. He hurried on, "If you're willing to take the risk, I think you should carry the papers, and also this . . ." From his pocket he drew out the other stolen passport. Paul Hahn, SS-Sturmbannführer, born Cologne, August 16, 1925. Three years younger than March, and looked it.

She said, "Why don't you keep it?"

"If I'm arrested and searched, they'll find it. Then they'll know whose identity you're using."

"You have no intention of coming."

"I have every intention of coming."

"You think you're finished."

"Not true. But my chances of traveling eight hundred kilometers without being stopped are less than yours. You must see that. That's why we go separately."

She was shaking her head. He came and sat beside her, stroked her cheek, turned her face to his, her eyes to his. "Listen. You're to wait for me—listen!—wait for me at the hotel until eight-thirty tomorrow morning. If I haven't arrived, you drive across without me. Don't wait any longer, because it won't be safe."

"Why eight-thirty?"

"You should aim to cross the border as close to nine as you can." Her cheeks were wet. He kissed them. He kept on talking. She had to understand. "Nine is the hour when the beloved Father of the German People leaves the Reich Chancellery to travel to the Great Hall. It's months since he's been seen—their way of building excitement. You may be sure the guards will have a radio in the customs post, and be listening to it. If ever there's a time when they're more likely just to wave you through, that's it."

She stood and unwrapped the turban. In the weak light of the attic room, her hair gleamed white.

She let the second towel drop.

Pale skin, white hair, dark eyes. A ghost. He needed to know that she was real, that they were both alive. He stretched out a hand and touched her.

They lay entwined on the little wooden cot and she whispered their future to him. Their flight would land at New York's Idlewild Airport early tomorrow evening. They would go straight to the *New York Times* building. There was an editor there she knew. The first thing was to make a copy—a dozen copies—and then to get as much printed as possible, as soon as possible. The *Times* was ideal for that.

"What if they won't print it?" This idea of people printing whatever they wanted was hard for him to grasp.

"They'll print it, all right. God, if they won't, I'll stand on Fifth Avenue like one of those mad people who can't get their novels published and hand out copies to passersby. But don't worry—they'll print it, and we'll change history."

"But will anyone believe it?" That doubt had grown within him ever since the suitcase had been opened. "Isn't it unbelievable?"

No, she said with great certainty, because now we have facts, and facts change everything. Without them, you have nothing, a void. But produce facts—provide names, dates, orders, numbers, times, locations, map references, schedules, photographs, diagrams, descriptions—and suddenly that void has geometry, is susceptible to measurement, becomes a solid thing. Of course, this solid thing can be denied or challenged or simply ignored. But each of these reactions is, by definition, a *reaction,* a response to something that exists.

"Some people won't believe it—they wouldn't believe it no matter how much evidence we had. But there's enough here, I think, to stop Kennedy in his tracks. No summit. No reelection. No détente. And five years from now, or fifty years, this society will fall apart. You can't build on a mass grave. Human beings are better than that—they have to be better than that—I do believe it—don't you?"

He did not reply.

He was awake to see another dawn in the Berlin sky. A familiar gray face at the attic window, an old opponent.

"Your name?"

"Magda Voss."

"Born?"

"October 25, 1939."

"Where?"

"Berlin."

"Your occupation?"

"I live at home with my parents, in Berlin."

"Where are you going?"

"To Waldshut, on the Rhine. To meet my fiancé."

"Name?"

"Paul Hahn."

"What is the purpose of your visit to Switzerland?"

"A friend's wedding."

"Where?"

"In Zürich."

"What is this?"

"A wedding present. A photograph album. A Bible? A

book? A chopping board?" She was testing the answers on him.

"Chopping board—very good. Exactly the sort of gift a girl like Magda *would* drive eight hundred kilometers to give." March had been pacing the room. Now he stopped and pointed at the package in Charlie's lap. "Open it, please, Fräulein."

She thought for a moment. "What do I say to that?"

"There's nothing you can say."

"Terrific." She took out a cigarette and lit it. "Well, would you look at that? My hands are trembling."

It was almost seven. "Time to go."

The hotel was beginning to wake. As they passed the lines of flimsy doors they heard water splashing, a radio, children laughing. Somewhere on the second floor, a man snored on regardless.

They had handled the package with care, at arm's length, as if it were plutonium. She had hidden it in the center of her suitcase, buried in her clothes. March carried it down the stairs, across the empty lobby and out the narrow fire exit at the rear of the hotel. She was wearing a dark blue suit, her hair hidden by a scarf. The hired Opel stood next to his Volkswagen. From the kitchen came shouts, the smell of fresh coffee, the hiss of frying food.

"When you leave the Bellevue, turn right. The road follows the line of the valley. You can't miss the bridge."

"You've told me this already."

"Try to see what level of security they're operating before you commit yourself. If it looks as if they're searching everything, turn around and try to hide it somewhere. Woods, a ditch, a barn—somewhere you can remember, a place where someone can go back and retrieve it. Then get out. Promise me."

"I promise you."

"There's a daily Swissair flight from Zürich to New York. It leaves at two."

"At two. I know. You've told me twice."

He took a step toward her, to hold her, but she fended him off. "I'm not saying good-bye. Not here. I'll see you tonight. *I will see you.*"

There was a moment of anticlimax when the Opel refused to start. She pulled out the choke and tried again, and this time the engine fired. She backed out of the parking space, still refusing to look at him. He had a last glimpse of her profile—staring straight ahead, her knuckles clenching the wheel—and then she was gone, leaving a trail of blue-white vapor hanging in the chilly morning air.

March sat alone in the empty room, on the edge of the bed, holding her pillow. He waited until an hour had passed before putting on his uniform. He stood in front of the dressing-table mirror, buttoning his black tunic. It would be the last time he wore it, one way or the other.

*"We'll change history."*

He donned his cap, adjusted it. Then he took his thirty sheets of paper, his notebook and Buhler's pocket diary, folded them together, wrapped them in the remaining sheet of brown paper and slipped them into his inside pocket.

Was history changed so easily? He wondered. Certainly, it was his experience that secrets were an acid—once spilled, they could eat their way through anything: if a marriage, why not a presidency, why not a state? But talk of history—he shook his head at his own reflection—history was beyond him. Investigators turned suspicion into evidence. He had done that. History he would leave to her.

He carried Luther's bag into the bathroom and shoveled into it all the rubbish that Charlie had left behind—the discarded bottles, the rubber gloves, the dish and spoon, the brushes. He did the same in the bedroom. It was strange how much she had filled these places, how empty they seemed without her. He looked at his watch. It was eight-thirty. She should be well clear of Berlin by now, perhaps as far south as Wittenberg.

In the reception area, the manager hovered.

"Good day, Herr Sturmbannführer. Is the interrogation finished?"

"It is indeed, Herr Brecker. Thank you for your patriotic assistance."

"A pleasure." Brecker gave a short bow. He was twisting his fat white hands together as if rubbing them with oil. "And if ever the Sturmbannführer feels the desire to do a little more interrogation . . ." His bushy eyebrows danced. "Perhaps I might even be able to supply him with a suspect or two?"

March smiled. "Good day to you, Herr Brecker."

"Good day to *you*, Herr Sturmbannführer."

He sat in the front passenger seat of the Volkswagen and thought for a moment. Inside the spare tire would be the ideal place, but he had no time for that. The plastic door panels were securely fastened. He reached under the dashboard until his fingers encountered a smooth surface. It would serve his purpose. He tore off two lengths of cellophane tape and attached the package to the cold metal.

Then he dropped the roll of tape into Luther's case and dumped the bag into one of the rubbish bins outside the kitchen. The brown leather looked too incongruous lying on the surface. He found a broken length of broom handle and dug a grave for it, burying it at last beneath the coffee dregs, the stinking fish heads, the lumps of grease and maggoty pork.

Yellow signs bearing the single word *Fernverkehr*—long-distance traffic—pointed the way out of Berlin, toward the racetrack autobahn that girdled the city. March had the southbound carriageway almost to himself—the few cars and buses about this early on a Sunday morning were heading the other way. He passed the perimeter wire of the Tempelhof aerodrome, and abruptly he was into the suburbs, the wide road pushing through dreary streets of red brick shops and houses, lined by sickly trees with blackened trunks.

To his left, a hospital; to his right, a disused church, shuttered and daubed with Party slogans. "Marienfelde," said the signs. "Bückow." "Lichtenrade."

At a set of traffic lights he stopped. The road to the south lay open—to the Rhine, to Zürich, to America . . . Behind him someone tooted. The lights had changed. He flicked the turn signal, swung off the main road, and was quickly lost in the gridiron streets of a housing estate.

In the early fifties, in the glow of victory, the roads had been named for generals: Student-Strasse, Reichenau-

Strasse, Manteuffel-Allee. March was always confused. Was it right off Model into Dietrich? Or was it left into Paulus, and *then* Dietrich? He drove slowly along the rows of identical bungalows until at last he recognized it.

He pulled over in the familiar place and almost sounded the horn until he remembered that this was the third Sunday in the month, not the first—and therefore not his—and that in any case his access had been revoked. A frontal assault would be needed, an action in the spirit of Hasso von Manteuffel himself.

There was no litter of toys along the concrete drive, and when he rang the bell, no dog barked. He cursed silently. It seemed to be his fate this week to stand outside deserted houses. He backed away from the porch, his eyes fixed on the window beside it. The net curtain flickered.

"Pili! Are you there?"

The corner of the curtain was abruptly parted, as if some hidden dignitary had pulled a cord unveiling a portrait, and there it was—his son's white face staring at him.

"May I come in? I want to talk!"

The face was expressionless. The curtain dropped back.

Good sign or bad? March was uncertain. He waved to the blank window and pointed to the garden. "I'll wait for you here."

He walked back to the little wooden gate and checked the street. Bungalows on either side, bungalows opposite. They extended in every direction like the huts of an army camp. Old folks lived in most of them: veterans of the First War, survivors of all that had followed—inflation, unemployment, the Party, the Second War. Even ten years ago, they had been gray and bowed. They had seen enough, endured enough. Now they stayed at home and shouted at Pili for making too much noise and watched television all day.

March prowled around the tiny handkerchief of lawn. Not much of a life for the boy. Cars passed. Two doors down an old man was repairing a bicycle, inflating the tires with a squeaky pump. Elsewhere, the noise of a lawnmower . . . No sign of Pili. He was wondering if he would have to get down on his hands and knees and shout his message through the letterbox when he heard the door being opened.

"Good lad. How are you? Where's your mother? Where's Helfferich?" He could not bring himself to say "Uncle Erich."

Pili had opened the door just enough to enable him to peer around it. "They're out. I'm finishing my picture."

"Out where?"

"Rehearsing for the parade. I'm in charge. They said so."

"I bet. Can I come in and talk to you?"

He had expected resistance. Instead the boy stood aside without a word and March found himself crossing the threshold of his ex-wife's house for the first time since their divorce. He took in the furniture—cheap but good looking; the bunch of fresh daffodils on the mantelpiece; the neatness; the spotless surfaces. She had done it as well as she could without much to spend. He would have expected that. Even the picture of the Führer above the telephone—a photograph of the old man hugging a child—was tasteful: Klara's deity always was a benign god, New Testament rather than Old. He took off his cap. He felt like a burglar.

He stood on the nylon rug and began his speech. "I have to go away, Pili. Maybe for a long time. And people, perhaps, are going to say some things to you about me. Horrible things that aren't true. And I wanted to tell you . . ." His words petered out. *Tell you what?* He ran his hand through his hair. Pili was standing with his arms folded, gazing at him. He tried again. "It's hard not having a father around. My father died when I was very little—younger even than you are now. And sometimes I hated him for that."

*Those cool eyes . . .*

". . . But that passed, and then—I missed him. And

if I could talk to him now—ask him . . . I'd give anything . . ."

*. . . all human hair cut off in concentration camps should be utilized. Human hair will be processed for industrial felt and spun into thread.*

He was not sure how long he stood there, not speaking, his head bowed. Eventually he said, "I have to go now."

And then Pili was coming toward him and tugging at his hand. "It's all right, Papa. Please don't go yet. Please. Come and look at my picture."

The boy's bedroom was like a command center. Model Luftwaffe jets assembled from plastic kits swooped and fought, suspended from the ceiling by invisible lengths of fishing line. On one wall, a map of the eastern front, with colored pins to show the positions of the armies. On another, a group photograph of Pili's Pimpf unit—bare knees and solemn faces, photographed against a concrete wall.

As he drew, Pili kept up a running commentary, with sound effects. "These are our jets—*rrroowww!*—and these are the Reds' AA guns. *Pow! Pow!*" Lines of yellow crayon streaked skyward. "Now we let them have it. Fire!" Little black ants' eggs rained down, creating jagged red crowns of fire. "The commies call up their own fighters, but they're no match for ours." It went on for another five minutes, action piled on action.

Abruptly, bored by his own creation, Pili dropped the crayons and dived under the bed. He pulled out a stack of wartime picture magazines.

"Where did you get those?"

"Uncle Erich gave them to me. He collected them."

Pili flung himself onto the bed and began to turn the pages. "What do the captions say, Papa?" He gave March the magazine and sat close to him, holding on to his arm.

" 'The sapper has worked his way right up to the wire

obstacles protecting the machine gun position,' " read March. " 'A few spurts of flame and the deadly stream of burning oil has put the enemy out of action. The flame-throwers must be fearless men with nerves of steel.' "

"And that one?"

This was not the farewell March had envisaged, but if it was what the boy wanted . . . He plowed on: " 'I want to fight for the new Europe: so say three brothers from Copenhagen with their company leader in the SS training camp in Upper Alsace. They have fulfilled all the conditions relating to questions of race and health and are now enjoying the manly open-air life in the camp in the woods.' "

"What about these?"

March smiled. "Come on, Pili. You're ten years old. You can read these easily."

"But I want you to read them. Here's a picture of a U-boat, like yours. What does it say?"

He stopped smiling and put down the magazine. There was something wrong here. What was it? He realized: the silence. For several minutes now, nothing had happened in the street outside—not a car, not a footstep, not a voice. Even the lawn mower had stopped. He saw Pili's eyes flick to the window, and he understood.

Somewhere in the house: a tinkle of glass. March scrambled for the door, but the boy was too quick for him—rolling off the bed, grabbing his legs, curling himself around his father's feet in a fetal ball, a parody of childish entreaty. "Please don't go, Papa," he was saying. "Please . . ." March's fingers grasped the door handle, but he couldn't move. He was anchored, mired. I have dreamed this before, he thought. The window imploded behind them, showering their backs with glass—now real uniforms with real guns were filling the bedroom—and suddenly March was on his back gazing up at the little plastic warplanes bobbing and spinning crazily at the ends of their invisible wires.

He could hear Pili's voice: "It's going to be all right, Papa. They're going to help you. They'll make you better. Then you can come and live with us. They promised . . ."

His hands were cuffed tight behind his back, wrists outward. Two SS men had propped him against the wall, against the map of the eastern front, and Globus stood before him. Pili had been hustled away, thank God. "I have waited for this moment," said Globus, "as a bridegroom waits for his bride," and he punched March in the stomach, hard. March folded, dropped to his knees, dragging the map and all its little pins down with him, thinking he would never breathe again. Then Globus had him by the hair and was pulling him up, and his body was trying to retch and suck in oxygen at the same time and Globus hit him again and he went down again. This process was repeated several times. Finally, while he was lying on the carpet with his knees drawn up, Globus planted his boot on the side of his head and ground his toe into his ear. "Look," he said, "I've put my foot on shit," and from a long way away, March heard the sound of men laughing.

"Where's the girl?"
"What girl?"

Globus slowly extended his stubby fingers in front of March's face, then brought his hand arching down in a karate blow to the kidneys.

This was much worse than anything else—a blinding white flash of pain that shot straight through him and put him on the floor again, retching bile. And the worst was to know that he was merely in the foothills of a long climb. The stages of torture stretched before him, ascending as notes on a scale, from the dull bass of a blow in the belly, through the middle register of kidney punches, onward and upward to some pitch beyond the range of the human ear, a pinnacle of crystal.

"Where's the girl?"

"What . . . girl?"

They disarmed him, searched him, then they half pushed, half dragged him out of the bungalow. A little crowd had gathered in the road. Klara's elderly neighbors watched as he was bundled, head bowed, into the back of the BMW. He glimpsed briefly along the street four or five cars with revolving lights, a lorry, troops. What had they been expecting? A small war? Still no sign of Pili. The handcuffs forced him to sit hunched forward. Two Gestapo men were jammed into the backseat, one on either side of him. As the car pulled away, he could see some of the old folks already shuffling back into their houses, back to the reassuring glow of their television sets.

He was driven north through the holiday traffic, up into Saarland-Strasse, east into Prinz-Albrecht-Strasse. Fifty meters past the main entrance to Gestapo headquarters, the convoy swung right, through a pair of high prison gates and into a brick courtyard at the back of the building.

He was pulled out of the car and through a low entrance, down steep concrete steps. Then his heels were scraping along the floor of an arched hallway. A door, a cell . . . silence.

They left him alone to allow his imagination to go to work—standard procedure. Very well. He crawled into a corner and rested his head against the damp brick. Every minute that passed was another minute's traveling time for her. He thought of Pili, of all the lies, and clenched his fists.

The cell was lit by a weak bulb above the door, imprisoned in its own rusty metal cage. He glanced at his wrist, a useless reflex, for they had taken away his watch. Surely she could not be far from Nuremberg by now? He tried to fill his mind with images of the Gothic spires—St. Lorenz, St. Sebaldus, St. Jakob . . .

Every limb—every part of him to which he could put a name—ached, yet they could not have worked him over for more than five minutes, and still they had managed not to leave a mark on his face. Truly, he had fallen into the hands of experts. He almost laughed, but that hurt his ribs, so he stopped.

He was taken along the hallway to an interview room: whitewashed walls, a heavy oak table with a chair on each side; in the corner, an iron stove. Globus had disappeared; Krebs was in command. The handcuffs were removed. Standard procedure again—first the hard cop, then the soft. Krebs even attempted a joke: "Normally, we would arrest your son and threaten him as well, to encourage your cooperation. But in your case, we know that such a course would be counterproductive." Secret policeman's humor! He leaned back in his chair, smiling, and pointed his pencil. "Nevertheless. A remarkable boy."

" 'Remarkable'—your word." At some point during his beating, March had bitten his tongue. He talked now as if he had spent a week in a dentist's chair.

"Your ex-wife was given a telephone number last night," said Krebs, "in case you attempted contact. The boy memorized it. The instant he saw you, he called. He's inherited your brains, March. Your initiative. You should feel some pride."

"At this moment, my feelings toward my son are indeed strong."

Good, he thought, let's keep this up. Another minute, another kilometer.

But Krebs was already down to business, turning the pages of a thick folder. "There are two issues here, March. One: your general political reliability, going back over many years. That does not concern us today—at least, not directly. Two: your conduct over the past week—specifically, your involvement in the attempts of the late Party Comrade Luther to defect to the United States."

"I have no such involvement."

"You were questioned by an officer of the Ordnungspolizei in Adolf-Hitler-Platz yesterday morning—at the exact time the traitor Luther was planning to meet the American journalist, Maguire, together with an official of the United States Embassy."

How did they know that? "Absurd."

"Do you deny you were in the Platz?"

"No. Of course not."

"Then why were you there?"

"I was following the American woman."

Krebs was making notes. "Why?"

"She was the person who discovered the body of Party Comrade Stuckart. I was also naturally suspicious of her, in her role as an agent of the bourgeois democratic press."

"Don't piss me about, March."

"All right. I had insinuated myself into her company. I thought: if she can stumble across the corpse of one retired state secretary, she might stumble across another."

"A fair point." Krebs rubbed his chin and thought for a moment, then opened a fresh pack of cigarettes and gave one to March, lighting it for him from an unused box of matches. March filled his lungs with smoke. Krebs had not taken one for himself, he noticed—they were merely a part of his act, an interrogator's props.

The Gestapo man was leafing through his notes again, frowning. "We believe that the traitor Luther was planning to disclose certain information to the journalist Maguire. What was the nature of this information?"

"I have no idea. The art fraud, perhaps?"

"On Thursday you visited Zürich. Why?"

"It was the place Luther went before he vanished. I wanted to see if there was any clue there that might explain why he disappeared."

"And was there?"

"No. But my visit was authorized. I submitted a full report to Oberstgruppenführer Nebe. Have you not seen it?"

"Of course not." Krebs made a note. "The Oberstgruppenführer shows his hand to no one, not even us. Where is Maguire?"

"How should I know?"

"You should know because you picked her up from Adolf-Hitler-Platz after the shooting yesterday."

"Not me, Krebs."

"Yes, you, March. Afterward, you went to the morgue and searched through the traitor Luther's personal effects—this we know absolutely from SS surgeon Eisler."

"I was not aware that the effects *were* Luther's," said March. "I understood they belonged to a man named Stark who was three meters away from Maguire when he was shot. Naturally, I was interested to see what he was carrying, because I was interested in Maguire. Besides, if you recall, *you* showed me what you said was Luther's body on Friday night. Who did shoot Luther, as a matter of interest?"

"Never mind that. What did you expect to pick up at the morgue?"

"Plenty."

"What? Be exact!"

"Fleas. Lice. A skin rash from his shitty clothes."

Krebs threw down his pencil. He folded his arms. "You're a brainy fellow, March. Take comfort from the fact that we credit you with that, at least. Do you think we'd give a shit if you were just some dumb fat fuck, like your friend Max Jaeger? I bet you could keep this up for hours. But we don't have hours, and we're less stupid than you think." He shuffled through his papers, smirked and then played his ace.

"What was in the suitcase you took from the airport?"

March looked straight back at him. They had known all along. "What suitcase?"

"The suitcase that looks like a doctor's bag. The suitcase that doesn't weigh very much, but might contain paper. The suitcase Friedman gave you thirty minutes before he called us. He got back to find a telex, you see, March, from Prinz-Albrecht-Strasse—an alert to stop you from leaving the country. When he saw that, he decided—as a patriotic citizen—he'd better inform us of your visit."

"Friedman!" said March. "A 'patriotic citizen'? He's fooling you, Krebs. He's hiding some scheme of his own."

Krebs sighed. He got to his feet and came around to stand behind March, his hands resting on the back of March's chair. "When this is over, I'd like to get to know you. Really. Assuming there's anything left of you to get to know. Why did someone like you go bad? I'm interested. From a technical point of view. To try to stop it happening in the future."

"Your passion for self-improvement is laudable."

"There you go again, you see? A problem of attitude. Things are changing in Germany, March—from within—and you could have been a part of it. The Reichsführer himself takes a personal interest in the new generation—listens to us, promotes us. He believes in restructuring, greater openness, talking to the Americans. The day of men like Odilo Globocnik is passing." He stooped and whispered in March's ear, "Do you know why Globus doesn't like you?"

"Enlighten me."

"Because you make him feel stupid. In Globus's book, that's a capital offense. Help me, and I can shield you from him." Krebs straightened and resumed, in his normal voice, "Where is the woman? What was the information Luther wanted to give her? Where is Luther's suitcase?"

Those three questions, again and again.

Interrogations have this irony, at least: they can enlighten those being questioned as much as—or more than—those who are doing the questioning.

From what Krebs asked, March could measure the extent of his knowledge. This was, on certain matters, very good: he knew March had visited the morgue, for example, and that he had retrieved the suitcase from the airport. But there was a significant gap. Unless Krebs was playing a fiendishly devious game, it seemed he had no idea of the *nature* of the information Luther had promised the Americans. Upon this one, narrow ground rested March's only hope.

After an inconclusive half hour, the door opened and Globus appeared, swinging a long truncheon of polished wood. Behind him stood two thick-set men in black uniforms.

Krebs leapt to attention.

Globus asked, "Has he made a full confession?"

"No, Herr Obergruppenführer."

"What a surprise. My turn then, I think."

"Of course." Krebs stooped and collected his papers.

Was it March's imagination, or did he see on that long, impassive face a flicker of regret, even of distaste?

After Krebs had gone, Globus prowled around, humming an old Party marching song, dragging the length of wood over the stone floor.

"Do you know what this is, March?" He waited. "No? No answer? It's an American invention. A baseball bat. A pal of mine at the Washington Embassy brought it back for me." He swung it around his head a couple of times. "I'm thinking of raising an SS team. We could play the U.S. Army. What do you think? Goebbels is keen. He thinks the American masses would respond well to the pictures."

He leaned the bat against the heavy wooden table and began unbuttoning his tunic.

"If you want my opinion, the original mistake was in '36, when Himmler said every Kripo flatfoot in the Reich had to wear SS uniform. That's when we were landed with scum like you and shriveled-up old cunts like Artur Nebe."

He handed his jacket to one of the two guards and began rolling up his sleeves. Suddenly he was shouting: "My God, we used to know how to deal with people like you. But we've gone soft. It's not 'Has he got guts?' anymore, it's 'Has he got a doctorate?' We didn't need doctorates in the East, in '41, when there was fifty degrees of frost and your piss froze in midair. You should have heard Krebs, March. You'd have loved it. Fuck it, I think he's one of your lot." He adopted a mincing voice. " 'With permission, Herr Obergruppenführer, I would like to question the suspect first. I feel he may respond to a more subtle approach.' Subtle, my ass. What's the point of you? If you were my dog, I'd feed you poison."

"If I were your dog, I'd eat it."

Globus grinned at one of the guards. "Listen to the big man!" He spat on his hands and picked up the baseball bat. He turned to March. "I've been looking at your file. I see you're a great one for writing. Forever taking notes, compiling lists. Quite the frustrated fucking author. Tell me: are you left-handed or right-handed?"

"Left-handed."

"Another lie. Put your right arm on the table."

March felt as if iron bands had been fastened around

his chest. He could barely breathe. "Go screw yourself."

Globus glanced at the guards and powerful hands seized March from behind. The chair toppled and he was being bent headfirst over the table. One of the SS men twisted his left arm high up his back and wrenched it, and he was roaring with the pain of that as the other man grabbed his free hand. The man half climbed onto the table and planted his knee just below March's right elbow, pinning his forearm, palm down, to the wooden planks.

Within seconds, everything was locked in place except his fingers, which were just able to flutter slightly, like a trapped bird.

Globus stood a meter from the table, brushing the tip of the bat lightly across March's knuckles. Then he lifted it, swung it in a great arc, like an ax, through three hundred degrees, and with all his force brought it smashing down.

He did not faint, not at first. The guards let him go and he slid to his knees, a thread of spit dribbling from the corner of his mouth, leaving a snail's trail across the table. His arm was still stretched out. He stayed like that for a while, until he raised his head and saw the remains of his hand—some alien pile of blood and gristle on a butcher's slab—and then he fainted.

Footsteps in the darkness. Voices.

"Where is the woman?"

Kick.

"What was the information?"

Kick.

"What did you steal?"

Kick. Kick.

A jackboot stamped on his fingers, twisted, ground them into the stone.

♦

When he came to again, he was lying in the corner, his broken hand resting on the floor next to him like a stillborn baby left beside its mother. A man—Krebs, perhaps—was squatting in front of him, saying something. He tried to focus.

"What is this?" Krebs's mouth was saying. "What does it mean?"

The Gestapo man was breathless, as if he had been running up and down stairs. With one hand he grasped March's chin, twisting his face to the light. In the other he held a sheaf of papers.

"What does it mean, March? They were hidden in the front of your car. Taped underneath the dashboard. What does it mean?"

March pulled his head away and turned his face to the darkening wall.

*Tap, tap, tap.* In his dreams. *Tap, tap, tap.*

Sometime later—he could not be more accurate than that, for time was beyond measurement, now speeding, now slowing to an infinitesimal crawl—a white jacket appeared above him. A flash of steel. A thin blade poised vertically before his eyes. March tried to back away, but fingers locked around his wrist, the needle was jabbed into a vein. At first, when his hand was touched, he howled, but then he felt the fluid spreading through his veins and the agony subsided.

The torture doctor was old and hunchbacked, and it seemed to March, who brimmed with gratitude toward him, that he must have lived in the basement for many years. The grime had settled in his pores, the darkness hung in pouches beneath his eyes. He did not speak. He cleaned the wound, painted it with a clear liquid that smelled of hospitals and morgues, and bound it tightly in a white crepe bandage. Then, still without speaking, he and Krebs helped March to his feet. They put him back into his chair. An enamel mug of sweet, milky coffee was set on the table before him. A cigarette was slipped into his good hand.

In his mind March had built a wall. Behind it he placed Charlie in her speeding car. It was a high wall, made of everything his imagination could collect—boulders, concrete blocks, burned-out iron bedsteads, overturned tramcars, suitcases, prams—and it stretched in either direction across the sunlit German countryside like a postcard of the Great Wall of China. In front of it, he patrolled the ground. *He would not let them beyond the wall.* Everything else, they could have.

Krebs was reading March's notes. He sat with both elbows on the table, his chin resting on his knuckles. Occasionally he removed a hand to turn a page, replaced it, went on reading. March watched him. After his coffee and his cigarette and with the pain dulled, he felt almost euphoric.

Krebs finished and momentarily closed his eyes. His complexion was white, as always. Then he straightened the pages and laid them in front of him, alongside March's notebook and Buhler's diary. He adjusted them by millimeters into a line of parade-ground precision. Perhaps it was the effect of the drug, but suddenly March was seeing everything so clearly—how the ink on the cheap pages had spread slightly, each letter sprouting minute hairs; how badly Krebs had shaved: that clump of black stubble in the fold of skin below his nose. In the silence he actually believed he could hear the dust falling, pattering across the table.

"Have you killed me, March?"

"Killed you?"

"With these." His hand hovered a centimeter above the notes.

"It depends on who knows you have them."

"Only some cretin of an *Unterscharführer* who works in the garage. He found them when we brought in your car. He gave them directly to me. Globus doesn't know a thing—yet."

"Then that's your answer."

Krebs started rubbing his face vigorously, as if drying himself. He stopped, his hands pressed to his cheeks, and stared at March through his spread fingers. "What's happening here?"

"You can read."

"I can read, but I don't understand." Krebs snatched up the pages and leafed through them. "Here, for example—what is 'Zyklon B'?"

"Crystallized hydrogen cyanide. Before that, they used carbon monoxide. Before that, bullets."

"And here—'Auschwitz/Birkenau.' 'Kulmhof.' 'Belzec.' 'Treblinka.' 'Majdanek.' 'Sobibor.' "

"The killing grounds."

"These figures: eight thousand a day . . ."

"That's the total they could destroy at Auschwitz/Birkenau using the four gas chambers and crematoria."

"And this eleven million?"

"Eleven million is the total number of European Jews they were after. Maybe they succeeded. Who knows? I don't see many around, do you?"

"Here: the name 'Globocnik' . . ."

"Globus was SS and police leader in Lublin. He built the killing centers."

"I didn't know." Krebs dropped the notes onto the table as if they were contagious. "I didn't know any of this."

"Of course you knew! You knew every time someone made a joke about 'going East,' every time you heard a mother tell her children to behave or they'd go up the chimney. We knew when we moved into their houses, when we took over their property, their jobs. We knew but we didn't have the facts." He pointed to the notes with his left hand. "Those put flesh on the bones. Put bones where there was just clear air."

"I meant: I didn't know that Buhler, Stuckart and Luther were involved in this. I didn't know about Globus . . ."

"Sure. You just thought you were investigating an art robbery."

"It's true! It's true!" repeated Krebs. "Wednesday morning—can you remember back that far?—I was investigating corruption at the Deutsche Arbeitsfront: the sale of labor permits. Then, out of the blue, I am summoned to see the Reichsführer, one to one. He tells me retired civil servants have been discovered in a colossal art fraud. The potential embarrassment for the Party is huge. Obergruppenführer Globocnik is in charge. I am to go at once to Schwanenwerder and take my orders from him."

"Why you?"

"Why not? The Reichsführer knows of my interest in art. We have spoken of these matters. My job was simply to catalog the treasures."

"But you must have realized that Globus killed Buhler and Stuckart?"

"Of course. I'm not an idiot. I know Globus's reputation as well as you. But Globus was acting on Heydrich's orders, and if Heydrich had decided to let him loose, to spare the Party a public scandal—who was I to object?"

"Who were you to object?" repeated March.

"Let's be clear, March. Are you saying their deaths had nothing to do with the fraud?"

"Nothing. The fraud was a coincidence that became a useful cover story, that's all."

"But it made sense. It explained why Globus was acting as state executioner, and why he was desperate to head off an investigation by the Kripo. On Wednesday night I was still cataloging the pictures on Schwanenwerder when he called in a rage—about you. Said you'd been officially taken off the case, but you'd broken into Stuckart's apartment. I was to go and bring you in, which I did. And I tell you: if Globus had had his way, that would have been the end of you right there, but Nebe wouldn't have it. Then, on Friday night, we found what we thought was Luther's body in the railway yard, and that seemed to be the end of it."

"When did you discover the corpse wasn't Luther's?"

"Around six on Saturday morning. Globus telephoned me at home. He said he had information Luther was still alive and was planning to meet the American journalist at nine."

"He knew this," asserted March, "because of a tipoff from the American Embassy."

Krebs snorted. "What sort of crap is that? He knew because of a wire tap."

"That can't be—"

"Why can't it? See for yourself." Krebs opened one of his folders and extracted a single sheet of flimsy brown paper. "It was rushed over from the wire tappers in Charlottenburg in the middle of the night."

March read:

*Forschungsamt* *Top Secret State Document*
*G745,275*
*2351 hours*

Male: You say: What do I want? What do you think I want? Asylum in your country.

Female: Tell me where you are.

Male: I can pay.
Female: [Interrupts.]
Male: I have information. Certain facts.
Female: Tell me where you are. I'll come and get you. We'll go to the embassy.
Male: Too soon. Not yet.
Female: When?
Male: Tomorrow morning. Listen to me. Nine o'-clock. The Great Hall. Central steps. Have you got that?

Once more he could hear her voice; smell her; touch her.

In a recess of his mind, something stirred.

He slid the paper back across the table to Krebs, who returned it to the folder and resumed, "What happened next, you know. Globus had Luther shot the instant he appeared—and, let me be honest, that shocked me. To do such a thing in a public place . . . I thought: this man is mad. Of course, I didn't know then quite why he was so anxious that Luther shouldn't be taken alive." He stopped abruptly, as if he had forgotten where he was, the role he was supposed to be playing. He finished quickly, "We searched the body and found nothing. Then we came after you."

March's hand had started to throb again. He looked down and saw crimson spots soaking through the white bandage.

"What time is it?"

"Five forty-seven."

She had been gone almost eleven hours.

God, his hand . . . The specks of red were spreading, touching; forming archipelagoes of blood.

"There were four of them in it altogether," said March. "Buhler, Stuckart, Luther and Kritzinger."

"Kritzinger?" Krebs made a note.

"Friedrich Kritzinger, Ministerialdirektor of the Reich Chancellery. I wouldn't write any of this down if I were you."

Krebs laid aside his pencil.

"What concerned them wasn't the extermination program itself—these were senior Party men, remember—it was the lack of a proper Führer Order. Nothing was written down. All they had were verbal assurances from Heydrich and Himmler that this was what the Führer wanted. Could I have another cigarette?"

After Krebs had given him one and he had taken a few sweet draughts, he went on, "This is conjecture, you understand?" His interrogator nodded. "I assume they asked themselves: why is there no direct written link between the Führer and this policy? And I assume their answer was: because it is so monstrous, the head of state cannot be seen to be involved. So where did this leave them? It left them in the shit. Because if Germany lost the war, they could be tried as war criminals, and if Germany won it, they might one day be made the scapegoats for the greatest act of mass murder in history."

Krebs murmured, "I'm not sure I want to know this."

"So they took out an insurance policy. They swore affidavits—that was easy: three of them were lawyers—and they removed documents whenever they could. And gradually they put together a documentary record. Either outcome was covered. If Germany won and action was taken against them, they could threaten to expose what they knew. If the Allies won, they could say: look, we opposed this policy and even risked our lives to collect information about it. Luther also added a touch of blackmail—embarrassing documents about the American ambassador to London, Kennedy. Give me those."

He nodded to his notebook and to Buhler's diary. Krebs hesitated, then slid them across the table.

It was difficult to open the notebook with only one hand. The bandage was sodden. He was smearing the pages.

"The camps were organized to make sure there were no witnesses. Special prisoners ran the gas chambers, the crematoria. Eventually, those special prisoners were themselves destroyed, replaced by others, who were also destroyed. And so on. If that could happen at the lowest level, why not the highest? Look. Fourteen people at the Wannsee conference. The first one dies in '54. Another in '55. Then one a year in '57, '59, '60, '61, '62. Intruders probably planned to kill Luther in '63, and he hired security guards. But time passed and nothing happened, so he assumed it was just a coincidence."

"That's enough, March."

"By '63, it had started to accelerate. In May, Klopfer dies. In December, Hoffmann hangs himself. In March this year, Kritzinger is blown up by a car bomb. Now Buhler is really frightened. Kritzinger is the trigger. He's the first of the group to die."

March picked up the pocket diary.

"Here—you see—he marks the date of Kritzinger's death with a cross. But after that the days go by; nothing happens; perhaps they are safe. Then, on April ninth—another cross! Buhler's old colleague from the General Government, Schöngarth, slips beneath the wheels of a U-bahn train in Zoo Station. Panic on Schwanenwerder! But by then it's too late."

"I said that's enough!"

"One question puzzled me: why were there eight deaths in the first nine years, followed by six deaths in just the last six months? Why the rush? Why this terrible risk, after the exercise of so much patience? But then, we policemen seldom lift our eyes from the mud to look at the broader picture, do we? Everything was supposed to be completed by last Tuesday, ready for the visit of our good new friends, the Americans. And that raises a further question—"

"Give me those!" Krebs pulled the diary and the notebook from March's grasp. Outside in the passage: Globus's voice . . .

"Would Heydrich have done all this on his own initiative, or was he acting on orders from a higher level? Orders, perhaps, from the same person who would not put his signature to any document?"

Krebs had the stove open and was stuffing the papers in. For a moment they lay smoldering on the coals, then ignited into yellow flame as the key turned in the cell door.

"Kulmhof!" he shouted at Globus when the pain became too bad. "Belzec! Treblinka!"

"Now we're getting somewhere." Globus grinned at his two assistants.

"Majdanek! Sobibor! Auschwitz-Birkenau!" He held up the names like a shield to ward off the blows.

"What am I supposed to do? Shrivel up and die?" Globus squatted on his haunches and grabbed March by the ears, twisting his face toward him. "They're just names, March. There's nothing there anymore, not even a brick. Nobody will ever believe it. And shall I tell you something? *Part of you can't believe it either.*" Globus spat in his face—a gobbet of grayish-yellow phlegm. "That's how much the world will care." He thrust him away, bouncing his head against the stone floor.

"Now. Again: where's the girl?"

Time crawled on all fours, broken-backed. He was shivering. His teeth chattered like a clockwork toy.

Other prisoners had been here years before him. In lieu of tombstones they had scratched on the cell's walls with splintered fingernails. "J.F.G. 2-22-57." "Katja." "H.K. May 44." Someone had gotten no further than half the letter "E" before strength or time or will had run out. Yet still this urge to write . . .

None of the marks, he noticed, was more than a meter above the floor.

The pain in his hand was making him feverish. He was having hallucinations. A dog ground his fingers between its jaws. He closed his eyes and wondered what time was doing now. When he had last asked Krebs it had been—what?—almost six. Then they had talked for perhaps another half hour. After that there had been his second session with Globus—infinite. Now this stretch alone in his cell, slithering in and out of the light, tugged one way by exhaustion, the other by the dog.

The floor was warm to his cheek, the smooth stone dissolved.

♦

He dreamed of his father—his childhood dream—the stiff figure in the photograph come to life, waving from the deck of the ship as it pulled out of the harbor, waving until he dwindled to a stick figure, until he disappeared. He dreamed of Jost, running on the spot, intoning his poetry in his solemn voice: "You throw food to the beast in man, / That it may grow . . ." He dreamed of Charlie.

But most often he dreamed he was back in Pili's bedroom at that dreadful instant when he had understood what the boy had done out of kindness—*kindness!*—when his arms were reaching for the door but his legs were trapped—and the window was exploding and rough hands were dragging at his shoulders . . .

The jailer shook him awake.

"On your feet!"

He was curled up tightly on his left side, fetuslike—his body raw, his joints welded. The guard's push awoke the dog and he was sick. There was nothing in him to bring up, but his stomach convulsed anyway, for old time's sake. The cell retreated a long way and came rushing back. He was pulled upright. The jailer swung a pair of handcuffs. Next to him stood Krebs, thank God, not Globus.

Krebs looked at him with distaste and said to the guard, "You'd better put them on at the front."

His wrists were locked before him, his cap was stuffed onto his head and he was marched, hunched forward, along the passage, up the steps, into the fresh air.

A cold night, and clear. The stars were sprayed across the sky above the courtyard. The buildings and the cars were silver edged in the moonlight. Krebs pushed him into the backseat of a Mercedes and climbed in after him. He nodded to the driver: "Columbia House. Lock the doors."

As the bolts slid home in the door beside him, March felt a flicker of relief.

"Don't raise your hopes," said Krebs. "The Obergruppenführer is still waiting for you. We have more modern technology at Columbia, that's all."

They pulled out through the gates, looking to any who saw them like two SS officers and their chauffeur. A guard saluted.

Columbia House was three kilometers south of Prinz-Albrecht-Strasse. The darkened government buildings quickly yielded to shabby office blocks and boarded-up warehouses. The area close to the prison had been scheduled for redevelopment in the 1950s, and here and there Speer's bulldozers had made destructive forays. But the money had run out before anything could be built to replace what they had knocked down. Now, overgrown patches of derelict land gleamed in the bluish light like the corners of old battlefields. In the dark side streets between them dwelled the teeming colonies of East European *Gastarbeiter.*

March was sitting stretched out, his head resting on the back of the leather seat, when Krebs suddenly leaned toward him and shouted, "Oh, for fuck's sake!" He turned to the driver. "He's pissing himself. Pull over here."

The driver swore and braked hard.

"Open the doors!"

Krebs got out, came around to March's side and yanked him out. "Quickly! We haven't got all night!" To the driver: "One minute. Keep the engine running."

Then March was being pushed—stumbling across rough stones, down an alley, into the doorway of a disused church, and Krebs was unlocking the handcuffs.

"You're a lucky man, March."

"I don't understand—"

Krebs said, "You've got a favorite uncle."

*Tap, tap, tap.* From the darkness of the church. *Tap, tap, tap.*

♦

"You should have come to me at once, my boy," said Artur Nebe. "You would have spared yourself such agony." He brushed March's cheek with his fingertips. In the heavy shadows, March could not make out the details of his face, only a pale blur.

"Take my pistol." Krebs pressed the Luger into March's left hand. "Take it! You tricked me. Got hold of my gun. Understand?"

He was dreaming, surely? But the pistol felt solid enough . . .

Nebe was still talking—a low, urgent voice. "Oh, March, March. Krebs came to me this evening—shocked! so shocked!—told me what you had. We all suspected it, of course, but never had the proof. Now you've got to get it out. For all our sakes. You've got to stop these bastards!"

Krebs interrupted, "Forgive me, sir, our time is almost gone." He pointed. "Down there, March. Can you see? A car."

Parked under a broken streetlamp at the far end of the alley, March could just see a low shape, could hear a motor running.

"What is this?" He looked from one man to the other.

"Walk to the car and get in. We've no more time. I count to ten, then I yell."

"Don't fail us, March." Nebe squeezed his cheek. "Your uncle is an old man, but he hopes to live long enough to see those bastards hang. Go on. Get the papers out. Get them published. We're risking everything, giving you a chance. Take it. Go."

Krebs said, "I'm counting: one, two, three . . ."

March hesitated, started to walk, then broke into a loping run. The car door was opening. He looked back. Nebe had already disappeared into the dark. Krebs had cupped his hands to his mouth and was starting to shout.

March turned and struggled toward the waiting car, where a familiar voice was calling, "Zavi! Zavi!"

# *FÜHRERTAG*

♦

The railway to Krakau continues north-east past Auschwitz (348 kilometers from Vienna), an industrial town of 12,000 inhabitants, the former capital of the Piast Duchies of Auschwitz and Zator (Hotel Zator 20 bedrooms), whence a secondary railway runs via Skawina to Krakau (69 kilometers in three hours) . . .

BAEDEKER'S *General Government,* 1943

Midnight peals of bells rang out to welcome the day. Drivers whipped past, flashing their headlights, hammering their horns, leaving a smear of sound hanging over the road behind them. Factory hooters called to one another across Berlin, like stationary trains.

"My dear old friend, what have they done to you?"

Max Jaeger was trying to concentrate on driving, but every few seconds his head would swivel to the right, in horrified fascination, toward the passenger seat beside him.

He kept repeating it: "What have they done to you?"

March was in a daze, uncertain what was dream and what reality. He had his back half turned and was staring out of the rear window. "Where are we going, Max?"

"God only knows. Where do you want to go?"

The road behind was clear. March carefully pulled himself around to look at Jaeger. "Didn't Nebe tell you?"

"Nebe said *you'd* tell *me.*"

March looked away, at the buildings sliding by. He did not see them. He was thinking of Charlie in the hotel room in Waldshut. Awake, alone, waiting for him. There were still more than eight hours to go. He and Max would have the *Autobahnen* almost to themselves. They could probably make it.

"I was at the Markt," Jaeger was saying. "This was about nine. The telephone rings. It's Uncle Artur. 'Sturmbannführer! How good a friend is Xavier March?' 'There's nothing I wouldn't do,' I said—by this time, the word was out about where you were. He said, very quietly, 'All right, Sturmbannführer, we'll see how good a friend you are. Kreuzberg. Corner of Axmann-Weg, north of the abandoned church. Wait from quarter to midnight to quarter past. And not a word to anyone or you'll be in a KZ by morning.' That was it. He hung up."

There was a sheen of sweat on Jaeger's forehead. He glanced from the road to March and back again. "Fuck it, Zavi. I don't know what I'm doing. I'm scared. I'm heading south. Is that okay?"

"You're doing fine."

"Aren't you glad to see me?" asked Jaeger.

"Very glad."

March felt faint again. He twisted his body and wound down the window with his left hand. Above the sound of the wind and the tires: a noise. What was it? He put his head out and looked up. He could not see it, but he could hear it overhead. The clatter of a helicopter. He closed the window.

He remembered the telephone transcript: *"What do I want? What do you think I want? Asylum in your country."*

The car's dials and gauges shone a soft green in the darkness. The upholstery smelled of fresh leather.

He said, "Where did you get the car, Max?" It was a Mercedes: the latest model.

"From the pool at Werderscher-Markt. A beauty, yes? She's got a full tank. We can go anywhere you want. Anywhere at all."

Then March began to laugh. Not very hard and not for very long, because his aching ribs soon forced him to stop.

"Oh, Max, Max," he said, "Nebe and Krebs are such good liars, and you're so lousy, I almost feel sorry for them, having to have you on their team."

Jaeger stared straight ahead. "They've pumped you full of drugs, Zavi. They've hurt you. You're confused, believe me."

"If they'd picked any other driver but you, I might almost have fallen for it. But you . . . tell me, Max: why is the road behind so empty? I suppose, if you're following a shiny new car that's packed with electronics and transmitting a signal, you needn't come closer than a kilometer. Especially if you can use a helicopter."

"I risk my life," whined Jaeger, "and this is my reward."

March had Krebs's Luger in his hand—his left hand, it was awkward to hold. Nevertheless he managed a convincing enough show of digging the barrel into the thick folds of Jaeger's neck. "Krebs gave me his gun. To add that essential touch of authenticity. Not loaded, I'm sure. But do you want to take that risk? I think not. Keep your left hand on the wheel, Max, and your eyes on the road, and with your right hand give me your Luger. Very slowly."

"You've gone mad."

March increased the pressure. The barrel slid up the sweaty skin and came to rest just behind Jaeger's ear.

"All right, all right."

Jaeger gave him the gun.

"Excellent. Now, I'm going to sit with this pointed at your fat belly, and if you try anything, Max—anything—I'll put a bullet in it. And if you have any doubts about that, just sit there and work it out. And you'll conclude I've got nothing to lose."

"Zavi—"

"Shut up. Just keep driving on this road until we reach the outer autobahn."

He hoped Max could not see his hand trembling. He rested the gun in his lap. It was good, he reassured himself. Really good. It proved they had not picked her up. Nor had they discovered where she was. Because if they had managed either, they would never have resorted to this.

Twenty-five kilometers south of the city, the lights of the autobahn looped across the darkness like a necklace. Great slabs of yellow thrust out of the ground bearing in black the names of the Imperial cities: clockwise from Stettin, through Danzig, Königsberg, Minsk, Posen, Krakau, Kiev, Rostov, Odessa, Vienna; then up through Munich, Nuremberg, Stuttgart, Strasbourg, Frankfurt and Hanover to Hamburg.

At March's direction, they turned counterclockwise. Twenty kilometers later, at the Friedersdorf intersection, they forked right.

Another sign: Liegnitz, Breslau, Kattowitz . . .

The stars arched. Little flecks of luminous cloud shone above the trees.

The Mercedes flew down the slip road and joined the moonlit autobahn. The road gleamed like a wide river. Behind them, sweeping around to follow, he pictured a dragon's tail of lights and guns.

He was the head. He was pulling them after him—away from her, along the empty highway toward the east.

Pain and exhaustion stalked him. To keep awake he talked.

"I suppose," he said, "we have Krause to thank for this."

Neither of them had spoken for almost an hour. The only sounds were the hum of the engine and the drumming of the wheels on the concrete road. Jaeger jumped at March's voice. "Krause?"

"Krause mixed up the rotas, ordered me to Schwanenwerder instead of you."

"Krause!" Jaeger scowled. His face was a stage demon's, painted green by the glow of the instrument panel. All the troubles in his life could be traced back to Krause!

"The Gestapo fixed it so you'd be on duty on Monday night, didn't they? What did they tell you? 'There'll be a body in the Havel, Sturmbannführer. No hurry about identifying it. Lose the file for a few days . . .' "

Jaeger muttered, "Something like that."

"And then you overslept, and by the time you got to the Markt on Tuesday I'd taken over the case. Poor Max.

Never could get up in the mornings. The Gestapo must have loved you. Whom were you dealing with?"

"Globocnik."

"Globus himself!" March whistled. "I bet you thought it was Christmas! What did he promise you, Max? Promotion? Transfer to the Sipo?"

"Fuck you, March."

"So then you kept him informed of everything I was doing. When I told you Jost had seen Globus with the body at the lakeside, you passed it along and Jost disappeared. When I called you from Stuckart's apartment, you warned them where we were and we were arrested. They searched the woman's apartment the next morning because you told them she had something from Stuckart's safe. They left us together in Prinz-Albrecht-Strasse so you could do their interrogation for them—"

Jaeger's right hand flashed across from the steering wheel and grabbed the gun barrel, twisting it up and away, but March's fingers were caught around the trigger and squeezed it.

The explosion in the enclosed space tore their eardrums. The car swerved across the autobahn and up onto the grass strip separating the two roadways and they were bouncing along the rough track. For an instant, March thought he had been hit, then he thought that Jaeger had been hit. But Jaeger had both hands on the wheel and was fighting to control the Mercedes and March still had the gun. Cold air was rushing into the car through a jagged hole in the roof.

Jaeger was laughing like a madman and saying something, but March was still deaf from the shot. The car skidded off the grass and rejoined the autobahn.

In the shock of the blast, March had been thrown against his shattered hand and had almost blacked out, but the stream of freezing air pummeled him back into consciousness. He had a frantic desire to finish his story—*I only knew for certain you'd betrayed me when Krebs showed me the wiretap: I knew because you were the only person I'd told about the telephone booth in Bülow-Strasse, how Stuckart called the girl*—but the wind whipped away his words. In any case, what did it matter?

In all this, the irony was Nightingale. The American had been an honest man; his closest friend, the traitor.

Jaeger was still grinning like a lunatic, talking to himself as he drove, the tears glistening on his plump cheeks.

Just after five they pulled off the autobahn into an all-night filling station. Jaeger stayed in the car and through the open window told the attendant to fill the tank. March kept the Luger pressed to Jaeger's ribs, but the fight seemed to have gone out of him. He had dwindled. He was just a sack of flesh in a uniform.

The young man who operated the pumps looked at the hole in the roof and looked at them—two SS-Sturmbannführer in a brand-new Mercedes—bit his lip and said nothing.

Through the line of trees separating the service area from the autobahn, March could see the occasional passing headlight. But of the cavalcade he knew was following them: no sign. He guessed they must have halted a kilometer back to wait and see what he planned to do next.

When they were back on the road, Jaeger said, "I never meant any harm to come to you, Zavi."

March, who had been thinking about Charlie, grunted.

"Globocnik is a police general, for God's sake. If he tells you 'Jaeger! Look the other way!'—you look the other way, right? I mean, that's the law, isn't it? We're policemen. We have to obey the law!"

Jaeger took his eyes off the road long enough to glance at March, who said nothing. He returned his attention to the autobahn.

"Then, when he ordered me to tell him what you'd found out—what was I supposed to do?"

"You could have warned me."

"Yes? And what would you have done? I know you: you'd have carried on anyway. And where would that have left me—me, and Hannelore and the kids? We're not all made to be heroes, Zavi. There have to be people like me, so people like you can look clever."

They were driving toward the dawn. Over the low wooded hills ahead of them was a pale glow, as if a distant city were on fire.

"Now I suppose they'll kill me for allowing you to pull the gun on me. They'll say I let you do it. They'll shoot me. Jesus, it's a joke, isn't it?" He looked at March with wet eyes. "It's a joke!"

"It's a joke," said March.

It was light by the time they crossed the Oder. The gray river stretched on either side of the high steel bridge. A pair of barges crossed in the center of the slow-moving water and hooted a loud good morning to each other.

The Oder: Germany's natural frontier with Poland. Except there was no longer any frontier; there was no Poland.

March stared straight ahead. This was the road down which the Wehrmacht's Tenth Army had rolled in September 1939. In his mind, he saw again the old newsreels: the horse-drawn artillery, the Panzers, the marching troops . . . Victory had seemed so easy. How they had cheered!

There was an exit sign to Gleiwitz, the town where the war had started.

Jaeger was moaning. "I'm shattered, Zavi. I can't drive much longer."

March said, "Not far now."

He thought of Globus. *"There's nothing there anymore, not even a brick. Nobody will ever believe it. And shall I tell you something? Part of you can't believe it either."* That had been his worst moment—because it was true.

A *Totenburg*—a Citadel of the Dead—stood on a bare hilltop not far from the road: four granite towers, fifty meters high, set in a square, enclosing a bronze obelisk. For a moment as they passed, the weak sun glinted off the metal, like a reflecting mirror. There were dozens of such tumuli between here and the Urals—imperishable memorials to the Germans who had died—were dying, would die—for the conquest of the East. Beyond Silesia, across the steppes, the *Autobahnen* were built on ridges to keep them clear of the winter's snows—deserted highways ceaselessly swept by the wind . . .

They drove for another twenty kilometers, past the belching factory chimneys of Kattowitz, and then March told Jaeger to leave the autobahn.

He can see her in his mind.

*She's checking out of the hotel. She says to the receptionist, "You're sure there've been no messages?" The receptionist smiles. "None, Fräulein." She has asked a dozen times. A porter offers to help her with her luggage, but she refuses. She sits in the car overlooking the river, reading again the letter she found hidden in her case. "Here's the key to the vault, my darling. Make sure she sees the light one day . . ." A minute passes. Another. Another. She keeps looking north, toward the direction from which he should come.*

*At last she checks her watch. Then she nods slowly, switches on the engine and turns right onto the quiet road.*

♦

Now they were passing through industrialized countryside: brown fields bordered by straggling hedgerows; whitish grass; black slopes of coal waste; the wooden towers of old mine shafts with ghostly spinning wheels, like the skeletons of windmills.

"What a shithole," said Jaeger. "What happens here?"

The road ran beside a railway track, then crossed a river. Rafts of rubbery scum drifted along the banks. They were directly downwind of Kattowitz. The air stank of chemicals and coal dust. The sky here really was sulfur yellow, the sun an orange disc in the smog.

They dipped, went through a blackened railway bridge, then over a rail crossing. Close, now . . . March tried to remember Luther's crude sketch map.

They reached a junction. He hesitated.

"Turn right."

Past corrugated iron sheds, scraps of trees, rattling over more steel tracks . . .

He recognized a disused rail line. "Stop!"

Jaeger braked.

"This is it. You can turn off the engine."

Such silence. Not even a bird call.

Jaeger looked around with distaste at the narrow road, the barren fields, the distant trees. A wasteland. "But we're in the middle of nowhere!"

"What time is it?"

"Just after nine."

"Turn on the radio."

"What is this? You want a little music? *The Merry Widow,* perhaps?"

"Just turn it on."

"Which channel?"

"The channel doesn't matter. If it's nine they'll all sound the same."

Jaeger pressed a switch, turned a dial. A noise like an ocean breaking on a rocky shore. As he scanned the frequencies the noise was lost, came back, was lost and then came back at full strength: not the ocean, but a million human voices raised in acclamation.

"Take out your handcuffs, Max. That's it. Give me the key. Now attach yourself to the wheel. I'm sorry, Max."

"Oh, Zavi . . ."

*"Here he comes!"* shouted the commentator. *"I can see him! Here he comes!"*

He had been walking for a little over five minutes and had almost reached the birch woods when he heard the helicopter. He looked back a kilometer, past the waving grass, along the overgrown tracks. The Mercedes had been joined on the road by a dozen other cars. A line of black figures was starting toward him.

He turned and continued walking.

*She's pulling up at the border crossing—now. The swastika flag flaps over the customs post. The guard takes her passport. "For what purpose are you leaving Germany, Fräulein?" "To attend a friend's wedding. In Zürich." He looks from the passport photograph to her face and back again, checks the dates on the visa. "You are traveling alone?" "My fiancé was supposed to be with me, but he's been delayed in Berlin. Doing his duty, Officer. You know how it is." Smiling, natural . . . That's it, my darling. Nobody can do this better than you.*

He had his eyes on the ground. There must be something.

*One guard questions her, another circles the car. "What luggage are you carrying, please?" "Just overnight clothes. And a wedding present." She puts on a puzzled expression: "Why? Is there a problem? Would you like me to unpack?" She starts to open the door . . .*

*Oh, Charlie, don't overplay it. The guards exchange looks . . .*

Then he saw it. Almost buried at the base of a sapling: a streak of red. He bent and picked it up, turned it over in his hand. The brick was pitted with yellow lichen, scorched by explosives, crumbling at the corners. But it was solid enough. It existed. He scraped at the lichen with his thumb and the carmine dust crusted beneath his fingernail like dried blood. As he stooped to replace it, he saw others, half hidden in the pale grass—ten, twenty, a hundred . . .

*A pretty girl, a blonde, a fine day, a holiday . . . The guard checks the sheet again. It says here only that Berlin is anxious to trace an American, a brunette. "No, Fräulein"—he gives her back her passport and winks at the other guard—"a search will not be necessary." The barrier lifts. "Heil Hitler!" he says. "Heil Hitler," she replies.*

Go on, Charlie. Go on . . .

*It is as if she hears him. She turns her head toward the East, toward him, to where the sun is fresh in the sky, and as the car moves forward she seems to dip her head in acknowledgment. Across the bridge: the white cross of Switzerland. The morning light glints on the Rhine . . .*

She had escaped. He looked up at the sun and he knew it—knew it for an absolute, certain fact.

"Stay where you are!"

The black shape of the helicopter flapped above him.

Behind him, shouts—much closer now—metallic, robot-like commands:

"Drop your weapon!"

"Stay where you are!"

*"Stay where you are!"*

He took off his cap and threw it, sent it skimming across the grass the way his father used to skim flat stones across the sea. Then he tugged the gun from his waistband, checked to make sure it was loaded and moved toward the silent trees.

# AUTHOR'S NOTE

Many of the characters whose names are used in this novel actually existed. Their biographical details are correct up to 1942. Their subsequent fates, of course, were different.

Josef Buhler, state secretary in the General Government, was condemned to death in Poland and executed in 1948.

Wilhelm Stuckart was arrested at the end of the war and spent four years in detention. He was released in 1949 and lived in West Berlin. In December 1953 he was killed in a car "accident" near Hanover: the "accident" was probably arranged by a vengeance squad hunting down those Nazi war criminals still at large.

Martin Luther attempted to oust the German foreign minister, Joachim von Ribbentrop, in a power struggle in 1943. He failed and was sent to Sachsenhausen concentration camp, where he attempted suicide. He was released in 1945, shortly before the end of the war, and died in a local hospital of heart failure in May 1945.

Odilo Globocnik was captured by a British patrol at Weissensee, Carinthia, on May 31, 1945. He committed suicide by swallowing a cyanide capsule.

Reinhard Heydrich was assassinated in Prague by Czech agents in the summer of 1942.

Artur Nebe's fate, typically, is more mysterious. He is believed to have been involved in the July 1944 plot against Hitler, to have gone into hiding on an island in the Wannsee and to have been betrayed by a rejected mistress. Officially, he was executed in Berlin on March 21, 1945. However, he is said subsequently to have been sighted in Italy and Ireland.

Those named as having attended the Wannsee Conference all did so. Alfred Meyer committed suicide in 1945. Roland Freisler was killed in an air raid in 1945. Friedrich Kritzinger died at liberty after a severe illness. Adolf Eichmann was executed by the Israelis in 1962. Karl Schöngarth was condemned to death by a British court in 1946. Otto Hoffmann was sentenced to fifteen years' imprisonment by a U.S. military court. Heinrich Müller went missing at the end of the war. The others continued to live in either Germany or South America.

The following documents quoted in the text are authentic: Heydrich's invitation to the Wannsee Conference; Göring's order to Heydrich of July 31, 1941; the dispatches of the German ambassador describing the comments of Joseph P. Kennedy; the order from the Auschwitz Central Construction Office; the railway timetable (abridged); the extracts from the Wannsee Conference minutes; the memorandum on the use of prisoners' hair.

Where I have created documents, I have tried to do so on the basis of fact—for example, the Wannsee Conference *was* postponed, its minutes *were* written up in a much fuller form by Eichmann and subsequently edited by Heydrich; Hitler did—notoriously—avoid putting his name to anything like a direct order for the Final Solution but almost certainly issued a verbal instruction in the summer of 1941.

The Berlin of this book is the Berlin Albert Speer planned to build.

Leonardo da Vinci's portrait of Cecilia Gallerani was recovered from Germany at the end of the war and returned to Poland.

Look in my face; my name is Might-have-been.

Dante Gabriel Rossetti

Grateful acknowledgment is made to the following for permission to reprint previously published material:
GLOCKEN VERLAG LIMITED: Six lines from *The Merry Widow* translated by Christopher Hassall. Copyright © 1959 by Glocken Verlag Ltd. Rights throughout the British Commonwealth of Nations, its Protectorates, Dependencies and Mandated Territories, Eire, and all the United States of America by Glocken Verlag Limited; published in all other countries by Ludwig Doblinger (Bernard Herzmansky). Reprinted by permission.
UNIVERSITY OF CALIFORNIA PRESS: Excerpt from the translation of "Marschliedchen" from page 191 of *Hitler and the Final Solution* by Gerald Fleming. Copyright © 1984. Reprinted by permission.

**City of Gold**
by Len Deighton

A riveting story of espionage and high-voltage suspense, set amid the turmoil of World War II in Egypt, as Rommel's forces sweep across the Sahara and the fate of the free world hangs in the balance.

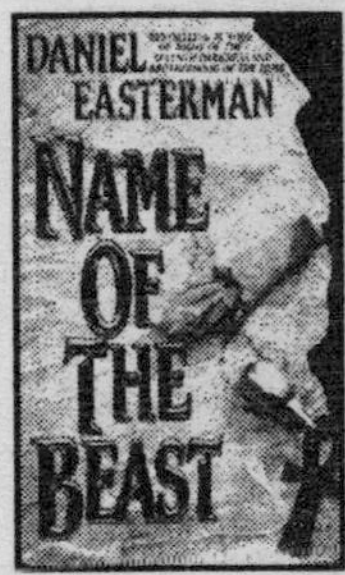


**Name of the Beast**
by Daniel Easterman

Ex-British agent Michael Hunt, and noted archaeologist A'isha Manafaluti, are driven to the truth about the mysterious Al-Qurtubi, who some call the saviour—others the Antichrist.

Buy 4 or more and receive FREE postage & handling

Visa & MasterCard holders—call 1-800-331-3761 for immediate service

MAIL TO: **HarperCollins Publishers**
**P.O. Box 588 Dunmore, PA 18512-0588**

**Yes! Please send me the books I have checked below:**

❑**The Fighting Man** 109257-6 . . . . . . . .$5.99 U.S.
❑**Dead Halt** 100825-7 . . . . . . . . . . . . . .$5.99 U.S./$6.99 CAN.
❑**Secret Missions** 109239-8 . . . . . . . . .$5.50 U.S./$6.50 CAN.
❑**City of Gold** 109041-7 . . . . . . . . . . . .$5.99 U.S.
❑**Name of the Beast** 109149-9 . . . . . . .$5.99 U.S./$6.99 CAN.

**SUBTOTAL** . . . . . . . . . . . . . . . . . . . . . .$________
**POSTAGE AND HANDLING** . . . . . . . . . .$________
**SALES TAX (Add applicable sales tax)** $________
**TOTAL** . . . . . . . . . . . . . . . . . . . . . . . .$________

Name____________________
Address____________________
City__________State______Zip______

Order 4 or more titles and postage & handling is **FREE!** Orders of fewer than 4 books please include $2.00 postage & handling. Allow up to 6 weeks for delivery. Remit in U.S.funds. Do not send cash. Valid in U.S. & Canada. Prices subject to change. H12211